She stepped into the masculine environs of dark wood walls and forest green draperies. Though unoccupied, the room breathed Grayson's familiar scent, a heady mingling of the earthy outdoors and genteel grooming, entirely masculine, vaguely unsettling and undeniably arousing.

To her right stood a bureau, wide and high, its top littered with Grayson's personal effects. She couldn't help running her fingers over a comb and brush, his silver pocket watch. A cravat lay coiled beside his watch. She picked it up, the fine linen leaving traces of dampness across her fingertips.

"How odd."

"Indeed."

At the sound of the rumbling baritone, Nora yelped. Her gaze searched the dusky corners; at first she didn't see him. But she felt him. Oh, she felt his presence filling the room and surrounding her like a physical embrace.

He stood in the dressing room doorway, taking shape from the surrounding gloom like an apparition materializing from thin air. A full day's growth shaded his jaw in baleful reflection of the shadows beneath his eyes. His clothes, a white shirt lying open at the neck and tight breeches tucked into riding boots, seemed to adhere to his body like a second skin. She saw a scratch at the corner of his eye, another across the bridge of his nose.

Had he been brawling?

As he returned her stare, his nostrils flared and his stark blue eyes simmered with . . . anger, displeasure . . . desire? Whatever it was both chilled her and lit a smoldering fire inside her . . . and made her want to defy her fears and go to him. Go to him and kiss the scrapes on his face, soothe the wounds in his heart.

He pushed forward into the room. "Good afternoon, Lady Lowell. Perhaps you'd care to explain what the blazes you're doing here."

## Praise for *Dark Obsession*

"Allison Chase's *Dark Obsession* dishes up a wonderful story in a charming, romantic tradition, complete with a handsome and tortured hero, real conflict, and a touch of mystery! Anyone who loves . . . a well-written historical romance will relish this tale."　　—Heather Graham

"A compelling and exquisitely written love story that raises such dark questions along the way, you've no choice but to keep turning the pages to its stunning conclusion. Allison Chase is a master at touching your heart."　　—Jennifer St. Giles, author of *Silken Shadows*

"Intriguing! A beguiling tale. Moody and atmospheric."
　　　　—Eve Silver, author of *Dark Prince*

"A haunted hero and a determined heroine create sparks in *Dark Obsession*. With a nod to Daphne du Maurier, this sexy story weaves together irresistible romance and ghostly warnings that lead to the truth hidden in a wounded heart. Filled with adventure and danger, deception and desire, this is a book you won't forget."
　　　　—Jocelyn Kelley, author of *Kindred Spirits*

# Dark Obsession

## ALLISON CHASE

### A NOVEL OF BLACKHEATH MOOR

A SIGNET ECLIPSE BOOK

SIGNET ECLIPSE
Published by New American Library, a division of
Penguin Group (USA) Inc., 375 Hudson Street,
New York, New York 10014, USA
Penguin Group (Canada), 90 Eglinton Avenue East, Suite 700, Toronto,
Ontario M4P 2Y3, Canada (a division of Pearson Penguin Canada Inc.)
Penguin Books Ltd., 80 Strand, London WC2R 0RL, England
Penguin Ireland, 25 St. Stephen's Green, Dublin 2,
Ireland (a division of Penguin Books Ltd.)
Penguin Group (Australia), 250 Camberwell Road, Camberwell, Victoria 3124,
Australia (a division of Pearson Australia Group Pty. Ltd.)
Penguin Books India Pvt. Ltd., 11 Community Centre, Panchsheel Park,
New Delhi - 110 017, India
Penguin Group (NZ), 67 Apollo Drive, Rosedale, North Shore 0632,
New Zealand (a division of Pearson New Zealand Ltd.)
Penguin Books (South Africa) (Pty.) Ltd., 24 Sturdee Avenue,
Rosebank, Johannesburg 2196, South Africa

Penguin Books Ltd., Registered Offices:
80 Strand, London WC2R 0RL, England

First published by Signet Eclipse, an imprint of New American Library,
a division of Penguin Group (USA) Inc.

First Printing, May 2008
10  9  8  7  6  5  4  3  2  1

Copyright © Lisa Manuel, 2008
All rights reserved

SIGNET ECLIPSE and logo are trademarks of Penguin Group (USA) Inc.

Printed in the United States of America

*For Sara and Erin.
Remember, kids, when you work
hard enough, dreams come true!*

# ACKNOWLEDGMENTS

Many thanks to my editor, Ellen Edwards, and my agent, Evan Marshall, two extraordinary members of the publishing industry who have inspired me to look closer and dig deeper to produce my best work. Your enthusiasm and encouragement are appreciated more than you can know.

Heartfelt thanks to an incredibly talented group of authors whom I am especially lucky to call friends: Zelda Benjamin, Nancy J. Cohen, Sharon Hartley, Karen Kendall, and Cynthia Thomason. You have all kept me going through times when it might have seemed easier to quit.

And special thanks and my love to Paul, who has shown me and continues to show me in countless ways what being a real hero is all about.

## *Chapter 1*

*London, 1830*

Today promised to be a day of singular distinction—
indeed, the finest day of Honora Thorngoode's
life. In a few short moments she would finally step
out from behind her parents' long and admittedly
awkward shadows and become her own person, recognized and possibly even admired by those who had
discreetly snubbed their noses at those "upstart Thorngoodes" all her life.

Best of all, she would achieve the one thing she'd
craved for as long as she could remember, a thing she
dreamed about and rehearsed, alone in her bedchamber, since she was a little girl. Yes, today would be
her triumph.

Upon arriving at the Marshall Street Art Gallery,
however, the upsurge of anticipation that had buoyed
her while dressing that morning and prevented her
from eating so much as a morsel at breakfast ebbed
liked the seaward tug of the Thames.

Two strides in and she sensed an appalling lack of
everything she had envisioned for this moment. There
should have been exclamations, applause, glasses of
champagne. . . .

The gallery should have teemed with admirers of
Signore Alessio di Paolo's masterpieces. Oh, the *ton*

had arrived en masse, to be sure. Yet the Italian master's oils proclaimed his genius to empty air, while a veritable throng stood crowded into a lone corner of the gallery, the huddled figures concealing from view the single artwork that had so utterly captured their attention.

An abrupt and deadening silence blanketed the room as the street door closed behind Nora and her parents. As thick as cheese, that silence, as heads turned and stares fell like tumbling dominoes upon her face.

Oh yes, something was very wrong indeed.

As the seconds ticked by, she scanned the faces for a smile, a wink of encouragement. She found none, only an awful gawking that scalded from head to toe.

Surely her *Portrait of a Southwark Madam*, the one Alessio had promised to include in the viewing, could not have engendered so much controversy, so much . . . enmity. But even as the thought formed, the horde of judgment across the room stiffened and, seemingly as one, took a decisive shuffle backward, as if to put as much distance as possible between it and her.

Was her painting as wretched as all that?

She darted a glance to her right. Her mother's expression held its usual mingling of self-satisfaction and simpering opportunism. Millicent Thorngoode had never approved of Nora's connection to Signore Alessio. For years now she had bemoaned Nora's dabbling in a man's occupation, as she'd put it, and disdained with wearisome sighs the paint that always found its way beneath Nora's fingernails. Still, Mama had hoped today might present her daughter in a more fashionable light. Might even, with a bit of luck, entice some eligible young bachelor to offer for her.

At the moment Nora wasn't feeling particularly fashionable, nor did a blessed one of those glares seem in the least bit enticed.

Her father, flanking her left side, perceived it too,

or his rough-hewn features would not have realigned so instantly from a moue of indulgent pride to one of icy challenge, as if daring the first insult to fly.

"Where on earth is Signore Alessio?" Her mother's query jarred the stillness. A speculative fluster fanned through the crowd.

Where indeed. Alessio should be here to greet his guests and admirers, and to unveil the painting he had praised as Nora's first true masterpiece. What manner of ill fortune would have kept him away today of all days?

She had one choice—only one. Proceed with chin held high across that gallery and learn what everyone else so obviously knew, or at least apparently agreed upon.

The assemblage parted at her approach, slowly opening a narrow path that lengthened with each step she took. Her parents trailed behind. Ahead, through the spreading crowd, the colors and shapes imprinted on a rectangular canvas began to take form—a form categorically *not* that of *Southwark Madam*.

The madam's portrait contained no sweeping expanses of crimson, nor did its colors fade into dark, velvety oblivion at the painting's edges as this one's did. Within the scarlet tones of this work, strokes of fairest rose blended with smoothest ivory. A sheen of gold added luster to a swath of rich chestnut. . . .

"He's a dead man!"

Zachariah Thorngoode's shout drowned out Nora's strangled cry, an outpouring of dismay that left her mouth agape. Eyes aching in their sockets, she gawked—like her audience—at a portrait depicting, in mortifying detail, her very self sprawled on satin bed linens, as naked as the day she entered the world.

Horror bloomed, ran riot within her. The images seared like molten lead that solidified in the pit of her stomach. Good gracious, the thighs were parted, breasts exposed. . . . One hand cupped her private parts. . . . The other arm—long and slender like her very own—stretched behind her head, fingers tangled in locks of hair. . . .

Within seconds, indignation worked its way past her dumbfounded shock. "I didn't. I never. That is *not* me."

Across the room, a brocade curtain swept open to reveal the stout figure of Signore Alessio. With a tug on his tailcoat he stepped forward. One fine-boned hand extended toward her, a rose balanced on the ends of his long fingers.

"Now you see how much I love you," he said in his accented English. His gaze shifted. "And now you, Signore and Signora Thorngoode, have no choice but to allow me to marry your daughter."

"Then, by the devil, she'll be married and widowed in the same instant!"

Her father's pounding footsteps and Alessio's scampering ones muffled but did not entirely mask the swish and thud of Millicent's senseless body swaying, then hitting the floor.

Beyond a doubt this had proved the worst day of Nora Thorngoode's life.

"Marriage."

"But, Papa—"

"Immediately." Millicent Thorngoode's high-pitched pronouncement reverberated up the parlor's walls. The crystal chandelier above their heads tinkled, a sound as brittle as Nora's taut nerves.

"Now, Mama, we mustn't act rashly."

"Rashly?" Her mother's hand flew to cup her forehead, as if in preparation of repeating her earlier swoon. "You're a fine one to speak of acting rashly. Perhaps you should have considered the notion before posing—"

"It wasn't me—"

"—nude and shameless for all the world to—"

"I did *not* pose for that portrait!"

At a warning twitch of her father's eyebrow, she bit down on her tongue and laced her fingers tight, as if that might rein in her galloping anger, her staggering frustration.

Oh, how *could* that man have done this to her? Perhaps she shouldn't have raced after Papa at the gallery; perhaps she *should* have allowed Alessio to meet his just end for disgracing her. . . .

Several breaths passed before she trusted herself to speak. "As I've explained countless times, Mama, that portrait came entirely from Alessio's imagination. I had no part in it. We therefore needn't speak of marriage—"

"There's no other way, Nora." Her father scowled. "Real or imagined, this debacle has struck your reputation an irreparable blow. By Christ, there can be no recovering from it. If only the whoreson hadn't slipped off to God knows where, he'd be supping with the devil this very moment."

Nora reached across the table and slipped her hand over his, the thick-veined, coarse-haired hand of a commoner. "Papa, he *did* slip away, didn't he? I mean, you haven't . . ."

Her mother's palm slapped the tabletop. "Of what are you accusing your father, Honora?"

She chewed her lip. Nearly all her life she'd heard whispers about her father's travels across the world as a young man convicted of thievery; how he'd escaped the Australian penal colony and fought his way back to England via the Americas with the makings of a fortune in his pockets. Once home, he had allowed no one to stand in his way as he forged a veritable golden path from one end of London to the other, or so the rumors had it.

She had always wondered what, precisely, people meant by his not allowing anyone to stand in his way. . . .

With a sigh, she stared into her father's murky blue eyes and answered her mother's question. "I am not accusing Papa of anything."

"Trust me, sweeting." His gravely voice gentled as it once had when he'd soothed her childhood hurts or lulled her to sleep. "Wherever that scoundrel may be, as God is my witness, he arrived there by his own power, not mine."

Her gaze fell and she nodded.

"He's likely halfway to Florence by now, if he knows what's good for him." Her mother plucked a pear from the Meissen bowl at the center of the polished walnut table. Juice sprayed as she bit into the fruit; more dribbled onto her chin as she said, "And you, child, *will* be married just as soon as your father and I can find a suitable groom."

"A suitable groom?" Nora swallowed an ironic chortle. Finding a son-in-law had been her mother's one and only goal these past five years, since Nora's eighteenth birthday. She'd virtually scoured the *ton* from top to bottom and sideways in pursuit of an eligible candidate—not that there hadn't existed a surfeit of wellborn bucks in the city. There were plenty. Just none that wished to marry Nora.

The dismal fact had once convinced her, despite Papa's sincerest assurances to the contrary, that she lacked the physical attributes necessary to attract a man. And it *was* true that she'd been a rather late bloomer, with the awkwardness of adolescence lingering several years longer than she would have preferred.

But nowadays her mirror professed the truth, that while perhaps not having achieved extraordinary beauty, time had nonetheless softened a reedy figure, smoothed unruly hair and whitened a freckled complexion. She could only conclude that perhaps it wasn't any deficiency on her part, but rather Mama's voracious, often embarrassing efforts—and yes, Papa's shadowy reputation too—that drove the young men away.

Perhaps they should have allowed her to marry Alessio. The thought barely concluded before a shudder skipped across her shoulders. As a painting master he'd fulfilled her heart's desires. But as a husband . . .

No, she had never felt so much as a twinge of desire in that respect. Not to mention that the brute had proved himself a scoundrel beyond redemption this very afternoon.

"Perhaps a trip abroad." She brightened at the notion. "What a charming adventure Paris would present, and I could study painting with some of the most celebrated—"

"Painting—bah!" Tiny pieces of pear accompanied her mother's outburst. She leaned as though taking aim from across the table; indeed, she pointed her half-bitten pear at Nora. "You'll never paint again, young lady, not if I have anything to say about it. Art has utterly ruined you! Great bloody heavens, displayed before all of London like a common—"

"Now, Milly, Nora says it wasn't her, and I believe her."

"Thank you, Papa."

"You're welcome, child. You're a good girl and I never doubted you. But London will—make no mistake. And if you think to escape by running off to Paris, think again. Scandals are fleet of foot, my dear. This one will arrive in any city of consequence long before you've even packed your bags. No, the only way to diffuse the barrage is for you to marry—marry well and marry swift."

"Yes, but with whom? A butcher's son?" Millicent shut her eyes and groaned as if about to be ill. "After all my efforts to see her well connected . . ."

"No, my dearest, she'll not marry a butcher, baker or candlestick maker. Our Nora will have her nobleman yet, for I believe I know just the man we seek."

"Who?" Nora and her mother exclaimed as one.

"Sir Grayson Lowell."

A gasp flew from Nora's lips, but Papa didn't notice. No, he was too busy leaping from his chair and running to aid his wife, slumped over onto the table in a dead faint for the second time that day.

Grayson stood at the edge of the headland, renamed Tom's Tumble by the villagers, as if this outcropping of dirt and stone confronting the Atlantic Ocean were a site of frolicsome sport rather than a place of death and the personal hell it had become for him. But even to those who had devised the moniker, the term held no jest; it was merely a simple, grim remembrance of what had occurred here nearly a year ago.

Squinting against the winds shuddering off the water, he peered out at the whitecaps riding the sea like ghosts on a midnight gale. His brother, Thomas, Earl of Clarington—dead these many months. Right from this spot he had slipped, among the heather and gorse and bluebell, on a sparkling summer's day, a day the ocean shone so bright it seemed the sky itself had drifted to earth in a billowing waft of silk.

The sun hadn't shown its weary face since, or so it seemed to Grayson. No, a perpetual dusk had descended over Blackheath Grange that day, over the hills, the moors and the sea. Over him. And over ten-year-old Jonathan, orphaned and silent ever since, little more now than a shadow and a huge pair of eyes that slid over Grayson to imprint his guilt deeper and deeper still. . . .

He backed away from the cliff, intending to head home. He'd found no answers here, not that he'd expected any. Tom was dead and it was his fault. *His*.

The knowledge fanned an ember inside his chest, a constant, searing reminder of those last awful days. . . . The despicable words Grayson had blurted upon his discovery that the estate was bankrupt, the Lowell family nearly penniless. Grayson might have offered his understanding, his compassion, his assistance in rectifying his elder brother's disastrous financial decisions. Instead he'd . . .

Young Jonny was earl now, but of what? An empty title, a shell of an estate. And who to look after him but his shell of an uncle, haunted, guilt ridden and shriveled of heart.

"Ah, Tom, forgive me. . . . Forgive me. . . ."

A thrash of his heart tore the whispered words apart. A chill slithered beneath his skin, raked the hairs on his arms and neck. He whipped around to view the headland behind him, gripped by a sense of being watched.

Again.

Pulse lashing in his wrists, he scanned the rocks and wildflowers, the hillocks that cast craggy shadows into the grassy hollows. Once more he felt the oppressive weight of a presence that watched him, that seemed always to hover just over his shoulder.

Limbs trembling, he raised a reluctant gaze to the more distant trees. In their summer-heavy branches he saw movement, an assemblage of shape and form that was not tree, not shadow, neither solid substance nor a figment of the wind.

And it was, indeed, watching. As it had twice before.

"Thomas?"

Dread pooled thick in his throat, cutting off breath. His legs fell out from beneath him and he landed on his knees in the weeds, head slumped between his shoulders. His right hand fisted, and as though to yank the pain from his being he rent purple blossoms from the earth.

But the pain and the horror of that day had become his boon companions. What would he be without them? His quaking fingers opened, offering a token to the wind.

The flowers spiraled from his palm and soared above the water as if intent on meeting the gulls and cormorants flapping over the tossing waves. But the breeze faltered and the flowers dipped, disappearing over the cliff to float gently to the rocks below.

Tom hadn't floated gently down. No, he'd . . .

Grayson sucked a breath through his teeth and stumbled to his feet. He stared into the trees and saw nothing, not even the trees themselves; only shadows and emptiness. Had he truly seen something or merely taken a glimpse inside himself?

Sleep. He sorely needed some, but ever since that day he hadn't been able to steal more than two or three hours' slumber at a time, and restless ones at that.

Slowly the breath began moving freely in and out of his lungs. His vision cleared. His resolve, like the apparition itself, reaffirmed and took shape inside him.

"I'm going to marry her, Tom. For Jonathan's sake. Her dowry will restore the Grange and the earldom and give your son a future—the grand one he deserves. He'll have everything a boy can want. And he'll never know how close we came to losing everything. That's my promise, Tom. I swear it on my life."

Ah, such paltry security for his pledge. For what worth did his life hold now? Soon to be shackled to a woman he didn't know, much less love. And while the optimist might hope love would grow over time, Grayson held no such illusion.

He had appealed to Zachariah Thorngoode for a loan. He'd come away with unlimited funds. . . . And betrothed to the man's daughter.

London's notorious Painted Paramour, as the *ton* had dubbed her. Rumor held her to be bold enough to make the most seasoned demimonde blush. He deserved her. They deserved each other. A sardonic chuckle broke from his lips.

Ah, what a glorious couple they would make.

\*      \*      \*

Grayson alighted from his curricle just beyond the front steps of the Earl of Wycliffe's Park Lane town house. Raising a gloved hand, he adjusted his beaver hat and stepped onto the pavement. "You needn't wait," he said to his driver. "I'll more than likely stay the night."

If not, he'd walk home to Clarington House, a mere half dozen streets away. His driver nodded and clucked to the matching grays.

"Should tonight go badly," Grayson added under his breath as he watched the gig recede, "I don't know how much longer you'll be in my employ."

But how could the evening be anything less than an unqualified success? He was here at his closest friend's home to officially offer for Honora Thorngoode, a little farce they would play out for appearance's sake. Never mind that all of London knew the truth of it: theirs was a union fashioned out of desperation and nothing more.

Thorngoode had assured him of his daughter's hand, insisted she was delighted with the match. Of course, that was merely another way of saying there could be no backing out for the chit, not with her reputation in such tatters. Nor could there be for him, not with Jonathan's future equally laid to waste.

He placed his foot on the bottom step, then went utterly still. From the dark void of the park across the street, a strange hissing rode the wind. He heard it sift through the branches overhead, felt it scour the street. Beneath his clothing, his flesh prickled. From a chilling wisp of breeze, an eerie murmur uncurled.

*Gray . . .*

He clenched the railing. "Who's there?"

His eyes strained in the darkness. In the fog prowling Hyde Park's lawns, did he see . . . ?

No. There was no one. Nothing. No gathering of

shadows, no eyes glaring in accusation. Merely branches fluttering in the mist.

As the thumping of his heart ebbed, he stood a moment longer, relieved the swirls held no hint of anything more sinister than a London night typically contained. He'd heard the wind, not words. Foolish of him to believe it could be anything more.

*It* had only ever happened at Blackheath Grange, if indeed *it* had happened at all. What had he seen that day on the bluff or those other times in the house? Shifting shadows, a trick of the light. Or was he going mad?

The grind of coach wheels halted his speculation. Could this be his betrothed? He held his breath, waiting with clenched stomach.

A barouche drawn by no fewer than three matched pairs, their glossy coats a continuation of the vehicle's lustrous black lacquer, turned the corner and ambled in his direction. Some four houses away, the coach came to an abrupt stop. The driver remained stiffly at attention in the box.

Grayson exhaled, a long and deep release. Surely if that barouche carried the Thorngoodes they would have pulled up in front of Wycliffe House rather than linger halfway down the street. Good. He didn't wish to meet her here, in the dark emptiness of the street; he would far rather be inside among familiar surroundings, with his longtime friend at hand.

Oddly, though, the coach seemed to be trembling on its wheels, was presently listing back and forth as though an altercation were taking place inside. The horses pawed the road fitfully. From inside came muffled voices but no screams, no shouts for help.

With a sigh, he mounted the town house steps two at a time. Soft lamplight spilled from the windows; the muffled sound of voices seeped through the door. His nerves settling, he raised the brass knocker and let it fall with a resounding clang.

\*    \*    \*

"Good heavens, can that be *him*?" Nora pressed her nose to the barouche window as she peered down the street at the man standing on the steps of Wycliffe House. "Is that the man I must marry?"

The front door opened just then, spilling golden light onto the figure silhouetted on the threshold. In a top hat and a two-tiered cloak that billowed languidly around him, he was a study in shades of black— charcoal, ebony, raven's wing, obsidian—forbidding and devoid of light, yet as fascinating as a fitful dream.

She could make out no distinct details, only lean, graceful lines, broad and tall, filling the doorway with an aristocratic confidence she could never hope to emulate. As he stepped inside, his cape eddied in an inky wave behind him. He seemed . . . otherworldly, a phantom born of Hyde Park's mists, here to sample human pleasures before returning to vapor at dawn.

Those night mists had always frightened her as a child; she had always wondered what mysteries lay hidden within. . . . What secrets, what sins.

What dangers . . .

"Is that Grayson Lowell?" she whispered, wondering what lay hidden beneath the gentleman's exterior.

Her father leaned over her shoulder to follow her gaze. "Aye, that looks to be him."

A sinister little chill raised gooseflesh down her back.

"Stop the coach." She rapped twice on the ceiling, their driver's signal to rein in the team.

"What the blazes are you doing?" Her mother reached up and knocked once, the signal to drive on. The horses lurched into motion.

Nora just as quickly countermanded that order with a second series of raps. The horses stopped, started, stopped again as she and her mother waged a battle against the coach ceiling.

"That will be quite enough. This little game is far from amusing."

"Nor is it meant to be, Mama." No, something inside her—instinct, intuition or perhaps merely her heart's desire—had dug in its heels. "I'm not going through with this. There is no reason for me to meet this man tonight because I am not going to marry him. And there's an end to it."

"Don't be ridiculous. The Earl of Wycliffe has graciously lent his home for the occasion. One does not keep an earl waiting, Honora."

"Make my apologies." She reached for the door handle. "And don't worry about me. I shall hail a hackney."

She succeeded in opening the door an inch or two before her father's fingers encircled her wrist, holding her gently but fast. "Use your head, girl. Without this marriage there's no future for you."

And what future would she have with a murderer? She didn't say the words aloud, but her father nonetheless seemed to read her mind. Holding her gaze, he said evenly, "Have you been listening to the same gossips that branded you a fallen woman?"

With a gasp, her mother snapped open her fan and whisked it back and forth in front of her face.

Zachariah stilled her with his free hand. "Both claims are hogwash, Milly, so don't work yourself into yet another lather. Lowell's no more a killer than our Nora is compromised."

The coach door hovered partly open, wavering back and forth as Nora considered her father's assertion. Most gossip constituted nothing more than the imaginings of the bored and idle. She of all people understood that. Still . . .

"How can you be so sure about him, Papa?"

"The magistrate declared him innocent."

SUSPICION MARKS THE EARL OF CLARINGTON'S DEATH. HIS OWN BROTHER UNDERGOES QUESTIONING. . . . Last summer's scandal sheets had brimmed with the sensational details. But no conclusions.

"He wouldn't be the first nobleman to get away with murder."

Her father grasped her chin and turned her face to his. His dark eyes penetrated the shadows, searing in their intensity. "I've met Grayson Lowell and I can vouch for him. He is not a murderer. It isn't in him. I would know if it were. A murderer's black heart reflects in his eyes, but Lowell's eyes are clear."

Her forearms prickled; the hairs on her nape rose. It was said Grayson Lowell never denied the crime, that he'd had little to say during the investigation. It was said the magistrate exonerated him because there simply hadn't been enough evidence to place Sir Grayson at the scene of the death.

Part of her wished to demand how her father knew exactly what to look for in a man's eyes to judge his innocence or the lack of it. But to ask would be to pry into things about Papa's past she didn't wish to know. Perhaps couldn't bear knowing.

"Goodness, Nora, all this fuss." Fingering the sapphire and diamond necklace around her neck, her mother tsked. "After all that's happened, you should be grateful a nobleman will have you. A baronet, knighted for his services to the poor. So he's got a bit of a past. What nobleman doesn't have a skeleton or two rattling about in his closet?"

True enough, he'd earned his knighthood for helping establish schools for Cornwall's poor. All well and good, but her mother's blithe dismissal of the rest made her eyes go wide with disbelief. "How many of those skeletons happen to be the nobleman's brother?"

"Oh, drivel-dravel. Your father has arranged a brilliant match, all things considered. Stop complaining and do as we ask."

It wasn't her mother's peevish command that convinced her to release the door handle and rap once on the ceiling. It was her father's quiet entreaty.

"Trust me, Nora."

At those simple words, the storm inside her quieted. Papa had once been a criminal—that much she knew—and God alone knew what secrets he carried within him. But to her he had never been anything but kind, loving and completely straightforward.

If Zachariah Thorngoode said Grayson Lowell was not a murderer, then by God, she could wager her finest sable paintbrush that the Earl of Clarington died by far less sinister means.

She hoped.

"All right, Papa." She drew a breath. "You win. I'll marry him."

"There's my bonnie good girl."

Yes, but then she wasn't Zachariah Thorngoode's daughter for nothing. She'd marry Grayson Lowell, but she would do so on her own terms, as the man would very shortly discover.

## Chapter 2

Grayson was about to knock again when the paneled oak door creaked open a few circumspect inches. The butler's stern face appeared in the gap. "Ah, Sir Grayson. Good evening." He swung the door wide. "Do come in, sir."

Grayson smiled as he stepped into the foyer. "Good evening, Harris. Why so vigilant?"

"One can never be too careful, sir." The elderly man gave a disdainful sniff as he went on to explain, "There have been vagrants about of late. His lordship has issued the strictest instructions not to admit anyone who appears the least bit suspicious."

"I'm sure the earl is quite safe with you at hand."

"Indeed, sir."

The mingled aromas of roasting meats, tangy sauces and sweet desserts wafted from below stairs, stirring an appetite Grayson had not thought he would experience tonight. He swung his cloak into Harris's waiting arms, then added his top hat and gloves to the bundle. "Is his lordship in the drawing room?"

"His lordship is right here." Chadwell Rutherford, Earl of Wycliffe, stopped halfway down the staircase, one manicured hand resting on the banister, the other curled in a fist on his hip. Light from the chandelier above him picked out gold glimmers in his freshly trimmed hair. He raised one slightly darker eyebrow and grinned. "I'd all but given you up for lost. What the blazes kept you?"

Grayson frowned. "Kept me? I was about to apologize for being unforgivably early. In fact, I'd rather hoped there'd be sufficient time for my host to offer me a fortifying brandy before feeding me to the wolves."

"The wolves should be here any moment, and they're sure to be hungry. Ravenous enough, in fact, to find even the sorry likes of you palatable."

"You're enjoying this, you insufferable swine." Grayson started up the stairs.

"Enjoying watching you land yourself a stunning little package of wealth and wit?" Chad shrugged. "I'll admit I shan't weep for you, my friend, though I do understand what's causing you to dig in your heels. No man likes to feel dragooned. Why not try pretending this was all your idea, rather than Thorngoode's?"

When Grayson reached his lifelong friend, he stopped and faced him levelly. "Remind me that I have no choice, Chad."

"You have no choice, Gray."

"Say it as though you mean it."

Chad clapped a sympathetic hand on his shoulder. "You're looking downright ghoulish, old boy. Not ill, are you?"

He was quick to shake his head. "Only at heart. I could use that brandy, damn it."

"And you shall have it." Chad's eyes reflected the many years of their friendship, their countless confidences, their infinite trust of each other. "See here, as I've told you at least a dozen times already, if there's any way I can help you . . ."

"No."

Chad's hand slid from his shoulder. "I only meant . . ."

Grayson made an effort to soften his tone and relax his stance, which had tensed to battle readiness a moment ago. "I know. And you've already helped me more than you'll ever guess. When Thomas died . . . if you hadn't been on hand, well, I don't know . . ."

"I'm still on hand, old chap. Always will be."

The truth of that statement resonated with him. He could count on his oldest friend. But not even Chad knew about . . . *it*. No one did.

"Then you'll see me through this evening." Grayson conjured a grin. "I'm depending on you."

"To what? Ensure you don't go sneaking out through the kitchen door? Come. My sister and Albert are waiting for us in the drawing room, bless their hearts. I suggest we join them and present not only a united front when your intended arrives, but a contented domestic scene as well."

The two men climbed the carpeted stairs to the spacious hall above, their steps thudding in companionable rhythm. "Seriously, Chad, thank you for arranging this evening. How did you manage it, by the way? I should have thought Thorngoode would prefer to face me down on his own turf."

"Manage it?" Chad gave a sniff that made him sound rather like his butler. "All I had to do was send my card and my compliments, and dear Millicent Thorngoode was on me like sugar glaze on a roast goose. Oozing and sticky sweet."

"But it's my goose that's cooked." Grayson crossed the landing, heading for the drawing room.

Chad stopped him just before the threshold. "Look, I consider both Thorngoodes as bordering on the absurd. Like caricatures in the Sunday papers. But to tell you the honest truth, I find their daughter charming."

"The Painted Paramour? *Charming* is not a word that leaps to my mind."

"She's talented. She's surprisingly intelligent. And she *is* beautiful."

"As half of London has had the privilege of witnessing."

Chad laughed. "Has it occurred to you that she might not be the demirep she's reputed to be? After all, since when have you and I put any stock in scandal-sheet prattle?"

A wave of chagrin swept Grayson's shoulders. He certainly knew what the scandal sheets had to say about *him*. He knew too that behind every rumor there existed at least a particle of truth.

*The Earl of Clarington was pushed. . . .*

Must a push be physical?

He cleared the darkness from his mind with a quick shake. "Dozens of people *were* treated to the sight of Honora Thorngoode's unabashedly naked body. The scandal sheets didn't make *that* up. Not to mention the buggers who are lining up claiming to have been with her."

"Besides that Alessio chap?"

Grayson nodded, his expression grim.

"Who?"

"Bryce Waterston, for one."

*"No."* Chad pushed a low whistle through his teeth. "Don't tell me the bloke had the audacity to tell you to your face."

"He bragged about it at White's. Everyone knows."

"Jealous, are we?" With athletic grace, Chad ducked Grayson's halfhearted fist. "All I'm saying is keep an open mind. At the worst, you've found yourself a lusty bedmate, and a deuced comely one at that. With my luck I'll end up chained to some vapid little virgin who'll do her duty until she produces an heir and a spare and then forever bar her boudoir door. Sorry, but I've no pity for you at present."

"I'm worried about Jonathan," Gray said on a more sober note. "He doesn't need any further heartache."

"Then keep the new Lady Lowell clear of Cornwall. Meanwhile, enjoy your marriage for what it's worth."

"You're simply trying to prevent me from slipping

out through the kitchen and spoiling your dinner party, aren't you?"

"The wolves must be fed, after all." Chad flashed the smile Grayson had always envied, the one that had gotten him out of scrapes, made him a favorite at Eaton and, later, won the hearts of ladies. "Besides, it seems I am indebted to Mrs. Thorngoode. The woman addresses me as *your grace*. Odd, but I thought only the king could elevate an earl to duke."

"She wrote to me last week, addressing me as *your worship*. That's rather a step down, I should think."

"Ouch." Chad shook his head. "New money."

"So new one can smell the ink, not that my creditors will complain."

Chad gestured toward the open doors of the drawing room. "Chin up, old boy. Almost time to face the front lines."

Zachariah Thorngoode closed the door to Chad's private study and drew back the gilded armchair that faced the desk. "Sit, my boy."

The gruff invitation sounded more like a command, and Grayson wasted no time folding himself into the exotic, Egyptian-inspired piece.

He had met his bride-to-be not five minutes earlier, exchanged a bow, a how-do-you-do and a polite kiss on the hand before her father stepped between them. Without preamble Thorngoode had grasped his elbow and abruptly ushered him from the drawing room. Indeed, one might say *grabbed* his arm and *hauled* him without being accused of a gross exaggeration.

He'd barely had time to form the slightest impression of the young woman. Except for her hair. Rich, dark chestnut. Streaked with gold. So glossy he'd wager it hung perfectly straight when not coaxed into the curls that danced about her shoulders tonight.

Of her face he'd noticed little but its heartlike

shape—full in the cheeks, pertly narrow at the chin. And her eyes. He'd glimpsed them just before her father yanked him away. Though their exact color escaped him—greenish, perhaps hazel—it was their exotic slant that produced a little jolt of . . . he didn't know . . . interest? Curiosity? Perhaps even a begrudging desire to know more of her.

Then again, why shouldn't he find the Painted Paramour desirable? Most of London already did.

Like a prowling footpad Thorngoode noiselessly circled the desk, his gaze pinned on Grayson with all the subtlety of the flat of a dagger, not exactly cutting into flesh—yet—but cool and flinty all the same.

Grayson tried to focus on his surroundings, the rich oak paneling, the deep tones of burgundy and hunter green. The mellow scent of pipe tobacco permeated the air, mingling with the essence of leather-bound books and a hint of fine aged brandy. It was a room he knew well, having spent many a late night sitting up with his friend, talking, smoking and imbibing some of that excellent brandy.

Even as a boy, this had always been Grayson's favorite room in Wycliffe House. Chad's father, the previous earl, had from time to time invited the boys in for a taste of what he'd termed a man's last haven, refreshingly devoid of all feminine influence.

It didn't present much of a haven now, not with Thorngoode glowering at him like a pile of hot coals about to burst into flame. He supposed it was for effect, the man's way of establishing who was in authority here and who was not.

This was all for Jonathan, Grayson reminded himself. Thorngoode's money would restore the boy's inheritance. If only it could repair Jonny's wounded heart as well, and give him back all he'd lost.

Thorngoode cleared his throat. "I've ordered the improvements to Blackheath Grange. The outbuildings, the paddocks, the silos. It'll all be repaired, along with the tenant farms damaged by the flooding last autumn. Livestock will be replaced. Your brother's debts here in London are being handled even as we speak."

*Handled.* Grayson knew better than to ask what exactly that meant. And as for the rest, the repairs would restore production, but would they renew the local people's faith in the land? Dead livestock, failed crops—many believed Tom's death had brought a curse upon them all.

He forced the thought from his mind. "Thank you, sir."

"It's lucky you came to me when you did. Mending structures is one thing, but restoring a dwindling fortune is devilish tricky business. As things lie now, it won't be easy to undo so many years of neglect."

"My brother never neglected his responsibilities," Grayson snapped, sudden ire pulsing in his temples. Whatever else his brother might be accused of, and Lord knew Tom had his faults, disregard for those in his care for damn certain wasn't one of them. "He did his best—"

"What your brother neglected," Thorngoode interrupted, "is the same matter so many of your kind have ignored since Boney's wars ended. It's not entirely his fault. Your father was equally guilty. You aristocrats shrink from dirtying your hands in trade and finance, but while you were all promenading through the park, the world changed. A fortune can't be supported by the home farm any longer. You've got to stop living large and thinking small."

He paused, running a speculative glance over Grayson that ended with a clearly doubtful lift of one coal black brow. "Tell me, have you got the faintest idea how much cotton is produced by this country's Caribbean plantations? Or how many countries we export that cotton to?"

"I ah . . ."

Thorngoode leaned back in his chair. "No, I didn't think you did."

A weighty silence ensued while the other man continued his critical if silent appraisal. Grayson swallowed and then wished he hadn't when Thorngoode's gaze converged on his twitching Adam's apple. The tiniest gleam of amusement entered the man's eyes. Grayson wanted to crawl under the nearest settee.

For the life of him he didn't know why Zachariah Thorngoode made him feel this way, as if his life hung by a cobweb. He'd never seen the man behave with anything other than his peculiar brand of unrefined civility. Nor had he ever heard Zachariah Thorngoode raise his voice. He didn't have to. Somehow he exuded more intimidation in a murmur than most men could muster with bellowed threats.

Not to mention his way of wangling others to his will by means so subtle a man's signature would appear on a contract before he even realized he'd taken up the pen. Take Grayson's own predicament.

He'd never meant to agree to marry Honora Thorngoode, had intended simply to negotiate terms for a loan no reputable bank would extend. He still didn't quite know what had happened.

Across the desk, the man laced his craggy fingers together and cracked the knuckles. Loudly. Grayson sat up straighter.

"Now, my boy, about my daughter." The East London influences on Thorngoode's speech thickened to an ominous drawl. And his eyes—so dark a blue and so recessed they seemed nearly black—honed directly on Grayson like dual pistol barrels about to discharge.

Suddenly Grayson envisioned himself in a dockside alley at midnight, surrounded by brigands. He didn't move. Or breathe.

"I wish to set a thing or two straight." Thorngoode paused and aimed a crooked forefinger at Grayson.

He felt an urge to duck. Instead he said, "Yes, sir."

"She's a good girl, my Nora. Innocent of what people say about her. Don't you for one instant believe otherwise."

"No, sir." His denial slipped out a beat too swiftly, and the other man's expression hardened.

"The very least I expect is for you to ensure her safety and keep her content." The misshapen forefinger jabbed the air. "Can you do that?"

Was Thorngoode having second thoughts? Regrets about aiming so low on his daughter's behalf? Not that Grayson could be blamed for that. If Honora had considered her reputation before suspending it from a wall for public viewing, she might now be marrying a nobleman rather than a nobleman's second son, of questionable character himself.

Her father waited for an answer, and none too patiently if the drumming of his fingers on the desk gave any indication.

But he wondered—did he have what it took to content the Painted Paramour? He cleared his throat. "I'm certain your daughter and I can come to terms that will be mutually satisfying to us both."

"She's a woman, not a scrap of real estate." Thorngoode's wide nostrils flared, accentuating a nose undoubtedly broken on more than one occasion. "Be good to her. So help me, if you ever flaunt a mistress in front of her or lay an unkind hand on her, I'll have your hide."

The threat, delivered smoothly in a controlled tone, all too vividly conjured an image of Thorngoode peeling Grayson like a piece of fruit. "Understood. Sir." Some indignant part of his ego prompted him to add, "It isn't in my nature to harass or abuse women."

"Then you and I shall get on famously."

Thorngoode gripped the arms of the chair and pushed to his feet. Grayson should have been overjoyed at the prospect of escaping this little téte-à-tête, but one question had nagged from the very beginning, and now it demanded an answer.

"May I ask you something, sir?"

Thorngoode sat back down.

"Why me?" He looked down at his hands, not daring to meet the other man's eye. "Surely you've heard the rumors. Aren't you . . . concerned?"

After all, any father should be.

Thorngoode had the audacity to laugh. Nearly doubled over the desk. Grayson didn't know whether to be relieved or insulted.

"You haven't even asked me if there's any truth to those rumors," he added.

Thorngoode sobered. "By Christ, boy, if I needed to ask, do you think I'd be handing my daughter over to you? The gossips can go straight to the devil, along with the creditors who've been banging at your door."

He extended his hand across the desk. Grayson grasped it, instantly aware of the protrusion of the veins, the prominence of the knuckles, the calluses on the fingertips and palm. With those gnarled hands, Zachariah Thorngoode had clawed a fortune out of nothing. His was a grip that could strike an honest bargain or squeeze the life out of Lucifer himself. As Grayson shook that hand, he speculated on which it would be for him.

At the rumble of approaching male conversation, the air abandoned Nora's lungs in a whoosh facilitated by a forceful thrust of her heart. Would she finally exchange more than a word of greeting with Sir Grayson Lowell? And if so, what exactly would those words be?

*Delighted to meet you, Sir Grayson, but tell me, did you murder your brother?*

Oh, dear. Such thoughts wouldn't do. Not here, not now, especially in such company. But she would have a word with him at the first opportunity.

"Grayson is a splendid rider. Do you ride, Miss Thorngoode?" The question came from the Earl of

Wycliffe's beautiful sister, Lady Belinda Stockwell, perched on the settee beside her.

Apparently the lady had known Sir Grayson since childhood and considered him a capital fellow. In the past few moments she had listed more attributes than any one man had a right to possess, and Nora couldn't help wondering which were true and which were invented to impress her. Still, she could fault Lady Belinda for neither her loyalty nor her enthusiasm. Having such a friend of her own would have made this all so much easier, but Nora's only close friends were artists, and Mama would take up arms before she permitted any of them through the door again.

"I'm afraid I haven't ridden in quite the longest time," Nora replied with a little sigh. "Not since I was a child visiting my grandparents in Kent."

"Oh, what a shame. Perhaps Grayson will persuade you to take up the reins again." Lady Belinda's smile remained perfectly intact. "What entertainments do you enjoy?"

Nora's hesitation lasted only as long as it took to realize the prudence of not mentioning her painting—as if anyone here needed reminding. "I'm a passing fair chess player."

She heard none of Lady Belinda's next comment, for Papa and Sir Grayson had entered the drawing room. At that moment Nora wanted nothing so much as to jump up from the settee, claim her fiancé's attention and state her opinions concerning their impending marriage.

Instead she discreetly craned her neck to see around Lady Belinda's high coif, an effort that rendered her little satisfaction, for her father's craggy profile blocked her view.

Their introduction earlier had happened too fast, her nerves in far too tight a tangle for her to form more than a general impression of the man. Perfect grooming, stylish clothing, impeccable poise. On closer inspection, would she find him appealing? Or would she dread waking every morning to the sight of cold eyes, a disdainful mouth or the constant censure of a glowering eyebrow?

"Ah, Zachariah. Sir Grayson. May we assume you've concluded your business agreeably?" Seated across the way beside Lady Belinda's husband, Nora's mother sat up straighter, her features pinched with nervous expectancy.

Nora sighed. In spite of everything—Alessio's crushing betrayal and Grayson Lowell's dubious past—Mama simply could not hide her elation at Nora's marrying into an aristocratic family. She would not relax until the vows were spoken.

"Most agreeably, Mrs. Thorngoode," Sir Grayson said, his voice smooth and carefully polite.

"Oh, your worship, I am so pleased to hear it."

Nora swallowed a groan. Chomping at the bit would best describe Mama's reaction to that news, and would she *never* learn to address the nobility correctly? A subdued chuckle drew her gaze to the Earl of Wycliffe, who lowered his face to conceal a grin.

She experienced a moment of ambiguity toward the man, and not for the first time. He treated her amiably enough, but she could not shake the feeling that there was more to the earl than appearances suggested. Tonight and on the previous occasion they had met, some underlying . . . she didn't know . . . tension, perhaps . . . seemed to strain his nobleman's poise, as though he were walking on ice and afraid of falling. She couldn't quite put her finger on it. . . .

Catching her gaze and apparently realizing he'd been caught smirking at her mother's foible, his smile tilted apologetically. He pushed away from the hearth and helped both Nora and his sister to their feet. "I believe congratulations are in order."

He continued holding Nora's hand after his sister drifted to her husband's side. He raised it to his lips, and then leaned to whisper in her ear, "I'm very happy about this match, Miss Thorngoode. I believe you'll do Gray a world of good. And God knows he deserves a turn for the better."

She should merely have thanked him. Instead, she listened in a sort of dreamlike, detached mortification as words darted from her tongue, words spawned by the many humiliations she'd suffered since that afternoon on Marshall Street. "Are you mocking me, my lord?"

Eyes gone wide, the earl flinched as if she'd smacked him, yet he did not, as she might have expected, drop her hand. "Good heavens, no, Miss Thorngoode. I assure you I am sincere." The appearance of a grin, broad, disarming and utterly forgiving, sent a wave of confusion to singe her cheeks. She began stammering an apology, but he waved it off. "Come, and I'll show how sincere I am."

A glass of champagne was pressed into her hand. As the others gathered around, everyone raised their glasses. Sir Grayson took up his proper position beside her. Once again deprived of any clear view of him, she yet became very much aware of him—keenly aware that he stood nearly a head taller than she, that his arm, broad and muscular inside his expensive coat, nearly touched her bare shoulder, and that even with no physical contact his presence seemed to engulf her. He smelled of something sharp, clean and vitally masculine.

The Earl of Wycliffe's eyes twinkled in the lamplight. "It has been my good fortune," he began, "to have been blessed with the dearest of elder sisters, who never balked at pinching my ear from time to time as the need arose." This raised a titter of laughter. "I've also been fortunate in having a brother. Not of the blood, perhaps, but if our boyhood penchant for mischief wasn't conceived of the same spirit, then I am utterly at a loss to explain it."

This heralded a few more chuckles. The earl raised his glass. "To the best of friends, who has these many years been a brother to me, and to his lovely bride-to-be, whom I am most honored to welcome as a sister . . . a sister in spirit, and in our shared regard for this boorish lout she has so graciously consented to marry. Remember, Miss Thorngoode, the occasional pinch to the ear will help keep the old boy honest. I wish you both health, happiness, and a lifetime of contentment together."

At those words, the earl rose immeasurably in Nora's estimate. Yet the toast dragged her spirits lower than ever, for his warm sentiments and easy humor could not be farther from the truth of this marriage, and no amount of pretending could change the facts.

Beside her, Sir Grayson stood stiffly, ill at ease, uttering correct phrases and occasionally raising a hand to her elbow with as much show of affection as he could apparently muster. That made her sadder still.

With a false smile she sipped her champagne and accepted congratulations, which lent her just the opportunity she needed to sidestep, turn, and finally study the man who would be her husband.

She very nearly wished she hadn't. Her pulse quickened, trounced, would have made her giddy even without the champagne. Grayson Lowell was . . . startling. All bold planes and sharp contours. Handsome, certainly, but with a rugged severity that rivaled Papa's, though softened by youth and privilege. His was a face that made her yearn for paints and canvas, for to an artist, it is the flaws in beauty that fascinate and inspire.

A peculiar rippling caressed her insides. Earlier, standing in his flowing black cloak on the front steps of Wycliffe House, he had seemed not quite of this world. A creature of darkness, of secrets and mysteries. She sensed those things now—intensely—in the set of his mouth and in the shadows beneath eyes that were pale blue and as stark as moonlight.

*Oh, do stop it!* With an inner shake she looked away and pretended to smile at whatever Lady Belinda's husband, Lord Albert, had just said.

So her affianced possessed interesting looks and a brooding sort of charm. That was no reason to let her imagination run rampant; no reason, surely, to lose sight of her goals. She had a plan, and at the very first opportunity she intended sharing the details of that plan with Sir Grayson. In the meantime, however . . .

"Dinner is served."

Nora found herself seated across the table from him. Lord Albert occupied the seat to her right, her father the one on her left. The earl and his sister presided from the head and foot of the table, while Nora's mother sat across the table, to Sir Grayson's right.

Even as she attempted to consume a respectable portion of her capon with gooseberry sauce, Nora's fingers persisted in curling delicately around her fork, anticipating the feel of her brush and planning exactly what strokes would capture the energy that lurked beneath Grayson Lowell's exterior. Or were mere paint, canvas and her fledgling skills equal to the task?

"I understand you are an artist, Miss Thorngoode."

Her fork clattered to her plate in response to Lord Albert's offhand remark. An immediate silence descended, strained and heavy—the art gallery all over again. Grayson Lowell choked while sipping his wine, sputtering a few ruby droplets onto the table linen.

Was Lord Albert joking? Taunting? Condemning her for the fallen woman she was reputed to be? Then again, she'd jumped to the same conclusion only moments ago with the Earl of Wycliffe, who had happily proved her wrong.

She stole a swift glance around the table, meeting

expressions of shock and disbelief. Her father's eyes
smoldered dangerously. But Lord Albert's affable face
revealed nothing more menacing than polite interest.
Nora's spiraling pulse drifted slowly back to earth.

Across the table, her mother cleared her throat and
treated the earl to a fawning look. "Tell me, your
grace, do you summer in London or at one of your
many country estates?"

Before Lord Wycliffe could bite back a smirk, Nora
reached a decision and turned to her supper companion. "As a matter of fact, Lord Albert, I *am* an artist.
A painter, specifically."

"How stupendous. Watercolors, I presume? I do believe landscapes are always a popular subject for ladies. Is that not so?"

"I do occasionally dabble in watercolors, but I much
prefer oils. They are bolder. More substantial. And
I've a passion for both landscapes and portraits."

Great good heavens, what made her dare use the
word *passion*? A wave of scarlet crept over her mother's face, while beneath the table she felt the gentle
but distinct pressure of her father's foot on hers.

At the cool touch of Sir Grayson's speculative gaze,
she felt a moment's uncertainty, a wish to end the
conversation immediately, as her mother had tried to
do. Oh, but why should she feel ashamed to admit the
truth? Why *shouldn't* she speak of her one true love—
possibly the only love she'd ever know?

"Ah, yes indeed. Portraits." Lord Albert dabbed his
lips with his napkin. "I myself am a huge admirer of
Gainsborough. Whom do you emulate, Miss Thorngoode, if I may be so bold as to ask?"

"I don't know that I emulate anyone," she said with
a modest chuckle. "But I especially admire the works
of Joseph Mallord William Turner."

"Turner," the Earl of Wycliffe repeated. "I must
confess I'm not certain I understand his work, Miss

Thorngoode. With his muddled colors and indistinct forms, I sometimes think I could manage it myself."

Nora nodded. "Yes, he makes it all look easy, doesn't he, when in fact it's a brilliant technique. One I strive to master . . . though with limited success, I must confess."

"Ahem." Mama's throat clearing was followed by several loud coughs and an emphatic glare.

Nora glowered back as another awkward hush blanketed the table. Good heavens, it wasn't as if she had initiated the conversation, and surely even Mama couldn't expect her to be rude to their hosts.

Lady Belinda settled the matter. "Perhaps you'd care to elaborate further, Miss Thorngoode, on what it is Mr. Turner does so well."

"Of course. You see, Turner focuses his attention on the emotion of his subject, rather than on particular details."

"Ah, but how does one relate to emotion," Lord Albert interrupted, "without the details to enlighten one?"

"My lord, have you never experienced an overwhelming sensation—deep down inside—that could not quite be expressed in words? Through color and composition, Mr. Turner conveys the overall mood of his subject to create an emotional response within the viewer.

"Because he leaves so much to the imagination, each viewer's response will be uniquely his own. In effect, there are two artistic processes at work—that of the painter's perspective and that of the viewer's interpretation."

She paused, astonished to discover the others at rapt attention. Even her parents. Sir Grayson was leaning forward over his plate too, his compelling features locked in such probing intensity that she experienced the beginnings of a blush and a most disconcerting tingle.

In that instant she decided his eyes were not merely blue, but a hue that inspired poets to scramble for new metaphors and had artists mixing and remixing their palettes for just the right intensity. Yet those eyes were not beautiful, not in a typical sense. An icy edge prevented it, a steely quality that nearly made one flinch.

She quickly looked away.

"That is what Turner achieves in his paintings," she concluded, annoyed at the slight tremor in her voice. "The result is ingenious. Miraculous, really."

"I, for one, shall certainly view all paintings from an entirely new perspective from now on," Lord Albert declared. "Thank you indeed, Miss Thorngoode."

"Not that Honora intends to continue her little hobby," her mother said with a nervous titter, "what with the responsibilities of being a new wife and all."

Nora's mouth hung open. Despite Mama's insistence that she never take up her brushes again, that painting had been the source of all her troubles, she positively had no intention of relinquishing her principal source of solace and personal pride.

Bother anyone who might think her rude and headstrong, this was one argument from which she would not back down. Not now, not ever. She gathered breath to say so. . . .

"If Miss Thorngoode wishes to paint after we are married, I certainly have no objection."

Her mouth remained open, her eyes agape. For the span of a single breathless heartbeat she wished to throw her arms around her betrothed and bestow endless kisses upon him for supporting her in her greatest aspiration. But the truth lurked in the indifferent cast of his handsome features, the aloof tone of his voice. Even the way he spoke her name, Miss Thorngoode, held a stiff-lipped hint of distaste.

He simply didn't care what she did. She assumed

she could paint or go to the devil and not particularly affect Sir Grayson's day.

She acknowledged him with a quietly begrudging "Thank you."

Another silence drifted over the group, punctuated by the clink of silverware against porcelain as they finished supper.

Lady Belinda suddenly looked up. "Why, Chad, we must show Miss Thorngoode the Holbein." She turned to Nora with an animated smile. "You must see it immediately after supper. It is a portrait of one of our ancestors, Lady Cecilia Francis, who was a lady-in-waiting to Princess Mary Tudor when she became the Duchess of Suffolk. We consider it one of the Wycliffe treasures. Don't we, Chad?"

An eager *ooh* slipped from Nora's lips. She experienced that lift of heart that so often occurred in relation to her "little hobby," as her mother had put it, whether resulting from viewing a masterpiece or reaching a new level of proficiency in her own work.

The earl raised his wineglass and swirled the rich claret. "I'm afraid Miss Thorngoode is to be disappointed."

"Disappointed?" Belinda blinked. "What ever do you mean?"

"It isn't here. Not presently."

Nora's anticipation drained in a shoulder-slumping sigh.

"Where on earth is it?"

Lady Belinda was not the only person taken aback by the earl's disclosure. Gawking at his friend, Sir Grayson held his fork aloft as if to spear his closest neighbor, in this case Nora's mother, whose blank expression declared her complete ignorance of what a Holbein might possibly be. Apparently, the portrait being anywhere but in this house was a singularly peculiar event.

"It's out on loan." The Earl of Wycliffe set his wineglass down and brushed at imaginary crumbs on the tablecloth. "For an exhibit."

"Exhibit," his sister repeated.

"Yes. In Oxford."

"Oxford." It seemed Lady Belinda could do nothing but echo her brother's replies.

"Precisely. We'll get it back, of course, when the exhibit concludes." The earl offered what Nora supposed was meant to be a reassuring smile. Beneath it lurked a ghost of uncertainty, clearly visible to Nora and, she was certain, to Lady Belinda. He sipped his wine, and when he looked up again his stony expression declared the subject closed.

Lady Belinda exchanged a look with Sir Grayson. He merely shrugged, apparently dismissing the matter as none of his business, which of course it wasn't.

He directed a second shrug to Nora and she wondered what the gesture was meant to convey. Empathy? Or indifference? But what could he know of it? To be able to study a masterpiece, truly study it without well-meaning attendants interfering with "helpful" information about the painting, as if she, a woman, could have no sense of an artwork's importance. Or worse, standing behind her, clearing their throats to remind her she should move on and allow other patrons a look.

Oh, this itinerant Holbein constituted a missed opportunity of vast proportions.

The conversation drifted to other matters as the servants served dessert, and Sir Grayson spared her not another glance. No, he entered into a lively conversation with Lady Belinda, all traces of his former apathy vanishing from his expression. More than that, his stark eyes sparked each time Lady Belinda laughed or simply smiled, or when she briefly laid her hand on his coat sleeve.

Watching them, a burning sensation crept through her. Good heavens . . . jealousy? No. Resentment.

Yes, for having to marry against her wishes, for finding herself saddled with an arrogant, disinterested creature of darkness who may or may not have murdered his brother, despite Papa's claims.

Oh, may Signore Alessio's oils harden to rock and his canvases crumble to dust for the fate to which he'd consigned her!

*Chapter 3*

Grayson experienced difficulty in rising from his friend's dining table upon conclusion of the meal, a predicament due to another and quite persistent rising that he attributed to Miss Honora Thorngoode's influence.

They didn't call her the Painted Paramour for no reason, for the woman was nothing if not bottled sensuality steaming for escape. A passion for portraits indeed. With her talk of overwhelming sensations and unique responses, she'd all but likened art to physical intimacy in a way that made his blood simmer, his appetites yearn.

Though she maintained her innocence throughout, he couldn't help wondering if the famed Signore Alessio had been the victim, snared in a carnal web of Miss Thorngoode's making.

He had tried seeking refuge in a conversation with Belinda, pretending to hang on her every word while his gaze shifted countless times against his will to Miss Thorngoode. To her pretty mouth, her delicate bosom, those graceful arms he'd very much like to feel wrapped around him.

Hence his present difficulty, and blast the other men for so blithely leaping to their feet and dispensing with the tradition of port and cigars following supper. That might have given him sufficient time to collect his composure and tame the beast even now straining for a good thrust or two with the lady in question.

But the women were about to stand, and that left him no choice. He eased to his feet, buttoning his coat and attempting to smooth it as well as he could, considering.

"Sir Grayson, there is a small matter I should like to discuss."

He discovered her standing at his shoulder. His pulse spiked, though not so much due to her proximity as the fragrance she bore with her, sweet, heady, with a hint of something spicy. He couldn't name the scent. He knew only that it danced through him like fingertips over harp strings.

"I thought perhaps the terrace . . ." She gestured toward the French doors at the far end of the room. "If you would."

"A moment alone—a splendid idea." Mrs. Thorngoode beamed, displaying a decidedly crooked front tooth. "You poor dears have barely exchanged a word all evening. Come. In the interest of propriety, I shall serve as your chaperone."

With a giggle the woman fluttered her hand at her husband, who stood waiting to return with the others to the drawing room. "Go on, go on. These children have some settling to do between them and they certainly have no need of an audience." She cupped her hand over her mouth as if to muffle her next words, spoken nonetheless as audibly as the rest. "Don't worry, Zachy, I shall be close at hand."

Willingly enough, Grayson followed the Paramour across the room. He was curious, really, as to what she could possibly wish to speak with him about. Theirs was a simple transaction, with little left to haggle over as far as he could see.

As they neared the threshold he slowed, caught by a familiar sight, one he'd grown so accustomed to over the years he typically paid it scant regard.

Until now.

To the left of the French doors, in a carved frame some four feet in length and three in height, hung an oil-color depiction of Blackheath Grange. It had been a gift from his parents to Chad's many years ago. Now he found himself arrested by images of a summer morning so removed from present circumstances no one at the time could possibly have imagined them. How innocent they were then, how unaware of what would come.

The scene filled his gaze, then seemed to enlarge, breathing as if alive, stretching paint and canvas nearly to cracking as the view expanded to engulf him, absorb him. Birdsong wafted from swaying trees, a warm breeze ruffled his hair, a child's voice beckoned from the house. . . .

*Gray.*

Like the whisper he'd heard outside tonight.

A strangled oath rose in his constricted throat, fighting to push past his lips. He wrestled it back, but only just. He squeezed his eyes shut.

He opened them to brushstrokes on canvas and nothing more. As paintings were wont to do, this one tilted a bit to one side. He raised a hand to move it back in place, a task complicated by his shaking fingertips.

Miss Thorngoode swept to his side and grasped his hand. "This way, Sir Grayson, if you *please*."

Her warm touch anchored him firmly in the here and now while her impatience forced him into motion. He gladly abandoned the unsettling memories of his country home in favor of Chad's elegant terrace, where nothing irregular, much less calamitous, had ever occurred.

Wine and too little sleep. Last night he'd tossed his way through countless restive dreams. Fatigue never mixed well with spirits. He must have consumed too much during supper, though he hadn't thought so at the time. And there'd been that brandy earlier. Good thing they had skipped the port.

He expected Mrs. Thorngoode to follow them as they stepped outside, but the woman merely took up a position beside the threshold, hands folded at her waist, her sharp profile silhouetted by the lights behind her. He felt an odd sense of betrayal, as if she had been supposed to safeguard him but had shirked her responsibilities.

Not that he needed safeguarding from her daughter. He supposed he could handle Honora Thorngoode well enough, Painted Paramour or no. But what irked him, what tossed him so off kilter that he was hearing things and imagining paintings leaping out at him, was the loss of control over his life.

Because of the desperate straits he'd found himself in, he must now jump at every word spoken by these Thorngoodes and pretend he enjoyed it.

He dragged in a breath of night air and suppressed the rising anger—the futile, irrational, selfish anger he couldn't help feeling despite his every effort not to. If only Tom hadn't lost everything. If only he'd had better sense.

If only he were still alive.

With another tug, Miss Thorngoode propelled him beneath the sheltering overhang of a spacious walnut tree. He couldn't help but notice how small and smooth her hand felt against his. What a comfortable fit it made. How the pressure of her fingers conveyed qualities both ingenuous and seductive, and had him simmering with curiosity as to the purpose of their sojourn.

Branches dripping with greenery blotted out the moon and effectively concealed them from her mother's view. Apprehension tingled down his back, as so often happened in shrouded, shadowy places. But no, that was absurd. His peculiar visitations had surely been conjured from within, manifested by his grieving conscience.

A cool breeze stirred Miss Thorngoode's curls and sighed through the filmy layers of her evening gown. She released his hand and faced him.

"I wish to speak of this marriage we're about to enter into. It will benefit you in a singular way, will it not, Sir Grayson?"

Before he could reply, she revealed the rhetorical nature of her question by plowing doggedly on. "My dowry, not to mention the benefit of my father's business acumen, will allow you to restore the Clarington fortunes for your nephew."

"I can't deny that it will, Miss Thorngoode."

She gave a brisk nod that sent a loose tendril of fine, glossy hair floating in her face. Were they not acting out the pretense of two well-bred young people about to embark upon a respectable life together, and were he still the man he once was, he might have reached out and tucked that tendril behind her ear.

From there he'd have allowed his fingertips to trail over the warmth of her nape, make contact with the tender skin of her neck, smoothing, caressing, fondling ever so gently, all the while drawing her to him. It was a game he'd enjoyed countless times with countless willing vixens. Such a long time ago . . .

"Let us be frank, Sir Grayson. For me there is no such obvious benefit. In fact, I've yet to ascertain what advantage, if any, this marriage will render me."

She went on, but he heard only the prickliness of her voice. Good God, was he fated to marry a younger version of her mother and endure such harping the rest of his days?

His eyes narrowed, pinching her image between his lashes. "Excuse me, Miss Thorngoode, but there *is* the small matter of your reputation—"

Her jaw dropped for the briefest instant. "The matter of my reputation, sir, is the result of incorrect assumptions formed upon a contemptible hoax."

"Ah. I see."

Her eyes sparked venom; then she blinked. "Believe what you will. I've agreed to marry you to please Papa, but I refuse to live in any man's shadow. I will not be shut away or give up my painting or—"

"As I've already said, if you wish to paint—"

"I do not need your permission for that, sir, thank you ever so much. What I *would* appreciate, the thing I am trying to negotiate if you'd let me slip a word in edgewise is—"

"A negotiation—good. Here is something I can appreciate, Miss Thorngoode." Finally he recognized something of her father in her. And as he'd done with her father, perhaps they might shake hands in agreement before each went their own way, emotionally speaking, that is.

Of course, there would have to be the further pretense of the happily married couple. It had been part of his bargain with Zachariah. They must be seen together at the usual round of plays, symphonies and social events, all necessary to quell the gossip.

Then again, as Chad had so astutely pointed out, bedding this lusty morsel did not present a dismal prospect. He deserved some small compensation for his efforts, did he not? His eyes fell to her small though decidedly well-rounded bosom, snugly accentuated by the eager embrace of her shoulder-baring bodice.

When he'd first agreed to marry her, he had intended for them to live essentially separate lives. Once he fulfilled his role in raising the Painted Paramour from her fallen state, they would settle into happily divergent activities. He had planned to concentrate fully on his nephew's welfare. His dear wife, he'd told himself, might do whatever it was that pleased her.

Now that he'd met her, seen her, he wasn't as certain about that strategy.

"Pray, name this negotiation you speak of, Miss Thorngoode. If it is within my power to grant—"

"Yes, yes." A breath of impatience sent that loose tendril dancing about her impishly upturned nose. "Indeed it is quite simple, sir. I should like access to your Cornwall estate."

Wariness prickled his spine. "Blackheath Grange?"

"The very same. Particularly in the summer months, perhaps early autumn as well."

"I am afraid the favor isn't mine to grant." His words were clipped, curt. "I merely manage the finances and upkeep. The Grange belongs to my nephew."

She dismissed this with a careless shrug. "It *is* in your keeping for now, is it not? I wish to establish a summer retreat for fellow artists—"

"My nephew lives there," he ground out between jaws gone suddenly taut. He wondered—and for the first time cared—what she might have heard about him. Was she deliberately baiting him, using the one thing in his life still worth something—Jonny—for the sport of raising a reaction? "He does not take well to strangers."

"Most children don't." Her voice rose on a note of vexation. "But that shall pass soon enough and he'll undoubtedly benefit from the company of so many artistic individuals."

His shoulders tightened; a sudden pain lanced his neck. "Indeed he will not, Miss Thorngoode, due to the fact that not one of them shall ever set foot on the property. And neither shall you."

"Why not?"

"Why not? Why *not?*" He suddenly wanted to grab her by the shoulders and give her a hearty shake to force some sense into her. No wonder she'd gotten herself into such a muck-mire; the poor woman simply couldn't ascertain the obvious.

"My dear Miss Thorngoode, if you and your artist cronies wish to hold riotous orgies all summer long,

that is your concern. But I will not have you cor-
rupting the mind of an innocent child."

Silence shivered between them. Her eyes opened
wide, storm tossed, darkly shining. A bloodstained tide
swept her indignant features. He felt a moment's
uncertainty. . . .

"How *dare* you?" Her hand shot out, but before it
swiped his face he caught her wrist. She yanked and
tugged while expletives worthy of the saltiest old jack-
tar flew at him.

"Odd, but I don't hear a denial in this otherwise
colorful dissertation," he said. Her other hand came
up; he gripped it too. "Do you deny it?"

"Deny what? On which charge am I summoned to
plead?"

"How many are there? Signore Alessio, Bryce
Waterston . . . how many others have there been?"

"You're insufferable."

"That isn't an answer."

"You don't deserve an answer." She tried to pull
free as a shocking round of adjectives described his
person.

Enough. He tugged back and without warning her
weight fell against his chest. With a step backward for
balance, he grasped her shoulders, fully intending to
give her that well-earned shake, but something else,
something entirely unplanned, occurred.

Clutching her tightly, he raised her to her toes, causing her breasts to rub along his coat front and bringing
her lips on a level with his. He attributed the next
moments wholly to gravity and the mysterious forces
of electromagnetism, for surely he never would have
kissed her otherwise.

But there it was, there *they* were, lips pressing, moist
and searing, while rivers of heat poured through him
straight down to his toes, thoroughly flooding his loins
along the way.

Miss Thorngoode fought him for the briefest instant,

then shuddered and melted against him. He released
her shoulders and wrapped his arms around her. Like
twin serpents her arms coiled round his neck, lifting
her sweet, soft breasts high against his chest. Her fingers twisted in his hair.

Ah, he might have enjoyed the kiss, the heat, the
taste of Miss Thorngoode for the next hour or so, and
decency be damned, but it was pain and not propriety
as her teeth closed on his bottom lip that sent his head
jerking backward.

He thrust her to arm's length, her sudden release
of his hair inflicting further pain. "Why the devil did
you do that?"

"Why do you think?" Her fingers kneaded her
mouth as if it throbbed in pain—as his presently did.

"Don't act the innocent with me, my sweet Honora." He too raised a hand to his mouth, then held it
up to inspect for blood. There was none. "I might
have given you the benefit of the doubt, but I've had
my eye on you all evening. A contemptible hoax, my
foot. I saw how you warmed to the subject of art
during supper—your passion, you called it, speaking
of inner feelings and overwhelming sensations. As if I
didn't know what *that* meant."

"I was engaged in an interesting conversation about
a topic that inspires me. Where is the crime in that?"

"If you weren't flirting with Lord Albert, then . . .
I don't know what."

"Flirting? With Lord Albert? Are you demented?"

Yes, well, maybe she hadn't exactly been flirting
with Albert, per se, but she'd certainly courted seduction with someone at that table.

Chad? The notion sent a knifing pain to his temple,
a bitter taste to his mouth. For an insane moment he
loathed his friend's patrician good looks.

Her lips parted in a smirk both wry and accusing.
"And what of you and Lady Belinda?"

"What *about* me and Belinda?"

*"Please."*

"Belinda is practically my sister, and don't change the subject. You're no shrinking violet. You're down-right combustible, and no use denying it." He attempted to raise her chin in his palm but she shrugged away.

Then she tipped her face up to meet his gaze dead on. Her smile was shrewd, too filled with cunning for his liking. "Are you saying it matters to you?"

"What matters?"

"Me. What I do."

"Don't be absurd."

A knowing lift of her brows made him want to yank hair—his, hers, it wouldn't have mattered. He knew only that she was dangling him just this side of lunacy.

Good God, *did* he care what she did? The notion galled him, especially in light of that look on her face. Undoubtedly she'd use the knowledge against him, and he'd be as ruined as poor Signore Alessio. Or worse, should her father become involved.

He took a determined step back. "Do not flatter yourself, my dear. You may shag every garret rat in London and you'll not inconvenience me, so long as you stay away from my nephew."

She hissed a breath. Her obstinate expression dissolved into the last thing he expected—sheer unhappiness.

His conscience shoved at his anger, his self-righteousness and his damned perplexity, which admittedly did nothing but flourish in this woman's presence.

"I see." With a calm belied only by her flared nostrils, she raised her hems and started away, stepping out from the walnut's canopy.

It was her utter lack of wrath—wrath he deserved

no matter her past sins—that made him regret the past several moments. Whatever wrongs she may have committed, who was he, indeed, to judge?

"Miss Thorngoode, wait. I . . . I apologize."

She paused and half turned toward him. Moonlight poured across her features, illuminating a spot of moisture yet to dry on her bottom lip. Silver dollops swam in her eyes. She looked so frightfully young— young and despondent and undeserving of the blow he'd knocked her.

His appalling words reverberated through him and made him queasy. He wished she'd say something. Insult him. Take another swing. She merely lifted her shoulders, white and ethereal in the moonlight, and swept into the house.

He let go a breath. Had he misread her so entirely? Or was this sudden capitulation—this demureness after giving as good as she got—merely another strategy in her game of seduction? If so, her tactics threatened to succeed.

Not that she'd left him in his former rigid discomfort; no, his guilt over his utter boorishness precluded that. He wasn't hard. But, ah, God, he wanted to be. He yearned to feel her warm and feisty in his arms again. Wanted it in a way he hadn't wanted anything in a long time, since before . . . everything happened.

What did that mean? How had this woman, this ruined chit of a girl, managed to affect him so profoundly in so short a time? What was it about her that drove him to distraction? He'd already broken his word to her father, for he'd both harassed and abused her—albeit unintentionally—despite his promise not to. He wondered if Thorngoode would use a weapon or his bare hands to flay him.

Had it been her or her mention of Blackheath Grange that worked him into such a state? And was his refusal to allow her use of the manor truly about Jonny? Or about his own fears of returning to that

dismal place and facing the past. Unable—unwilling—
to seek the answer, he shook the questions away.

He paused to master his breathing before returning
to the house. Before facing his fiancée again. Heaven
help him, if the Painted Paramour was to be his wife,
he had damned well better determine how to be her
husband.

*Chapter 4*

The voices came at her as if from across a snow-smothered valley. *I will* echoed twice, first in a subdued rumble, his, then higher and softer, hers. Different yet equally uncertain. Unsteady. Both, one might even say, apologetic.

While the blood pounded in her ears in counter-rhythm to the flailing of her heart, her knees wobbled beneath a crashing conviction that she shouldn't be here. Shouldn't be doing this.

But the vows had been spoken. It did not matter whether the words were sincere, or that they had seemed to come from some source beyond herself. Indeed, perhaps they had.

Last night she'd slept fitfully, tossing, turning, slapping her pillows. Eventually she had dozed, dreaming of a fair-haired woman standing by her bed. In her dream Nora had sat up, frightened and trembling, clutching the bedclothes to her chin. *What do you want?* she'd demanded. The woman smiled, and for some inexplicable reason Nora's fears dissolved.

*You needn't be afraid. Marry him. He'll never hurt you.*

"Who are you?" But the woman had vanished, and Nora had awakened to find herself sitting up in bed, the linens balled in her fists.

Now she had given her consent, made her pledge,

because some nameless woman in a dream—a figment of her own wistful hopes—had said she should.

"I pronounce you man and wife. . . ."

She belonged to him now, for better or worse, for always.

Her veil came away from her face, swept back between Grayson Lowell's long, straight fingers. For an instant Nora marveled at the difference between those hands and her father's, once worn to bleeding on a regular basis in the effort to survive.

Vastly different from her own hands too. Sturdier, stronger. Hers were small and delicate but often paint stained, the nails and cuticles suffering from contact with powders and oils. And yet with her frail female hands she created, sifted life's singular moments through her fingers and set them to canvas. At least, she did so as best she could and with an open heart.

Could Sir Grayson make a similar claim? Had he ever created anything with those fine gentleman's hands?

His face came into focus and filled her vision, became the whole of her world while masculine scents settled over her. Lifting her veil did little to brighten the prospect before her, for the dusty church forbade entrance to all but the slenderest fingers of sunlight. Even close up her new husband seemed drawn from a midnight landscape, his startling blue eyes the only brilliance in his shuttered expression.

His lips were cool and smooth, just moist enough to leave a trace of dew across her own. She resisted the urge to flick her tongue across the spot while the rector concluded the ceremony. Resisted but could not quell the temptation to compare this kiss with the other one they'd shared.

She had bitten him. The memory nearly raised a grin. He'd deserved it, cad that he'd been. Though she must admit it hadn't been so much the kiss but the insults flanking it that had provoked her temper.

But . . . she'd made a shocking discovery that night, a little secret he must never learn. It lived inside her, a quivery predicament with the power to trip her heart, hitch her breath, send her better sense for a tumble.

The organist struck up the exit march, discordant notes that blared through the building and rattled inside her. With a hand at her elbow, Sir Grayson, her husband, turned her about and nudged her toward the back of the church.

What a sad affair their wedding was. Between her and Sir Grayson they'd mustered all of a handful of guests—the Earl of Wycliffe, the Stockwells, the odd assortment of elderly aunts and uncles, all of whom appeared just the tiniest bit confused.

Mama had insisted on the church, at the same time bluntly refusing to allow any of Nora's artist friends to attend. Somehow she saw Nora's downfall as their fault, even though not one of them had been involved in Alessio's deceit. Mama needed someone to blame, and in Alessio's absence her anger settled on anyone even remotely connected to the art world.

At the open doors of the vestibule, the morning sun hit Nora full in the face. She blinked and wished Sir Grayson would release her elbow. Did he believe her incapable of remaining upright on her own? A new, gleaming black phaeton pulled by a pair of matching bays—a gift from her parents—awaited them on the windy street. They ducked beneath a shower of rose petals and well-wishes and made their way to the vehicle's open door.

"After you, my dear." Again he nudged her elbow as if she were unable or unwilling to proceed on her own.

Feeling cross, she gathered her skirts and climbed inside, then experienced a heated sense of panic when he clambered in after her, filling the empty space with a bulk of shoulders, arms and legs.

The door closed, sealing them in dusky solitude, she

and this stranger. He was all muscle and rambling limbs with no particular regard for her own need for space. His knee tapped hers as the coach rocked forward. His coat sleeve brushed her bare forearm while his shoulder knocked solidly against hers. Even as she attempted to negotiate an inch or two between them, that little secret whispered to her pulse points, murmured its quivering message to deepest places inside her.

Her fingertips traveled to her lips, pressing ever so gently. . . .

"Thank heavens that's over."

Snapped from her musings, she scowled up at him. "Can you never refrain from insulting me?"

He regarded her blankly. Then his eyebrows gathered. "I did no such thing. You can't mean you enjoyed that?"

Her breath caught. Had he read her mind, somehow guessed . . . but then she realized which "that" he meant. The ceremony, not the kiss. A laugh of relief escaped her as she relaxed against the squabs. "Goodness no. It was torture."

"Deuced right." He paused. "Wait. You're not insulting *me* now, are you?"

Her gaze traced the strong lines of his face and she wished, for the briefest instant, that those vows they'd repeated hadn't rung with such hypocrisy. She merely faced forward again and shrugged.

"I suppose I'd deserve it."

She smoothed the layers of her lace and satin skirts. "Indeed you would."

From the corner of her eye she saw him studying her. She couldn't be certain, but she believed she detected the beginnings of a smile. With a tremor of anticipation she wondered what he was thinking, what he might be planning. As she'd learned at Wycliffe House, Grayson Lowell was nothing if not unpredictable.

When she braved a glance, however, the smile had vanished.

"I wish to apologize for my behavior that night at Chad's," he said, uncannily following her thoughts again. "I don't usually say or do those kinds of things."

"Oh?" She pulled the lace mitts from her hands and tossed them into her lap. The ring he'd placed on her finger only minutes before glimmered with indifference. "So you save that privilege specifically for me?"

"Not exactly." He released a breath. "I was angry but not at you. None of this is your fault."

"Meaning?"

"I had to marry. If not you, then someone else."

"Someone with a generous dowry."

He nodded.

"I suppose your options were limited."

Another nod, accompanied by a shrug.

She glanced at his profile, itself a fascinating world of jutting angles and rough planes, as inhospitable as any barren landscape. Several days ago she had begun a painting of him by memory. Now she realized she could never hope to capture a spirit as volatile as Grayson Lowell's.

She sighed. She had been his last resort, just as he had been hers. No one else would accept either of them. No wonder he was angry. She was angry too. But did he have to say it? Rub it in? Wouldn't a gentleman at least preserve the illusion of this day, make a gift of it rather than handing her an empty plate of reality and bidding her chew it well?

"Supposing you could have it without me, then? The money, I mean. What would you give in return?"

He shifted to peer down at her, one arm sliding across the squabs above her shoulders so that if she leaned her head back, it would rest in the crook of his elbow. He drew closer, searching her face until she pulled back. And then there she was, caught between his arm and his piercing regard. "Explain."

"I—I'll insist Papa give you full control over my dowry, in exchange for my being able to spend my time as and where I wish." Her breath trembled despite her effort to appear calm. "I had one hope for this marriage. One. And you dashed it that night at your friend's house."

"I have no idea what you're talking about."

"Your Cornwall estate."

"Ah, that again." A hard look entered his eyes, like a wall that could not be scaled. "Blackheath Grange."

"Yes. I'd hoped . . . you see . . . I've been to Cornwall. The light there is extraordinary, the scenery unmatched. I'd give anything . . . But you refused to allow it. Still, surely there must be another of your nephew's estates where I might bring fellow artists in the summer months. . . ."

She stopped, biting down and swallowing a sudden and mortifying urge to cry. How could this man understand how important this was to her?

An artists' retreat. For women only, of course. A place to study and experiment unhindered by society's eye, or by the disapproval of parents and husbands who considered a woman's constitution too delicate, too corruptible for any but the most trifling exploration of the art world. To have such freedom . . . oh, it would constitute a boon of immeasurable worth.

"It isn't possible." The words were decisive, his expression implacable.

"But why not . . . ?"

"Because there aren't any others. Estates, that is." His voice grated; his jaw turned stony. "Surely your father explained. Two have already been sold off. A third is being leased in the hope of saving it from the auction block. Blackheath is all that's left and . . ."

"And you won't allow us to corrupt the mind of a child." Oh, *blast* him for passing judgment. He didn't know her, didn't know her colleagues, yet he was determined to believe the worst. Did that mean she too should fall prey to rumor and condemn him whether innocent or no?

*He'll never hurt you. . . .*

He grasped her chin. "You must understand. Jonathan is the best of what is left of the Clarington name. He embodies our future—the whole of it. I won't take chances with his welfare. I will not risk him. Not for anyone. Therefore I must be certain—"

Tears pricking the backs of her eyes, she shoved his hand away. "If you believe I could ever harm a child in any way . . . then there is nothing more to discuss."

"Perhaps not," he replied softly. His hand engulfed her shoulder, his fingers clamping with an insistence that startled her. "Perhaps I simply don't like the terms of your bargain, Lady Lowell."

The term jarred her, for she'd not heard it spoken aloud before, nor had she once considered that it belonged to her. As her mind thrashed in confusion, he grasped her other shoulder and held her firmly against the squabs, then leaned in and set his mouth to hers.

The only points of contact between them were his hands on her shoulders and his open lips on hers, yet his touch kindled a fiery presence between her legs. Her thighs burned, turned to heated butter. Her bones dissolved and her breasts strained painfully against her bodice, seeking something unnamable, heretofore unthinkable.

As if he understood their mute cries for attention, his hands slid from her shoulders and covered her breasts, thumbs finding her nipples through all that satin, lace and linen. He rubbed them in rough, urgent circles that had her moaning into his mouth, squirming beneath him, had her pressing for more even as he deepened the kiss and explored the entirety of her mouth with his tongue.

Nothing existed beyond those kisses, beyond the desire that left her scorching, throbbing. And greatly fearing he *had* discovered her secret and planned to use it to his advantage.

For the truth was, she had enjoyed that kiss on Lord Wycliffe's terrace . . . and this one as well. More than enjoyed; she delighted in the sensation of his hands upon her, savored the taste and heat of him in her mouth and all through her.

He lifted his mouth from hers, so tenderly she again felt the inexplicable sting of tears. He propped a hand beside her head. The other cradled her cheek, effectively trapping her within his gaze, within the breadth of his arms.

"What I had been about to say before you so rudely interrupted me is that I must be certain of rendering the right decision. I may have been hasty that night. I shall think more about your request, and I shall take my time thinking about it, so do not ask again. You'll know when I've reached my decision."

He brushed his lips against hers, and the graze of his tongue raised shivers that left her weak and feverish. He pulled back again and his eyes, blazing in the dimness, held her immobile but for her trembling fingertips. "Never put words into my mouth, my dear. Your tongue, your lips, your sighs of pleasure, yes. But never words. I will not stand for it."

For the first time she felt afraid of him, truly afraid, and not because of anything anyone might have said about him. He didn't need rumors to make him fearsome. He need only kiss her and look at her like that.

Grayson poured brandy into a snifter, watching the coppery flow deepen the dimensions of the crystal. As the liquid heat poured through his body, his gaze drifted over the familiar dark furnishings of the study that had served the Clarington earls for generations.

By rights this should be his brother's haven. Tonight, Grayson's wedding night, Tom should have been here pouring brandy for both of them. Should have been grinning, slapping Grayson's back and toasting his nuptials in less-than-polite terms.

The brandy burned his nose and eyes and traced a searing path to his gullet. He took another long pull, knowing it would do little to numb his sense of loss. Nor would it transform the hours ahead into the sort of wedding night he'd always believed he would celebrate. A virginal young wife with a heart filled with love. A future filled with hope.

Not for him, those things.

He sauntered behind the desk and threw himself into the chair. Slipping into a slouch, he raised his glass again. The liquid set his lips aflame. Would Honora's kisses do likewise? All too well did he know their power to scorch. To make a man half-crazed with desire. Yes, he would have that if nothing else.

Leaning, he set his brandy on the desk. An object near it shimmered in the glow of the candle he'd brought. He frowned. Besides a few token items—glass quill holder and inkpot, a pewter letter rack, an inlaid stationery box—the desk had been cleared of personal articles. Except for a monthly dusting, no one ever entered this room but him, and then only rarely.

Puzzled, he reached forward.

His hand closed over a pocket watch. As he scooped it into his palm the chain scraped the desktop, the bleak sound producing a foreboding that prickled up his spine.

Tom's gold watch—a Clarington heirloom—had gone missing since the day of his death. . . .

Lurching forward, Grayson dragged the candle closer and shoved the timepiece into its erratic flicker. But even before his gaze traced the designs etched in the silver cover, the size and weight of the piece produced a less-than-reassuring certainty.

This was not Tom's watch, but his own. The one

he'd opted not to wear this morning, which he had left atop his dressing room bureau.

His breath rasped in a throat gone dry. How did his watch get here? Surely his valet would not have moved it.

The night air penetrated the window behind him, its cool breath raising the hairs on his arms. The crisp scent of lemons crept beneath his nose. Inhaling it, tasting it, he shoved backward until the chair hit the window frame. His heart thumped as an overwhelming sense of recognition swept over him.

"Charlotte?"

He pushed to his feet, eyes straining into the crouching shadows. He knew he wouldn't receive a reply; *couldn't* receive a reply. Charlotte, Thomas's wife, died nearly four years ago, along with their unborn child.

Tremors racked through him. The room suddenly felt like the wine cellar deep beneath the house. Snatching the candle in one hand and gripping his watch in the other, he nearly stumbled over his own feet in his haste to quit the room.

"Do stop, Mama. That hurts. I believe there might still be a pin or two in there somewhere."

Nora winced and leaned closer to the dressing table mirror as she ran her fingers through her hair, raking unsteady paths along her scalp. Tonight was her wedding night, and here she sat in an unfamiliar bedroom in Clarington House, where her unfamiliar husband would visit her all too soon.

She felt like a prisoner facing a life sentence. . . . And, indeed, that was exactly what she was.

Her mother's reflection frowned down at her. Holding the silver-backed hairbrush at her side, Millicent leaned to pluck one of the pins Nora had just located, pulling hairs along with it and pricking her scalp.

"Goodness, Honora, this mane of yours is so long and thick, it's quite like searching for reeds in a bushel of hops."

Millicent Thorngoode would know. Before her marriage, she'd been but a farmer's daughter, and her father was by no means a gentleman farmer. No, Grandfather Whipple had worked his tenant lands with his own hands, his own sweat. Mama had grown up amidst the hops fields and oasthouses of south Kent, helping to harvest the ripe bines and brew beer for the family's use and to sell at market.

Even now Mama's hands showed traces of the hard work, with calluses that would not be buffed away and knuckles that bulged as a lady's never should.

Nora found it nothing to be ashamed of, and she regretted the airs that prevented her mother from acknowledging her youthful past. The memories were vague, but if Nora concentrated she could almost catch the bitter scents of the ripened hops, or the dry, pungent heat rising from the oast houses, those round, pointed-roofed structures she had once mistaken for fairy dwellings.

A stroke of the hairbrush caught another pin and several more strands of hair. "Ouch! Enough, Mama! It reminds me of when I was little. I learned never to let you brush my hair when you were angry or nervous. So which is it tonight?"

"Neither." Millicent set the brush on the dressing table. "But . . . it's time we had a little chat. There are certain things you must understand about tonight and—"

"Oh, dear." A bit too quickly she pushed to her feet, forcing Mama to hop out of her way. The sensations Sir Grayson had aroused in her were constantly in her thoughts, but they certainly were not a topic she wished to discuss with her mother. "Really, Mama, it isn't necessary. I'm perfectly well aware—"

She broke off at the sudden alteration in her mother's expression, not to mention complexion, as a startling crimson blush flowered beneath several layers of powder.

"Oh, Honora, you promised . . . you swore you didn't . . ." Millicent whirled away and stumbled to the bed. She fell facedown upon it, sending the down tick hissing around her in a great heave. A long moan funneled through the bedclothes.

It took Nora only a moment to understand this sudden fit of vapors. Sweeping to the bedside, she sat and pressed a hand to her mother's shaking shoulder. "No, no, that isn't at all what I meant. Of course I didn't pose for Signore Alessio. My knowledge of . . . such matters . . . comes purely secondhand."

*Thanks to Kat,* she acknowledged silently. Kat was the upstairs maid at home. On several furtive occasions she wasn't particularly proud of, Nora had listened in on tales of the alluring servant's escapades with the Thorngoode's groom, their man-of-all-work and the lad who delivered the coal on Thursdays.

Of course she didn't dare reveal the source of her illicit knowledge to her mother, or Kat would be sacked come morning.

Millicent rose on her elbows and twisted round to peer at her through glistening eyes. "Lewd talk from those artist friends of yours, I daresay." She gave a quick sniffle. "I shudder to consider what horrors those creatures stuffed your head with."

Nora only sighed.

Her mother rolled over and sat up, whisking back the hairs that had fallen pell-mell from her chignon. "Ignore whatever those young hellions told you. You have nothing to fear tonight, my dearest. If your young man fails to treat you properly, you have only to tell Papa and he will set Sir Grayson straight, I warrant you that. For here's a secret you won't hear often, my girl—no, indeed not."

She took possession of Nora's arm and tugged her

down beside her on the bed. "It's considered a woman's duty, but such activities can be, that is to say, *should* be pleasurable, as much for the woman as for the man if he's going about it properly. Now, for instance . . ."

Nora felt a tiny burst of interest, gone just as quickly in the shuddering remembrance that this was her *parents* they were discussing.

She groaned.

"Yes, think of it rather like priming a pump. . . ."

"I'd truly rather not. . . ."

"At first it takes a few forceful thrusts to coax the water to flow. . . ." Her mother made hand motions that might have mimicked the working of a pump had they not been discussing something else entirely.

The thought of Sir Grayson's strong hands *priming* her sent a heated tremor through her, one she concealed with a cough. "Good grief, Mother. *Do* stop . . ."

"But once the initial reluctance is breached, shall we say, a slow and steady rhythm achieves the desired results, long pulls up and down that . . ."

Hands on her ears, Nora sprang from the bed and scurried to the window. Oh, she did *not* wish her wedding night reduced to instructions on operating a pump. She even considered bursting out in song to drown out Mama's unwanted advice.

Turning to see if Millicent would pursue her across the room, she backed up until the coolness of the panes penetrated her linen shift.

Would Sir Grayson's hands feel cool or warm when he placed them on her? Would he do these things her mother was trying to explain?

Did she wish him to?

A dull ache through her lower regions suggested the answer, but she concentrated on the chill at her back rather than on the improbable, *inconceivable* images her mother was presently conjuring, and with such gusto too.

Good heavens.

"Would you like me to show you, Honora?"

Her face snapped in her mother's direction. "Absolutely *not*. I . . . I understand all you've said, and I daresay I'm fully prepared for . . . whatever . . ."

She had little notion, really. Only jumbled expectations careening inside her.

Her mother stood and came toward her, brows knotted in concern. "Are you quite certain, dearest? The first time can be frightening. Especially if he—"

"I'm quite sure he won't. Truly. I'm not afraid at all. In fact, I think it's time you were off, Mama." She mustered a smile. "It's late. You and Papa should go on home now. I'll see you tomorrow."

"Oh, we're not going anywhere, child. We'll be right down the hall. Should you need us, you've only to call."

Nora spun about to gaze down on the street outside the window. "Good night then, Mama. See you in the morning."

Millicent lingered at her shoulder, one hand stroking up and down Nora's arm. "I do so wish you to be happy, Honora. As happy as your papa and I have been."

Was it possible? Could she find happiness with the brooding stranger she had married, that wandering creature of the mists?

She had offered him a bargain, her dowry in exchange for the occasional use of one of the Clarington estates. A simple business arrangement that would benefit them both. He had neither accepted nor declined that offer. Instead he had silenced her with the right of a husband, proving beyond a doubt that she now belonged to him.

The memory of his forceful kisses crowded her thoughts, seared her lips. While an achy heat squeezed her thighs and tugged at her breasts, her fears and uncertainties coiled round an extraordinary thought: it should be pleasurable, as much for the woman as for the man.

Could Mama be right?

She kissed Millicent's cheek. "Good night. And you needn't worry, I can handle Sir Grayson."

A gleam of pride illuminated her mother's appraising look. "As you wish, then, dearest . . . good night."

Nora nodded, then quickly turned back to the scene outside the window as brisk footsteps receded across the room. Mama meant well, but this was a tangle only Nora could unwind. . . . Nora and her puzzling husband.

She shivered. Papa had said Grayson's eyes were clear. . . . Clear of murderous guilt, perhaps. But not empty. Ah, no. She saw so much in those eyes—dread, hope, disdain, desire—but always with a silent warning not to get too close. If only she understood what lay at the heart of that admonition.

She stood, shaking slightly, at the window, as her nerves, bundled so carefully throughout the day, began to unravel. Outside a barouche lumbered by, followed by a lighter, swifter curricle drawn by two sleek dapple grays.

*Hmm.* Perhaps if a stagecoach happened by, she might climb out the window, catch the branches of the tree just outside, swing out over the road and land safely amid the luggage stashed on the vehicle's roof. Merely a matter of careful timing, a sure grip . . .

The bedroom door opened. Footsteps, too heavy to belong to her mother or even Papa, raised a wash of gooseflesh that left the hairs on her arms and nape bristling.

She drew in a breath, cooled by the night-chilled window. The time had come for her to become a wife in deed as well as in word.

# Chapter 5

On his way upstairs, Grayson told himself he was visiting her only to discuss the terms of their marriage.

Never mind that he simply didn't wish to be alone. Not after those unnerving moments in Tom's study.

Tomorrow he'd ask the servants if any of them had placed his watch in the study. He already knew what their answers would be. Tonight he didn't wish to think any more about it. He wished to forget the unnatural chill that had crept up his arms and seized his chest. Needed to forget all the strange occurrences these past weeks. What else could they mean but that his hold on sanity was slippery at best?

Yet hold on he must, for his nephew's sake. There were certain matters his new wife must be made to understand, and he must stand firm.

She was his wife now—*his*—and he expected her to act the part. No more Alessios, no more Bryce Waterstons. Finished. Forgotten. The sooner she learned that, the better. For the Clarington name. For Jonathan. Grayson would see to it there were no new rumors circulating about Jonny's aunt.

He reached her room, let himself in noiselessly. The air inside fairly pulsated with her sensual, spicy scent. Nothing lemony about it, thank heavens for that. Should he turn the key, lock the door? He couldn't but admit to an unfurling desire to seek the forgetfulness he craved within Honora Thorngoode Lowell's luscious flesh.

Would that be assuming too much with this enigmatic new wife of his? One minute simmering, the next frigid as a winter's dawn. Passionate . . . then downright demure. Which embodied the true Honora Thorngoode? Rampant rumor suggested the former. Yet some fragile quality behind those lovely eyes— he'd decided they were hazel—hinted at the latter.

Or was it merely the old guilt coloring his perceptions? Guilt and the constant fear of repeating past mistakes. But it wasn't his brother, Thomas, occupying this room, nor Tom's orphaned son, Jonny. This was Honora Thorngoode, Painted Paramour of London. Hers was a downfall for which he bore no blame.

He gave the key a resolute turn.

The room stood mostly in shadow, illuminated by a faceted lamp and the street lanterns outside. She was standing by the window, her back to him, so still and slight she hardly seemed real. Her hair flowed loose to her waist, a dark, glossy river glinting gold where it caught the light.

She wore only a nightgown, sleeveless and airy. The garment draped her torso in gentle folds that flared at her hips and hugged her bottom—her high, round, sweet bottom—in a way that set his feet in motion even before his mind formed the intention.

She didn't turn, but the stiffening of her bare arms against her sides told him she was aware of his presence, his approach.

He was but a foot away when she suddenly spun about. Her trailing hair tumbled over one shoulder and curved around her breast, framing its pert roundness with an invitation he could not ignore.

She breathed hard, lips plumped and parted. Her tilting eyes held a glittering beauty. His reasons for being there rolled to some back corner of his brain as he reached out and cupped her breast in his palm.

She gasped, but whether in pleasure or affront he couldn't say. She met his gaze with a challenging lift of her chin.

He should have released her. Instead he seized the opportunity of both that raised chin and her continued silence to press his lips to hers.

The petal softness of her mouth triggered a startling hunger inside him. Eagerly he leaned to widen the kiss, deepen the pressure. The fingers of one hand spread possessively across her cheek to hold her in place.

She exhaled a moan into his mouth, an involuntary burst that had his senses vibrating, his insides humming. Until, that is, he realized he felt neither resistance nor acquiescence. She simply bore his lust with stoic immobility.

Did she want him but wasn't sure how to proceed? Did she abhor him and detest his very touch?

Or was this simply an elaborate game, and his burden to discover the rules?

He pulled back, searching her expression. When he met her gaze again, her eyes hardened and narrowed. An eyebrow slowly quirked above the other, daring him to proceed.

As no virgin ever would.

An instant's consideration was all it took for him to accept that dare. The weight of her small breast trembled warmly in his palm; he rubbed his thumb across the nipple, ripe and dark beneath her thin linen shift. He stroked back and forth, around in little circles, feeling the bud tighten beneath the pad of his finger.

A spark flashed in her eyes and her nostrils gave a delicate flare. But still she stood motionless, letting him do as he wished.

Her acquiescence set him burning even as it piqued his temper. Why did she not respond? A smile, a sigh, a slap in the face. Why this stony, silent challenge? Did she not realize the temptation she offered? The carnal impulses rising inside him?

More likely, she knew very well.

He brushed a fingertip across her lips. "By God, you're a work of art," he murmured.

That roused her. She reeled a step backward, her arms swatting him away as though he were some loathsome insect. The action raised a grin. He couldn't help it. Did she enjoy less-than-gentle love play?

Her eyes appeared more catlike than ever above lips pulled in a feline sneer. "You might try speaking a civil word or two before pawing me."

Ah. It wasn't his inclinations that offended her then, but his methods. His grin widened.

"Forgive me." He dipped a little bow. "Good evening, dear wife. I trust you've found this room comfortable."

Her chin tipped with the merest hint of insolence. "Quite, thank you."

"You're very welcome," he said, echoing her mocking courtesy. "This was once my mother's bedchamber, but it's been refurbished in recent years. Should you care to make changes, you've only to ask."

"How kind of you." She scanned him appraisingly from head to toe. "And what other privileges might I enjoy as your wife? Or must I gain your permission for everything I do?"

The question angered him. His other sins aside, he was no tyrant, especially when it came to women. He didn't like her implying otherwise, didn't like her inferred accusations. He thought they'd established a kind of truce earlier in the coach, each admitting their lot wasn't the other's fault, but rather the result of an ironic, capricious turn of fate.

He gazed dispassionately out the window above her head. "You may do as you please, my dear, when you please."

"Except go to Blackheath Grange."

The comment jabbed like a hatpin. "Don't you d—"

"Oh, I'm joking. You can take a joke, can't you?" The shining tip of her tongue slid along her bottom lip. "But I suppose I shouldn't tease, especially in matters of consequence."

He regarded the path of moisture on her lip, wishing to follow it with his own. His spurt of anger flickered away, replaced by sheer perplexity coupled with a desire to kiss her senseless, emotions becoming increasingly familiar when it came to dealing with this woman.

She'd certainly used the right word—tease—for she *was* a consummate tease, a skillful tormentor. He raked the hair off his brow and blew out a breath. "I don't know what you want, Honora."

She shrugged. "Nor do I."

"Perhaps I might help you assess your choices."

He reached for her again, one hand claiming the small of her back, the other fisting in her hair. He tilted her head, exposing a creamy expanse of throat. Before his mouth made contact she shoved at his chest.

Now what? Panting, channeling those erratic breaths into snorts of indignation, each stood glaring at the other like adversaries with pistols at dawn. Confound it, what *did* the little seductress want?

"Is the concept of subtlety a completely foreign one to you, Sir Grayson?"

Oh. He hadn't thought of that. Why should he have? Displaying one's nude portrait in a public gallery did not particularly smack of discretion. Quite the contrary.

As he stood quite literally scratching his head, her bottom lip slipped between her teeth and an eyebrow quirked in an expression so ingenuous his heart constricted. And that left him more baffled than ever.

She set his blood on fire, then tugged his conscience like a naive girl.

Another game? Did she enjoy pretending each kiss was her first, each caress a new experience? Just as she feigned innocence about the portrait?

The notion had him grinning again.

"Just what do you find so amusing?"

He paused to choose his words carefully—*very* carefully. Because since entering the room he'd come to an emphatic realization. Few women had ever managed to arouse both his passions *and* his intellect the way Honora Thorngoode did. Certainly none had consumed his every waking moment as she had these past days.

He wanted this baffling, beguiling beauty in his arms and in his bed. And he was willing to do whatever he must to ensure her presence there.

"Me, Honora." He offered a lopsided smile. "I'm finding myself highly ridiculous at the moment."

Her eyebrows drew inward. With a shake of her head she crossed her arms and waited.

"Here I am behaving like a schoolboy. Groping for you like some green youth." Yes, he'd turn it around, blame himself. "I hope you can forgive me. For tonight and the other times as well. I can be an arrogant cad sometimes."

She gave her long hair a shake. "Apology accepted. I suppose."

He conjured a tender smile. "You know, it's your fault I've acted the ass."

"I beg your pardon."

"It's true. When I said you were a work of art, I wasn't mocking. I swear I wasn't." That much *was* true. He hadn't stopped to consider the obvious—that she would think he was referring to her nude portrait.

He moved closer. She went rigid, poised as if about to dart out of reach. But she held her ground, leaving them at a standoff of sorts. He supposed it was up to him to retreat or make the next advance. With a fingertip he lifted a strand of hair from the corner of her mouth and swept it behind her shoulder.

"You're incredibly lovely. Surely you know that. Just as you must know I'd give anything right now to kiss you again. Not an unreasonable desire, I trust, for a man on his wedding night."

He gave her no time to answer before striding forward and grasping her hands. A breathy *"oh"* escaped her, and the sweetness of the sound convinced every part of him except his brain that no man had ever touched her before. His arousal strained at his trousers.

He wanted all of her in his arms, but for now, while he played her game, a chaste hand-holding would do. He bent his head until his nose brushed hers. "May I kiss you, Honora?"

"You never sought my permission before."

"I'm seeking it now."

"Then . . . yes. I believe I wish you would," she whispered, her eyes luminous, her expression earnest.

He almost stepped away, ashamed at having turned his seductive skills on such an innocent. Then he remembered who she was, and the path that had led them both to this moment.

In the instant their lips touched, their hands broke apart. He slid his arms around her, feeling an odd thrill of triumph when she let him, when hers slipped around his neck.

He'd discarded his coat and waistcoat earlier, and now her torso, deliciously soft beneath wispy linen, arched like a sun-warmed kitten against him, a seduction so subtle as to seem entirely unintentional. Yet as he pressed her closer and deepened the kiss, he somehow felt it was she and not he in control of their kisses, of him.

"You're more skilled than I'd imagined."

"Am I?" Her lashes fluttered; her bottom lip drooped invitingly, gleaming and kiss-bruised.

"Not even Waterston told me of this."

"Who . . . ? Told you of wha—"

He silenced her with more kisses, the entirety of his

being absorbed into the heat of her mouth. Her fingers curled in his hair, triggering the memory of a certain bite on the lip, instantly forgotten when her sighs purred into him.

His heart pounded. His blood roared. He nudged her mouth wider and entered with his tongue, a quick dart, a soft caress. She responded with more counterfeit innocence, tasting him and offering a tenuous welcome to her sultry secrets. Her body melted so sweetly against him, his arousal throbbed as never before.

By God, he'd never been interested in virgins, but this make-believe maiden inflamed him. With his need to have her weakening his knees and trembling through his thighs, he swung her into his arms and blindly made his way to the bed, lost in the lustrous tangle of her hair.

She clung to his neck, her alluring little whimpers muffled against his shoulder. He backed onto the bed and settled her on his lap. Using his forearm he swung her hair out of her face and smoothed it down her back. His palm settled on her bottom and her eyes flashed with anticipation or, if he didn't know better, alarm.

"Isn't it time we dispensed with coyness, darling?" He bent his head and set about devouring her mouth while his free hand dipped beneath her neckline.

She broke the kiss, slid her lips to the corner of his mouth and uttered a breathy word. "Coyness?"

"You perform it brilliantly, but it's no longer necessary." Yet he found her game exquisitely erotic. He was like a barbarian imprisoned, a warrior shackled by a petite adversary who held him merely by the force of her whim and the fire in her fingertips.

"You have me utterly at your mercy." His tongue traced the curve of her ear, eliciting shivers, squirms, a breathy moan. "I surrender."

Her fingers combed in little stops and starts, one

might say shyly, through his hair, then went still. "What was that?"

"Just my tongue, darling. Nothing to worry about. You have the most adorable ear . . ."

"No." She tilted her head to one side, effectively removing the object of his present fascination from reach. "That noise."

"I don't hear anything." He caressed her nape, attempting to coax her into relaxing back into pleasure. "Is there anything about me you particularly like, Honora?"

"There it is again. That scratching sound."

Despite his frustration, he couldn't but admit he'd heard it that time too. Muffled and faint, the sound came from across the room.

"Do you have mice in your walls?"

He shook his head. "The man and his ferrets were here less than a fortnight ago. No mice."

With their arms entwined they sat silently and listened. Honora propped her chin on his shoulder in a gesture of such familiarity, he experienced another of those odd crimps in his chest. When she lifted her head and started to speak, he pressed a finger to her lips. "Shh. It's coming from the door. I fear there may be a spy in our midst. Wait here."

He slid her from his lap and stole noiselessly across the room. Ear pressed to the door, he quite distinctly heard the unmistakable shuffling of feet, the rustle of fabric. He flung a nod toward his wife, grabbed the latch, swiftly rotated the key and swung the door wide.

Millicent Thorngoode—no great revelation—yelped, flinched upright and removed her cupped hand from behind her ear. Her startled expression instantly rearranged into a broad smile. "Oh. I didn't mean to disturb you children. I just wondered . . . that is . . . would you like tea sent up?"

*Chapter 6*

"Mama, how could you!"
    Alternate waves of chagrin and fury scorched Nora's cheeks as she bore down on the most infuriating, interfering parent in the entire history of parenthood. "Have you been eavesdropping all this time?"

"I was doing nothing of the sort, Honora." She crossed the threshold, but Nora thrust up a hand.

"Not another step. Did I not tell you—"

"Yes, dearest, I know you said you could handle Sir Grayson but—"

Nora didn't know whether it was Mama's excruciating disclosure or Grayson's indignant snort that sent spots dancing before her eyes. Sweeping past Millicent and a flabbergasted Grayson, she leaned out into the corridor.

"Papa! Papa, please come at once! Papa!"

Perhaps she shouldn't have bellowed so. Perhaps she merely should have escorted Mama from the room and shut the door. In the next moment a door down the hall burst open and her father charged out.

He didn't stop charging until he'd breezed past both her and her mother, wrenched Grayson's arm behind his back and kicked his legs out from under him. She watched in dismay as her husband of but a few hours landed hard on his knees with a grunt of pain.

Papa stood glowering over him. "What have you done?"

Her mortification grew as she witnessed the resentment churning in Grayson's eyes, heard the jaw-clenching, emphatic precision with which he pronounced each word of his reply. "I. Merely. Opened. The. Door."

"Release him this instant, Papa. He didn't do anything. It's Mama. She's been listening in on us."

Millicent's hands flew up in self-defense. "I was merely checking on them, Zachy. A mother worries for her daughter. Especially when it comes to mysteries she knows nothing of."

"Good grief, Mama."

In scowling silence Papa took in all of them—Nora, her mother, and the top of Grayson's head. Slowly both his features and his grip relaxed. He offered Grayson a hand up.

"Sorry, lad. I heard my daughter's shouts and instinct overcame reason."

"No harm done." Grayson straightened his shirt-front and tugged his cuffs into place. His mouth was tight, bracketed, grim.

What must he be thinking? Of her parents, of her. Disappointment spread like the roots of an old oak. At his touch she had alternated between frenzied nerves, paralyzing doubt and pure fear. Oh, it had all been pleasurable, but she'd been entirely ignorant of what to do, how to react. Hadn't an inkling of what he expected of her.

She certainly did not want him leaving now, as he almost surely would. They had been on the verge of . . . something extraordinary. And she had been on the verge of answering some of those startling questions raised by her mother's earlier ramblings.

She longed to learn more of the singular things Grayson had been teaching her prior to Mama's bumbling interruption. The very notion tingled through her and sent fresh heat to her face, doubtlessly accompanied by a scarlet stain certain to betray her thoughts to the others.

Her father's midnight blue eyes settled on her until her discomfiture bordered on unendurable. *Why* didn't they leave?

As if reading her mind, Papa turned to her mother. "Come along Milly. These children don't need us here. It's their wedding night, after all."

At the reference her blush burned hotter—and no doubt brighter—as if she and Grayson had embarked upon something illicit.

Yet as husband and wife they were free of restrictions, free of the burdening disgrace others had heaped upon her when, in fact, she'd done nothing wrong at all.

Free to indulge and explore . . . there was something wholly liberating in that, something she very much wished to ponder, but without her present audience.

Her mother was uttering apologies and last minute bits of advice. Nora impatiently waved her off. She'd had enough of Mama's counsel for one night, and to be sure she'd discerned no resemblance between what she and Grayson had been doing and the priming of a water pump.

She pecked Mama's cheek and all but propelled her into the hall. She turned back into the room just in time to catch her father's all too audible whisper to Grayson.

"You gentle her proper or your arm won't be the only part of you I'll be twisting. Clear?"

Grayson's hands fisted at his sides. "Perfectly. Sir."

The door closed, and they were alone. Nora worried her bottom lip. Would he open that door once more and seek sanity elsewhere? She waited, certain she'd seen the last of him, at least for tonight. But he made no move. They stood staring at each other, the mo-

ments preceding the interruption crisp in the air between them, or so it felt to Nora. Then . . .

He burst out laughing. Loudly. Head thrown back,
mouth wide. The sound of it rang through the room;
the shock of it reverberated inside her. For what
seemed an eternity she stood frozen and mortified.
Was he laughing at her?

An instant later she was hugging her sides, doubled
over as the tensions and worries and even the trials
of her parents' farcical meddling tumbled free like
pearls from a broken strand. Yes, it was funny. All
of it—her parents, their snooping, their meddlesome
ways—everything about this situation. It had to be
funny, or it would be too, too tragic.

Still laughing, she clutched the edge of the dressing
table for balance and struggled to catch her breath.
"Did you see her face?"

"Did you see *his* face?"

"Heavens, yes. Did Papa hurt you?"

"Yes, as a matter of fact." He flexed his wrist. "Is
he always like that?"

Her laughter ceased as she looked doubtfully into
his handsome countenance. Then a fresh round of guf-
faws rolled from her lips. "Yes. As a matter of fact,
he is."

To her relief, Grayson's laughter engulfed her own.
She raised the back of her hand to wipe away mirthful
tears. In the aftermath of chaos and laughter she felt
a sudden glow, an entirely new, somewhat startling but
at the same time comforting impression that Grayson
Lowell had somehow transformed into more than the
man she'd been forced to marry.

That he was her . . . friend.

He held out a hand, large and broad, a tempting
place to rest her own. "Come," he said, his smile
equally broad and tempting.

She placed her hand in his, experiencing a surge of
heat when his fingers closed and claimed her. Her

breath hitched as he gave a sudden tug that yanked her against his chest. His lips plunged, hard and wet, leaving her breathless, drowning, just the tiniest bit frightened again.

His mouth came away with a rueful twist. "So you can handle me, eh?"

"I'd hoped that comment had escaped your notice."

"Perhaps I enjoy the idea of being handled." A devilish slant tipped his brows. "Perhaps I've finally determined how to handle you."

His baritone dipped on a note that ran under her flesh, raking her nerve endings and stealing her newfound ease. Comfortable? A mere friend?

No, Grayson Lowell was anything but. Right now he was a sensual rival, a seductive foe. Looking down at her with that rapacious gleam in his eye, he seemed predatory, bent on satiating an appetite she was only beginning to comprehend.

A shivering current hovered between them. She tried to widen the gaps between their bodies. His arms locked around her, giving no quarter.

"My mother misspoke. You must not think—"

"Don't be indignant." His fingers stroked up and down her bare arm, raising telltale goose bumps that revealed her confusion. He grinned. The strokes became longer, deeper, a lusty rhythm that swept through her, seizing control of her heart and pulse, her breathing, her thoughts.

"I'd say my methods of handling you were well under way to reaping some rather interesting rewards— for both of us. Until a little mouse put a halt to things, that is."

She felt the same paralyzing fear as before. He was moving too fast, exceeding her understanding, her ability to make sense of the sensations threatening to overwhelm her. And while part of her longed to be overwhelmed, another part needed time. Needed gentling, as her father had said.

Why must he push, rush so? Yes, they were married, but couldn't he court her? Even just a little? Could he not understand her inability to simply leap into this new sphere of pleasure?

His hand rose to trace the curve of her cheek. "Shall we carry on where we left off?"

He felt a quiver beneath his fingers just before she broke away, showing him a smooth, bare shoulder.

"Carry on? You make it sound tawdry."

Teasing again. The aloofness emanating from the elegant line of her neck, the arch of her back, had him pining for her again. Painfully. Ah, the woman truly was an artist, an expert at the arts of seduction.

He slid a hand beneath her hair onto her warm nape and drew her toward him. "Don't turn away from me, and yes, we'll be tawdry if it pleases us to be so."

The look she cast him scorched. Ah, this woman played a far different game than any he was accustomed to, but he was more than willing to follow her lead.

He didn't remove his hand from her nape, but eased as close as he dared. "I meant no offense. I merely thought we were enjoying ourselves rather much. If I am mistaken, tell me and I'll bid you good night."

A little ridge formed above her nose. Her lips parted, the bottom a pouty morsel he wished more than anything to suck between his own. He resisted the temptation, but brushed his nose against a silky lock of hair. "I'd prefer to stay if you'll permit me."

He waited, and was rewarded when she ever so slowly listed toward him, arching her neck and turning her face until her lips hovered an inch or two from his. He chanced a sweeping caress along her bare arm, ending at the satin curve of her shoulder. There his fingers lingered in a seductive dance against her skin.

"Stay," she whispered, and closed the space between their lips.

His hand slid into her hair, sifting the heavy gloss through his fingers as their limbs entwined, their mouths merged. She wilted against him. His blood caught fire. As he'd done earlier, he scooped her into his arms and brought her back to the bed.

Once there he distracted her with kisses while he set about undoing the buttons down the front of her nightgown. He went slowly, careful not to raise her ire, as he seemed more than adept at doing.

"My neckcloth . . . untie it." He remembered to add a "please," and she tugged at the knot, making surprisingly short work of it. Soon his collar sprang open. She raised a poignantly uncertain gaze. He grinned, warming once more to the charade, thoroughly enjoying it now. He nodded and whispered, "The buttons too."

Meanwhile her neckline dropped a fraction more with each button he released, exposing the valley between her breasts. When she didn't flinch or send him a severe look, he dipped his head and nuzzled. "Tell me what you like, Honora," he murmured against her.

"I'd . . . like you to call me Nora."

He nodded, rubbing his nose up and down her supple flesh. "You may call me Gray if you wish. All my very closest friends do."

"Gray," she obeyed breathlessly.

"There, that brings my list of closest friends to two. You and Chad."

She gave a dubious chuckle, as if disbelieving his little confession. He let it drop and whispered, "Tell me what you want, Nora. Tell me what you wish me to do and I'll do it."

He risked allowing his tongue to graze the cleft of her bosom. She shuddered, her breasts quivering against his face, cutting off breath for one delicious instant.

Desire thundered inside him. He released another two buttons. Her nightgown slithered over her shoulders, as exquisite as fine bisque. He kissed his way from one to the other.

"Do you like this, Nora?"

The word *yes* rode a tremulous breath.

"I'd like it if you touched me too."

Her hands found their way beneath his shirt and inch by inch she raised the hem. He helped her bare his stomach and chest, grasping her hands and raising them until together they stripped the garment over his head.

With a trembling sigh she grazed the muscles of his torso, making them quiver. Her eyes were wide, darkly dilated. He tossed the shirt away, then peeled the remaining scrap of nightgown from her breasts and pressed her to his naked chest.

"By Christ . . ." His oath tore from deep inside. He gripped her waist, fingers of both hands splayed across her hips, and rocked her against his arousal. Only this demure game they were playing prevented him from tossing her down and plunging into her.

He set his open mouth to her neck, sucking gently but deeply, sure to leave a mark. Against the thrashing pulse in her throat he murmured, "Command me, my darling."

Her words were garbled, thick with passion. Her lips, hot and swollen, worked silently, and then he quite distinctly heard, ". . . the first time."

Ah yes, he understood. "You wish it to be as your first time."

She went still in his arms and stared back at him, her eyes fever bright. Her cheeks were burnished, her breasts flushed and ruby-tipped with passion.

He smiled. "And so it shall be, my lady."

Slowly, meticulously, he lowered her to the bed. He eased the nightgown over her hips until it slid down her legs and floated to join his shirt on the floor.

"Ah, Nora, such legs." His pulse gave a lurch. As petite as she was, those legs seemed endless in proportion. Smooth and long, pleasingly round in the knee, enticingly plump at the thighs. Her skin glowed coppery in the lamplight. He raised his gaze. . . .

And swallowed a gasp of admiration. He could have lost himself in the silhouette of her hip, the contour of her stomach, the dusky silk at the junction of her legs. He ran a fingertip through the curling hairs, then drew it back. His desire for her throbbed, but it was too soon to venture there.

Her eyes became huge and filled with questions, with the uncertainty she mimicked so well. That look bore the power to undo a man—if only it had been real.

She wished to pretend, and he was more than happy to accommodate those wishes. Sliding his feet to the floor, he stood above her and ran his hands the length of those generous legs. With the utmost care he stroked her ankles, circled her calves, caressed behind her knees. He raised her foot and set his lips to the delicate instep, smiling when he felt a ticklish current run through her.

Alternately he used his fingertips and his open palms, his lips, his tongue, drawing inward as he reached the tops of her thighs.

She uttered a cry. He gripped her hips and raised them from the bed, pressing kisses to her belly. His lips strayed lower, to the tender skin in the bend of her thigh. He used his tongue and even his teeth for a sensual nip. She rocked beneath him, sighed, grabbed handfuls of the counterpane.

"Tell me all you wish me to do, Nora."

Her hands glided to her breasts, her fingers closing over her nipples.

"Ah, you want to feel my hands there, is that it?"

A "yes" made itself heard between panting breaths. Her small breasts filled his hands, burned beneath his palms. Her eyes were closed, her lips parted and gleaming. She arched into him, splintering his control.

"Sweet Nora, you are far too tempting. . . ." He spoke until his mouth reached her breast. Then his tongue grew too busy for words, learning the shape and taste of her nipple, molding it into a tight little peak. His teeth closed around it. She cried out.

Her head came off the mattress and she gaped at him. He expected sharp words, a shove. Waited for her to crawl out from under him. His lust both raged and cringed as he anticipated the rebuke. Could he head it off?

"By God, Nora, I'm sorry. I didn't mean to—"

"Hurt me?" She shook her head wildly. "You didn't. That was . . . astounding. Gracious, I . . ." Her head fell back. Her eyes drifted shut. "Can you do it again?"

"I'll try my best."

He had her moaning within seconds, had himself breathless with urgency. But he neglected nothing, not a part of her, until her hands tore at his trouser buttons and her legs wrapped around him, drawing him close and making her desires clear.

"Finish it," she breathed against him. "Teach me all of it."

Her fingers tightened, digging into his buttocks with an insistence that spurred him. But once again he fought the urge to hasten inside her.

Instead he grasped her knees and eased her legs from around his waist. Backing the necessary few inches away, he held her thighs apart while he kissed his way between them. With his tongue he prepared her, adding his own moisture to the already damp folds. He searched out the hidden globe of flesh and with his lips adored it, revered it, pleasured it until Nora thrashed and clenched her fists against the mattress.

Her apparent readiness and his own voracious need sent him sprawling over her.

"No more pretending." Pressing the head of his

arousal against her, he braced his arms on the bed and pushed.

Instead of the effortless sweep he expected, he encountered the very last thing he'd imagined or wished—a barrier. Even before his mind processed its meaning, he felt the sudden break, then a heated rush of fluid and Nora's stifled cry against his shoulder.

He went utterly still, his heart clenched around an awful certainty.

*She is a virgin. Was a virgin.*

God help him.

Her hands clutched at his arms and a mewling sound, part anguished, part imploring, vibrated through him. Her legs once more encircled his waist, holding him, impelling him.

Even as the magnitude of how thoroughly he'd wronged her howled through him, he thrust forward. Because she wanted him to. Because he needed to. Through the resistance, past the tightness of untouched muscle and farther, he buried his length, his mind, his being into soul-damning bliss.

She uttered a faint "yes' and he thrust again, losing himself to the tempo, to the savage song echoed from his lips to hers. The mingling notes built, became louder, insistent, sweeping him over a devastating brink.

## Chapter 7

Nora felt a splintering . . . a shattering . . . a burst of fiery color. Flaming scarlet, sizzling amber, blistering ocher . . .

A chasm yawned and gaped, and the receding pain was replaced by a lustrous shaft of spiraling ecstasy; by a knowledge both heady and frightening. Her world shifted, careened and broke apart while the girl she'd been flickered away, cast to oblivion by Grayson's thrusts.

She gripped him with arms and legs, as inside her a woman emerged, one with desires and demands she'd never imagined. She opened her eyes and looked up at him. He was . . .

Beautiful. Intense. Gleaming with energy, trembling with controlled power and restrained fury. The very sight squeezed droplets from her eyes. Despite all her misgivings, she wanted this man. Wished to possess him as he possessed her, teach him as he taught her. Minutes ago she could not have conceived of the lesson. Now her body knew just what to do.

No longer the passive recipient of his lovemaking, she moved beneath him, arching, contracting her muscles to meet his thrusts and return them in kind. He held her hips in his large hands, guided her, breathed into her, became part of her.

Every thought, every feeling, every sensation became a twisting sphere of fire that quite suddenly fractured, consumed her whole, reshaped her and left her his.

*His.* For better or worse. From now until death. She listened for hypocrisy, and for the first time heard none.

Afterward they lay entwined in silence, until Grayson adjusted his arms around her. He cupped his hand round the back of her head as if she were a child or a fragile thing of great worth, and gently pressed her cheek to the hollow of his shoulder. Feeling his lips traveling through her hair, hearing the rumbling sigh deep in his chest, she knew contentment such as she'd never dreamed.

"Nora . . ." The solemn timbre of his murmur stole a portion of her joy. "Nora, forgive me. I am so—"

She whisked her hand to his mouth. "If you say you're sorry, I shall leave this instant and never come back."

She didn't mean it. She simply could not bear either of them regretting what they'd done.

He kissed her palm before grasping it and holding it against his chest. "I should have known. I should have believed you."

"Yes, decidedly so. It was rather foolish of you, wasn't it, to listen to rumors when the truth was right before you." His body tightened beneath her. She turned her face to his chest and kissed a taut pectoral muscle. "But I didn't believe in you either."

"And now?"

"I do."

Again that somber sound, billowing from a cavernous place inside him—a gathering of breath, a desultory rumble.

"Do stop that. You're being like Mama."

He stiffened. "Just how the devil am I—"

"By being melodramatic. That's Mama's field of expertise." She hugged him, grinning, liking the way his chest hairs tickled her cheek. "I thought it was all rather nice. Not nearly as bad as I'd feared."

"I believe I've just been deeply insulted."

"What I mean is, I didn't think you liked me at all, so I was afraid that . . . what we've done . . . might not turn out to be particularly pleasurable. For either of us."

He rolled with her until they lay side by side, then propped his chin on his hand and gazed down at her. His other hand smoothed up and down her arm, from wrist to shoulder and back. "What made you think I didn't like you?"

"Oh, everything you've said and done since we met."

He sighed, nodding. For a moment his hand stopped traveling her arm, then took up its journey again. "I acted the buffoon precisely because I was growing to like you. . . . But didn't wish to."

"Ah. You mean you were afraid to."

He didn't answer. She could all but hear the ruminations of his brain as he worked that one over. She supposed he didn't much like the notion. Yawning, she hid a smile behind her hand.

"Let's go to sleep," he finally said, sounding just the faintest bit tetchy. And that made her smile too.

He awoke to the silver prod of moonlight spearing through the western windows.

They hadn't drawn the curtains. They hadn't done a lot of things. Such as that discussion he'd been determined to have with her. He had intended making demands, insisting upon a certain standard of behavior, the proper decorum for a wife of the House of Clarington.

Thank heavens he hadn't gotten any of that hypocritical claptrap out of his mouth. Recent memories, warm and softly blurred from sleep, flowed through his body.

He reached for her . . . and found her gone. The shock of the empty bed beside him awakened him fully. He sat up. The mattress still held the imprint of her body. The bedclothes were rumpled but no longer warm. They'd been turned down and shoved aside.

Even as he scanned the room, hoping to find her, his heart rattled a panicked tune. A hundred thoughts, mostly recriminating, ran through his brain. What had he said wrong, done wrong? Had the euphoria with which he'd drifted to sleep been an illusion? Had Nora, appalled and resentful, waited stiffly beside him for her chance to flee?

He was on his feet, searching for his trousers. Her nightgown was nowhere in sight. He discovered his shirt half kicked beneath the bed. He dragged it over his head and loped to the door.

In the upper gallery he groaned a huge sigh of relief. Nora, emerging from shadow, came into view at the top of the staircase. Balancing a cup and saucer in one hand and holding her nightgown free of her feet with the other, she started toward him. His relief, vast and palpable, drummed through him.

He held out his arms to her. "You shouldn't traipse through the house in the dark. Better yet, you should have woken me. I'd have gone with you."

"I didn't wish to wake you." With her satin robe billowing softly behind her, she floated into his embrace, careful not to jostle her teacup. "And anyway, one of the servants made me tea and walked me to the foot of the stairs. Didn't you hear her bid me good night?"

"No." He glanced down the staircase but saw no candle glow receding from the hall below. "Who was awake at this hour?"

"Funny, she never spoke her name, and I didn't think to ask." She stepped away, carefully balancing her cup and saucer as she made her way back into the bedroom.

Lightly he stepped over the threshold behind her, gripped with an unsettling sensation as he watched her circle the bed and set her tea on the bedside table. He came to a halt, disoriented and swathed in goose-flesh. In the silver cast of moonlight, she appeared ghostlike, a shimmering apparition drifting through the room.

His breath turned icy in his lungs. Then shook his head and dismissed the very thought of ghosts. Or at least refused to pay it heed. He crossed the room and slid into bed beside her. This was his wife, his lovely, passionate yet virtuous wife. Flesh and blood. She was his future.

The past was dead.

Or so he fervently wished to believe.

It was then the whisper arose inside him. *You don't deserve her. You deserve the Honora from rumor, not this ingenuous, unsullied young Nora.*

The undeniable truth squeezed his throat. Reaching for her with both arms, he gathered her to his side and kissed her brow, her hair. She let out a murmur. Her breath tickled his chin and she smiled at him as she draped an arm around his waist. "She was quite beautiful. Should I be jealous?"

Baffled, he blinked. "Of whom?"

"Your servant, of course. The woman I met in the kitchen."

A wary alertness seized him. "Who was this person? Describe her."

"She's tall and blond. And quite charming. She had the loveliest accent. Irish, I believe. I'm not positive of that, but it was neither London nor Kentish. Quite musical." She braced her forearms on his chest and lifted herself to gaze down at him. "She's obviously someone long in your employ. She seemed to know rather much about you."

A chill swept his shoulders. "Such as?"

"She gave me advice . . . on how to handle you."

Her brows knitted at the memory. Then she grinned, obviously remembering her mother's slip of the tongue and the conversation that followed afterward.

"What exactly did she say?" He couldn't help asking, though the better part of him didn't wish to know.

"She told me you needed looking after."

"Indeed? Did she elaborate?"

"No, nothing specific. But . . ."

"But what?"

"Now I think of it, she seemed familiar. I can't place where I've met her before. . . ."

Her uncertainty echoed through him. His mind leapt to the unexplainable occurrences since his brother's death: that day on the cliffs, the disembodied whispers, the appearance of his pocket watch in the study, the sensation that Charlotte had been in that room with him. He felt a sudden urge to rush below stairs and find this woman, just to reassure himself she was flesh and blood.

Nora's arms went around him. She leaned her cheek against his shoulder, and suddenly it seemed easy to dismiss all of it as no more than the fatigue and imaginings of a man under too great a strain.

He seized upon an explanation. "Franny."

"I beg your pardon?"

"The cook's assistant. She has blond hair and sometimes works late. And the accent you heard—Franny hails from Cornwall."

She gave a nod, an agreement shadowed by a faint crease above her nose. "Yes, it was probably her, then."

What other conclusion could there be? The house was locked secure each night. No one could have stolen in, and even if someone had, what sort of intruder made tea for the occupants before robbing them?

He thought of asking Franny herself, but how would it look for the master of the house to inquire of a servant about his wife's nocturnal wanderings, especially in light of the rumors that already existed? Before long half the servants in London would be gossiping. And Nora had endured gossip enough for a lifetime.

"Next time you raid the kitchen at midnight, sweetheart, wake me and bring me with you." He tightened his arms around her, and vowed to keep her safe.

"What the devil is all this? I haven't placed any orders recently. Certainly none to warrant this tower of crates."

"From Thorngoode Continental, sir."

At the top of the stairs, Nora heard the name of her father's shipping company, followed by Grayson's grumbled reply.

*Oh, not now,* she thought with a sinking stomach. Please, don't let some difficulty or misunderstanding arise between Grayson and her parents. Not today.

She'd awakened in his arms earlier. He had already been awake, not wishing to disturb her, he'd said, but waiting for her. Then he'd kissed her and covered her with his body, sinking deeply into her and filling her with his warmth. Unlike last night, this had been leisurely, tinged with an enticing languor. But no less consuming. No less glorious.

Could something beyond money and reputation be brewing in this forced marriage of theirs?

Below, the unfamiliar voice said, "Shall I haul it all away then, sir?"

"No. No, I'll sign for it."

She hurried down, intending to ward off trouble if she could. She saw Grayson handing the deliveryman a bill of lading and a coin. He looked tired, his features drawn and his eyes framed by shadows.

They'd gotten precious little sleep last night, after all.

He cocked his head at her as she reached the bottom step. "And what might you know of all this?"

*All this* signified a good dozen crates of various sizes, each stamped with her father's emblem and company initials. "I'm sure I haven't the foggiest. Let's open one."

"No need. I can tell you what's inside." Her father strolled into the hall from the drawing room. "Art supplies and paintings, my girl. Yours."

Her hand flew to the base of her throat. "My paintings!"

"Yes, and brushes and canvas, all your powders and those foul-smelling jars of oil."

"Oh, Papa." She ran to him and threw her arms around his neck. He responded with gentle pats at her back, his nose poking her hair as he kissed her. "Thank you, Papa. You're such a darling. But . . ."

She released him, her eyes narrowing. "I thought Mama had it all tossed in the trash bin."

"I did." Her mother walked out from the drawing room. Standing beside her husband, she slipped her hand around the crook of his elbow. Her mouth tilted in disapproval, but she said nothing more.

"I had it all collected back out and stored at the wharf." Papa pursed his lips, stole a glance at his wife and breathed a long-suffering sigh. "Didn't see the point of your having to buy all new. And the paintings . . . could never replace those." He made a sweep of his hand, encompassing the boxes crowding the hall. "Talent the likes of yours must not go wasted. No, indeed."

Mama gave a snort.

Nora blinked away tears. Her paintings and supplies . . . it was all too good to be true. Everything beginning with the moment Grayson took her in his arms and kissed her last night had been too perfect to be true.

She turned to him, standing patiently by, if looking a little bemused. He had told her more than once she might continue painting if she wished. Would seeing all this clutter in his home change his mind?

"Where shall we put it?" she asked.

He gave a shrug. "That's for you to decide. I suppose you'll have to traipse through the house and decide which room lends the best light."

As they all filed into the morning room for breakfast, a thread of unease wound through her happiness. Traipse . . . Last night Grayson had warned her against traipsing about the house alone in the dark. But she hadn't been alone, had she?

The blonde—Nora *had* met her before. She remembered now. The woman in the kitchen last night had been the same as in her dream the night before her wedding. The one who had reassured her about marrying Grayson.

But how could that be?

Could she have fallen asleep at the kitchen table and dreamed the woman again? Still been dreaming when she believed the woman walked her to the stairs?

Grayson said she must have been Franny, who worked in the kitchen. Nora had met Franny upon her arrival here for the wedding breakfast yesterday. The maid bore no resemblance to her elusive companion.

Besides, she hadn't mentioned to Grayson the last bit of advice the blonde had imparted last night—a suggestion she doubted a kitchen servant would ever think to make.

*To learn more about him, persuade Grayson to take you to the National Gallery.*

## Chapter 8

"That was wonderful of Papa, wasn't it?" Nora murmured. Yet even as the traveling coach listed over a bump in the road, her thoughts veered to a far different matter.

Beside her, Grayson nodded his agreement. "Nice to see he has a tender side, though my guess is only you can bring it out."

"Mama can too," she replied absently. Storefront after storefront darted past her window; she felt half inclined to signal their driver to stop at any one of them.

What did she expect to find at the National Gallery? Insight into her husband's character? Something that might reconcile her initial impression of a brooding creature of darkness with the gentle, loving man capable of awakening her deepest passions? What could that possibly have to do with Grayson's taste in art?

Then again, she was following the advice of a complete stranger . . . or someone envisioned in a dream. Yes, surely it had been a dream. Lifelike, lingering, but a figment of her imagination all the same. No other explanation made sense.

"This outing is a capital idea." His observation startled her out of her reverie. "Glad you suggested it."

"I almost didn't. I thought perhaps the National

Gallery would be the last place you'd wish us to be seen, after what happened with Alessio's portrait."

But that was only half the truth. The other half involved her failing to tell Gray everything her mysterious lady had said last night, and that made her feel rather like a liar. Certainly she was bringing him along under false pretenses. But wouldn't he think her rather dotty to be listening to a dream?

He was shaking his head and smiling at her. "Alessio and his antics are behind us now, my darling. You are an artist. It only makes sense we'd wish to spend an afternoon viewing the exhibition."

Reaching an arm around her, he pulled her closer to his side, then tipped her chin to view her face beneath her bonnet brim. "For the life of me, I don't understand why you hedged so about it earlier and why I practically had to pry it out of you."

"Yes, well, I haven't been here all season, and I've been longing to study the Rubens works again, but I feared you wouldn't approve." She sighed and allowed the pitching coach to nudge her more firmly against him. "It's art that landed me in such a quagmire, isn't it?"

"Are you inferring that being married to me constitutes a quagmire?"

She couldn't help laughing as his expression wobbled between indignant and tragic. "I confess I thought exactly that. Until last night, that is."

"Ah. So I do have my charms, under certain circumstances at least."

Her misgivings retreated to a distant corner of her mind as she found herself tipped precariously back in his arms, her mouth ravaged by his lips. When a button on her carriage jacket sprang open and his warm hand slid inside her bodice, her better sense reluctantly reared its intrusive head.

"Gray, no . . ."

"Ah, but the way you say no sounds suspiciously similar to a yes." Before she knew it, he'd loosened her bodice. One of the laces that held her gown to her corset popped free.

"How on earth did you do that?"

"I've a multitude of tricks up my sleeve." His hand burrowed beneath her shift and slid across her breast, raising exquisite friction against her beaded nipple.

Her breath hitched. "That you're quite the magician became abundantly clear last night, but now is not the time."

And yet her body contradicted the sentiment. Appropriate or no, desire steamed like an urgent kettle, steeping her in aching heat.

She slapped at him playfully, wishing they were anywhere but rumbling down crowded Regent Street. "We're almost there. Help put me back to rights."

With a boyish pout he obeyed, refastening all but the errant lacing inside her gown. That would have to wait till later. In the meantime she must simply move carefully to prevent her bodice rumpling.

"There. Good as new." He ran his palm over her jacket, pausing again over her breast, tight and swollen in response to his teasing.

The quelling look she tried to conjure melted into a grin of complicity.

The coach rolled to a stop. She shook out her skirts, concentrated on drawing steady breaths in and out and did her best to ignore the persistently lustful gleam in his eye.

They'd arrived at Pall Mall, at a house not much larger than her parents' own in Belgravia. It never failed to confound her that the country's foremost collection of European art should be crowded into this inadequate building, formerly the home of one Julius Angerstein.

Now, after only a few short years, the collection threatened to exceed its allotted space. She could not help hoping there might be room someday for a work or two of hers.

But wishes aside, her feet stilled on the walkway and she stared in apprehension at the gallery's brick facade. A voice inside her suggested she climb right back into the coach and forget this little outing. Insisted nothing good could come of it. Debated the wisdom of pushing her luck by walking through the doors of any art gallery.

"Darling, you needn't be afraid." He wrapped an arm about her waist. "This is the best defense of all. Go exactly where people least expect us to show our faces and prove to them we've nothing to hide and nothing to fear. You'll see how quickly the gossip fades."

"I do hope you're right. Oh, but of course you are. I'm being silly." It was only a building filled with paintings, thankfully none of them of her. There would be no appalling surprises, certainly nothing to send her running like a coward.

Passing through the main hall, they entered what was once the ballroom, spacious and ornate, with wide marble pilasters dividing the walls into smaller viewing sections. Sheer silk curtains draped the wide windows, admitting filtered but indirect light. Gas lamps along the walls helped illuminate the artwork.

Several small groups of patrons milled slowly from painting to painting, their hushed tones traveling up the walls to echo against the carved ceiling. A man and woman stood gazing at a pair of Rembrandts; three ladies inspected a Reynolds; another group compared examples of the Dutch and Flemish schools.

Nora strode to the center of the room and stopped, gazing around and wondering what on earth she might learn about her husband by staring at art. She had been here many times before, had seen these very paintings countless times. Could one of them have been donated by the Lowell family?

She felt Grayson's solid presence at her back and turned to face him. "Do you have any particular favorites?"

He shrugged. "I like certain works better than others, though I confess I'm not always sure what distinguishes one school from another."

He stepped closer, filling her vision and bringing the masculine scent of his shaving soap to tantalize her senses. His eyebrows wiggled suggestively. "Perhaps you'd like to teach me a thing or two. Tell me what it is that excites you. About art, of course."

"Art indeed. All right, then. Come this way."

Taking his arm, she led him through an archway. If he truly wished to learn, she'd be more than happy to share her favorite masters with him. Perhaps that was their reason for being here, so that he might come to understand exactly what it was about art she so revered.

They were almost into the adjoining parlor when a whisper hissed liked an arrow through the hushed room.

"Why look there, it's that lewd painting come to life."

"The Painted Paramour. How utterly shameless."

The blood roared in Nora's ears as mortification prickled like hot needles on her cheeks. A few yards away, two women and a gentleman seemed no longer interested in viewing the George Beaumont landscape before them. No, apparently she and Grayson offered a much more fascinating prospect.

"I must say I'm rather surprised to see her still alive."

"No doubt they find each other highly engrossing— a murderer and his paramour. . . ."

"Yes, well, *she* of all people would be capable of holding his attention, succeeding where his poor brother failed."

Her breath filled her lungs in dagger-sharp bursts.

A bolt of fury followed, one that left her limbs trembling. No one spoke of her husband that way. Indeed, for her own part she could hardly blame them for believing the worst. Her nude portrait had, after all, hung on public display in the Marshall Street Art Gallery.

But after last night, the thought of Grayson Lowell ever harming another individual was preposterous, impossible. How could the rest of the world be so blind to the obvious?

She gathered breath to utter the sharpest retort her indignant mind could devise, but Grayson's hands clamped her shoulders and propelled her forward into the next parlor.

"Don't listen to them." His lips pressed against her ear. "Slanderous idiots, all of them. They dishonor themselves far more than they ever could us with their insipid prattling."

"Why should they say such hurtful things?" Her pulse points thudded as frustration filled her to bursting. "What pleasure do they derive from being cruel?"

He brought them to a halt. His palm cupped her chin, raising it until her watery gaze met his, unwavering and filled with a firm conviction that soothed away the greater portion of her anger.

"I don't give a tinker's damn what they say about me," he said, "and we both know what they say about you isn't true."

The disparity of his words struck her. He believed in her innocence, but what of his own? Merely that he didn't care what people said. She wanted to ask him, opened her mouth to do so, but a forbidding shadow darkened his features. She shivered in a sudden chill.

The shadow lifted and his arms went around her. "Devil take them all. We've just as much right to be here as anyone. Their venomous tongues can't force us out."

The pressure of his embrace, the kiss he pressed to the top of her head, exposed her misgivings for the serpents they were and sent them slithering away. She knew who she was; knew her husband for the man he was too. No scandal sheet or drawing room gossip could alter the truth or poison her happiness.

Her chin came up. "Be assured I've no intention of leaving. Not until we are good and ready."

"There's my brave, stalwart girl."

Nora beamed up at him, wondering if this is why her dream had directed her here today—to show her that together she and Grayson were stronger than all the gossip London could concoct. Didn't it make sense, then, that her mind would devise such a dream, sending her back to the art world where she'd once been so happy and so filled with plans for the future? A future that now included the man at her side.

Taking his hand, she led him into what had been the formal dining hall, a lengthy expanse flanked by hearths at either end and a bank of windows along one wall. Landscapes lined the wall opposite.

They were the room's sole occupants, and for that she breathed a sigh of relief. Not only would they be free of wagging tongues, but they might take their time without being jostled along. Why did it always seem that whichever painting captured her interest suddenly became the most coveted object in the entire gallery?

"Claude Gellée," she murmured fondly, walking closer to a landscape featuring the lovers, Narcissus and Echo, entwined in a tree-shaded foreground. Yet it was the brighter, rose-hued distance she leaned to examine. "The colors produce the most remarkable effect, don't you think?"

"I confess I'm more interested in what those two are up to." He gestured toward the lovers.

"Yes, but see how the brighter distance offers a

subtle reminder of a wider world beyond their intimacy."

A faint look that might have been concentration or puzzlement creased his brow.

"I'm convinced Turner must be influenced by Gellée's work."

He harrumphed and brushed his chin with the backs of his fingers.

"Come look at this one." She tugged him along, pausing next before a canvas by another Frenchman. "Now, Nicholas Poussin learned his use of color from Titian. Can you see it in the golden tones of the road and the wall?"

"Now that you mention it . . ."

"See how the man at the fountain is washing his feet? He has found a place of comfort and rest. It is at once sensual and safe, rather like a trusted lover's embrace."

But Grayson was no longer regarding the artwork. He was looking at her and grinning. His hand came up to stroke her cheek, cradle her chin. His thumb grazed circles beneath her bottom lip. "I believe it is not the colors but you that make these works sensual."

She blew out a mildly exasperated breath and would have explained further, had he not leaned beneath her bonnet brim for a kiss. His tongue darted against her lips, and a flame of desire leapt inside her.

She pushed against him. "Not here."

"Let's be off, then."

Shaking her head as if at an incorrigible child, she suddenly spotted the very painting she had most longed to see.

"There it is!" Lurching out of his arms, she swept away and hurried to an oblong panorama by Peter Paul Rubens. "I've needed to see this for ages."

"*Needed* to see?" He joined her at the painting. His shoulder brushed hers, then lodged firmly against it with an intimacy she delighted in, luxuriated in.

Such a solid shoulder, strong and rock hard and everything her own slender shoulder was not. Didn't that simply make them a perfect fit, his hardness against her softness. . . .

She stifled a scandalized giggle and ducked beneath her hat brim. When *did* she start having such lascivious thoughts?

Sometime last night, she supposed.

She cleared her throat and took a half step forward. "It's Rubens's use of light that fascinates me. I've been trying . . . oh, but not quite getting it . . . look here. How does he do it?"

She swept a hand in the air. "See how the foreground is dark and muted—much like the Gellée we just saw. But then how quickly the eye is drawn to the distant hills and those brilliant clouds. It's as if by entering into the landscape of this painting, the viewer is whisked from comfortable yet unenlightened familiarity to a gleaming, glorious realm of hope, of possibilities and potential. . . ."

At her back, he slipped his arms around her, lodging them just beneath her breasts. "I believe you're all the gleaming, glorious hope I need," he said against her neck.

His hot breath raised an ardent tremor. Even so, she twisted to flash him a mock scowl. "Don't you long to run across these hills and stand beneath that golden light?"

He shrugged, grinned, held her tighter. "Are you there waiting for me?"

And just like that she turned in his arms, yielded to his lips, melted against him.

A moment later she broke free of the kiss and darted wild glances first at one doorway, then the other.

He grasped her chin. "There's no one here. To hell with them anyway."

His lips prodded hers open. Against them he ground, "We're already lost to scandal. Why not make it the most glorious scandal ever to take London?"

His hands were everywhere, touching places she'd never been touched, nor dreamed of being touched, in daylight hours. Standing in this very public place had the shocking effect of heightening her senses, sharpening her desire. Of sending her hands to search brazenly inside his coat.

She lifted her face and smiled up at him, and glimpsed, beyond his shoulder, a sight that stopped her blood cold. Her hands dropped to her sides. Grayson spoke but she didn't hear, too intent on the strange, otherworldly light flickering from the next room.

In an instant she realized she'd grown all too familiar with the nature of that light. Twice now, in her dreams, it had glowed with the brilliance of a Rubens masterpiece.

Pushing away from Grayson, she set off, her footsteps clacking on the marble floor. Back into the small parlor . . . she entered just in time to see a glimmer of blond hair, the billowing luster of lavender silk.

Yes, now she remembered—on those two previous occasions her mystery lady had worn that very dress and had seemed to stand in the full noon sun.

This was no dream. She broke into a trot, dispensing with decorum as she pattered into the ballroom. Puzzled stares followed her. Whispers dashed after. Behind her, Grayson's footsteps hastened in pursuit.

"Nora, what is it? Where are you going?"

From the main hall she scurried up the stairs, where her chase ended in what had once been the billiard room. Panting for breath, she stumbled in from the landing in time to catch a fading shimmer of light, nothing more. She stopped on the threshold and gripped the door frame for balance.

The room was nearly empty but for a lone man in a tweed cloak. But how could that be? There was only one doorway out and Nora was standing in it.

The gentleman turned from the painting he'd been viewing. He was young, about Grayson's age. From above a hawkish nose, his pale eyes regarded her with the bland expression common to the wealthy and bored.

She half expected some snide comment like those that had greeted her in the ballroom. But he merely nodded politely, turned back to the paintings and side-stepped to a portrait of two children.

"Excuse me, sir," she called, "but did you see a lady enter just now? Dressed in lavender?"

He shook his head. "I've quite had the room to myself," he drawled in London's most aristocratic West End accent.

Puzzled, she was about to retreat when a wall came up against her back and an arm snaked round her middle. Grayson's breath fell heavy against her neck.

"What the devil was that cat-and-mouse chase all about?"

Before she could answer, his arm fell away. His torso stiffened rocklike against her.

"Waterston."

Grayson moved her aside, not rough but insistent. Features rigid with steely accord, he took the room in four great strides. He raised an arm, formed a fist.

The man in tweed cried out. His head snapped backward and he staggered against the force of the blow. Hitting the wall behind him, he sagged to the floor, slumping into a heap of arms and legs. Blood trickled from his lip. Above him, the portrait of the two children tilted drunkenly.

Nora too felt suddenly drunk, dizzy, thrust into a nightmare. Grayson advanced on the man, fist taking fresh aim.

Roused from bewilderment, she caught his arm in

both hands, forestalling the blow by putting all her strength into holding him still.

"What are you doing? Good heavens, you hurt that man. Grayson . . . Gray . . . look at me!"

His head turned. He gazed past her, through her. His eyes were chilling and vacant. She called his name again. His eyes shifted to her. Focused and thawed.

"Nora . . ."

"What have you done?"

Beneath her hands, the stubborn rage drained from his muscles. His fist uncurled.

Voices flooded in from the hall. A surge of people spilled through the door. There were shuffling feet, cries of dismay. A woman shrieked. Startled observations flew.

"Good gracious, it's *those* two."

"Yes, and he's in one of his murderous rages. . . ."

A masculine voice announced to no one in particular that a guard must be summoned.

Ignoring them all, Grayson glared down at the bleeding, cowering man. "The next time you choose to spew lies, perhaps you'll consider the consequences."

With that he pivoted and caught Nora's hand. As if only just registering the presence of their audience, he hesitated and drew a breath through his teeth. "I suggest someone get him to a physician."

He started walking, pulling Nora past the appalled stares.

"But that gentleman . . ."

"Is lucky I don't call him out."

But for the shocked, accusatory looks, they were not challenged as they made their way downstairs. Through a blur of confusion she was tugged along, her hand aching in the bluntness of his grip.

Such anger. Even now her mind couldn't fathom what he'd done or why. The look on his face, the glacial blaze in his eyes . . . If Papa had seen his eyes today, would he still maintain that Grayson's eyes were clear of guilt?

Remembered snippets of gossip mocked her with each hurried step toward the street. *They say he flew into a rage and strangled his brother, then threw his body over the cliff.*

As they stepped out into the gray glare of the overcast sky, other words added their taunt: *to learn more about him, persuade Grayson to take you to the National Gallery.*

Was this her intended lesson? That her initial fears about marrying Grayson Lowell were not entirely unfounded?

*Chapter 9*

"Don't you think it's time we talked?"

It was Nora's implacable stance—chin up, arms crossed, feet planted wide—and not her question that forced Grayson's eyes from the book he hadn't been reading.

"You didn't say a word on the ride home," she persisted.

No, after his temporary loss of sanity at the gallery there had been only silence and bleeding knuckles, Nora's pinched features and her unasked questions.

Odd, but there was no sign of that pinched look now. A new look had entered her eyes, one of conviction. Steadiness. Trusting certainty.

On second thought, it wasn't new, that look, for he'd seen it before. Last night, after making love for the first time. Or perhaps the second. She'd had that steady look in her eyes when she told him she believed in him.

The stubborn angle of her chin now declared the unlikelihood of his postponing this confrontation a moment longer.

Reluctantly he closed the unread book in his lap, placed there merely to prevent any staff entering the library from disturbing him. "I thought if you wished to speak of it in the coach you would have said something."

"I'm not the one who cuffed a man without apparent reason. What happened today?"

He clenched his jaw until it ached. What could he tell her? He had no words of reassurance, only confirmation of what she'd seen with her own eyes: a man with a tenuous grip on his temper, at times his sanity, likely to lose that hold with the slightest provocation.

He had thought—hoped—that here in London, away from the memories, he might manage an acceptable level of civility.

*Damn you, Thomas, how could you have been such a sodding idiot? You've lost everything, let us all down. What of your son? What will Jonny inherit? How could you have been so bloody irresponsible?*

He shook the memory away, wishing for the thousandth time he could go back and change things, be a better man, a better brother. Understand and forgive and help find a solution. . . .

An unutterable weariness stole over him. "Must we discuss this now?"

Even as he spoke she came closer, slid onto his lap and slipped an arm about his shoulders.

"Indeed, we must." Her warm scent engulfed him. Her lips and those tilting cat's eyes snared him with their power to captivate. The soft swell of her bottom against his thighs threatened to end any conversation they might have before it ever started.

She placed her other hand against his cheek. "Now that I have your complete attention . . . that man you hit, you called him Waterston. The name is familiar to me."

His pulse spiked while his earlier madness pinched, jabbed, murmured insidious suggestions. "How do you know him?"

It was all he could do to wait patiently for her answer, to not grab her shoulders and shake the truth out of her.

"I do not know him," she replied calmly. "But I remember you mentioning his name to me last night."

The madness receded into swirling relief. Of course she didn't know Waterston. The man was a liar, just like the rest of London.

"I recall it quite distinctly," she went on, while the throbbing in his wrists and temples settled to dull spasms. "You said, 'Waterston never told me of this.' Told you of what? I assume it has some connection to me."

His head tipped back against the chair. He'd blurted the stupid admission last night while still under delusions concerning her character, before he'd realized the injustice and plain wrongness of the rumors.

"It was nothing," he said dully. "Forget it."

"It was indeed something. And I have a theory." Obviously not about to take his advice, she grasped his chin and pulled his head down, forcing him to meet her gaze.

"At the gallery you told me to ignore the insults. You called those people slanderous idiots and pulled me away before I could reduce myself to their level. Yet you attacked a man who'd neither said nor done anything objectionable."

*Leave it alone,* he thought, but aloud he said, "And your theory is?"

"That he has, within your hearing, insulted me. Unforgivably."

Dear God, she was good at reading him. Too good. Soon enough she'd see the whole truth and know him for the man he was.

He gazed out a window in want of cleaning into a sky turned leaden. He wished for a downpour, a deluge to wash away the past. Wished to be free to devote his heart and every waking moment to this ingenuous beauty who didn't have the good sense to be afraid of anything in this life, least of all him. Part of him considered warning her not to be so reckless.

"Am I right?" she demanded.

"Let it go."

She leaned in and kissed him on the mouth, nudging his passion, yes, but more. Claiming him. Demanding he recognize her claim. Insisting he pay her heed. She pulled back and shot him a shrewd look. "I believe you were protecting me."

He wished he could say it were so. True, he'd attacked Waterston because of his lies about her. But in the instant of contact, even in the impetus that drove him across that room, there had only been fury. No thoughts for her, none for honor. Only the blind, black need to strike.

She lifted his guilty hand from the arm of the chair. Holding it in her warm palm, she used a fingertip to trace the two knuckles rubbed raw from the punch. "He told you he'd seen my portrait. Yes?"

He admitted as much with a twitch of his brow. She brought his hand to her mouth, her pretty lips puckering just beside the wounded skin. Then she turned his hand over and pressed kisses to his palm, working her way to the tip of his forefinger and sending streaks of heat through him. His arousal throbbed beneath the soft weight of her thigh.

"I don't think you'd have hit him for that alone." She suckled his middle finger. His heartbeat raced, but whether from wanting to toss her on the nearby settee or from fear of her nipping too close to the truth, he couldn't say. He watched her silently as she continued her sensual interrogation.

Her lips nibbled at his ring finger. "Perhaps he said he'd been with me. . . . He wouldn't be the first to make the claim."

He pulled his hand free. He couldn't stand it—couldn't endure that gleam of certainty wrapped around an eagerness to excuse his abominable behavior.

"You think you know me after a single day of marriage?"

"I'm trying to." Her voice faltered. She lifted her chin.

He turned his face away. She hadn't begun to scratch the surface of what he was. He dreaded the day she burrowed deeper.

"Well?"

He expelled a breath. "Well what?"

"Aren't I right about this Waterston fellow, darling?"

The endearment sliced at his conscience. He shut his eyes. He didn't deserve her. Nor did she deserve him. No, she deserved a young man whose greatest sin lay in occasionally imbibing too much brandy and wagering too high at cards.

He felt her hand, cool and petal soft, against his cheek. But upon opening his eyes he saw she hadn't moved. Both her hands lay in her lap.

*Go home, Gray. . . . Go home . . .*

Holding Nora at the waist, he shot to his feet, lifting her so suddenly that she gave a startled cry.

He released her and darted a gaze about the room. "Did you hear that?"

"Hear what?" She looked baffled, hurt.

Had he heard anything? Or merely his own inner voice acknowledging it was time to face his fears? He spoke to the wall behind her. "Go and pack your things."

She hesitated, then asked, "Where are we going?"

Where are *you* going, he wanted to amend. Should have amended. *Home, where you belong, where you'll always be safe*. But the fool inside him, the one who had just that afternoon attested to her being his one gleaming, glorious hope, simply couldn't let her go. Not even to save her.

"It's no good here," he said in a lame attempt to explain. "I thought perhaps we might prevail over the gossip, but I was wrong. It isn't fair to you. You shouldn't have to hear . . . shouldn't have to endure the taunts."

"All right." She stood before him calmly, head tilted, eyebrows a little raised. Her very posture declared she wasn't nearly taking him at face value, that she knew quite well there was more to this story but had decided to humor him for now. "Where are we going, then?"

"To Blackheath Grange."

*He is running, trying to, dragging his feet through sucking mud and the sodden weeds tangling around his ankles. Thistles snare his clothing, tear it ragged. He pushes on, mouth gaping and lungs shrieking for air. Up ahead he sees Tom, beyond his reach, running swifter than Grayson can manage.*

*Closer and closer to the sea they race. Where is Tom going? Grayson shouts to him, but Tom doesn't answer, doesn't pause. As Grayson gathers breath to try again, the words sear his throat but go no farther.*

*In dread he watches his brother reach the headland. Panic grips him as Tom leans out over the cliff as if daring the sea to reach up and seize him.*

*Tom, no!*

*Grayson must reach him, must tell his brother how sorry he is. That everything will be all right.*

*A burst of wind heaves a mighty push, and Grayson finds himself on the headland too. Mere inches from Tom he grinds to a halt, nearly colliding and sending them both over the ledge. Slowly Tom turns, his features tight, pained, his eyes beseeching. Words of conciliation form in Grayson's mind.*

*Aghast, he hears other words torn from his lips by the wind:* your damned stupidity . . . we're ruined . . . all your fault . . .

*Helpless, Grayson watches his own hands encircle Tom's neck. Horror sends bile to his throat as his grip*

*tightens, controlled not by him but by a murderous
demon that possesses him. Back and forth he shakes
his brother while he watches Tom's face darken from
red to purple, his eyes bulge grotesquely. Only in some
detached part of his brain does Grayson register the
fact that Tom offers no resistance. . . . As if he too
believes he deserves to die . . .*

*Grayson snatches his hands away. "Oh, God. My
God, Tom, forgive me. I'm so sor—"*

*Before the last word forms, the soggy ground gives
way with a sickening lurch that drags Tom with it.
Frantically Grayson grapples with thin air as Tom, still
gazing at him, slides backward over the cliff and down,
down to the jagged rocks below. . . .*

A scream yanked Nora from sleep. No, not *a* scream
but many, blending into one long wail of terror. She
bolted upright, then realized where she was—a coach-
ing inn in Devon, just east of the Tamar River. She'd
had a bad dream. . . . But no, those awful moans
continued echoing through the room.

Beneath her, the mattress quaked. Reaching in the
darkness, her hand collided with Grayson's flailing
arm. She grasped it, then threw herself across his body
to still his thrashing.

"Gray, wake up! It's all right. You're having a
nightmare." She cupped his face in her palms and felt
the perspiration pouring off him in rivulets. "Darling,
it's all right. Please wake up."

In the scant moonlight she saw a vein in his temple
throbbing, his lips stretched taut across his teeth. His
eyelids fluttered. The thrashing subsided and gradually
his moans quieted.

His eyes opened. "I—what—Nora?"

"Yes, I'm here. It's all right. You were having a
nightmare."

He shoved out a shaky sigh and threw an arm across
his eyes. "Good God. It was . . . hideous."

"Do you want to tell me about it?"

She felt him go completely still. "No."

She wished he would, thought he needed to. But in his present state, she didn't insist. "Well, it's over now. Can you sleep?"

He hesitated. "No."

"Perhaps I could make you some tea."

She started to sit up, but his hand shot out and clamped her wrist.

"Stay here. Please." He pulled her to his chest and wrapped his arms around her, squeezing like a frightened child. "Don't leave me."

"Of course I won't."

His trembling echoed inside her. She was about to say more to comfort him when suddenly he rolled, flipping her onto her back. His weight pinned her to the mattress and his mouth covered hers with a hunger that took her aback.

His hands roved insistently, purposefully, so much less gentle than previously. Within seconds her nightgown was stripped away. His mouth dragged across her breasts, and she gasped with shock and pleasure both as his teeth closed around a nipple, as his hand shoved her thighs apart.

A single-minded haste unlike she'd experienced with him before accompanied each action. Desperation emanated from the tension of his muscles and the force with which he held her fast.

"You're frightening me a little."

"Perhaps you should be."

"What?"

"Just love me tonight, Nora. Let go and don't think. Forget who I am—who we are. Forget everything. Just love me. For tonight."

"You know I will. Always."

Grayson took her pledge into his open mouth as if starved, but for sustenance far different than food. His tongue besieged the interior of her mouth even as his erection pushed through folds of flesh gone torrid with an intensity of desire she'd not yet experienced or imagined.

Yes, it frightened her, for it reminded her of the violence she'd witnessed in him so recently, and of her growing fear of what crouched inside the gentle man she'd married.

Yet it thrilled her too, darkly, dangerously. As his body moved inside her, as he pinned her with his pale, fierce eyes, she fought past her doubts and let go, freed her mind of all constraints as he'd bade her do.

His thrusts were like a gathering storm, building to a raging tempest. She wrapped herself around him and clung, urging him deeper. Harder. She wanted this brusque, indecorous lovemaking, discovered she needed it perhaps as much as he. She relished the intimacy that broke all barriers of civility and left nothing concealed.

Yet as her cries were muffled by his greedy lips, and as he echoed those cries moments later with a staggering surge of his body, the fierceness of his passion crashed through her—jarring, volatile, violent. A passion a thousand times more shattering than she had ever bargained for.

The tang of the sea, borne on a soupy mist, filled the interior of the coach and brought with it the bitter taste of Grayson's colossal mistake.

Outside the window to his left, the lush farmland of Helston had given way to the rugged sweep of the Lizard Peninsula, a high, rolling vista studded with outcroppings of granite and occasional thrusts of the area's peculiar, green- and red-veined serpentine rock. From here, Blackheath Moor, the brooding stretch of land that hugged the boundaries of his Cornish home and gave it its name, surged westward to meet the upward swell of the Goonhilly Downs. The heather and gorse were in bloom, though today their vibrant purples and golds struggled to be noticed beneath the blanketing fog.

In weather such as this, a man could lose his way within moments amid the hills and moors, wander for hours or even days, only to find himself trudging in circles.

He closed his eyes to the sight, then turned his head to gaze out the window on Nora's side. There the land edged away in a steep, wind- and rain-gouged descent to the cliffs, followed by a sheer drop to the sea. He sighed. Both views revealed a stark landscape, equally beautiful. . . . But as Grayson also knew, equally treacherous to the unsuspecting.

He considered rapping for his driver to swing the team around. Too late he realized he should have sent Nora to Cornwall on her own and remained in London. Or gone anywhere else on earth but where the memories were still so alive that they blew their clammy breath down his nape.

What had he been thinking?

He knew damned well what he'd been thinking. That Nora deserved better than being chained to a man like him. Her own tarnished reputation had proved falser than paste jewels, and would therefore fade as people observed, as he did, her gemlike qualities.

That would never be true for him. It wasn't false that Tom was dead. It was excruciatingly real. As irrevocable as the part Grayson had played in what had happened.

But he'd yearned to give her something, some rare gift in exchange for the man he wanted to be—for her—who he *had* been for a few short hours on their wedding night.

Blackheath Grange was the only gift he could think of that might hold value for her. That might fill the gaps where her husband and lover and friend should be.

She sat gazing out the window on her side, watching the sodden scenery roll by. He wondered what she thought of Cornwall so far. Was she rethinking her desire to be here? Did she find it as dismal and inhospitable as he did? Precious few words had passed between them today, leaving only the weighty silence that had become like a third traveling companion.

When they first set out from London she'd sat close, her body warm and pliant against his side. He'd wrapped an arm around her, tossed her bonnet to the opposite seat and indulged in more than a few sultry kisses.

They'd made love in the inn last night. Frenzied, mindless lovemaking that ended in slick bodies, wildly beating hearts and a look of alarm on Nora's lovely face. She'd assured him he hadn't hurt her, but he didn't believe it. Didn't his own bruised rib prove otherwise?

The dream. He'd been half-mad when she'd prodded him from sleep. All he had wanted was to hold her close, bury himself in sweet kisses and warm flesh, reveal his dark secrets and find her willing to understand.

But some ungovernable passion had sprung up from the madness. His other side had come plundering out. The side he wished she would never come to know.

A low roll of thunder growled in the distance. He glanced across the carriage seat to discover her studying him, her expression speculative.

"We must be nearly there," she said. "You look as though something is about to happen."

The observation speared him. She was becoming far too adept at reading him. Since that afternoon in the gallery, and then later in the library at home, he'd had the unsettling sense she was gaining the ability to steal inside his brain and sift through his thoughts.

He angled a look out the window, though he knew this road so well he could identify where they were

by the ruts and curves tossing the coach about. "We'll
be turning up the drive any moment."

"I can hardly wait." Yet her shadowed features
hinted of apprehension, of perhaps finding disappointment in her fondest wish. Disappointment in him. And
the disappointment of realizing she desired more now,
so much more than the barren bargain she had once
offered: her dowry for Blackheath Grange.

He hated that, essentially, that was the bargain
they'd made.

Swerving, the coach maneuvered a bumpy course
through an open pair of iron gates flanked by two
fluted pillars. A stone gatehouse stood to the right.
The roof, shiny from the rain, showed dull in spots
where slate tiles were broken or missing altogether.
One more repair that needed attending.

The weather-lined face of Elliot, the gatekeeper, appeared in the open gatehouse door. The man grinned
and waved his cap in the air as the coach rumbled
past. "Welcome home, Master Grayson."

He forced a smile and returned the wave. How
ironic that even at twenty-eight he was still Master
Grayson here, as he had been from his earliest days.

As they rounded a bend, the oaks and elms planted
generations ago, along with encroaching rowans, fell
away to reveal the sloping park bordered by rhodo-
dendrons so in need of trimming they spilled their
heavy blossoms onto the lawn. They turned again and
the house appeared in his window, its stone facade
and timber-trimmed peaks gaunt against the afternoon
sky. Steely clouds reflected in the mullioned windows,
lending them the rheumy gleam of eyes gone blind.

Grayson's stomach clenched at the familiar sights.
He was home, yet that word had long ceased to evoke
comfort or safety. He might as well be alone on a
stormy sea with nothing but his own chaotic fears to
guide him.

Why on earth had he returned?

Because had they remained in London, it would have been Nora who suffered for his mistakes. The incident at the gallery had convinced him of that.

"It's not as ancient as I'd thought," she said, leaning at his shoulder to peer around him. Her cheerful tone rang as hollow as the felled tree they had just passed. "Not medieval at all."

"Fire destroyed the manor in the 1520s. They razed what was left and used the original stones to rebuild. I apologize for its being so gloomy."

"Gloomy? Hardly. It's a glorious piece of history. I'll wager there's a maze of back stairwells and secret passages, for I've read the people of that age reveled in spying on one another." A faint smile hovered about her lips. "I wouldn't be surprised if there's even a . . ."

"A what?"

A horrified spark ignited in her eyes. "N-nothing."

The unspoken word shivered in the air like a breath from the grave. She needn't say it. Back stairs, secret passages . . . a ghost.

Was there one at Blackheath? Surely, but was it a tormented soul crying out from beyond this world, or merely his own tormented soul?

He faced stiffly straight ahead, avoiding both Nora and the scenery outside his window. He felt rather than saw her peeking at him from under her lashes. A frothy tension settled between them. She thought he was angry. True, but not at her. At so much else; at everything else but her.

For her at this moment, he felt only sorrow.

# *Chapter 10*

Nora could barely contain her excitement as the coach maneuvered the final turn in the drive. Her fingers, laced tightly in her lap, tensed to aching as she took in the lofty Gothic arch of the front door, presided over by the forbidding glare of a griffin's head carved into the oak.

The door opened and a tall female figure, thin and angular beneath thick folds of black broadcloth, descended the steps.

"That is Mrs. Dorn, our housekeeper," Grayson murmured as a footman hurried down from behind the woman and opened the coach door. Grayson stepped down first, then handed Nora carefully to the drive.

Considerate. Gentle. But nonetheless distant. Last night he had asked her to love him—and she had, willingly and wholeheartedly, even when their passion had spiraled too high for safety.

She supposed he felt contrite for the ungentlemanly way he'd treated her, but rather than reassure, his behavior only tightened those growing knots in her stomach. Where was that passion now? Surely not hiding within this placid stranger.

A chill breeze churned her skirts and nipped at her ankles as Grayson retrieved her reticule from the coach seat. Meanwhile a middle-aged man with peppered hair and a slight stoop joined the house-keeper at the foot of the steps. With his craggy features and pitted skin he reminded Nora of the shadowy characters that often slipped in through her parents' kitchen door at night to have a quiet word with her father.

"Welcome back, Master Grayson."

"Thank you, Gibbs. I'd like to present my wife, Lady Lowell. Nora, this is Mr. Gibbs, our steward."

"At your service, madam." Contrary to his looks, the steward spoke with the careful inflections of a London-bred gentleman. His smooth bow rivaled any in polite society. From just behind him the elder woman emitted a cough.

"And Mrs. Dorn, of course," Gray continued, "who has ruled over Blackheath Grange with an iron fist these thirty-odd years."

Up close the woman appeared nearly emaciated, her shoulders sharp within the severe cut of her sleeves. Clasping skeletal fingers at her waist, she dipped a stiff curtsy. "How very lovely to have you at Blackheath Grange, Lady Lowell," she said in the clipped burr particular to Cornwall. Her flinty eyes narrowed as she took in every detail of Nora's wrinkled carriage dress. Hers was a gaze that conveyed little affability, permitted no excuses. At least that was how she made Nora feel. "I do hope you'll enjoy your stay."

Nora gave an internal harrumph, for by those words it seemed Mrs. Dorn chose to view her as a guest rather than Blackheath's new mistress. Yet until young Jonathan Lowell came of age, mistress of this place was exactly what she would be.

"Thank you," she said. "I do hope you'll be good enough to show me about later."

"As you wish, madam." Her voice, like the lowest string of a violin slightly out of tune, set Nora's nerves further on edge. "Of course we had precious little warning of your arrival, and—"

"I'm sure we'll find everything satisfactory," Grayson interrupted. "Come, Nora."

He placed her hand gingerly—as if it might break—in the crook of his arm and escorted her up the front steps. Over his shoulder he asked, "Where is my nephew?"

"Down at the stables." Mrs. Dorn clambered up the steps after them, walking briskly behind as they entered the main hall. "Where he's been spending most of his time."

Grayson stopped in a shaft of multicolored light sifting from a stained-glass window above the front door. Yet his face was as pallid as moonlight as he turned and asked, "Has he . . . ?"

The housekeeper exchanged a glance with Gibbs, who had followed them inside. Mrs. Dorn shook her head. "Not a word, sir."

Grayson nodded with an air of resignation. Nora's nape tingled. She'd once heard her own servants at home whispering about young Jonathan Lowell. *The earl's son saw it all. He hasn't uttered a word since. They say he'll have none of his uncle Grayson.*

"Her ladyship and I will freshen up," he told the housekeeper, "and then I'd like to see him."

"There's a fire already lit in the library."

"No." Both Mrs. Dorn and Nora flinched at his tone. Even Gibbs, on his way down a corridor to parts unknown, paused in his stride. Grayson made a visible effort to gather his composure. "We won't be using the library."

"Not use the library? Not at all?" Nora's blurted question echoed like a raven's cry against the high, carved ceiling. The library at home had always been her favorite room in the house, where she spent nearly all her time when she wasn't painting.

Grayson's mouth settled into a grim line. "You're free to use the library if you wish, of course. But it happens to be a room I abhor. Mrs. Dorn, we'll see Jonny in the parlor."

Though Nora's curiosity bounded, his shuttered expression forbade questioning him further. For the time being, at any rate.

But as soon as she could, she intended to visit that library, and discover what had succeeded in penetrating Grayson's calm facade when all day she could not.

Grayson could hear her voice sifting through the wall. No distinct words, merely a welling of sound like distant bells or a rushing brook—high, clear, melodious. Oddly compelling. The sort of sound one instinctively followed straight to its source. He moved closer to the door, one only he knew existed, an innocent-looking panel of wall, which, for those who knew its secret, slid open to allow access into Nora's room. Grayson leaned and pressed his ear to the panel.

Again, Nora's lovely voice penetrated the wall, followed by Mrs. Dorn's stern reply. He thought he heard something about the adjoining dressing rooms. Silence fell. He stood with ears pricked, hand splayed upon the secret door, waiting to hear Nora one more time before heading back to his own room.

When it came, he heard not the words so much as the hesitancy, the tentative quality of her response. A sense of misgiving he could not explain fell over him.

Then all at once he was gripped with a sense of the wrongness of what he was doing, the shame of having skulked to this spot where he stood spying on his wife. As if he could not approach her openly, speak with her honestly or touch her intimately without risking— what? The truth coming out? His world falling apart? Her regard transforming to loathing?

He backed away, moving as quickly as he dared without raising a telltale clamor. He should seal this passageway—seal it and forget it ever existed. Because despite the oath running through his head—that he would not betray his wife's trust by using it again—he knew he would. Knew he would not be able to prevent himself.

The housekeeper opened the door upon a brightly appointed room, festooned with an array of feminine details that contrasted sharply with the glowering skies and dripping trees outside the window. Crossing the threshold, Nora took in the paneled squares of flowered wallpaper that matched both the curtains and the canopy of the four-poster, the tufted chairs upholstered in berry and cream–striped moire, the large wardrobe painted in soft hues of gold and mossy green. Stepping farther into the room, her feet were cushioned by the luxurious weave of a Persian rug.

Yet for all its appeal, the room somehow exuded a sense of loneliness . . . of faltering hope, as if awaiting the return of a mistress who would never come. Though the room was spotless, Nora nonetheless sensed the cheerlessness of gathering cobwebs and gloomy neglect.

But she would not appear ungrateful. Moving about, she fingered the fine curtains, smoothed a hand along the counterpane, opened and closed a drawer in the delicately carved dressing table.

"It's charming. Utterly lovely." She turned an appreciative smile upon the housekeeper, then acknowledged the futility of the gesture. Not one iota of austerity eased from the woman's features. Nora sighed. "I do thank you for your trouble, Mrs. Dorn."

"No trouble, madam. The master's orders, after all. Though had he sent notice earlier than yesterday, I might have had time to properly air the curtains and rug."

"Never mind. It's perfect as it is."

The woman nodded in her curt way, then briskly crossed the room. She threw open a door and gestured with a clawlike hand. "The dressing room, madam, connects with Master Grayson's."

The disclosure sent a little tremor through her, one she hoped Mrs. Dorn didn't notice.

Nora peered into the open dressing room. Would she and Grayson make frequent use of this portal between their chambers? After last night . . . she shivered, unable to deny a breath of misgiving concerning Grayson's less-than-gentle lovemaking.

Then again, part of her had welcomed it, quivered now to think of it. As if it were a dare, a heady risk, a heart-stopping ride. Or rather like intending to paint a delicate bouquet of flowers but somehow mixing deeper, darker hues—blood crimson, glowing russet, velvety plum—then choosing her boldest brushes to capture images infinitely more sensual.

A flame curled inside her. Would he steal in tonight? His behavior today made her doubt it very much. But if he did, which lover would he be? Tender, solicitous and patient—the lover of her wedding night? Or demanding, hungry? Angry.

She suddenly became aware of Mrs. Dorn waiting silently on the dressing room threshold, her arm still extended, her face grimly expectant. She was a looming figure in black and gray, thin and colorless, almost . . . bloodless.

"Ah yes . . . very good." Nora cleared her throat and willed her hands to cease fidgeting with her skirts. "I'm sure I'll be most comfortable here, Mrs. Dorn. Thank you."

Declining the woman's offer to help her change her clothes, she couldn't help heaving a sigh once the housekeeper left. Her maid from home and the rest of the luggage should arrive tomorrow, but she decided she would rather make do on her own than suffer Mrs. Dorn's taciturn company a moment longer than she must.

She spent an inordinate amount of time in selecting

a fresh frock and tidying her hair, fussing far more than usual over her appearance.

For Grayson? No. In fact, she realized with a start, she barely gave her apparel a second thought when it came to her husband. At first she hadn't particularly cared what he thought of her. More recently it simply hadn't seemed necessary—he admired her in any attire.

Or, as was the case today, he simply didn't notice.

No, her efforts now were all for his nephew. Silly of her, really, for what boy ever noticed or cared what ladies wore? Still, she very badly wished to make a good impression. The right impression. Both her brother and sister had died many years ago from illness; thus Jonathan Lowell presented her one and only chance to ever be an aunt.

The notion forced a raw lump into her throat. She desperately wanted the child to like her.

With barely a sound the boy appeared in the parlor doorway, hands crammed in his trouser pockets, head and eyes turned toward the floor.

"Jonny. Come in, lad."

It was the moment Grayson had longed for and dreaded. He sat near the windows in one of the overstuffed chairs at the chess table, hoping against hope he might entice Jonathan to sit opposite. Jonny used to enjoy chess, had become rather good at it for a youngster.

Rain slapped the window beside his chair, and as Grayson waited and searched for something friendly to say, Jonny too stood waiting, apparently intending not to say anything at all. That was how it had been since Thomas died. Grayson groping for the right words, and Jonny avoiding words at all cost.

He drew a breath that tasted of disappointment. "It's good to see you, Jonny. Please come in."

Small shoulders bunched within a brown tweed suit coat. The boy wore matching trousers meticulously tucked into polished riding boots. His shirt collar ringed his neck tightly, secured by the crisp bow of the linen cravat Mrs. Dorn had probably fashioned for him. He was a little man, the very image of his father at that age.

A pain pressed Grayson's breastbone. No child—at least no boy at his country home—should ever be so flawlessly neat. Nary a hair on his dark head curled out of place. Whatever happened to that cowlick his nurse used to bemoan?

Grayson stood, intending to go to the boy, slip an arm around his shoulders and draw him to the settee. With several paces still between them, Jonny flinched and pulled back. His gaze darted to Grayson's face, his blue eyes large and swimming in gleaming pools of white. Fear and remorse and an urgent desire to make everything different flickered in those eyes, and for a heart-stopping instant, Grayson saw Thomas. . . . Thomas on that last day, uttering the truth of how deeply the estate had sunk into financial ruin. Tom had been so damned sorry, but all Grayson had felt, all he could convey to his brother, was rage. . . .

Jonny's lashes fell. Grayson stood a few feet away, arms dangling at his sides, heart racing, breath suspended in a pair of icy lungs. Outside, a gusting breeze carried faint rumbles of thunder.

What should he do? What could he say?

"Do forgive me for being late, gentlemen. Why, good afternoon, sir. You must be Jonathan." Sweeping across the threshold, Nora circled the boy and faced him. Ruffling his hair, she stooped to smile into his face.

"Or am I to call you Lord Clarington?" She chuckled lightly, smiled gaily. "I am your new aunt, Nora, and I'm very pleased to make your acquaintance."

The sound of her voice filled Grayson with relief. She would be the buffer between them, providing neutral terrain where each might tread, however carefully.

At the same time, seeing her natural amiability with the child made him feel like a failure, a coward. And indeed he was, afraid to look his own nephew too closely in the eye for fear of seeing the brother he'd wronged.

And for fear of perceiving Jonny's loathing, his accusations. He had been just outside the library door that last day, listening while his uncle and father argued. . . .

*Damn you for this, Tom. How could you have been so stupid?*

*Yes, you must wish I'd never been born.* . . .

But Nora was here now, brave Nora who wasn't afraid of anything, not even a boy who refused to speak.

She knew Jonny wouldn't. Grayson had told her that much when they set out from London. She hadn't reacted with the slightest surprise. But then, Jonny's silence was no secret.

*The Earl of Clarington was pushed. His young son hasn't uttered a word since.* . . .

With a shudder Grayson dismissed the old gossip and moved closer to his nephew and Nora. Ignoring the boy's rigid posture, he reached for her hand.

"You look lovely," he told her. A gross understatement, yet he'd meant it with all his being. In her frock of sunny muslin she was a dazzling flower after months of drab winter. He brought her hand to his lips and kissed it.

She flashed him a look of earnest appreciation, as if she truly doubted her ability to make a man foreswear his chosen vices in favor of a single moment at her side. Then she was chattering to Jonny again, leading him with a hand on his shoulder to the settee near the bay window. Rain poured in rivulets down the glass, making a streaky watercolor of the brick terrace outside with its iron furniture and ivy-draped trellises.

Nora perched on the settee and with pretty motions settled her skirts around her. Jonny remained standing, hovering at her side and looking uncertain, a little lost. Overwhelmed, perhaps, by this beautiful aunt who seemed inordinately delighted with everything.

There was a clattering in the hallway. Mrs. Dorn wheeled in a cart of tea and refreshments.

Grayson scanned an assortment of cold meats and breads, fruit preserves and tarts. Mrs. Dorn had included a bowl of clotted cream and another filled with pure white sugar. The silver teapot sent out jets of pearly steam.

"Well, now, doesn't this look delicious." Nora set out the cups and saucers. She lifted the teapot and began pouring. "I must confess I'm famished after our journey. Why, we haven't eaten since early this morning, all the way back in Devon." She glanced up at Grayson, her cheeks blushing scarlet with the uneasy memory they shared of the previous night.

"Have you ever been to Devon?" she asked, turning her face to Jonny as she finished filling the last teacup and set it on the sofa table.

He lifted his blue eyes—huge and bright as an autumn morning—to Mrs. Dorn, who was just then plumping the cushion on the chair Grayson had vacated. The child looked as if he desperately wanted her to intervene on his behalf. The housekeeper considered a moment, then gave a quick nod.

"So you have." Nora spooned sugar into her teacup. "It's breathtaking country, though not quite as dramatic as Cornwall." She patted the cushion beside her. "Won't you sit down?"

He didn't move. A beat of silence became two, then stretched uncomfortably. Grayson felt an urge to yank the hair from his own head. "Jonny," he said, then stopped, shocked by the sternness in his voice. He hadn't meant to be harsh. He'd merely wanted to help coax the boy onto the sofa.

Instead, Grayson sat in a chair opposite Nora and lifted his teacup, hoping that seeing him thusly occupied might encourage Jonny to relax his guard. "I'm counting on a game of chess later. What do you say, Jonny? Wipe your Uncle Grayson's pieces clean off the board like you used to?"

Silence.

*Please answer,* he willed the boy. *Please say anything, even if it's to curse me. . . .*

"I play winner," Nora declared. She hefted her chin when he flashed her a glance. "I'm a passing fair strategist, I'll have you know."

"That shouldn't surprise me in the least," he said with a laugh and a surge of warmth. How did she do it, show him these glimpses of happiness when everything around him seemed steeped in melancholy?

She raised a hand in Jonny's direction. "Your uncle told me a secret about you."

He experienced a twinge of panic—what secret was she about to divulge? That they had discussed his ponderous silence? How would the boy react to that?

"I understand you're especially fond of sweets," she said, and Grayson's pulse settled. Not that he'd told her any such thing, but now that he thought about it he knew it to be true. How had she guessed?

"I shall confess to you I am equally guilty of indulging in that particular vice." Grasping a pair of silver tongs, she plucked a tart from the tray and placed it on a plate. "As if this weren't sweet enough, shall I sprinkle some sugar on it for you?"

After a moment's hesitation and another look at Mrs. Dorn, who was now adjusting the mantel clock, the child eased onto the sofa beside Nora.

Did he nod? Grayson couldn't be sure, but Nora smiled like a coconspirator and sprinkled a spoonful of glistening crystals onto the plum tart. She handed the plate to Jonny.

He twisted round again to where Mrs. Dorn had moved to straighten the lace arm covers on the wing chair.

Grayson had had about enough. It was as if Jonny feared so much as blinking without permission from the housekeeper. "That will be all, thank you, Mrs. Dorn." He glanced pointedly at her in the event his tone hadn't sufficiently conveyed the dismissal.

She and Jonny exchanged one last enigmatic look before she retreated from the room.

After watching her disappear into the hall, Jonny bit off a corner of his tart. Nora watched him and smiled.

"Something else your uncle told me was that you're quite a skilled rider. Living mostly in London all my life, I've never had a horse of my own, but my grandfather kept a Shetland pony for me to ride whenever I visited. Is yours a Shetland?"

Silence, marked by quiet chewing. But just as Grayson despaired of Nora receiving an answer, Jonny shook his head. He shoved more tart into his mouth, sprinkling crumbs onto the sofa. He stiffened with a look of alarm.

"Oh, never mind." Nora flicked the crumbs onto the rug at their feet. "No, I don't suppose you would have a Shetland, as grown up as you are. Your uncle Grayson tells me you turned ten last March, but were you to inform me you were twelve I'd thoroughly believe you."

Jonny only chewed and stared back.

"His horse is a Welsh cob," Grayson said.

"Oh, such an elegant breed. Shall I guess his name, then?" Nora tilted her head and considered. "I called mine Scotty, because the Shetland Islands are in Scotland, but such a name wouldn't do for a Welsh horse. So let me see. . . . Llewelyn?"

To Grayson's amazement, Johnny immediately shook his head. Not verbal, but an answer all the same.

"Urien?"

"Puck," Grayson supplied, knowing they could go on guessing all day without Jonny offering up the answer.

"Oh!" Nora's hands came together with a clap. "Are you a fan of Robin Goodfellow's?"

"One of Jonny's favorite characters."

Her eyes never left the boy's face, for all it was Grayson speaking for him. "Mine too. I adore how he confounds both mortals and fairies alike." She slipped an arm around his shoulders. "I do hope you'll show me Puck when the rain stops. Tomorrow, when my things arrive, I'll show you something I enjoy very much. Tell me, Jonny, do you like to draw?"

A slight shrug comprised his answer.

"I have boxes full of sketching pencils, paints and brushes of all shapes and sizes. If it's all right with your uncle, we shall set up in a sunny room and paint pictures together. Would you like that?"

An eager nod, followed by what could almost have been termed a smile, brought a pang to Grayson's chest.

"Gray?" Nora looked to him for approval.

"By all means. Any room you like."

# Chapter 11

Nora started at the brittle click that broke the silence of her bedchamber. She had been drifting into the hazy beginnings of a dream, lulled there by the soothing singsong of a woman's voice. Now her eyes sprang open, straining to see into the unfamiliar shadows.

At the edge of the curtained window she detected a shimmer, a flicker of movement. She bolted upright.

"Who's there?" But she saw nothing more, only the shadows tossed against the curtains by the swaying trees outside.

Still, her heart throbbed in her throat. What woke her? Her mysterious lady? Had yet another visitation been interrupted by Nora's sudden awakening?

The creak of an opening door and a footstep sent her thoughts scattering. Her back hit the headboard as she whisked the coverlet to her chin. The sudden glow of a candle sent blinding shoots of light into her eyes. She shut them, then heard a voice—this time decidedly masculine.

"It's only me."

When she opened her eyes, Gray was shutting the dressing room door behind him. The shadow of his robed figure filled the wall beside him, hulking like a sleek wolf tensed to pounce. Shivering, she instinctively arched her neck, apprehensive of his touch, yearning for it too.

He stalked closer, the light of his candle undulating across his features. She couldn't bring herself to speak, didn't trust her voice not to reveal her unease. Yes, she wanted him, but . . .

Not that he had hurt her at the inn. Not that he hadn't introduced her to new sensations, intense and exhilarating.

Or so it might have been, if not for what she had sensed rippling beneath his passion. Anger. A need to strike. Oh, not at her, but at something she had yet to understand, something he seemed unwilling or unable to share. Just as when he hit that Waterston fellow at the museum.

In silence he reached the bed and set the candle on the end table. As if in a dream she watched him, a moving shadow gilded gold where the candlelight touched him. He was watching her too, his eyes hooded and unreadable, deeper shadows within the dusky planes of his face. She felt his gaze like a weight upon her, heated and pressing. Desire slithered like a serpent through her, hissing and fierce, but lithe and graceful as well.

He yanked loose the sash of his robe and shrugged his arms free. As the brocade garment thudded to the floor, she received a full view of his naked body. Her pulse leaping, her gaze traced the masculine lines of muscle and sinew down to where they seemed to originate, to that inevitable place of heat and hardness and passion.

She bit back a gasp. Yes, he apparently wanted her, lusted for her. Her insides simmered with anticipation.

His long fingers grasped the bedclothes and slowly peeled them back. The coverlet slipped from her shaky fingers, exposing her sheer shift from the waist up. Her nipples contracted in the cool kiss of night air, in the expectation of his kisses upon them.

She trembled, feeling vulnerable, undressed. Breathless. He slid in beside her, his naked body spreading heat through the linens and through her. Desire coiled inside her. The hand she reached out to welcome him trembled slightly.

He caught it fast, enfolding it in his much larger one. "Is it all right that I'm here?"

"Of course it's all right." How surprisingly steady her voice sounded; how easily those words came. Because they were, for better or worse, the truth. "I'd rather hoped you would."

He brought her hand to his mouth and spoke against her fingers. "I wasn't sure. Not after . . ."

The inn. Yes. They were of the same mind, then, and he perhaps as confused as she by what had happened there. "You needn't ever doubt," she said. "If I wish to be alone I shall tell you."

"Yes. Promise me that, my Nora. Don't ever be afraid to send me away if it is your will to do so."

He kissed her knuckles, a long, lingering kiss that strayed beyond tenderness to encroach on the borders of something desperate, some tortured thought she wished to heaven he'd share. His lips were tight against her fingers; their tension traveled through her.

Then he released her, only to reach his arms around her as he lay down. His hands submerged in her hair, catching the long tresses and tangling them across their faces.

"How sweet you are. . . . So sweet . . ." With both hands he turned her face to his and gently kissed her brow and nose and cheeks. He wrapped his arms around her and rolled with her across the mattress, settling atop her. He swept the hair from her face, whisking it across the pillow. "We could be happy— so incredibly happy."

Before she could ponder his despairing tone, his face dipped. His lips hovered close, imparting their warmth, making her hunger for their taste. Like a magnet they drew her toward him, until she craned her neck and, trembling, strained upward.

With a growl he pressed his mouth to hers, the kiss ravenous and greedy. Painful. One kiss became many, consuming her breath while his body pinned her, helpless, to the mattress. Dark desire welled and swirled, swallowing her thoughts and sending her drifting on hot, aching sensation.

In the intensity of his passion she felt herself slipping away, lost in a wilderness of maleness and heat, becoming more and more an extension of him . . . and of that desperate bleakness inside him. It was too much, too uncontrolled.

"Gray . . ." Her hands closed over his shoulders and pushed. His lips broke away.

He rose on his elbows above her, panting, blinking as if to clear his head of a pounding ache. His features gleamed with perspiration. She too gasped for breath, and questioned him with a frown.

"I'm sorry," he said. "I didn't mean to be so . . ."

"Enthusiastic?"

He nodded, smiled guiltily, then rolled onto his back. The rush of cool air through her nightgown came as something of a shock and raised goose bumps. Beside her, Gray crossed slightly trembling arms behind his head and released a shaky breath.

In the silent gloom she shivered, struggling to separate fear from desire, desire from keen disappointment. She had wanted him—wanted him terribly much. The echo of it vibrated inside her still. She'd merely wanted him to slow down, give her own passion time to match his. Now the sudden lack of him left her feeling hollow and abandoned. Confused.

He reached for her hand, bringing her palm to his mouth for a kiss. "Welcome to Blackheath Grange."

She let go a laugh, a single taut note. "That was quite a reception, sir."

"Again, I'm sorry. You must be exhausted."

"Yes," she replied, knowing her level of energy had nothing to do with the past several minutes. That he would pretend otherwise made her feel wronged and cheated.

"Good night, then," he said. He closed his eyes, leaving her very much alone though she lay at his side.

Several times that night she awoke to the jostling of the bed beneath her. Gray's limbs twitched and spasmed against the mattress while low moans sputtered in his throat. Each time, she would stroke his arm or smooth his brow, rousing him faintly to redirect the nature of his dreams.

Once she jolted awake, expecting to soothe his nightmares again. Instead she discovered him lying rigidly awake, glaring unblinkingly up at the canopy.

"Are you all right?"

He gave a terse nod.

Turning onto her side, she reached out and with her fingertips traced the square line of his jaw. A sense of protective tenderness filled her. Her thoughts turned unexpectedly to her father—Zachariah, who had made a fortune from nothing, a man people whispered about, and who loved her and her mother fiercely. She loved him too, and whatever else Papa had done in his life, she believed there was good at the core of such a man. She could never bring herself to believe him capable of evildoing.

Suddenly she understood the feelings that had been plaguing her since the inn. No, before that, since Gray had hit Mr. Waterston. And she realized with a burning certainty that she was *not* afraid of her husband. But she was very much afraid *for* him. And of the demons that writhed inside him.

"You've had another nightmare," she whispered. "It might help to talk about it."

His eyes flickered like a starlit sea, revealing the barest hint of the turbulence beneath.

He slid closer and took her in his arms, nestling her

head in the hollow of his shoulder. "Go back to sleep."

He left her bed before dawn, feeling gaunt and exhausted. Empty. His head ached from his eye sockets to the roots of his hair. Sleep had all but eluded him, and when he *had* occasionally dozed he'd wished he hadn't. Each fleeting dream had roused images of his brother falling from that cliff, Jonny shrinking from his touch, Nora gazing at him in horror once she understood who and what he was.

Last night he'd gone to her, yearning to be with her, pulsing for her. Wanting to bury his guilt along with his body deep inside her. Yet each step that had brought him closer to her had set off a cadence inside his head: *you don't deserve her; you'll only hurt her.*

Wasn't Thomas proof of that? Wasn't Jonny? One dead, the other silent and hurting. What would happen to Nora if she stayed with him? How could he even attempt to use anything so lovely, so alive and unsullied, to try to salvage a piece of his dead spirit?

He could not. He knew that of a certainty now. From the moment he had taken her in his arms last night, something frightening and out of control had wrenched through him. A raging energy, like the mindless rutting of a stag in season. No, worse. A stag acted purely on instinct, all part of some divine plan to ensure its survival.

Not so for him. He seemed hell-bent on destruction, his own and that of everyone around him.

What was happening to him? Was he cursed? Did some evil spell hang over Blackheath Grange, as people whispered when Thomas died?

After pulling on clothes and ignoring the aromas rising from the kitchen, he mounted his favorite horse, a black Thoroughbred named Constantine, and set off across the moor. The sky overhead shone black and starless, lightened only in the far west where a pale

moon silvered the watery horizon. The air hung damp
and heavy, the landscape huddled in predawn shadows
and bathed in trailing wisps of fog.

A reckless impulse spurred him on. If Blackheath
was cursed, he'd put it to the test. At a breakneck
gallop he disturbed dozing cattle, sent sheep scattering
and raised angry shrieks from a roosting falcon. Bad-
gers and hedgehogs skittered through the damp grass,
frantically seeking their burrows. Grayson dodged
branches and splashed through streams, raising plumes
of mud in his wake.

It wasn't enough to shake loose his demons. To the
east, a cold sliver of sun struggled to penetrate the
clouds. In the wan light he saw Thomas's face
everywhere—in the shapes of the craggy hills, in the
long shadows they cast across the moors, in the swirls
of mist pooling in the bottomlands.

Thomas had loved this place, every blessed inch of
it, nearly as much as life itself. It had been from this
rugged, unpredictable, wide-open land that he had
drawn his energy, found fuel for his soul. Now, even
in death, Thomas was here, a visible, palpable memory
at every hairpin turn Grayson took at top speed.

A rock wall, some five feet high and three across,
separated one grazing pasture from another. Grayson
gave Constantine full rein and urged him on, taking
grim satisfaction in the lengthening strides beneath
him, the power of muscle and sinew bunching and
then stretching, elongating as the animal lunged and
left the ground.

For several exhilarating seconds he experienced the
liberating sensation of soaring, with a bracing wind in
his face and the graying sky arcing over him. Then
the jarring *oomph* of hooves hitting the ground,
pounding out the pace as, with nary a pause, they
continued across the fields.

He half hoped he'd be thrown and break his neck.
Yes, the very notion had spurred him over that wall

and pushed a defiant whoop from his lips. What was a neck, after all? Especially when nearly every bone in Thomas's body had broken in his fall from the headland . . .

Still, despite the urgency of his ride and his need to test fate, he wouldn't run his horse lame. He kept to higher ground, avoiding the low-lying wetlands where, without warning, firm terrain often gave way to perilous bogs that could bring a horse crashing down.

Finally, where Blackheath Moor rose to meet the Goonhilly Downs, he turned Constantine back toward the coast, slowing to a canter as they skirted the clusters of tenant farms near the tiny village of Millford.

Here lay the true evidence of the recent years' decline. Weathered cottages, once brightly whitewashed, dotted the winding lanes, their thatched roofs worn and thinning, many no longer able to keep out the rain. They needed replacing, but that took time away from the more important business of feeding families.

These particular fields had seen the worst of last autumn's flooding. A good portion of grazing pasture had washed away, while the crops had rotted from excess moisture. Even now many of the fields stood bare, their boundaries encroached upon by the heath rush and sedge grasses spreading from the moor.

The home farm hadn't escaped damage either. The herds were dangerously depleted, not only from harsh conditions and lack of feed, but also from a lingering malaise that had rendered many incapable of breeding.

He followed Millford's main road past the church, the blacksmith and carpenter's shops, the harness maker and the tannery. The stream meandering several dozen yards beyond the north side of the road provided power to the water mill about a quarter mile inland, where local farmers brought their grains to grind. Ironic that after the flooding, months of near drought had run the stream nearly dry. Even the most basic staples like bread had become scarce and expensive for months afterward.

At the foot of the sand dunes the road took a sharp turn, veering south where a curve in the shoreline hugged a small harbor. Fishing vessels, most little bigger than skiffs, bobbed stiffly at their moorings. A few sat anchored out beyond the breakwater, fishing lines cast to the murky tide. Most farmers in the area supplemented their dwindling incomes by fishing, which meant their farms suffered further neglect. But even the sea let them down; for unknown reasons, the bay's fish populations had diminished at an alarming rate.

Thinning herds, sparse crops, scant fishing . . . no wonder people whispered of curses; no great surprise so many believed the spirit of Blackheath Grange had died along with its young earl.

Grayson guided Constantine along a path twisting between the grassy dunes to the beach. Here, with nothing between him and the sea, the wind shuddered in off the water to slap his face and yank at his hair. Constantine bobbed his head, meeting each gust with a restless snort. Beneath deep stacks of clouds, iron gray waves rolled long and low until they reached the sandbar, where they frothed and shattered. A father and son waded knee-deep in the water, dragging in a net.

A few feet from the shoreline, a little girl with a head of tangled blond curls sat waiting with the buckets, absently sifting sand through her fingers. Tugging at the frayed shawl tied around her shoulders, she stood up as the other two trudged out of the water, their net swinging like a hammock between them. The catch dangling inside appeared modest at best.

Fishing was not the only opportunity offered by the sea. Traditionally, the earls of Clarington, Thomas included, had turned a blind eye to coastal smuggling, provided the activities didn't turn violent.

Some people believed that had changed in recent

times. About a year ago, a ship ran aground along this rocky stretch of shore. Grayson had heard rumors of wreckers being responsible, but as far as he knew the customs officials hadn't turned up any incriminating evidence. As long as there continued to be none, if local men wished to bypass import taxes by bargaining for black-market goods with foreign sailors, who was he to judge?

Then again, with Zachariah Thorngoode's money at work, the villagers would soon have little reason to trade illicitly or even fish for other than recreational purposes. But could mere money and new farm implements revive the heart of this place and restore faith in its future?

Reflecting on the tasks that needed immediate attention, Grayson sat watching the family until the boy happened to look up and see him. Both children grinned and waved as if they hadn't a care in the world. Wishing to God they hadn't, Grayson waved back. He walked Constantine over to them.

"Good morning. How's the fishing?"

A snap of emotion flashed in the father's bloodshot eyes, then vanished with a blink. Had Grayson imagined it? He believed he might have, especially when the man touched the brim of his cap in greeting and offered a smile that revealed two missing bottom teeth. "Fair enough, Sir Grayson, fair enough. Far better now than last winter, to be sure." He nodded at the silver bodies writhing and flapping in the net. "The missus'll fry these laddies up good and proper and make a fine supper tonight."

While they dumped the fish into the buckets, Grayson experienced a cool slither of embarrassment, for two reasons. One, that this villager knew his name, while he could not remember ever meeting this family before. Were they new here? Or had he simply failed to extend his notice to them, their farm perhaps hav-

ing not been among the Grange's more productive
properties even in good times?

The other reason for his discomfort had nothing to
do with such mundane matters as names or whether
he'd made someone's acquaintance. It was the fact
that this man, this hardworking father whose children
hovered but a few meals away from starvation, would
answer his question politely, even cheerfully.

Somehow, that stung more than any scalding accusations could have.

If Grayson had been alert to the signs of financial
decline sooner, would things be different now? If he
had been more of a help to Thomas, rather than the
aloof and critical scoundrel he'd been, could the disaster of this past year have been avoided? Even . . . that
last hideous day?

No, it would have been too damned easy to think
that, to believe things had gone wrong in a whirl of
events too quick to have been foreseen or avoided.
But he would have been lying to himself.

It had begun in their boyhood, the rivalry and the
antagonism, festering even in their schoolroom days
when Tom had struggled through the same lessons
Grayson had completed with cocky ease.

*Hang it, Tom, you dumb old turd, can't you manage
anything right? Or are you trying to get us stuck here
in the schoolroom all afternoon?*

*It's impossible, Gray. I've tried three times now and
got a different answer each time.*

And then there was Chad, usually with them during
the summer months, and always the mediator. *Gray,
you go distract old Norris—ask him a question or
two—and I'll let Tom copy my figures. No, don't
worry, we won't get caught. . . .*

A chill breeze shivered across the water. The slap of
waves broke Grayson's reverie, thankfully. Mercifully.
Once, he had told himself all brothers disagreed, that

their boyhood rows were merely part of what it meant to be brothers. He'd always assured himself that beneath it all Tom knew how much Gray had loved his older brother. . . .

He snapped his attention back to the villager, his children and their half-filled buckets of fish. The boy blew into his hands to warm them, stamped his bare, wet feet against the sand. His trouser legs were soaked through. His shirt and worn woolen coat could hardly have sufficed to shield his thin body from the wind.

"Can . . . can I do anything for you?" Grayson asked, feeling awkward. The Cornish were nothing if not proud, and he must couch his offer carefully. "I understand the flooding especially took its toll hereabouts. I'll be making a concerted effort in the coming year to bring the productivity of all the farms back to what it was in . . . well . . . in my father's day. If you need any assistance with repairs or buying seed or . . . anything . . . you come up to the house and see me."

"Well, now, thank 'e, sir. If need be, I'll do that."

The acceptance of the offer had come too quickly, too easily, to be sincere. He guessed nothing short of the impending death of one of his children would send this Cornishman seeking anyone's help.

He and his son began stretching out the net to drag it back into the water. From beneath their brows they angled impatient looks at Grayson, sentiments they'd never dare voice to a gentleman perceived to be their superior. He realized his presence only detained them from their task. They needed to get on with their fishing quickly, and return home to the farm chores awaiting them.

Grayson turned Constantine to go, but an altogether different impulse than the one that earlier had sent him over walls and splashing through streams prompted him to tug the reins and bring the horse to a halt.

The man squinted up at him. "Milord?"

He shook his head. "I'm no lord." He swung a leg

over the horse's neck and slid from the saddle. "Tell your son to go home and change into dry clothes. And a warm pair of stockings."

"But—"

Puzzlement turned to astonishment when Grayson relieved the boy of his edge of the net. Astonishment became gaping alarm when he gave the net a shake to dislodge a dangling ribbon of seaweed.

"Milord, surely ye can't be thinking o'—"

"I've already told you—I'm no lord. Besides, your boy's feet are nearly blue from cold."

"But those be fine London-bought boots, if ever there was. Ye can't be thinking of ruining the likes of those."

He'd bought them in Italy a year ago last spring, but he didn't think it worth mentioning. He gestured at the water. "The sun is nearly well up, and soon the fish will head for deeper water."

His allusion to their limited opportunity failed to produce the desired effect. The little family merely continued staring at him with horror-glazed expressions.

He stooped to address the boy. "What's your name?"

After a prod from his father, the youth replied, "Daniel, sir."

"Well, Daniel, you and your father make it look easy, but I've a hunch there's more to this than appearances suggest."

"Aye, sir. It's not so easy a t'all."

"I've a fancy to give it a go. You'd be doing me a favor, then, if you'd take your sister home, warm up, and return in half an hour's time to help carry the buckets in from the beach."

Daniel's indecisive gaze slid to his father, who gave a shrug and nodded.

Grayson tossed his coat over his saddle, pushed up his sleeves and spent the next half hour slogging through the waves. His companion drew the line at allowing Grayson to handle the fish with his hands, insisting on transferring their catch from net to buckets by himself. Still, by the end, Grayson's boots were more than likely ruined, for though the water would dry, the salt would undoubtedly corrode the buffed finish.

It didn't matter. What most assuredly did matter were the five-gallon buckets now brimming with cod and haddock—enough to fry for dinner today, with plenty left to salt as well. Dan Ridley, as he had introduced himself to Grayson, would not have to postpone morning chores on his farm for perhaps another week or more.

Grayson retrieved Constantine from the edge of the dunes, where the horse had wandered to graze on tough, wiry marram grass. Before climbing into the saddle, he extended his hand to Ridley. The man hesitated, then shook it and murmured his thanks.

"Sorry about those boots," he added.

"Forget it."

But Dan Ridley's shadowed expression said he would not forget it, that Grayson's ruined boots would weigh heavily on his conscience, as would, perhaps, his interference here on the beach. Perhaps he'd overstepped the bounds of familiarity, crossed a line he should not, as a nobleman, have crossed. Perhaps in lightening his own burden of guilt concerning the state of affairs in and around Blackheath Grange, he'd instead burdened this man with a sense of debt he could not hope to repay.

Wondering what Tom would have done here today, Grayson swung up into the saddle. "Good day to you, Mr. Ridley. Give my best to Mrs. Ridley." With nothing more to say, he clucked Constantine to a walk.

"Sir Grayson."

He swung the horse about and waited while Dan Ridley strode through the sand.

"My condolences to you, Sir Grayson. He was a good man, your brother. Generous to a fault. Always carried little treats for the children, and when anybody took sick he'd send down a good, hardy broth and made sure the doctor come. He's sorely missed round these parts, sir, and won't be forgotten anytime soon, as sure as the day is long. Just wanted you to know that, sir."

There it was, then, the reason a man like Dan Ridley could treat Grayson with a measure of cordiality, even respect. It was for Tom, in deference to his memory. The people here had loved him, still loved him, just as he had loved this place. Tom hadn't needed to cross the invisible barrier between nobleman and commoner to win their affections. All his life, Grayson had been the smart one, the handsome one, the charmed one. But despite his shortcomings, Tom had been loved.

And that look Grayson had initially glimpsed in Ridley's eyes? Fear. Fear of the man whispered to have robbed the people of their beloved earl, who had brought a curse upon them.

He spoke past the painful clenching of his throat. "Thank you. And don't forget to come see me. Bring the children. Cook always has a stash of sweets on hand."

Yes, he could offer sweets. He could fix their farms and occasionally deign to soak his boots while helping them haul fish. Perhaps, in time, he might overcome their suspicions and earn a measure of their trust. But would he ever have their love, as Tom surely had?

He moved on, turning Constantine's head toward home. He hadn't managed to outrun his demons, and all he felt now was unutterably weary. Everything he'd known as a boy was gone—the prosperous estate with its thriving farms, the proud family admired and respected by the local folk. He was all that was left—he and Jonny—and despite Zachariah's money, he greatly feared for the future of the Lowell family.

Back at the house, he passed Constantine's reins into the hands of a capable groom and quietly let himself into the house. Mrs. Dorn's voice stopped him in his tracks as he was about to enter the morning room.

"Master Grayson, a word, if you please. The matter is urgent."

## *Chapter 12*

Grayson sorely needed a cup of coffee; the hotter the better. Then he wished only to steal up to his chamber, change his clothes and see if he couldn't find a moment's peace. Or, rather, find a moment to make peace with himself—and his memories of Tom.

It was not to be, not yet. The housekeeper's brisk footsteps echoed along the corridor in his direction, raising the dull thudding in his head to an earnest ache.

"Can this not wait, Mrs. Dorn?"

"No, sir, it's about . . . well . . ."

It wasn't like Mrs. Dorn to hesitate when she had something to say. He scrubbed a hand across his eyes. "Do speak freely, Mrs. Dorn."

"It's about Lady Lowell." Her lips pursed to a tight ball. "Or what she's doing, specifically."

"And what would that be?"

"Destroying the house, sir."

Taken aback, he gazed up and down the corridor. "Doesn't appear to be crumbling about our ears at present. Could you be more precise?"

The housekeeper's eyebrows converged above her nose. "It's Lady Pricilla's bedroom."

"My aunt's old room? What of it?"

"She—Lady Lowell, that is—has completely disassembled it. The bed's been taken apart and brought up to the attic for storage. Much of the furniture as well."

"I hardly think Aunt Pricilla will mind, considering she hasn't occupied that room since her marriage some twenty-odd years ago." Wanting that coffee rather much and hoping it had stayed warm this long in the urn, he pushed at the door and started into the morning room.

"Yes, but the paneling, sir." Mrs. Dorn stayed him with a crablike grip on his shoulder, a gesture that had once held the power to render him immobile. "She—Lady Lowell—has hammered hooks into it. Hooks!"

"Whatever for?"

"To hang artwork, or so she said. Can you imagine? Into those lovely beveled squares of maple paneling? Why, I remember when your grandmother had it installed. Such an expert eye for decorating, Lady Clarington had, may she rest in peace. . . ." A dreamy look misted her eyes, then cleared just as quickly. "Sir, Lady Lowell's actions are more than destructive. They are positively irreverent."

He released a breath. "Mrs. Dorn, I can assure you my grandmother is beyond caring about the paneling, as is dear Aunt Pricilla. It all belongs to Jonathan now, and I sincerely doubt he gives a fig one way or the other. If it's ruined, we shall have it replaced. Now, if you'll excuse me."

Giving up on the idea of coffee and opting instead for some much-needed rest, he brushed past the housekeeper.

"Master Grayson," she said to his back, "I must point out that your brother would never have allowed . . ."

His jolting pulse sent blinding pain through his eyes, and he did something he'd always believed should never be done with servants. He raised his voice. "I am not my brother and there's an end to it, Mrs. Dorn."

He immediately regretted it, but simply couldn't

find the energy to stop and apologize. After an initial gasp, her continued grumbling about ruined treasures and not knowing what to expect next accompanied him to the end of the corridor, where he stepped through a door into the main portion of the house. No, he could not escape his demons today, or his many failings.

Yet as he headed up the stairs, he was taken aback to feel a sudden smile tugging at the corners of his mouth.

Hooks in the paneling indeed.

"Oh, dear. Perhaps I was a bit hasty."

Nora regarded her new studio and admitted that perhaps Mrs. Dorn had a valid point minutes ago when she'd stormed in, glowered at the clothesline stretching along one entire wall, delivered a tirade concerning the preservation of Blackheath Grange and stormed out.

What would Grayson have to say about it? Though her more pressing concern at present was where he had gone this morning, so early that none of the servants had seen him leave. Gibbs had reported his horse gone from the stables, and under ordinary circumstances Nora would have been content with the knowledge that Gray had simply set off on morning rounds of the estate.

But any hopes she'd entertained about normal circumstances had been dashed last night. Grayson's troubles ran soul deep, and she was beginning to despair of ever helping him overcome them.

She sighed, taking in all she and Jonny had accomplished that morning. Despite her worries, she couldn't help a surge of pride. Perhaps, after all, she could do something to help ease Grayson's burdens.

Strung along the clothesline Mrs. Dorn had so bemoaned were half a dozen pastels and watercolors she and the boy had worked on together: pictures of flowers, birds, different angles of the house, and a drawing of Jonny's Welsh cob, Puck.

She had spent the morning explaining and teaching. He had listened in his usual silence, but she could see his mind working, his imagination soaring. After a time his muteness no longer seemed unnatural. Nora did the talking and encouraging, while Jonny expressed his enthusiasm in the eager way he chose colors and spread them across paper. She had been delighted with his natural and rather impressive grasp of perspective. His artwork showed budding talent and no mistake.

"Bother the paneling." She plunked her hands on her hips. "Wouldn't you agree, my lord?"

Seated on a pillow on the floor and hunched over his latest work, young Jonny was just then adding a bit of charcoal shading to his rendering of the manor's central wing. He glanced up at the object of Nora's fretting and shrugged.

"Yes, precisely as I thought." Approaching footsteps, however, brought a smattering of doubt. She nipped her lower lip. "I do hope your uncle Grayson isn't vexed with me."

"Vexed? Why on earth should I be?"

He appeared in the doorway, leaning on the jamb and treating her to one of his rare but arresting grins. He was dressed for riding in a white linen shirt tucked into buff breeches that caressed every line of muscle in his thighs. His black broadcloth coat was tossed over one shoulder, held there by a forefinger hooked into its collar.

"Grayson . . . g-good morning," she stammered on a surge of elation at seeing him so relaxed and in apparent good spirits. He stepped from the hall shadows into the brighter room, and she saw the truth behind his smile. "Good heavens, Gray, are you all right?"

She went to him, hands closing over his shoulders.

She peered into his face, searching his taut features, the pinched look about his mouth. He looked . . . wounded, beaten, though she could find no bruises beyond the ashen ghosts hovering beneath his eyes and the gaunt hollows sharpening his cheeks. "Has something happened? Did you take a fall from your horse?"

"Certainly not." He leaned in and kissed her, whispered a throaty "Good morning" that, despite her alarm, poured through her like warm spiced wine. His skin smelled of the sea, crisp and briny, and a coating of salt glazed his boots.

"You've been to the shore."

He nodded with a slight frown and made a survey of the room. "You've certainly been busy while I was gone. One would never guess a boorish cad disturbed your sleep last night."

Memories of their interrupted passion streaked through her. She flicked a self-conscious glance at the boy, fast at work on his picture and paying them no heed. "I . . . no, you didn't . . . not at all."

His crooked smile acknowledged her white lie. His gaze caressed her, then swung to trace the artwork along the wall. "I hear there's been a bit of mischief afoot this morning."

"Oh. I suppose you've been speaking to Mrs. Dorn." Suddenly she saw the studio through his eyes—the strewn papers, the open paints, the heaped cloths, the paintbrushes soaking in jars of water. Not to mention those controversial hooks she'd banged into the wall. "I'm sorry if I've overstepped—"

"Never mind Mrs. Dorn." He tossed his coat onto the one settee remaining in the room. "She wouldn't understand, would she, my darling? She'll never understand you as I do."

The husky timbre of his voice stroked her nerve endings, igniting tense flares of desire. The look they exchanged bolstered her suspicion that this discussion wasn't limited to her artistic endeavors. That Grayson's mind—and hers—were on ventures of another sort entirely.

"No, I don't suppose she would."

But did he understand her? Could he see her willingness to accept him as he was—with his faults, his past and whatever mistakes he might have made? He need not change for her. He need only allow her to come closer and share, *truly* share, his life. Her throat squeezed around a sense of failure. Surely she'd been trying to convey just that to him since their wedding night. And just as surely she had failed to reach him.

He had continued his perusal of the room, and now issued a low whistle between his teeth. "I'd say Aunt Pricilla's bedroom has undergone a significant transformation since last I saw it."

"We have made a bit of a mess, I'm afraid. We'll tidy up as soon we're finished."

"Nonsense. This is your studio and you may leave it as untidy as you wish. I like it. The place fairly pulses with inspiration. With your passion for art." Again his voice dipped with a rumbling innuendo that melted her limbs like wax set to flame. His arm went around her, pulling her to him for another kiss, slower than the first, hungry and searching, seeming to implore something urgent from deep inside her. Something she ached to return, if only she knew how.

He released her with a lingering look, his hand sliding the length of her arm, ending with a little squeeze of her fingers that conveyed a reluctance to let her go. Then he moved away to lean over his nephew, still sitting on the floor, drawing. "Jonny, won't you show me what you've made?"

The swish of the child's charcoal across the paper hissed loudly in the stillness.

Nora reached for a rag and wiped a mottled sampling of chalk dust from her fingertips. She came up behind Grayson and rubbed a clean edge of the rag where her fingers had left colorful smudges on the shoulders of his white shirt; she succeeded only in smearing them more. "Jonny and I have dabbled with pastels, watercolors, and we did a bit of sketching."

"All in one morning?"

"He was very eager. And an avid learner."

He grazed her cheek with the backs of his fingers. "There is nothing quite as gratifying as an avid learner, is there, my love?"

Was he referring to their wedding night, and all he'd taught her then? His half-closed lids and pensive expression suggested he was, and heated tendrils unfurled inside her.

But with a quick glance down at the boy, she gestured to a watercolor near the end of the row. "That one is the view of the paddock and stables from the corner window. His skill with perspective is quite remarkable."

"Indeed. Jonny, this is extraordinary. I'd no idea you were so talented." He leaned again over the boy's shoulder. "And this is the front of the house you're drawing, isn't it? I can hardly believe it, but you've captured far more than just the building. Somehow this picture speaks of the Grange's history, the secrets and the intrigue. There's a mood about it. . . ."

As Grayson went on, Nora experienced a renewed burst of hope. He seemed genuinely pleased with his nephew's work, sincere in his admiration. Perhaps Jonny—and art—would provide a common ground where it didn't matter that they'd married for the sake of convenience, that they knew so little about each other, or that, except for a simmering physical attraction, most days they seemed hardly compatible at all.

"Yes, it's in the colors he chose." She gazed with pride at Jonny's work. "See how the clouds, the slate roof and the walls seem to blend into one another? We discussed how color can be very atmospheric."

Grayson's head snapped up. "You and Jonny discussed?"

"Well . . . I discussed." She tipped an apologetic nod, realizing she must learn to choose her words more carefully when it came to the child. "He listened and made good use of my advice. As you can see."

"I certainly can." Their gazes met, locked, heated by several degrees. His nostrils flared, and she could all but feel his desire curling like steam around her. But he didn't reach for her, didn't take her hand or lean in to kiss her again.

Abruptly he turned away and put several paces between them. "May I see what's on the easel?"

"No!"

He ground to a halt, hand freezing inches from the cloth that concealed the painting beneath. With an amused lift of his brows, he regarded her over his shoulder. "Nothing scandalous hiding under here, I trust?"

It wasn't his obvious reference to her nude portrait that sent flames to her face, but rather the fact that his curiosity showed no signs of abating. He continued around to the front of the canvas, prompting Nora to heft her skirts and hurry after him.

"It's nothing. Just a little project I started a few weeks ago."

"I'd love to see it."

"I'd rather you didn't. It isn't finished." She stood behind him, willing him away and hoping he wouldn't insist on unveiling the portrait she'd begun soon after they'd met.

It hadn't been the most flattering likeness at first, for she had allowed her anger and frustrations about the marriage to color her work. She'd since begun alterations—a lightening of the shadows here, a warming of color there—but she was far from satisfied with the results.

He reached behind him with both hands and

grasped hers. With a tug he pulled her arms around his waist. She leaned readily against him, her breasts pressing against his back in a way that made her wish they were alone.

He raised one of her hands to his mouth, nuzzling her fingers. "Show me," he whispered.

She breathed a sigh that ruffled the hair across his collar. "Oh, if you insist."

She stepped from behind him, grasped the edge of the cloth and tugged. "Voilà. But remember, it is a work in progress, so don't judge too harshly and don't say I didn't warn you."

He stepped forward—and went utterly still.

"I don't think it's a terrible likeness, do you?"

He didn't answer, wasn't listening. He just stood there glaring, a sheen of sweat glossing his brow and upper lip.

"Gray?" Prickles of unease raised the hairs at her nape. "It isn't that bad, is it? If you don't like it I could—"

"Good God." The whispered words seemed to shudder outward from some fissure deep inside him. The astonishment gripping his features hardened to something approaching horror. His mouth opened, forming a strangled sound that made no sense to her, that turned her blood to ice.

"Thomas."

# Chapter 13

"Gray, I don't understand."
  Nora reached for him, but the look of utter revulsion on his face made her drop her hands. Amid a rising perplexity, she searched the details of the painting. What did he see that she didn't?

"I told you I began it some weeks ago. I don't suppose it's very good—the tone is all wrong, but . . . Gray, why do you look like that?"

"Is this your bloody bad idea of a joke?"

"I don't know what you mean. . . ."

"Good God, not from you." His voice, thus far little more than a murmur, strengthened like gathering thunder, producing a current that ran beneath her skin. "I'd never have suspected this of you."

She stole a glance at Jonny, who tilted his head to study them from his place on the floor. "Please don't be angry."

"Angry?" His hands clamped her shoulders. He dragged her to him and pressed his face close until his labored breath lashed hot across her cheek. "And to think I'd begun to care . . . to trust . . . to . . ."

His fingers tightened, lifted her to her toes. In the position he held her, her breasts strained against her bodice. Her skin prickled beneath his scrutiny, devoid now of all tenderness, all affection.

His grip bit into her with a savage edge that frightened her. In the feral glint of his eyes, in his blanched and barren features, she saw a man surely slipping from sanity. A man she no longer knew in the slightest.

"Burn it." He abruptly released her, sending her staggering backward until her shoulder hit the edge of the portrait.

Hints of doubt and remorse flickered beneath the anger blazing in his eyes. He pivoted and strode from the room.

Heart thrashing, Nora stood frozen, her shoulder pinned to the canvas where she'd struck it and tipped it askew. Slowly she mastered her breathing, caught control of her shaking hands by fisting them in her skirts. Then she turned and righted the painting on its easel.

"Jonny, please come here."

The boy set his charcoal aside.

"Tell me what you see," she urged in a trembling whisper when he stood beside her. Then she remembered he would tell her nothing. She draped an arm around his shoulders and struggled to remain calm. "Look at this painting. Do you see anything but your uncle Grayson?"

Without hesitation he shook his head. His bright blue eyes brimmed with questions. She smiled down at him, hugged him tighter.

"Does the face remind you of anyone besides your uncle Grayson?"

Another shake of the head.

She had to be sure, had to risk upsetting the boy in order to understand fully what had just happened. "Other than the fact they were brothers, does this picture remind you very much of . . . your father?"

His small chin lifted against her side, prodding her ribs as he gazed steadily up at her. He shook his head.

"Oh, Jonny . . ." *What are we to do?* Wrapping her other arm around his slight frame, she pressed him to her and held on tight.

Grayson fled down the corridor, blind to all but the taunting, damning image burned into the corneas of his eyes.

When Nora unveiled the portrait, he'd seen his own likeness for the briefest instant. Then it was Thomas filling his view—Tom with his limbs flailing, his lips stretched in horror and the sea raging beneath him.

It hadn't been a mere illusion, could not have been slanting sunlight working with his state of mind to transform one image into another. He *had* seen his brother's face on that canvas, distinct and indisputable.

He forced his feet to move, dragged one after the other until he reached the stairs. As he groped his way down, he struggled to draw breaths through the choking mire that clogged his throat. He could swear the gargoyles carved into the newel posts snickered as he passed. What in this forsaken house didn't mock him, didn't accuse him of the most unforgivable of crimes?

The clunking of his boots on marble told him he'd reached the hall. The front door—escape—awaited mere paces away. But the hellish images chased him, and the faster he went the clearer it became that there was no escape.

Gravel shot out from beneath his feet and pelted the flower beds as he strode the pathway around the house. The same instinct that had sent him galloping across the moor earlier now brought him stumbling over the cobbles in the stable yard, groping his way to the wide double doors of the main entrance. He tugged at one of the handles, only to have the door stubbornly refuse to open. He backed up and kicked the door in.

"Get me a horse," he shouted to the dust motes inside. His demand met with the agitated snorts of the horses. "Devil take it, does anyone hear me? Have you all gone daft? I said I want a horse. Now!"

He stood panting, chest heaving, pain slicing at his temples. The scents of damp hay and dung stung his nostrils and prickled his throat. Just as he was about to shout again, a voice drifted down the line of stalls.

"I hear you, sir. I haven't yet finished brushing Constantine down. Will another do?"

"Just bring me a horse and make it fast. I don't need a damned saddle."

Edgar, one of the groom's young assistants, came out of Constantine's stall, holding a brush. He eyed Grayson with a puzzled expression, and seemed about to question his command.

Grayson forestalled him with a simmering glare and a terse, "Do as you're told."

"Yes, sir." The young man set the brush down and trotted up the aisle into the tack room. Within moments he'd harnessed a roan gelding and was leading him to Grayson.

It was then he heard Nora's shouts.

"Gray! Don't leave. Please, we need to talk."

Framed in the open stable door, he saw her running down the path, a flurry of muslin, petticoats and streaming hair. He didn't want to see her; couldn't face her just now. Snatching the reins from the groom's hand, he led the horse outside to the mounting block, ignoring Nora as he climbed onto the horse's back.

She came to a halt, bending at the waist to catch her breath. Then she moved quickly forward and caught hold of the bridle. "Don't run off again like you did this morning."

"Stay away from me, Nora." He clucked to the horse and tried to swing its head around to loosen her grip.

"No." She dug in her heels and held fast, knuckles whitening around the leather straps. "Not until you explain."

"You can't understand."

"I'll toss the portrait in the hearth if you want. Just tell me why it upset you so."

"You can burn it or tear it to pieces. It won't change anything." His voice eased a fraction. Despite what his eyes had told him, he knew she hadn't painted Tom. Couldn't have painted Tom. Never mind that she'd never met him. Gentle Nora would never do such a thing. He'd known that even as he had stood gaping at the portrait.

The alternative had been too ghastly to contemplate. Too . . . impossible. Yet he could not but believe that what he'd seen was a message from Tom himself, an admonition from the grave.

He sat atop the gelding, head bent and shoulders bunched, palms pressed to his forehead. Guilt burned his gullet while a relentless, throbbing pain threatened to tear his skull in two. Nora was talking, pleading, her voice a distorted echo in his ears. Nausea roiled, threatened to rise.

Unable to stand it a moment longer, he swung down, landing hard on his feet on the cobbles. Nora jumped back with a startled cry, but came just as quickly back to his side.

Her hand closed on his arm. "I can help you if you let me. If you'd only—"

He spun away, glaring out over the green-carpeted paddock, seeing in its gentle tufts and hillocks the waves and rocks that had swallowed his brother. "You can't help me. Destroying the painting can't help me. I'll be damned just the same."

"That isn't true. It can't be true."

That fragile show of faith set off a tempest inside him. He whirled, lurched, caught her wrists as she attempted to back away. "Why didn't you listen to the truth when you heard it?"

"I never heard anyone speak the truth. Not about me and not about you."

Such guileless trust undid him. He thrust his face in hers, his features clenched in painful knots. She shuddered but stared back as if daring him to say the worst. So be it. "They spoke the truth. At least about me."

"I don't believe it. I never will. Your brother's death has left you distraught. . . ."

"It's because of me he's dead."

"No."

"Do you believe he could have fallen from that cliff by accident? He knew every inch of Blackheath Grange like the back of his hand. He could have maneuvered up or down that headland with his eyes closed. We'd done it a thousand times as boys."

She went completely, utterly still. "What are you saying?"

His hands fell to his sides. He raised his face and spoke to the clouds scuttling overhead. "Thomas was pushed."

Mute, she gaped, the whites of her eyes gleaming around irises gone deadly black. It was her very silence that challenged him, defied him, to finally speak the truth. All of it.

"My brother is dead by my hand. Can I make it any plainer? I sent him over that cliff."

The color leached from her face.

"Tell me now how you feel about your husband. Will you defend me to the gossipmongers? Will you write your mama about how wildly happy we are? Will you welcome me into your bed at night—me, with my guilty heart and my murderous hands?"

The silence stretched, filled with the ironic gaiety of birdsong. He shut his eyes and listened to the crashing hammer of his heart. Why had he done that? Why hurt Nora so irrevocably? To ease his guilt? It hadn't worked. No, God, he only felt more alone, more desolate.

Of its own volition his hand came up. "Nora . . . forgive me. . . ."

A cool breeze skimmed his fingers. He opened his eyes and saw her retreating back, her fluttering hair, her skirts swirling around her ankles. He heard her muted footsteps as she ran toward the house.

"There you are, dear heart." Nora tucked the coverlet beneath Jonathan's chin and leaned to kiss his forehead, hoping he wouldn't feel the trembling that hadn't subsided since her encounter at the stables with Grayson.

Her wrists still bore the faint imprint of his madness. His . . . derangement. She couldn't call it anything else. He'd seen something in her portrait that simply wasn't there. Had reacted irrationally to something altogether imagined. He'd confessed . . .

Suppressing a shudder, she cupped Jonny's cheek in her palm. As much as she might wish herself away from this troubled house, this turbulent marriage, she was at least glad she was here for the boy. Someone had to keep him safe, and if not her, who?

Mrs. Dorn? The housekeeper held an oppressive influence over Jonny, one Nora could neither explain nor dismiss.

She kissed him one last time. "Good night and sleep well."

He responded with a look of such open affection her heart squeezed. It was a look that said he needed her, counted on her not to let her down. She patted his shoulder through the bedclothes, then rose and crossed the room.

"Under no circumstances are you to leave him

alone," she whispered to Kat, who had arrived along with her belongings from home that morning.

A maid some five years in the Thorngoode's employ, the buxom, dark-eyed Kat wasn't always known for the strictest morals, nor did she typically take pains to hide the evidence of her dalliances from anyone but Nora's mother. Still, her lusty appetites aside, Kat was honest. In her work she'd never been anything but efficient and conscientious. And through the years she had kept a secret or two for Nora, earning Nora's trust.

"Lock the door behind me and do not open it till morning."

"Yes, ma'am."

She found a measure of confidence in the young woman's steady look. More assurance, certainly, than she felt in Mrs. Dorn's overbearing guardianship of the child.

She blew Jonny a kiss. "Sleep well, dearest."

With solemn eyes he blew one back.

Mrs. Dorn met her in the corridor as though she'd been lurking. Her stern features drawn tighter than usual, she blocked Nora's path. "Lord Clarington is accustomed to sleeping alone, madam. Why lock him in with a stranger?"

"Thank you for your concern, Mrs. Dorn. Kat is wonderful with children. I'm sure Jonny will take to her quite readily."

"I'm afraid I can't agree. His lordship is a retiring child. I think it advisable—"

"I am Jonny's guardian, Mrs. Dorn, and I shall do as I think best."

"Master Grayson is Lord Clarington's guardian."

"And I am *Sir* Grayson's wife." The words burned her throat and raised a queasy sensation in her stomach. Had she pledged her life to a madman?

But her assertion did have the desired effect of rendering the housekeeper speechless. Nora brushed by, making her escape. "Good night then, Mrs. Dorn."

She retreated to her bedchamber and with unsteady fingers locked the door. Held her breath as she tested the knob to make certain it was secure. Turned to regard the door to the adjoined dressing rooms.

Fear sent an icy wave through her. There was no key in that lock. But of course there wasn't—why on earth would a wife need to lock out her husband?

With the answer knocking a frigid rhythm in her heart, she dragged the chair away from the dressing table and wedged it as tightly as she could beneath the knob. She gave the door a tug. Grayson would pay her no visits tonight.

Would she lock herself in every night? Deny her husband that which he had every right to demand? A ribbon of heat curled round her belly, squeezed her thighs. His fierce lovemaking had set her aflame. But it had frightened her too. She realized now she had every reason to be afraid.

But even if she barred him by night, what of the daytime hours? How was she to set about being mistress of Blackheath Grange and caring for Jonny, never knowing what might arouse Grayson's ire, or when?

Wrapping her arms across her chest, gripping each elbow until her fingers dug into the flesh, she faced into the room. What must she do?

She moved to the window and stared out at the stark moonlight, at the silver-tipped trees casting glimmering shadows across the lawns.

*Don't you long to run across those hills and stand beneath that golden light?* she had asked him that day at the National Gallery.

*Are you there waiting for me . . . ? You're all the gleaming, glorious hope I need.*

Were those the words of a murderer? Could a villain have made her feel more beautiful, more alive, more cherished than ever before?

Oh, but then he'd attacked that man, that Waterston fellow. . . .

*My murderous hands* . . .

Could a killer's hands have coaxed such shuddering, vibrant responses from her body? From her heart?

Her raised fist slammed the window frame, rattling the glass. Her fears were like a fist upon glass, pressing to the breaking point.

"Take Jonny and steal away." The answer was so simple, yet so monumental and onerous she couldn't help voicing it aloud. Leave her husband . . . and take his nephew with her. Such an act would be considered a crime. Kidnapping. She would become a wanted woman. A *hunted* woman.

And yet . . . contrary to everything logic told her, the very notion of never seeing Grayson's face and never again knowing his touch left her as desolate as an empty canvas.

But what other choice? Her husband was . . . he was . . .

Surely mad. She pressed a shaking hand to her mouth, then just as quickly dropped it to her side. She swallowed, blinked back tears and stood up straighter. Jonny needed her resolute and in control.

"Papa will know where to send us. He can ensure no one ever finds so much as a trace—"

*"No."*

The word filled the air and vibrated like an organ note against the ceiling. Nora jumped, then spun to face the room. Her nerve endings tingling, she searched the shadows for the source of the strangely musical voice.

"Who's here?"

*"Don't run away. Stay and be brave."*

Nora knew that voice, was certain she'd heard it before. Seeing no one, she stumbled backward, shoulder blades hitting the window. Groping for balance, she gripped the curtain, only to tear it from the rod.

Flowered silk rained down, half covering her. She clawed it like cobwebs from her face.

"Kat? Mrs. Dorn?" But she knew neither of them occupied the room with her.

A few feet from the locked door, a glimmering radiance that had nothing to do with moonlight or the table lamp unfolded from the shadows. Nora's instinct was to run, but astonishment held her paralyzed. The shimmer grew, elongated, took form. Human form. A head, shoulders, arms, the flowing lines of a gown.

A lavender gown.

Recognition sapped the strength from her knees. She sagged to the floor. "I'm going mad as well. . . ."

Behind the figure the door was still visible, obscured as though by a veil of cloud. Elegant if insubstantial features softened to a smile. *"You aren't mad. Not in the least."*

A transparent person telling her she wasn't mad—surely proof she was.

"What do you want with me?" Nora clutched the skirt of her gown, nearly renting the fabric as waves of incredulity made her dizzy. "Wh-who are you? *What* are you?"

The image, as solid now as Nora herself but still glowing as if the sun shone full upon her, smiled again. *"I am a woman who once lived here at Blackheath Grange. That is all I can tell you. The rest is for you to discover."*

"Discover what?"

*"The truth."*

"How?"

*"By searching, of course."*

Nora started to protest, but the woman held up a hand to silence her. *"Do not run away, Nora. Do not give up so easily. The people here need you. Desperately. My . . ."* She paused and clasped pale, slender hands at her waist. *"Your husband's nephew . . . his father as well."*

"Jonny's father?" Fascination overcoming a portion of her fear, Nora pushed to her feet and eased away from the window. "Thomas Lowell is dead. How can he possibly need me? What can I or anyone do for him now?"

*"Free him from this place. Set his spirit to rest."*

"His spirit . . ." she whispered more to herself than to her otherworldly visitor. "He haunts this house. He's been haunting Grayson." Yes, for Grayson had seen his brother's image in the portrait she painted. . . .

She shook her head. "There are no such things as ghosts."

A pair of shimmering golden eyebrows arched delicately but nonetheless emphatically. *"Are there not?"*

Nora scowled as disbelief warred with the evidence standing before her eyes. Who was this woman, and why had she been manipulating Nora since before her wedding, albeit within the guise of her dreams? Was tonight another attempt at manipulation, and would it lead to yet another travesty, such as when Grayson hit Mr. Waterson?

"Your riddles grow wearisome. If there is some truth I must know, tell me what it is. Tell me and leave me in peace."

*"I cannot."* Those exquisite lips again curled in a smile, one Nora found eerily familiar. *"The wounds at Blackheath Grange are scored too deeply for mere words to heal them. You must find the truth that will free you all. You must see it with your own eyes, know it, believe it with your mind and heart and soul."*

"And if I cannot?" A sudden bleakness made Nora shiver. What was it this apparition demanded she learn? Whether or not her husband had committed murder? Was that a truth she wished to know? "What if I cannot believe as you say I must? What if there is always doubt?"

All trace of the woman's smile vanished. She said nothing, only regarded Nora with eyes grown large and luminous in her fine-boned face. The light surrounding her faded, and the room fell once more to shadow. Nora stood staring at nothing but her bedchamber door.

She rushed forward. "Wait. Please don't leave yet. I don't understand. . . ."

A pounding at her door cut her pleas short.

"Y-yes, what is it?"

"Is anything amiss, madam?" Mrs. Dorn spoke from the other side. "I thought I heard you calling."

What was the woman doing skulking above stairs at this hour? She should have been completing plans for the morning with Cook and the rest of the staff before retiring to her own rooms near the servants' dining hall.

Crossing the room on shaky legs, Nora turned the key and opened the door a couple of inches. "I'm fine, thank you. Just a dream. Sorry to have bothered you."

"No bother, madam." The housekeeper eyed her curiously, no doubt taking note of the day gown Nora still wore. "May I bring you anything? Tea, perhaps?"

"No, thank you. I'm going to try to go back to sleep now."

"Good night then, madam."

"Good night, Mrs. Dorn."

But after Nora relocked the door and faced the empty room, she knew that what had happened had been no dream, nor did she expect to enjoy anything resembling a good night because of it.

*Chapter 14*

With no more sound than the house's ordinary night creaks, Grayson eased his way into Nora's bedchamber, his eyes pinned to the four-poster where she lay sleeping. The glow of his candle kissed the highlights in her hair, a glossy river burnished with gold. Grayson loved her hair, adored the gossamer glide of it through his fingers, over his cheeks, across his chest and torso, followed by her silken touch and her moist lips.

Yet as he reached the bed, he resisted the urge to run his fingers through the errant locks that beribboned her breasts. He tore his gaze from the nipples outlined beneath thin linen that, far from concealing, invited further exploration.

His hand shook, rustling the notepaper he held. Nora stirred. Without a sound he folded into a crouch beside the bed, set the candle on the floor and cupped his free hand around the flame.

Darkness once more claimed the room. From this position his face came level with hers, separated only by the rumpled bedclothes. Her lips were softly parted. His gaze traced the delicate bow of the upper lip, the kissable swell of the lower. He shut his eyes against a stab of desire.

Reaching, he placed the note on her nightstand where she would find it upon waking. Once she read it she would know she must leave Blackheath Grange. If this afternoon hadn't sent her packing, his written wishes should. And if that still didn't suffice, the fact that he had gained entry to her room despite two locked doors would.

He stole another glimpse at her mouth. *Kiss me,* her sweetly slackened lips said directly to the part of his brain that housed his lust. He groaned and pressed his forehead against the edge of the bed. The imagined words echoed, spiraling inside him, spinning all other thoughts to oblivion.

*Kiss me, kiss me. . . .*

"Gray . . ."

His head shot up. Was she awake? He remained stock-still but for the flick of thumb and forefinger that extinguished the candle.

"Grayson, dearest . . ."

His eyes adjusted to the darkness, enough to perceive her outline against the ivory bedclothes. Her eyes were closed, her features relaxed with sleep.

"Please, my love . . ."

Reason fled. Something else entirely—instinct, lust, lunacy—propelled him to peel the bedclothes back and ease in beside her. She did not resist when he reached his arms around her. She barely moved but to snuggle her cheek against his shoulder.

Ah yes . . . to simply hold her for a few moments and think of nothing else but how lovely she was, how good she smelled, how soft she felt against him.

"My dearest, sweetest Nora." He spoke in a whisper no louder than the far-off murmur of the sea. "My heart."

He tucked his chin atop her head, breathing in her spicy scent—he'd learned recently that she used cinnamon sticks to scrape the paint from around her fingernails. It was an aroma that tempted him to suckle each delicate finger.

"Mmm." She snaked an arm across his chest and buried her nose against his neck.

"How like a child you sleep." He brushed his lips against her hair while his better sense urged him to leave before it was too late.

He didn't. With a barely steady fingertip he traced her from the arch of her hip to the curve of her throat, then ever so gently lay his open hand upon her breast.

Her hand came up, settling on his. "Ahh."

Daring more, he smoothed his thumb across her nipple, and the sensation of it beading through her cool linen shift set loose a devil that seized the remnants of his sanity.

Her mouth opened to release a soft and sultry "Yes . . ."

Razor-sharp urgency sent him leaning over her, lifting her nightgown above her hips. Careful not to jostle the bed, he straddled her, anchoring his weight on his arms on either side and ready to roll away should she wake. Her breathing came in sharp little bursts, but her eyes remained closed. He dipped his head, lips nudging a careful sampling of hers.

Fingertips as smooth and sweet as the night breeze glided beneath his shirt. He shivered as liquid heat rained through him. She found his shoulders and with gentle insistence tugged him closer. A moan of longing spilled from her lips, hot across his cheek.

Obedient, he lowered himself carefully against her, his flesh barely touching hers. Her knees came up to cradle his thighs.

Perhaps they were both asleep, sharing the same dream. For it could only be a dream, he decided. Reality held no room for such madness as this.

Why resist?

Balancing on one arm, he fumbled open his trouser buttons. He positioned himself, kissed her lightly and . . .

Stopped. Horrified.

Good God. What kind of fiend would do such a thing?

Nora's eyelids fluttered. His heart plummeted to his stomach, then ricocheted to his throat and stuck.

"Gray . . ."

Please God, let her have been awake the whole time, playing along. . . .

"Mmm . . ."

Or let her still be asleep.

Silent, thoroughly aghast, he watched her and listened. Her breathing continued deep and steady. With excruciating care he inched away, his swollen member throbbing in protest. The bed creaked. Nora's breath hitched in a little gasp.

Working his buttons closed, he slid to the side of the bed, watching her for any movement. With a soft groan she turned her face to the pillow. Her eyes opened.

His feet hit the floor and he knelt, hoping to God the shadows hid him. That she would close her eyes and roll back into slumber, all memory of him sliding away into new dreams.

Her gaze found his, held it as a furrow formed between her brows. He didn't so much as breathe.

Then she rolled until her back faced him. "Just a dream," she murmured. "Oh, Grayson . . ."

Some two hours later, unable to sleep, he stood in Aunt Pricilla's former bedchamber, now Nora's studio. A candle fluttered in the holder he gripped in one unsteady hand, sending his shadow into grotesque gyrations upon the wall. Before him stood the portrait she had unveiled earlier, hidden once more beneath the folds of the cloth.

He had to know if what he'd seen that morning bore any resemblance to what was actually imprinted on the canvas. Yet now as his fingers made contact with the concealing cloth, they went stiff. What answer could possibly lie beneath? That he'd lost his mind? That his brother's spirit truly haunted him? That for either reason, no one near him was safe?

He jerked his hand away and started backing toward the door.

The crisp scent of lemons stopped him cold.

*Lift it.*

His head snapped up, eyes straining in the candle-light. Had the whisper been real, or had he merely thought the words?

A cool breeze grazed his forehead, ruffling his hair. A hasty glance at the window confirmed what he feared—the curtains were drawn and motionless, the casement beneath shut tight.

That set his feet in motion, but as he neared the door a blow to the chest emptied his lungs and sent him sprawling on the hardwood floor. The candle clattered away, sputtering and thrusting him into darkness.

As he lay immobile, he heard nothing, could perceive no movement in the blackness but the pounding of his own heart. Oddly, despite the shock he'd suffered his chest didn't hurt. What had felt like a collision had knocked him down but left no lingering bruise.

Hair on his nape bristling, arms erupting in goose-flesh, he sat up, then pushed to his shaking legs. "Charlotte? Tom? Are you both haunting me now? Then show yourselves."

He scrubbed a hand across his eyes, aching now from lack of sleep. "For God's sake, show yourselves and tell me what you want."

*"Do what you came here to do."*

The whisper again reverberated inside his skull so that he didn't know if he'd heard it or imagined it. But the message was clear.

He made his way first to the window, opening the curtains wide to the moonlight. Then he dragged the

easel closer. There could be no question, no ambiguity
caused by a lack of light.

His fingers closed on the cloth. He tugged . . .

And gazed upon his own unmistakable image. Not
Tom falling to his death, but Grayson, or the Grayson
he'd become these past months.

It was his hair, his eyes, his mouth. His face, pinched
with grief. With guilt. And with greed. Yes, the same
greed that kept him at Nora's side, that had sent him
to her chamber tonight when he knew—*knew*—she'd
taken pains to keep him out. And when he knew he
didn't deserve her, couldn't be trusted to keep her safe.

Oh yes, that knowledge, along with his selfish disregard, was etched in the creases around his eyes, the
slope of his brow, the dispassionate curve of his
mouth. Nora had captured it all brilliantly. It was like
gazing into a mirror that showed not the features he'd
grown accustomed to all his life, but the face now
shaped by the soul beneath.

A strident laugh broke from his lips, jarring in the
silence. "Is this what you wanted? Did you think I
needed this portrait to know what lies inside me?"

*"Go to the cliffs."*

An iron band clamped his chest. "The cliffs?"

*"Go to the base of the cliffs."*

"To die?" As Tom did. It would be justice.

But the hollow reply offered no satisfaction.

*"Go."*

Nora spread paper across the dining table, then
reached into her basket for pens and pots of ink. Beside her Jonny stood waiting as she set out their art
supplies, showing neither impatience nor enthusiasm
to return to the picture he'd been sketching in the
garden when sudden raindrops drove them indoors.

"Now, then." She smiled down at him. "Where
were we when the weather so rudely interrupted us?"

He stepped up to the table and traced a finger

across the still-damp lines of his drawing, dragging a smear through a cluster of primroses. He shrugged.

"Growing rather bored with this one, are we?"

A second shrug provided the opportunity she'd been waiting for. Given the task of searching out the truth in this enigmatic house, what better place to start than with the one person who seemed to harbor the most secrets, secrets so onerous they had robbed him of his voice?

But as she well knew, there were other, infinitely more vivid ways of expressing oneself than with mere words.

Untying her bonnet, she set it on the table and then pushed aside a silver candelabrum. When she pulled out a chair and gestured to the boy, he scooted up onto his knees and leaned his elbows against the inlaid edge of the mahogany table.

"I've been hoping you might draw something special for me today," she said as casually as her taut nerves would allow. She didn't particularly relish cajoling information from a child, but discovering the truth about his uncle might well prove Jonny's salvation.

And perhaps Grayson's as well.

What better moment would there be, with Grayson presently gone from the house. She had knocked on his door earlier—pounded, really—to confront him about the perplexing letter he'd somehow left on her bedside table last night despite two secured doors. And to inform him he wouldn't be rid of her that easily.

He'd brushed by her, mumbling an apology about having to meet with a tenant farmer. He had hardly seemed fit to meet anyone, with his hair on end, his cravat askew and his wrinkled shirt hem trailing inside the same coat he'd worn yesterday.

And his eyes—sunken and glinting with a recklessness that frightened her. Frightened her nearly as much as the startling images that gripped her as she stared at his receding back.

His hands sizzling on her skin, his heated weight pinning her, his lust howling through her. *Had* he been in her room last night? Touching her? Covering her? Had she dreamed him, or had the real Grayson left her with tingling breasts and an insatiable need throbbing between her thighs?

Dream or no, he hadn't been her only visitor last night. Earlier, her lavender lady had seemed so substantial, so irrefutable. Yet upon awakening this morning, rising to the realities and responsibilities of a new day, how ludicrous it all seemed. Ghosts? She knew better.

As for the curtain she had found puddled on her floor . . .

She combed her fingers through Jonny's hair. "I'd like you to draw me a picture of your Uncle Grayson, if you would be so kind."

She held her breath. Would he balk at the notion, as he so often balked at Gray's efforts to be friendly? "Will you do that for me, dearest?"

His dark eyebrows knotted above his nose as he picked up a pen.

Nora eased the lid from one of the inkpots. "Perhaps you might make a picture of the two of you. I could hang it in my bedchamber."

He dipped the pen, blotted it and set it to the paper. Nora took up another pen and tried to concentrate on capturing the scene directly outside the dining room's broad windows. Or at least pretend to, lest Jonny sense her staring over his shoulder.

Try as she might, her lines went awry until the rain-blackened oaks she attempted to draw more resembled hulking monsters creeping up the front park. She was far too intent on the images forming beneath Jonny's busy hand to concentrate on the form and detail of her own efforts. When he finally looked up and pushed his paper toward her, she stifled a gasp.

She struggled to betray nothing with her expression

while searching for the right words to frame the questions rifling through her mind. "Well done, Jonny. Thank you."

The abrupt angles and smudged eyes produced a remarkable—and disturbing—likeness to Grayson. Jonny hadn't simply captured his uncle's features, but his turbulent state of mind. A state no child should ever have to witness in someone he depended upon.

And yet, that was not what troubled her most. While Jonny had drawn Gray large and in the forefront, he had placed his own diminutive image in the lower corner, with something resembling a tall rock between them.

Or . . . was it a headstone? Perhaps not, for a circle dangled from one side of the structure as if by a chain. Some sort of shackle?

She coughed to conceal a shiver. "You're, ah, rather small here. Are you playing hide-and-seek?"

He shrugged, offering not even a ghost of a smile.

"Do you like to hide sometimes? I know I do. My favorite place to do so is behind my easel. I especially like to retreat to my paints when the people around me are angry or upset."

He nodded.

She reached for his hand. "Dearest, does your uncle sometimes seem upset?"

His eyes grew large. She took that as an admission. "It troubles you, doesn't it?"

He lowered his gaze and traced his thumbnail along the grain of the table. A tiny shrug followed.

Nora took his hand in both of hers. "Are you sometimes afraid of Uncle Gray? It's all right to say so," she added in a whisper. "I promise I won't tell."

He leveled his bright blue eyes on her and surprised her with his answer. An adamant shake of his head.

It was the certainty of his response that most took her aback. No hesitation, not an ounce of reluctance. She had been prepared to coax his reply, to prompt him with hypothetical situations and reassure him that admitting the truth would not be a betrayal of any kind.

*Oh, but then why do you hide from him, Jonny? Why do you always bear the look of a frightened fawn whenever Gray enters the room?*

Her questions dissipated into the wide-open gaze trained on her; into soft, little-boy cheeks with the faintest of dimples winking at her as he waited, as he always did, to take his cue from her mood.

She kissed one of those precious, warm, dimpled cheeks.

"Good heavens!"

She and the child both jumped. Turning, Nora beheld a crimson-faced Mrs. Dorn poised rigidly in the doorway.

"Not on the inlaid dining table!" The woman stormed into the room with an expression not unlike that of a provoked bull. "Not on my Lady Clarington's precious ivory and mahogany table brought all the way from Florence."

Nora eased to her feet and stood in front of Jonny, lending him the protective camouflage of her skirts. "We were drawing on the terrace, Mrs. Dorn, but it began to rain. This seemed the most convenient room at the time."

"And that chair." Mrs. Dorn's finger shot out, the tip trembling as she thrust it toward Jonny. "He's got his feet up on the fabric. He knows better than that. The damask was woven by the Sisters of St. Adelaide in Brussels and cannot, simply *cannot* be replaced."

"Perhaps the sisters would appreciate a commission for new seat covers."

"It was well before the war, and they were elderly then." Mrs. Dorn's gaze burned with unmistakable fury. "They surely will have all passed away by now."

Nora sighed. "The chairs and everything else in the room belong to Jonny. I'm quite certain we haven't ruined anything, but really, what is a chair compared to a young boy's imagination?"

The woman's thin lips opened on an indignant breath and then clamped tight. She did an about-face and stalked out the door. "A young boy's imagination—bah!"

Despite her relief that the confrontation had ended, a notion sent Nora dashing after the housekeeper. "Mrs. Dorn, another moment, please."

The woman turned back into the room with a look of pained resignation. "Yes, madam?"

Nora nodded to Jonny first. "Dearest, run along and wash up for tea, won't you? Cook told me she baked a special treat just for you today."

With an eager look he trotted off, though whether his enthusiasm was for his special treat or to elude the fuming housekeeper, Nora couldn't say.

She took a moment to gather her thoughts, until Mrs. Dorn cleared her throat. "You have a question, madam?"

"Yes, I do. It's . . . well . . ." There was no delicate way to put it. "Can you tell me where Jonny was found the night his father . . . ah . . ."

"Died?"

Nora clasped her hands together and nodded.

"That is not a time I wish to recall, madam. It is better left in the past."

"If indeed it were in the past. But these events are still very much with us in the form of a little boy who will not speak." *And in the form of his uncle, mad or guilty or both.*

"He'll speak when he's ready, madam."

"You sound frightfully certain of that." Nora studied the woman, well aware she was using her position as lady of the house to back the servant into a corner. "Is there something you know about this matter, Mrs. Dorn?"

The look she met scorched with defiance. "No, madam."

"No. That is your answer? Nothing to add?"

"No, madam."

"Mrs. Dorn, if you cannot or will not answer my questions, I will be forced to interrogate the other staff. Or perhaps I'll seek out the local magistrate. I believe these details are on record, are they not?"

The housekeeper's scowl admitted defeat. "Very well. Young Lord Clarington was found not far from the headland, just within the tree line."

"Who found him?"

Mrs. Dorn's glare wilted away. She plucked at her apron and scurried to a nearby sideboard. Her back to Nora, she fussed with the lace runner, then repositioned a crystal vase and a Chinese porcelain bowl.

"Was it my husband?" Nora followed her, too intent on having answers to let the woman slip away. "Please, Mrs. Dorn. I'd never use the information to harm Jonny in any way."

The woman swung around to face her. "The Earl of Wycliffe."

Nora jolted. "He was here then?"

"He had been here all that week."

"Visiting Grayson," Nora murmured.

"Visiting both Master Grayson and his brother, madam. The two earls often went out riding together in the early mornings." A faint trace of tears clouded Mrs. Dorn's eyes, banished in an instant with a terse sniffle. "There is nothing more I can tell you, madam. I don't care to think about it."

"No, of course not," Nora agreed, taken aback by the housekeeper's brief show of emotion. "Thank you, Mrs. Dorn. And I apologize about the table and chair. We'll be more careful in future."

"The objects in this house are not all you need be careful with, madam." With that, Mrs. Dorn strode from the room, the terse warning echoing in Nora's startled ears.

# Chapter 15

Lungs burning, Grayson lengthened his strides along the trail leading to the headland. He'd left Constantine safe in his stall; Lord knew, he'd ridden the Thoroughbred hard enough yesterday, and had been lucky despite taking too many chances. He would not risk injuring the horse this morning. Not with what he had to do, what he had to face.

Beyond the murmur of the rain-encumbered breeze, the forest seemed unnaturally quiet, muted by low, rolling clouds that created a blanketing melancholy, as if everything here—trees and plants and even the birds—hung suspended in silent mourning.

On either side of him, towering maples and gray poplars bowed with the weight of the rain, the thrust of the wind. Sodden branches hung over the trail, swiping his face and showering drops across his shoulders. Further off the path, squat rowans afforded garish splashes of color to an otherwise somber palette, their scarlet berries glistening like splattered blood against the leaves.

Some two dozen yards in either direction, the forest dimmed to nothingness, only those murky, prowling shadows that sped Grayson's pulse and hastened his steps. Every breath of wind seemed to carry a whisper; every squelch of his boots a strangled cry from the grave.

*Go to the cliffs.*

So he had been ordered last night. All right, then, yes, he'd go . . . go to the very edge of the headland and see what fate planned for him. Up ahead, a tangle of bramble choked the pathway. He fought through it, thorns snagging his coat sleeves. A tendril whipped up and caught him across the bridge of his nose; another snapped up to sting his brow. He scored his palm as he tore the vines aside and kicked his way past.

The headland spread before him.

Heather and gorse, foxglove and red campion, shivered on their stems across the exposed bluffs. Free of the forest, he slowed but kept walking, afraid that if he stopped even for a moment he'd lose his momentum, his courage. With eyes focused on the churning, wind-whipped horizon, he made his way to the cliff edge.

It was there, with the ocean billowing beneath him, that the familiar dread robbed his limbs of strength. Even with feet braced wide, he swayed with the swirling gusts, dizzied, almost wishing . . .

If he simply let himself fall, would he hit the ledge partway down, or would he freefall to the salt-blanched shingle where they'd found Thomas? Rain splattered his face as the memory of that day sent waves of nausea spinning through him. The skewed angles of the arms and legs, the hideous twist of the neck, the bloody river that emptied, as all rivers do, into the sea.

"I'm here," he shouted. He opened his arms to the clouds, heavy and rumbling, pressing down as if to sweep him over the edge. "What do you want of me? Do you wish me to jump? Is that it?"

Would he? If Thomas appeared to him out of that roiling sky to point a condemning finger, would Grayson accept his sentence? Did he have that strength?

*Nora.*

The word hurled his heart against his ribs. Even

now she might be gone from Blackheath. He'd wanted her to go, had told her as much in writing. But when faced with the reality of it—the dismal reality—he knew he could not let her. Nor could he leave her. Especially not like this, as Tom had left him. Without a chance to mend what was broken. To ask forgiveness. To at least say farewell.

"I won't do it. You'll have to push me over."

He stepped back from the cliff as a soft sound burst in his ear, a single, faint note.

Laughter?

He pivoted, glancing wildly about. "Who's here?"

*"Go down. Not over. No one wants you dead. Not yet."*

"Charlotte? It's you, isn't it?" He flung dripping hair from his eyes. Chills rippled between his shoulders. "It was you last night. Where's Tom? I've seen him here and at the house. Why won't he speak to me?"

*"Go down to the beach."*

"At least tell me what I'm supposed to do there."

This time his only reply was a howl of wind and the slap of rain in his face.

"No answers for me, then? I'm to play your game and be good about it, am I?"

Something flashed in the corner of his gaze, a scrap of blue like the flick of a coattail. He scrubbed the rain from his lashes and strained his eyes, thought he saw more of that dark blue take form farther along the headland. It hovered motionless, silhouetted against the stormy sky, then disappeared down the slope of the promontory toward the beach.

"Tom? Tom, wait."

Feet squishing in his boots, he trudged along the cliff to the sloping trail he, Tom and Chad had secretly scraped out many years ago. Their parents would have throttled them had they known. But it had remained their secret, their private challenge.

Always that competition between them, the subtle strife fueled by their very different natures and very different stations in life. Tom, the eldest and the heir, should have been the leader. The instigator. The one with courage built upon a young aristocrat's confidence. Yet it had always been Grayson doing the prompting, along with Chad, who had never hesitated to test his limits—who, indeed, had never believed he had any.

Tom, meanwhile, had always hung back, assessing and cautious, joining in at the last minute only because he'd lose face with the younger boys if he didn't.

*Don't be afraid, Tom, we won't fall. . . . Let's swim out over our heads. Chad and I'll drag you back if you get tired. . . . Go inside the cave, Tom, we dare you. . . .*

Grayson half stumbled, half slid his way down the channel of loose stones and oozing mud that plunged to the beach, setting off little landslides in his wake. At the bottom he pushed off onto the mucky sand.

"Now what?" he said through chattering teeth. His clothes were soaked, his body chilled through.

A memory flashed as vivid as a painting held up before his eyes.

*I'm Captain Morgan! Chad is my first mate and you, Tom, are the Spanish. We capture you in the name of King George.* Using driftwood weapons, a sword fight would ensue, with Chad and Grayson always triumphant. *Now, into our secret cave, you swine!*

Their cave . . .

The cliffs along this beach were riddled with fissures once used by real pirates. They'd grown up on the stories, and at the ages of twelve, ten, and ten and a half respectively, Thomas, Grayson and Chad had discovered one of the legendary hideaways and made it their pirate lair. During the next few years they had stashed all manner of salvaged treasure: shells, fish bones, driftwood and odd articles of clothing and debris washed up from passing ships.

Is that where he was being sent? Could the cave somehow shed light on Tom's death?

The encroaching tide would soon send the waves sweeping into the cavern's mouth. He'd have to hurry.

Only a narrow crevice opened onto the beach, and Grayson stooped to enter it. Several yards in, the ceiling rose to accommodate his height. Despite the tide having been out all morning, the rocks glistened and the sound of dripping echoed like high notes on a pianoforte. As he'd discovered as a boy, extensive fissures penetrated the cliff face, letting water seep down on rainy days as well as providing enough light to see without a torch in the daytime.

He groped a hand along the wall beside him, the rough stone abrading his already lacerated palm. Within a dozen more paces, a smaller chamber would open off to his right. Inside, the floor sloped high enough to remain dry even at high tide. That was the grotto they'd claimed as boys.

He counted his steps, but where the dusky light should have yielded to the gaping blackness of an opening just large enough to admit a man, Grayson's probing fingers encountered rock. Not solid rock, but stones piled to seal the entrance.

Why? And by whom?

He crouched, feeling around with both hands. He hadn't been inside this cave for fifteen or more years, nor had he believed anyone else had. He certainly didn't remember a barricade here. The old tales of pirates flashed in his mind, but he dismissed them. Those seafaring brigands had long since gone the way of knights and troubadours.

"Think you can keep me out, do you?"

His words hissed off the rocks. Easing to his feet, he felt his way to one of the smaller stones lodged near the top of the gap. Carefully he fit his fingers into its jagged outlines. A bit of wiggling had it falling into his palms within moments.

He dislodged another just as easily and concluded this barricade had been erected by someone who hadn't particularly expected intruders to come poking around. Apparently, someone had simply wished to disguise the grotto entrance on the off chance some Sunday picnickers happened to stumble upon the main cave.

He shifted a few more stones until he opened a hole large enough to climb through. From outside came the steady crash of the sea, louder now, swallowing more beach as each moment passed.

He hesitated while debating the wisdom of returning later when the tide ran back out. Then he scrambled inside.

His foot came in contact with something hard, but with enough give to assure him it wasn't another boulder. He bent at the waist, hands closing around wooden slats. When he straightened, the dim illumination from the outer cave revealed what he'd already deduced: he'd found a crate.

Curious.

He gave it a shake, feeling the heavy contents thud and then settle with a jolt. He set the container down and jiggled the lid.

Nailed shut.

His eyes, adjusting now to the deeper darkness of the inner chamber, began to make out countless more crates stacked along the walls. Feeling his way about, he came upon the polished contours of some ten or so barrel-shaped casks crowded into a corner. Stooping, he put his ear to one and rapped his knuckles on its wooden surface. From inside came a faint slosh of liquid.

Apprehension churned in his gut. He returned to the first crate and stood, considering it a moment. Then he lifted a foot and slammed it into the slats, once, twice, a third time, until the wood splintered beneath his heel.

The contents clunked in protest. He dropped to his knees, tore the broken planks aside and clawed tufts of straw packing out of the way, all the while ignoring the jabs to his fingers. Holding his breath, he swept aside the last wisps.

A metallic gleam caught his eye. His hands closed around cool metal. Grayson lifted a silver platter and held it up to the light silhouetting the entrance.

He frowned as he examined it, running his fingertips along elaborate engravings. He set it aside and delved into the crate again, counting two dozen platters in all. Packed around them he discovered silver goblets etched to match the plates.

Choosing another crate at random, a larger one this time, he again kicked through the wood. The straw inside yielded a pair of six-branched candelabra. Three more pair lay beneath successive layers of packing.

Grayson sat back on his haunches. He had seen enough. Silver, casks containing brandy or wine . . . whatever else lay concealed undoubtedly shared one basic characteristic: stolen goods. Had to be. Why else the secrecy? But his conclusion did little to solve the greater part of the mystery. How had this booty gotten here, and who would someday come to claim it?

One answer crashed through every possible theory. Smugglers still made regular runs along the Cornish coast, secreting black-market goods in and out of the country to avoid the rising excise taxes. But why here, on the private property of the Earl of Clarington?

He pressed a palm to his temple. *No.* He refused to consider it. It couldn't be possible.

Not *his* brother.

But . . . if Tom *had* resorted to criminal activities, it would have been because he, Grayson, pushed him to it, because he forced Tom's hand by not raising his own to help when he should have.

Pushed him . . . pushed him over the brink . . .

The rushing in his ears made him light-headed, sickened, until he realized the sound wasn't caused merely by his guilt-ridden thoughts. He went still, ears pricked. The tide was fast approaching, the waves now echoing inside the main cave. He set a goblet aside from the rest, intending to take it with him when he left. The engravings might help him identify where the spoils had come from. If he were lucky, he'd discover a silversmith's mark on the bottom. And if luckier still, he'd learn enough to absolve his brother.

And himself, at least of this particular crime.

Quickly he tucked the other items back into their crates, replaced the straw, and balanced two intact crates on top of the ones he had broken, rearranging as best he could to conceal his intrusion into the lair. Satisfied, he clambered back through the opening, a goblet weighting his coat pocket.

The sea heaved at the mouth of the cave, venturing in, rushing out, stretching farther inside at each return. He'd be ankle deep if he left now. But he couldn't leave. Not until he replaced the barricade and erased his presence here. Hastily he began shoving each rock back into place.

The rain had stopped, and not long ago Nora had left Jonny under the supervision of the head groom while the boy exercised his Welsh cob in the closest paddock. She stayed long enough to express her admiration for the spirited, misty-coated Puck. After urging Jonny to be careful going over the jumps, she hurried back to the house to take advantage of yet another opportunity.

Now she stood in the center of her room, contemplating its four walls. They appeared solid enough. But last night Grayson had somehow gained entry through two locked doors. She was not mistaken. He *had* been here. Every thrumming nerve in her body, every tingle along her skin, assured her so.

He hadn't entered through the dressing rooms, for

the chair had still been wedged beneath the knob this morning. A duplicate key to the main door? But the key she had turned last night had still protruded from the lock in exactly the position she had left it. If Grayson had unlocked the door from the other side, her key would have been pushed free and fallen to the floor.

Then how on earth? Through a window? No balcony or ledge ran between their chambers.

*I'll wager there's a maze of back stairwells and secret passages.* Those were her own words the day she arrived at Blackheath Grange. Her eyes narrowed as she studied the wall separating the bedrooms.

Rushing forward, she ran her palms over the plasterwork and framed panels of wallpaper. Carefully she inspected every reachable inch of wall to the right and left of the wardrobe closet, which was far too heavy to be moved. Perhaps one of these papered rectangles . . .

Solid. All of it. Hands on hips, she stepped back, a rueful grin curling her lips.

Secret passage indeed. She was merely letting the mysteries of the house affect her judgment, just as she had last night in believing she'd seen a ghost. Of course she had merely fallen asleep in the chair by the window. It wouldn't be the first time she'd dreamed vividly, which explained her tugging the curtain until it fell.

That curtain had been restored earlier by the upstairs maid. She walked over to it, inspecting the rod and brackets, when an airy rustle of silk sent her gaze darting back to the wall she had just scrutinized.

Her pulsed throbbed in her wrists as she stood utterly still, listening. Waiting. Holding her breath.

At least a full minute passed and nothing more occurred. As she was about to dismiss her fears as beyond silly, a thought struck her.

Her bedroom was a perfect square. The two dressing rooms lay between her room and Grayson's, but they were small and set against the outer wall of the house. Then . . . what else lay between the two bedrooms?

There had to be something she had missed. She stood in front of the wardrobe, considering. It towered some eight feet high and surely weighed a ton.

Her gaze dropped, and a discovery sent her sinking to her knees. The piece sat on three, not four wheels. The left rear leg was different. On hands and knees, then, she crawled to inspect what turned out to be a sort of pivot.

Gathering her skirts, she pushed to her feet. A tight frown tugged her brows as she opened the doors, peered inside, closed one and gripped the edge of the other with both hands. With a quick little prayer that she wasn't about to make a colossal mistake and bring the massive cupboard crashing down on top of her, she gave a fierce tug.

And was rewarded when, after an initial hesitation, the wardrobe swung away from the wall as easily as an opening door. Which perhaps it was.

Heart thumping with the excitement of her discovery, not to mention the outrage of Grayson's subterfuge, she studied yet another tall, wallpapered rectangle. While it appeared innocent enough at first, further inspection revealed it to be slightly different from the rest. By nearly pressing her nose against the paneling, she could detect a hairline gap between the molding and the wall itself.

She pressed the flats of her hands against the panel and pushed. It didn't budge. In the same position, she tried sliding the panel to the right, then to the left.

On the second try she felt a tiny shift, as if the panel were held by some sort of latch. She peered closely . . . and saw it—a miniscule recess near waist height at the edge of the panel, just large enough for a fingertip. She placed her forefinger into it, pushed . . . and heard a faint click.

Her jaw dropped even as she slid the panel open. Goodness. With all her searching, she hadn't truly expected to find anything. With one hand braced against the wall and ready to pull back should the need arise, she leaned and peered inside. Detecting no immediate dangers, she stepped over the foot-high threshold into a stairwell swathed in shadow.

The hairs on her arms bristled. She tossed a wistful look over her shoulder to the safety of her room. Then she lifted her skirts and placed a foot on the bottom step. It gave a creak, loud in the stillness, a jarring counterbeat to her racing pulse.

The darkness thickened as she climbed, pressing in around her. Once she stopped to peer down at the light spilling in from her bedchamber, just to assure herself the sliding panel hadn't somehow closed, sealing her in. Slowly she ascended to the top . . . to find nothing but a dead end.

There was nothing, merely a small landing. A staircase to nowhere? Indeed, if the past half hour had taught her anything, it was not to put stock in the obvious.

She debated going back down and returning with a lamp, then discarded the notion as one that would take too much time. Bother the darkness, for it couldn't hurt her. Only this house's secrets had the power to do that. She wanted answers, and she wanted them now.

As she had done below, she ran her hands over the walls on either side of her, flinching and stifling a cry when her fingers tangled in a sticky web. She quickly wiped them on her skirts and continued her search. On the wall to her left, her fingertips detected a tiny catch similar to the one downstairs. She pressed, and this wall too slid open. Dusty light from inside bathed the stairwell.

Again she paused. What would she find inside, and did she truly wish to know? She entertained no doubts that Grayson had used this passage to steal into her room last night. Perhaps other nights as well. Could he be hiding something here, something she might regret discovering?

Vague fears slid like ice through her, raising goose bumps. Pausing to draw a fortifying breath into her lungs, she stepped into a narrow room, cramped beneath the sloping roof of the house and illuminated by a single recessed window. A faded rug partially covered the wide pine floorboards. A small escritoire with a glass bookcase occupied one corner. Against the back wall, an exposed mattress slumped like an idle slattern. That was all.

A secret hideaway, but for what purpose? An unpleasant sensation gripped her. She nudged the mattress with her toe, raising a puff of dust. Seeing neither blanket nor pillows anywhere, she decided the bed could not have been used in a long time, and dismissed unsavory thoughts of her husband, midnight trysts and anonymous women.

By the direction she'd come, she deduced herself to be standing directly above her dressing room. If she crossed to the other side and found yet another sliding panel, surely she would descend to Grayson's chamber.

She had never entered his bedroom before. A kernel of trepidation skittered through her, yet in a deeper, darker place inside her, desire stirred.

But Grayson would not now be in his room. He had left the house early again on another of his mysterious errands, and hadn't yet returned.

Like a seasoned thief she stole across the room, treading lightly and going utterly still when a loose floorboard shifted beneath her weight. Hearing nothing beyond the blood rushing in her ears, she continued on. Easily she opened the room's second sliding door, all the while marveling at the astounding ingenuity that had gone into concealing the little garret.

Once more in semidarkness she felt her way down the predicted second set of stairs. By the time she reached the bottom, accessing the final hidden latch felt nearly as natural as opening any other door in the house.

No wardrobe or other piece of furniture blocked her entry into the adjoining chamber. A note of mixed triumph, indignation and pure fascination set her ears ringing. Until this moment, a tiny part of her had clung to the threadbare hope that the passage did not lead to Grayson's room, and that she had merely imagined him in her room last night, dreamed of his heated presence, his fiery touch.

She stepped into the masculine environs of dark wood walls and forest green draperies, of furnishings dominated by heavy English oak. A headboard carved with a lion's head at its center towered above a massive bed, hung with folds of green and gold velvet gracefully gathered and secured with tasseled cords to the bed's four tapering posts.

Though unoccupied, the room breathed Grayson's familiar scent, a heady mingling of the earthy outdoors and genteel grooming, entirely masculine, vaguely unsettling and, as Nora breathed it in deep, undeniably arousing. Had she not known this to be his room, she would have guessed correctly. His imprint was everywhere—in the dark intensity of the colors, in the hulking furniture, in the brooding silence broken only by the rain against the windows.

Detecting movement at the corner of her eye, she jumped, then calmed when she realized the source. Outside, rain traced wavering patterns down the windowpanes, throwing writhing shadows across the floor.

To her right stood a bureau, wide and high, its top littered with Grayson's personal effects. She couldn't help running her fingers over a comb and brush, his silver pocket watch—funny he didn't have it with him—and a pair of onyx cuff links. A cravat lay coiled beside his watch. She picked it up, the fine linen leaving traces of dampness across her fingertips. Bringing it close to her nose, she breathed in a faint salt tang.

"How odd."

"Indeed."

At the sound of the rumbling baritone, Nora yelped. Spinning about, she whisked her hands behind her like a child caught stealing. Her gaze searched the dusky corners; at first she didn't see him. But she felt him, oh, she felt his presence filling the room and surrounding her like a physical embrace.

He stood in the dressing room doorway, taking shape from the surrounding gloom like an apparition materializing from thin air. A full day's growth shaded his jaw in baleful reflection of the shadows beneath his eyes. His clothes, a white shirt lying open at the neck and tight breeches tucked into riding boots, seemed to adhere to his body like a second skin. She saw a scratch at the corner of his eye, another across the bridge of his nose.

Had he been brawling?

As he returned her stare, his nostrils flared and his stark blue eyes simmered with . . . anger, displeasure . . . desire? Whatever it was both chilled her and lit a smoldering fire inside her . . . and made her want to defy her fears and go to him. Go to him and kiss the scrapes on his face, soothe the wounds in his heart.

He pushed forward into the room. "Good afternoon, Lady Lowell. Perhaps you'd care to explain what the blazes you're doing here."

*Chapter 16*

"I . . . I . . ." As though cornered prey, Nora backed against his bureau, hands twisting behind her. Guilt glittered in her eyes while mortification flamed her cheeks. She looked about to turn and bolt the way she'd come.

He wished she would, wished with all his being that she wasn't here now, staring at him with her wide, innocent eyes and her open, ingenuous spirit.

What would she see? How lost his brother had become in his last months of life? And how indifferent Grayson had been during that time?

Even if Thomas hadn't been directly involved in smuggling, someone had been using his land for criminal purposes. The Tom that Grayson had known, the honest, generous earl who had cherished Blackheath Grange above all else but his wife and child, would never, *ever* have allowed such an outrage.

That he *had* allowed it, or had remained ignorant of it, gave testimony to how far his life had fallen apart, how desperate and distracted he had become in the end. That is what the ghosts wanted Grayson to know when they led him to the headland today. . . . The full consequences of his actions, or lack of them, in the year—no, years—leading to his brother's death.

And now, with Nora cowering against his bureau, her beautiful face filled with alarm and uncertainty, his culpability for her and for Tom and Jonny, felt like a jagged weight of granite cutting into his shoulders.

He crossed to the corner of the bed, leaned against the curtained post and folded his arms across his chest. He supposed the pose made him look cavalier. In reality he needed that post to shore him up, because he feared his strength might fail him, that he might land flat on his face.

"If you wished to speak with me," he said with false calm, "you might have simply knocked on my door. Even if you had merely wished to snoop about my room, I'd have let you in."

That produced an instantaneous transformation. Her shoulders squared, her chin swung up and her eyes fired off hot little flares that singed his flesh.

*"Knock?"* A hand shot out from behind her back, flailing his soggy neckcloth at him. "Did *you* knock before breaking and entering my chamber last night?"

"I broke nothing when I entered, and yes, I did try knocking first." When she looked thoroughly unconvinced he added, "Softly, and at both doors. I didn't wish to disturb you if you were sleeping. I also tried both knobs, but you seemed intent on barring my way."

"Oh, and so you took it upon yourself to steal in like a common thief?"

"On the contrary, I stole nothing and left something. Did you see my note?"

"Yes, I saw it."

"And?"

His gut clenched as he waited for her reply. He had been so certain when he wrote that missive last night that he was doing a noble thing in urging her to leave. Today he felt more convinced than ever.

But the desire to grab her and hold on tight pulsed through him as the silence stretched. As he watched an inner battle toss shadows across her lovely features, he questioned his ability to ever let her go, to face the rest of his life—and his demons—without her quiet strength and steady faith to anchor him.

All the more reason for her to fly free. For in the end he'd only drag her down, as he'd dragged Tom. . . .

She stepped away from the bureau. "Are you wet?"

"No."

"You are. You're soaked through. Especially your trousers. Where were you? Out in the rain?"

"It doesn't matter."

"You'll catch your death."

"I doubt it." He ran his fingers around his decidedly damp collar, then wished he hadn't.

"What have you done to your hand? How did you get those scratches on your face?"

He balled the injured hand in to a fist. "You read my note, Nora. What are you going to do about it?"

"Yes, well, I'm not leaving."

"It would be for the best if you did." Even to his ears, the statement lacked the smallest shred of sincerity, while the intensity of his relief convinced him he hadn't a noble bone in his body.

"I resent your telling me what I should and shouldn't do," she said.

"Never mind what I tell you. Haven't the past several days spoken well enough?" He pushed out a grim laugh. "Surely you can't deny having had the inclination to end this unfortunate marriage of ours."

"I did not marry you expecting heaven-sent bliss."

"To say the least."

"But things have changed since then." She twisted his neckcloth between her hands. "I've discovered you don't despise me any more than I do you."

"Perhaps you should."

"No." She came closer, and he pressed tighter against the bedpost. "Don't you see? There is something here worth holding on to."

Yes, *her*. She was worth holding on to. But what

would she have in return? Something empty and in-substantial. A lie of a husband.

"If you'd only talk to me, tell me the truth of what's troubling you. I know what you said about your brother but—"

"You didn't believe me? Did you think I spoke met-aphorically about pushing my brother over that cliff?"

"I don't believe you did any such thing. You're not capable of . . ."

Her words faltered as he shoved away from the post. She backed away quickly, hitting the bureau with her shoulders and rattling the drawers.

"Aren't I, sweet Nora?" Reaching her, he wrapped his hands around her slight hips and tugged her against him. "How can you be so certain?"

She went rigid against him, but didn't pull away. "I know perfectly well—"

He dipped his head and cut her assertion short by covering her mouth with his. He kissed her hard, pain-fully, teeth biting into lips. Her muffled protest vi-brated inside him while her hands slid up between them. He only held her tighter while his tongue pushed into her mouth to duel with hers.

He heard the catches in her throat, felt the tension of her resistance. But he watched himself go on fright-ening her with his devouring kisses and crushing em-brace. Just as he had once watched himself beleaguer Tom with angry words. Unable to stop. Loathing him-self. Wishing he were different, stronger, better.

And then . . . it all changed. *She* changed. Took control somehow, slowing their kisses until each one lingered sweetly, softly. Until his senses swam in plea-sure. Until his anger and grief melted into the fire smoldering between their joined mouths.

Just as he began to believe he might warm his frigid heart in her arms, she broke the kiss and pushed him to arm's length. Dampness from his shirt darkened the front of her dress, making it cling to her breasts in wanton invitation.

She panted for breath but regarded him unblinkingly, one eyebrow quirked above the other. "I think you need me more than you know."

"And more than I wish to." The words escaped before he could catch them. Triumph sparked in her eyes.

With a scowl he pulled free of her grasp. "Go, Nora, get out," he commanded, knowing he must be adamant or he'd end up gathering her in his arms and burying his soul in her lusciously willing body. *Losing* his soul, and endangering hers. "Leave Blackheath Grange."

"I'm not going anywhere." Slipping his cravat around the back of his neck, she held the trailing ends and pulled him close. Her breath heated the cold skin inside his sodden collar. "I married you and I'm in this for keeps, despite your attempts to frighten me away. You didn't murder your brother—"

"Damn it, Nora—"

"No, damn *you* for feeling so guilty about his death that you're willing to punish everyone around you for it."

"That isn't what I'm doing."

"Yes, it is." Her fingers encircled his arms, digging in. Tipping her chin, she peered fiercely into his eyes. "Tell me the truth. How did your brother die?"

He yanked free, turned and stumbled to the bed. Sinking onto the edge, he dropped his head into his hands. "I don't know for certain."

"What do you *think* happened?"

She had followed him, stood so close her scent floated dizzily through his head.

"I think he jumped. Jumped because he'd got himself into trouble he couldn't get out of, and because I refused to be of any help."

He raised his face to her all-too-trusting one and willed himself to say what had haunted him for nearly a year. "Tom committed suicide because of me, Nora. Because when he bankrupted the estate, I told him he was a worthless failure. That he'd disgraced the entire family, shamed the Clarington name and failed his son. And so he went out to the cliffs that very day and repaid his debts with the only thing he had left—his life."

"Surely you can't know that for certain."

He nodded miserably. "I believe I found evidence today that Tom had resorted to extreme measures to recoup the funds and property he'd lost. He'd become desperate, and I . . ."

"No, Gray. It can't have been your fault. You can't be responsible for another man's actions, not even your brother's." Her hand came down on his shoulder, light, tender, filled with infinite compassion.

He couldn't endure such undeserved trust; it set off a fury inside him. Not at her, but at her damned propensity to believe the best of him despite the facts. He leapt to his feet.

"Don't patronize me, Nora. You've no idea what you're talking about."

"Oh, but—"

"No! This is who I am. This is your husband." Turning back to the bed, he grabbed the bedclothes in both hands and with a howl of frustration dragged them from the mattress and flung them to the floor. Pillows flew, sending a lamp on the bedside table crashing to the floor.

Nora bit back a cry of dismay. He whirled on her, backing her across the room. "See me for what I am and don't talk to me about what you do not understand. It doesn't matter if these hands pushed him or not."

He held them up as if to wrap them around a neck, sending her lurching out of reach. "It doesn't matter whether or not I wished him dead that day. The result is the same. I drove Tom over the edge. I'm the reason he's dead and all that's left of the Clarington name is a shadow of a boy who won't speak."

"Jonny can be helped. . . ."

"Not here. No one can be helped in this house." Advancing on her again, he trapped her against his writing desk. He framed her face in his hands, feeling the heat of her fear in his palms. "You know it too. You feel it. The very walls are closing in on us, strangling us with their history of death and obsession. This house is haunted by its past, and your only chance is to get away. Take Jonny and go somewhere you'll both be safe."

"Only if you come with us."

He released her with a sharp laugh. "Oh, no. I belong here. Here with my brother."

"Do you see him?" At her whispered query his heart went still. The blood drained from his head as she continued, "Does your brother's spirit appear to you?"

"What are you talking about?" But the tremor in his voice belied his show of ignorance.

"You just said it. This house . . . is haunted."

"I only meant—"

"Gray, I've seen a woman, late at night. . . ." She wrinkled her brow as if disbelieving her own words.

"What woman?"

"I don't know. She's appeared to me several times now, always wanting me to do something, go somewhere, find . . . something."

"You've been dreaming." Yes, he wanted her to be imagining things. . . . Couldn't bear the notion that his demons might be haunting Nora as well.

She shook her head. "I've told myself that, but this last time she seemed entirely real, and I know I was awake. She always wears a lavender dress and speaks in a lovely musical accent—"

"Charlotte." The name grated from his throat.

"Who?"

"Never mind. You have to leave, Nora. For your own safety."

At long last he knew the truth—his ghosts were real and he wasn't insane. But this could prove infinitely worse. If Tom's ghost haunted him, there would be justice, retribution. But if so, it must be his alone to bear. He would not see Nora or Jonny hurt by whatever price he must pay for Tom's death. That much he swore. "Leave now or so help me . . ."

"I won't run away. You need me—"

"Damn it, Nora, why won't you listen to me?" He grasped the nearest thing within reach, the clock on the desk, and hurled it against the far wall. Shattering glass, splintering wood and the brass workings showered the floor.

Nora's cry echoed through the room, in his ears. He saw the color leach from her face in the instant before her hands shot up in front of her to shield her from . . . from him. He started to reach for her, halting when her eyes widened around a feral kind of fright rimmed with dawning comprehension, with dismay. They stood immobile, panting, for several seconds. Then she did as he'd earlier hoped—she whirled and disappeared into the secret passageway.

Hearing her panicked tread creaking along the wooden floor above, his heart broke at the same time relief surged through him. Perhaps now fear of him would send her to safety.

He pressed both hands to his head, squeezing, trying to crush the memories, the pain, and the knowledge that in marrying Nora he had come agonizingly close to touching happiness again, only to have it pulled beyond reach forever.

Nora stumbled over the high threshold back into her room, catching herself against the side of the angled wardrobe. Hot tears rolled down her cheeks but she dashed them away. Knuckles blanched, fingers trembling, she pressed a fist to her stomach and choked back a sob. Her breath came in violent bursts. Chills racked her, brought on only partly by the dampness clinging to her dress, transferred there from Grayson's clothing when he'd kissed her.

Grayson. He was surely mad. Not because he was seeing ghosts, for if that branded him insane then she must wear the same label. No, that his tormentors were real she didn't doubt. But the violence that torment unleashed in him . . .

She shivered. The man at the National Gallery . . . that night at the inn in Devon . . . just yesterday when he'd viewed his portrait . . . each occasion had been shaped by uncontrollable impulses, fierce and powerful . . . frightening.

Yet even now, her lips burned from his bruising kisses, and her body ached with the desire to return to him, take him in her arms and heal him. Heal all that was wrong in this house and all that had gone awry between them. She yearned for the Grayson of their wedding night—a man she wasn't sure existed anymore, or ever existed outside of her dreams and hopes. This volatile stranger who had taken his place . . . was *this* the true Grayson?

Releasing her grip on the wardrobe, she about-faced and whisked the passage door closed. Then, heart throbbing in her throat, she darted around the huge piece of furniture, flattened both palms on the painted doors and shoved with all her weight. The thing swung on its pivot, coming to rest in its proper place inches from the wall.

Nora stepped back. She shoved loose hairs from her face and regarded the arrangement. Not good enough.

An idea sent her hurrying out to the corridor, passing the door to Grayson's room at a run. At the top of the stairs she paused, half breathless, searching the hall below. A footman was crossing from the dining hall to the drawing room. Nora called down to him.

"Please send Mr. Gibbs up to my room immediately," she said. "And tell him to bring a hammer, hooks and wire."

"My lady . . . ?"

"You heard me. Hammer, hooks and wire. Immediately."

Some ten minutes later she again stood beside the wardrobe, hammer in hand. Holding the end of a hook against the wall, she swung the hammer with all her strength. She missed, knocking a dent the size of a shilling into the plaster. The impact jarred her arm from wrist to shoulder. The hammer clunked to the floor.

"Devil take it," she murmured. But no wonder. With her shaking hands, she was in no condition to be handling tools.

Behind her, she could hear Mr. Gibbs's bafflement in the shuffling of his feet, the clearing of his throat. "Perhaps I may be of assistance, madam."

Scowling at the cavity she'd created in the wall, she bent to pick up the hammer. Without a word, she held it out to the steward and stepped aside.

Gibbs unbuttoned his frock coat and took his position. After pounding the first hook home, he turned to her with a quizzical look.

"Perhaps my lady would care to explain the rest of the task?"

"I wish another hook set into the panel."

"Into the wallpaper, madam?"

"Yes." She showed him where. "And then the two hooks tightly connected by the wire."

"I see. Very good, madam."

Of course it was evident he didn't see at all, that her strange request puzzled him no end. Apparently the man had no inkling of what lay beyond the wall.

Now that her initial fright had passed, she realized that to some extent Grayson's violent handling of his bedclothes and clock had been intentional, meant to frighten her away for her own good. Hadn't he told her he wanted her somewhere safe?

That meant he cared. . . . Perhaps . . . even loved her. A lump rose in her throat at the memory of his hollow expression and his haunted eyes as he'd told her to go, to get out. She took courage in believing he hadn't meant it, not deep down.

His explosive behavior alarmed her, and yes, she would take pains to ensure Jonny's and her safety, but she had no intention of leaving Blackheath Grange or Grayson. On the contrary, she was more determined than ever to stay and get to the bottom of what had happened months ago, as well as what was happening now.

"Will that be all, madam?"

She blinked, roused from her ruminations. Gibbs stood waiting, hammer in hand.

"Perhaps my lady wishes me to pound hooks elsewhere?" His wandering gaze lighted on her dressing table, headboard and nightstand.

His eyes sparked with astonishment when she said, "Yes, one more. Into the wardrobe, just here." She pointed to the back corner of the piece. If Grayson somehow managed to dislodge the hook in the sliding door, she could still prevent him from moving the armoire aside. "I want it wired to the wall, tightly."

"I . . . uh . . . yes, my lady."

He had just finished when a shadow fell across the threshold.

"What is all this racket? Gibbs, what in heaven's name are you doing? Oh, Lady Lowell, I didn't see you there."

Mrs. Dorn's black-clad figure stood framed in the doorway like an elongated spider suspended in its web. Her pinched features traveled over Nora, slid back to Gibbs, and to the hammer dangling at his side. Her pale gaze flitted over the room . . . and stopped.

Glaring at the wire stretching from the wardrobe to the wall, she crossed the threshold as gingerly as a black widow stalking its prey.

*Oh, not now,* Nora thought. After everything else, she didn't need a confrontation with Mrs. Dorn, and what business was it of the housekeeper's anyway?

Apparently the woman thought it very much her business. A decidedly shocking shade of red flooded her face. Her mouth opened to emit a series of gasping stutters. Nora braced for worse, but after mouthing words that might have been *inestimable, destruction* and *abominable,* the woman stomped out.

Nora nodded to Gibbs. "That went better than expected."

Moments after the steward left, she tested her improvised lock by tugging on the wardrobe. It didn't budge, nor could the sliding panel be opened.

A knock sounded at her open door. Kat's dark eyes regarded Nora solemnly. "You asked me to report any developments with his little lordship."

Nora clasped the maid's hand as she would a familiar friend and drew her into the room. "What is it, Kat?"

"It's about his speaking, ma'am. He does, you see."

The shock of the revelation prompted Nora to shush the other young woman and glance out into the hallway. Satisfied there was no one to press an ear to the door, she closed it and led Kat to the chairs beneath the window.

"He's spoken to you?" she whispered, quite overcome with the conviction that for now, no one else must know the child was talking.

"He didn't talk to me, not actually, ma'am." Hands folded primly in her lap, Kat perched stiffly in her chair, clearly uncomfortable with sitting like a guest rather than standing like a servant. "It was in his sleep. He tossed and fretted half the night."

Nora leaned forward eagerly. "What did he say?"

A ridge formed above the maid's nose. "I couldn't make much out. You know how folks mumble in their dreams. But I do believe I heard him mention your husband by name, and perhaps his father. And I quite plainly heard him say 'Don't.' "

"Don't," Nora repeated. She sat back in her seat, a cold misgiving prickling the hairs on her arms. Could Jonny be reliving the night his father died? Could his plea of "don't" have been aimed at a father intent on suicide? At a murderer?

At Grayson?

"Can you recall anything else he said?"

"There was something." Kat paused, frowning again in concentration. "I thought I heard him say 'Uncle had.' "

"Uncle had what?" Nora wondered aloud, wincing at the answers that pinched her throat. Pushed his brother over a cliff? Driven him to take his own life?

If either were true, she knew there could be no saving her husband, neither from the accountability nor the guilt. She refused to allow that possibility.

"Was there anything else, Kat? Think. Anything at all?"

Kat shook her head. "The rest was gibberish. But it does prove one thing beyond a doubt. Our young earl can talk."

"Yes, but he chooses not to."

A disturbing thought struck her. Mrs. Dorn had adamantly disapproved of Kat sleeping in Jonny's room. Perhaps he had spoken in his sleep previously. And perhaps Mrs. Dorn had heard him and learned something she did not wish Nora—or anyone else—to know.

She remembered meeting Jonny for the first time, and how he had seemed so dependent on Mrs. Dorn whenever Nora asked him a question. Could the housekeeper be enforcing Jonny's silence?

"I believe it's more than the trauma of his father's death that has silenced him," she said. "He's terrified of something—or someone—and his fears prevent him speaking. I must find a way to break the silence."

"Begging your pardon, ma'am, but if you ask me, you already have the answer. Your paints and all. Whenever there was a to-do in your parents' house, I always knew I could find you behind your easel."

"I've tried art with Jonny, but canvas and sketch books are too limiting."

Kat flashed a shrewd grin. "I've an idea if you care to hear it, ma'am."

"I'll try anything."

"There are plenty of plain white bedclothes up in the servant's linen room. I'd wager we could nip one on the sly with dismal Dorn none the wiser. We can stretch it across the floor of your studio and give our little earl the biggest canvas anyone ever saw."

"Brilliant!" Nora practically leapt out of her chair. "Oh, but Kat, let me do the pilfering. I wouldn't want you to get into trouble."

"That dried up old raven doesn't frighten me, ma'am."

Nora couldn't help a fleeting smile. "She does me. Kat, I want you to stay with Jonny when I can't be with him. Become his shadow and do not let him out of your sight."

"Don't fret, ma'am. They don't call me Kat for nothing. My eyes are keen and my ears sharp. That child won't so much as wink, nor will anyone wink at him, without my knowing about it and reporting directly back to you."

"Thank you, Kat. I knew I could count on you."

## *Chapter 17*

"A beach patrol, sir?"

"Yes. Twenty-four hours a day," Grayson explained to his steward the next morning. He'd spent another restless night wondering if he should go to Nora and apologize, reassure her he wasn't insane.

But he'd already told her the truth, that he believed he'd pushed his brother to his death, and if living with that weren't enough to drive a man to insanity, he didn't know what would. So what reassurances could he offer his wife?

He and his steward stood in his father's old study, a room rarely used by either him or Tom due to the memories the room evoked. Even now, the lingering hint of pipe tobacco made his stomach clench around unsettling memories, for it was typically here that he and his brother had been taken to task by their father for their boyhood transgressions.

More often than not, it had been Tom bearing the brunt of their father's displeasure. *I'll teach you to be a man, Thomas. I'll show you what it means to be the heir to the Earl of Clarington. . . .*

Grayson squared his jaw and silently cursed the portrait hanging above the mantel, an oil depiction of his father sitting between his two young sons. Alexander Lowell's painted expression exactly mirrored the one ingrained in Grayson's memory: stern, arrogant, uncompromising.

But having chosen this room because he knew they would not likely be interrupted here, he turned his attention back to his immediate concerns. "Break the surveillance into shifts," he told his steward. "I want both the headland and the inlet under constant observation, day and night."

Gibbs nodded his compliance, if not his understanding. "I will have dependable men posted by this afternoon. But if I may ask, sir, what are these fellows to be on the lookout for?"

"Trespassers. Either stealing in on foot or by boat. If anyone approaches the beach, I want to know about it immediately."

"Of course, sir." If the conversation startled or otherwise unsettled Gibbs in any way, his unruffled exterior gave no hint. "Shall I notify the magistrate in Falmouth?"

Grayson had been asking himself the same question. It would have been the logical thing to do, the safe thing. But if Tom *had* been involved, there would be questions. Talk. Eventually, Jonny would hear.

"No. Not yet. I want more information first." He went to the desk and retrieved the silver goblet he'd taken from the cave. Turning it over, he showed Gibbs the initials etched inside a tiny diamond pattern. "I want this traced. See if you can have the silversmith identified."

"Judging by the shape of the stem and the curve of the cup, it looks like it might be Sheffield silver, sir." Gibbs took the goblet from Grayson and held it up to examine it from several different angles. "Of a certainty English, at any rate. Perhaps Mrs. Dorn might be of service in this instance."

"Just don't tell her where it came from."

An amused gleam eased the severity of Gibbs's pitted features. "Even if I knew where this piece did come from, sir, I'd hardly take it upon myself to say so."

"I've given you scant information, Gibbs, and for that I apologize. It's not that I don't trust you . . ." Or did he? At this point he couldn't be certain whom he could trust. Until he had answers, no one was above suspicion, no one at Blackheath except Nora and Jonny.

After Gibbs left with the goblet, Grayson lingered in the study. Standing at the mullioned window and staring at the vivid greens of the park beyond, he tried to concentrate on what he needed to do next. All he could think about was Nora.

Since arriving here he'd done nothing but frighten her. Even his attempt at lovemaking had strayed perilously close to mistreatment. He'd created distance between them, confessed point-blank he was a murderer and ordered her to leave. Yet here she remained, stubborn and steadfast, and if the truth be told, he felt an almost strangling sense of relief that she still occupied a place in his life.

For that alone, he owed her so much. . . .

That thought sent him out to the stables, where he ordered his horse saddled. The three of them—he, Nora and Jonny—came preciously close to being a family, yet might never be one. Not if the past continued to stifle any hope of a future together. All along, he'd believed himself to be cursed, and a curse to them. He could wallow in that belief and lose all hope of ever helping his nephew and making his wife happy, or he could fight—claw his way past curses and guilt and build new possibilities for them all.

Mounted on Constantine, he cantered past the paddocks and broke into a gallop that took him out onto Blackheath Moor.

"I'll find the truth," he called aloud. His voice rode the open landscape to echo against the granite outcroppings on the high ground. He hoped his ghosts

were listening, hoped they recognized his words as the
challenge they were, burning through him and spur-
ring him on. "Do you hear me? I won't rest until I
know exactly how and why you died, Tom, and what
part our cave played in your passing."

This would not be another breakneck ride like the
other day, for a plan formed in his mind. He'd start
by seeking out the tenant farmers and asking questions, plenty of them. Someone had to have seen
something. Perhaps Dan Ridley would be willing to
answer his questions in exchange for the fish Grayson
had helped him catch the other day.

Then he'd revisit other places where he and Tom
played as boys. Would he find more pirated wares
hidden at the abandoned tin mine south of Millford,
or among the foundations of the Iron Age settlement
a mile in from Gunwalloe, a few miles to the north?

With the Ridley farm in mind, he had just turned
his horse south when thundering hooves across the
fields behind him brought him up short. Constantine
brandished his head and swung about, as eager as
Grayson to see who bore down on them with such
determination.

The Thoroughbred's ears flattened as the galloping
stride of a sleek chestnut ate up the ground between
them. The figure in the saddle bent low over the
horse's mane, and a spirited shout pierced the breeze
as the horse streaked across the landscape.

"I don't believe it," Grayson murmured, straining
his eyes to see into the distance. But as a rare beam
of sunshine slid past a break in the clouds, gold hair
flashed nearly as bright as the surrounding gorse.
"Easy, there, Constantine." He gave his agitated horse
a reassuring pat. "This is the first positive sign I've
seen in weeks."

Yes, he felt a burst of hope. Or, if not hope precisely, at least a scrap of relief yielded from the sight

of the Earl of Wycliffe clearing the last of the heather-
and gorse-covered hillocks between them.

"How the devil did you find me here?" Grayson
asked once his friend had managed to calm his horse
to a standstill.

"Saw you from the ridge on the Helston Road. Fig-
ured it had to be you. Who else from these parts
would be wandering aimlessly across the moors on a
day when there's work to be done?" Chad's broad
grin reminded Grayson of days long ago when the
two of them had frequently raced madcap across the
countryside. "Does the carpenter's wife still keep
her inn?"

"Calling it an inn is a bit of an overstatement." The
woman in question kept a room in her cottage for
travelers and could be called upon to serve tea or ale
beneath the shade of a wide old elm in her garden.
"But, yes, she does."

"Race you there." With a lift of his brows and a
challenging wink, Chad flapped his reins and set his
horse to a gallop again.

Grayson followed in close pursuit, but even allowing
Constantine his rein, he remained a good horse length
or two behind his friend. No one could outrun Chad
Rutherford on horseback. The man was fearless, had
been since boyhood.

The ground blurred beneath their horses' hooves,
and as they approached the mill stream, Chad, coat-
tails flapping and hair fluttering wildly, showed no sign
of slowing. Grayson saw that, rather than head down-
stream to where the watercourse narrowed, Chad
meant to leap the banks at their widest.

The water roared in his ears, and Grayson had a
split second to choose whether to follow or play it
safe. With a brash shout, Chad stole the decision. Like
hawks on the kill, both horses shot forward in a
breath-stealing burst of speed, heads down, tails

streaming and legs stretching to the limit of their strides.

In midair Grayson's heart hit his throat. That Constantine possessed the power to make it over, he didn't doubt. But with all the recent rain, the bank might not hold. Fear shot like a bullet through him until, an instant later, both horses pounded onto the far bank.

Relief snarled with anger as they continued on, slowing to a canter and finally a walk as they reached the stone walls and hedgerows of the first farm. Still fuming over what he perceived as an unnecessary and foolhardy risk, Grayson clucked Constantine up beside Chad's mount. Words of censure sat hot on his tongue, ready to singe the other man's irrepressible confidence. . . .

Until Chad leaned across the space between them and punched his upper arm. "Remember the first time you made us do that?"

Grayson's mouth hung open as the memory rushed back. He'd forgotten all about it, but he *had* instigated that jump, a long time ago. He had been fourteen at the time and, as was typical on a summer's day, had spent the morning riding with both Chad and Tom. As usual, Chad had outridden and outjumped both brothers all morning, until finally Grayson had experienced a rare twinge of jealousy.

So he had pointed across the moor to the stream and issued the challenge, his voice wavering with the slightest of catches as he contemplated having to make the jump himself. But once uttered, there had been no taking it back.

*I've done it before and so has Tom. Isn't that right, Tom?*

*I . . . er . . .*

*I'm for it, then!*

And, just as today, Chad had spurred his horse forward. All three of them had made it over, though the harum-scarum leap had left Tom visibly shaken for hours afterward, and Grayson secretly weak with relief.

"I'd thought certainly we'd all break our necks," Chad said now with relish, as if pleased by the prospect. "A wonder none of us did, especially as it was a first for all of us."

Grayson nodded, his lip curled in a guilty half grin. "Indeed it was, despite my claims to the contrary. But if you knew, why were you so eager to accept my challenge?"

"Why the devil not?" Chad shrugged and laughed as the sun once more pierced the clouds and flashed on his disheveled hair, thick and fair and thoroughly admired by every lady of their acquaintance.

Grayson couldn't help laughing along with him. They and their horses had survived the jump unscathed, and after so many days of rain and gloom and guilt, he snatched at this chance, however brief, to feel . . . normal, free . . . young again.

Well, if anyone could command both the weather and the moods of those around him, it would be Chad Rutherford, a man who glided effortlessly through life with his golden looks and a devil-may-care attitude.

A quarter hour later they were seated at Mrs. Caldwell's linen-covered table beneath the elm, sipping her home-brewed ale and munching on home-baked almond cakes.

"Damned decent ale," Chad commented after a long pull. He wiped a sleeve across his mouth. "One of the few things I actually miss in London society." He set the tankard down and leaned forward over the table, his gaze so intent it made Grayson want to shrink back into his chair, especially when Chad burst out with, "Good God, man, you look like hell."

"Nearly killing both myself and my horse will do that to me. Speaking of which, what did you mean when you said you saw me from the Helston Road? Where is your coach? Surely you didn't ride all the way from London."

"Of course I did. Coaches are for ladies and luggage, and people with nothing better to do than spend an eternity being jostled by the pitiful state of our country roads."

"Got someone's husband after you again, don't you?"

"My good man, I'll have you know I've been as chaste as a monk."

Grayson sniggered, earning him a wry look from Chad.

"The fact is, London turned drab as dirt after you and your wife made your hasty departure. Not that I've any intention of becoming a nuisance to you." He gave a sniff. "Newlyweds need their privacy, after all."

"You're coming back to the house with me and you'll stay as long as you like," Grayson replied perhaps too quickly, a bit too desperately. Did he really think his friend could defuse matters? Or find answers Grayson hadn't already considered and discarded? "Nora will insist," he added in an attempt to appear cordial, rather than distraught.

Chad regarded him pensively from over the rim of his tankard. "If you're quite certain. But just a quick stopover on my way to Grandview. As Belinda keeps reminding me, I've neglected my Cornwall estate long enough. She and Albert send their regards, by the way."

Grayson acknowledged the sentiment with a nod. "Thinking of settling in at Grandview indefinitely?"

"Good God, no." Chad gave a little shudder. "You know I find Cornwall infinitely dreary. No theaters, no parties to speak of, no gossip. A veritable wasteland."

"You liked it well enough as a boy."

"Yes, and we made our own adventures then, didn't we, Captain Morgan?"

After yesterday's discovery, Grayson could find no enjoyment in the memory of their long-ago amusements. He took a swallow of ale and glanced at his booted feet, crossed one over the other and stretched out at an angle to the table.

"Now, then . . . when are you going to confess?" Chad asked after a pause.

Grayson's ale sloshed, almost spilling onto his trousers. The mug clattered against the table as he set it down. "What do you mean?"

Chad studied him while he chewed and swallowed a bite of almond cake. "See here, old man. Neither shaking hands nor those thunderheads riding beneath your eyes speak much in the way of marital bliss. Either tell me what has gone amiss or I shall be forced to ask your wife."

Grayson conceded with a sigh. "Don't do that. This has nothing to do with Nora." He pressed the heels of his hands to his eyes. "And everything to do with her. Christ, Chad, I've made a riot of the poor woman's life. And I believe I'll burn for it."

"Egad. You love her."

"No."

"Yes, you do," the cad returned in a singsong of a murmur. "What I can't figure out is why on earth it's turning you so cadaverous. I can understand the lack of sleep. But love doesn't typically make a man look as if he's just climbed out of his own grave."

"Not my grave. Tom's."

"What the devil are you saying?"

"I'm saying I'm damned glad you're here. Because I've stumbled upon something, and I'm counting on you to help me make sense of it. Care to take a ride down the beach?"

Grayson felt infinitely grateful when, rather than asking questions, his friend set aside his ale and cake, poured a handful of coins onto the table and came to his feet. "Let's go."

*          *          *

*You're free to use the library if you wish, but it happens to be a room I abhor.*

Those were Gray's words the day they arrived at Blackheath Grange. Nora repeated them under her breath as she closed the library's double doors and tiptoed to the center of the room. There she came to a stop, hands at her sides, afraid to breathe lest she break the silence. Despite Gray's permission to be here, she felt like a thief and a sneak.

Earlier, after breakfast, she had spent the morning in the schoolroom with Jonny, appalled to discover his studies had been abandoned these many months. No more. Together they had read about the Roman emperor Augustus, pored over a map of London before the Great Fire, and added and subtracted columns of figures. The boy might not speak, but his mind was quick and his interests varied, if only someone bothered to encourage him.

Afterward she ushered him into her studio, delighted to see his eyes widen at the sight of his new, virtually endless canvas. After assuring him it was perfectly permissible to fill the linen sheet as he wished, she had provided charcoal and a palette of paints and left him in Kat's care.

Now, then . . . why does Grayson abhor the library? What happened here in this room? What secrets did these walls and bookcases harbor? Whether it had been a dream or a real episode, her lavender lady had told her she must search. . . .

*You must find the truth that will free you all. You must see it with your own eyes, know it, believe it with your mind and heart and soul.*

Yes, somewhere within Blackheath Grange answers waited to be found. Before his death, Thomas Lowell had plunged his estate into profound debt and decline. And though Grayson held himself responsible for all of it, Nora didn't believe him capable of deliberate malice any more than she believed Jonny to be of blame. Something had to have been overlooked, some vital clue as to what had happened to Thomas in his last days.

With a finger tapping at her bottom lip, she shrugged off her qualms and walked to the nearest bank of shelves.

Grayson watched his friend exit the cave and stride to the water's edge. Shoulders knotted, head down, Chad stared out at the waves as he took his time absorbing everything he'd just been shown.

After a few minutes Grayson joined him where the waves lapped the shore. "Your boots are going to soak through."

"I can't believe this of Tom." Chad's mouth was tight, his eyes bleak. "I knew he'd run into difficulties, but . . ."

"His debts ran deeper than anyone could have guessed. Even months after his . . . his death, bills arrived from creditors I'd never heard of." He drew a breath laden with the bitterness of ocean brine. "You're certain he never even hinted to you—"

"Of course he didn't." Chad's usually affable features blackened with ire. "What do you take me for? Don't you think I'd have said something?"

Grayson placed a hand on his friend's shoulder. "I'm sorry. Of course you would have. I only thought . . . well, you and Tom had a bond I didn't share. You were both peers, both masters of vast estates. I'd hoped he might have confided in you."

"Would that he had, old man." Bending, Chad scooped up a stone and with a flick of his wrist sent it skipping erratically across the waves. "You know, there were times I thought it should have been you." A corner of his mouth pulled. "As earl, I mean. Tom was a good man, but not . . ."

"Not quite up to it. I know. He knew it too." Grayson pushed out a mirthless laugh. "God, how could he not have known it? Our father made a point of implying it often enough."

"Yes, I remember. I suppose the old gentleman thought he might shame Tom into being smarter, stronger."

"More like me?"

*Your brother can hit the target, Thomas. Why can't you? Be a man like Grayson, Thomas, and get back on that horse this instant.*

The memories, wrapped in his father's booming baritone and a haze of costly tobacco smoke, made Grayson queasy. How different everything might have been if Alexander Lowell had nurtured both sons rather than constantly demeaning one of them.

Or if Grayson had possessed the wisdom to understand his brother's silent pleas for help.

Back at the house, after leaving their horses with the groom's assistant, Chad ground to a sudden halt where a stand of birch trees shaded the tiered gardens. "Tom wasn't involved. That's the answer, plain and simple."

"I wish I could believe that," Grayson replied, "but goods are stashed on *his* beach. After Charlotte died he rarely left Blackheath Grange. How could he not have known?" He glared up at the house, at the windows reflecting the heavy clouds rolling in now off the sea. He wished to God he could believe Chad's theory. Not that it would change much. In fact it would change nothing. He would be no less culpable in Tom's death. But at least Tom's name would be cleared of wrongdoing.

Chad wasn't ready to concede his point. "Someone found and used that cave without Tom's knowledge. It's possible, Gray. You know it is."

"Not in this case. My brother wasn't one to spend his days in his drawing room. He was always abroad on the estate. He might not have managed the finances well, but he constantly had his finger on the pulse of Blackheath's activity." He shook his head, feeling as bleak as the storm gathering overhead. "He would have known."

He set off walking again, but his friend remained rooted to the spot. Grayson stopped and questioned him with a look.

"Suppose for one moment I'm right," Chad urged. "Suppose smugglers gained access to the beach and loaded that cave, thinking they were damned clever about it. And then suppose Tom stumbled upon them because, as you say, he was always abroad." He fell silent, the summation of his conjectures evident in his grim expression.

Grayson's breath tangled with his heartbeat. "You're suggesting that Tom's death was neither accidental nor suicide."

Chad nodded. "And if so, my friend, you, Nora and Jonny are no longer safe here."

*Chapter 18*

Nora had spent the better part of an hour poring through the library, pulling books from the shelves and fanning through them, opening drawers and littering the desk and the floor with their contents. She even got down on her hands and knees to inspect those contents.

Only now, when her growling stomach signaled the nearing of teatime, did she admit the futility of her endeavors. She had found nothing of importance. But for a few odds and ends, every drawer echoed of abandonment, and the pages of the books she had searched lay flat and unruffled by hidden notes. She had opened the beautifully painted bow-front music cabinet, the doors and drawers of the tall secretaire, the glass-front cupboards beneath the east windows. Apparently the room had already been scoured clean of memories.

Her efforts brought her no closer than before to understanding how Thomas Lowell had died. All that remained was the conviction rooted deep in her heart that Grayson could not have been responsible, neither actually nor metaphorically.

She perched on the mahogany desktop—as devoid of personal effects as the rest of the room—and drew her feet up under the hem of her skirts. Wrapping her arms around her knees, she battled a sinking feeling as she wondered what to do next. Raindrops splat-

tered the diamond-paned windows and her spirits
plummeted further, for even the morning's sun had
deserted her.

With no warning the library doors burst open. Startled, she found herself confronted by Grayson's perplexed expression, and her eyes widened around the
unsettling sensation of having been caught stealing—
again. The last time had been in his bedroom, and the
memory raised a chill of foreboding.

He took in the room while she studied the ever-
increasing fatigue dragging at his features. With each
shadowy bruise, each deepening worry line, her heart
broke a little more.

"Mrs. Dorn said I'd find you here," he said. His
tone held nothing of anger, nothing that heralded another frightening episode. Yet chills persisted in
sweeping her back, perhaps because his controlled
greeting seemed so artificial, so fragile and distant.

How she wished he would come to her, take her in
his arms and kiss her as only he could—until the
breath and strength drained from her body, leaving
hot, melting pleasure—rather than stand there in the
doorway, regarding her with the cold indifference of
a stranger.

Then his words sunk in and produced a frisson of
annoyance. "How in the world did Mrs. Dorn know . . .
oh, never mind. Yes, I've been exploring the texts."

"More than just the texts, I'd say." Was he accusing
her, or simply making an observation?

"Yes." She groped for excuses, but there were
none. . . . None but the truth. She raised her chin.
"I'd hoped to learn something more about . . . what
happened here last summer. Some clue that might be
of help to both you and Jonny. I hope you aren't
angry with me."

He stuffed his hands into his trouser pockets. "You
may do as you like, anywhere in this house you like."

She wanted to scream. She wanted to slap him,

shake him out of his complaisance. His former ranting suddenly seemed preferable to this . . . this nothingness. This lack of emotion and regard. It wrung her heart dry and tugged her temper at the same time, and before she knew what she was about she'd slid from the desk and strode to him.

Grabbing his lapels, she pulled him close and stood on tiptoe, face-to-face. "Don't you wish to know if I've found anything? Don't you care? Or have we reverted back to those dismal days before our wedding, when we were two strangers forced together by happenstance? Are we no better off now? Have we not progressed beyond mutual disregard?"

"Do not ask me such things, Nora." A vein lashed in his temple. Did it reveal an aversion to her touch, her nearness? Is that why she couldn't help him— because he didn't feel the way she did about their marriage?

"I won't be silent and I won't be frightened off," she snapped. More bitter words, desperate words, waited to be spoken but she bit them down, feeling a traitorous sob rise in her throat. Here, this close to him, she breathed his scent, felt his warmth, gripped the solidness of him beneath his clothing . . . and wanted him. Oh, Lord, she wanted him—against her, around her, *in* her. That and nothing else. No more grief or guilt or fatal secrets. Just the love she could not dismiss, the desire she could not refute no matter his sins, past or present.

"Nora, do not do this. I'll only hurt you." He was stiff and unmoving in her grasp, unblinking as he stared back at her, his features frozen in a grimace of dismay. It opened wounds inside her, that look, left her sore and bleeding.

"Hurt me, then," she urged in a whisper. "Let me feel what you're feeling. All of it. I'm not afraid"

"No." His chest convulsed once and went still.

She blinked away stinging tears and shook him.

When he merely stood there, rocklike, her resolve and her strength deserted her. She fell against him, fingers curled in his coat sleeves. "Is there nothing left between us? Was there ever anything but my own delusions?"

His hand shot out, groping for purchase on the open door. He caught the edge and wrenched out of her grip. "Not your delusions, Nora. My dream. God, such a beautiful dream. But I'm awake now and it's gone. Over. I cannot find my way back to it."

Her arms fell to her sides. He pulled farther away, hitting his back against the door, flattening both palms against it. A powerful emotion—fury, terror, love; she couldn't tell which—blazed in his eyes. It frightened her even as it filled her with relief. He wasn't empty and devoid of feelings. Wasn't indifferent to her after all.

Hope remained, as tenuous and indistinct as the ghosts haunting them, but real all the same.

"I'm sorry." She didn't know what else to say.

"No." His voice plunged to a husky note, a rumble from the earth itself. His hand rose, trembling, and found its way beneath her chin. The warmth of his fingers flooded her; the remorse in his eyes filled her. "I'm sorry, Nora. This isn't your fault. It's entirely mine. And mine to work out. Until I do . . ."

"Until you do, I will be here." With both hands she wiped the tears from her cheeks. "I am Zachariah Thorngoode's daughter. I neither frighten nor discourage easily."

She meant those words, found strength in them, but because of the way he continued gazing down at her, with shimmering eyes and a lost, mournful expression, she turned away before her tears might fall again. With no clear idea of where she was going, she hurried down the corridor of the east wing and to the main hall, where a sight in the drawing room stopped her in her tracks.

Grayson's footsteps echoed as he followed her into the hall. "I had a reason for coming to find you in the library." He gestured into the drawing room. "We have a visitor."

Indeed, seated in a wing chair beside the hearth, the Earl of Wycliffe came to his feet and bowed. "Good afternoon, Nora. I do hope you don't mind an uninvited guest."

A multitude of sensations swept through her. As Grayson's closest friend, perhaps the earl might succeed where she continued to fail miserably. He had certainly proved his goodwill toward this marriage that night at his London town house, when he'd welcomed her as a sister in spirit.

Then why did she once more experience a sense of unease, a vague prickling beneath her skin? Even his smile, wide and charming though it was, hinted at some unidentifiable quality at odds with his polished exterior. . . .

Or was there nothing more here to be found but a good-natured aristocrat, looking thoroughly amused as he waited for her to properly greet him?

"My lord, do forgive my manners." She blinked and walked to him with a hand extended. "This is such a surprise. You are always welcome, of course. How long can we persuade you to stay with us?"

"Perhaps just long enough to persuade you to stop calling me *my lord*." He met her partway, raising her offered hand to his lips. "I insist you call me Chad, for I fully intend to call you Nora. I'm afraid you'll find me an exceedingly brazen fellow, especially here in the wilds of Cornwall."

She found a smile for him. "Chad it is, then." An impulse, born of realizing she would no longer be alone in her efforts to help Grayson, prompted her to add in a heartfelt whisper, "I'm so very glad you're here."

He responded with a look of concern, even mild alarm. Her admission had disclosed more than she'd intended. Quickly she turned away, moving to the tasseled bellpull hanging in the corner.

Over tea, the news from London provided precisely five minutes of conversation. Then a rather ponderous silence weighted the drawing room, punctuated by the pointed looks Chad continually shot Grayson from beneath his brows.

Nora refilled her teacup and set the pot on the refreshment cart. "There is something afoot. I sense it from both of you, and I think one of you had better tell me what it is."

Grayson scowled at his friend, then met her gaze with what she could only term reluctance. "There is nothing—"

"Oh, come, Gray." Chad made an impatient gesture and rolled his eyes. "She's an astute one, this wife of yours. She has every right to know about your discovery and what it might mean."

She looked from one to the other. Grayson's eyebrows knotted above his nose. "Now is not the time."

"Not the time to warn your wife that there might be danger at Blackheath Grange?"

Nora set her tea aside and surged to her feet. "I'd like an explanation. This instant."

"Gray has found evidence," Chad explained, "of pirates using the caves along the beach to store their plunder."

"Good heavens. Is this true, Gray?"

"Smugglers." He pressed his fingertips to his brow, then pinched the bridge of his nose. "The term *pirate* is a bit overdramatic. And I hadn't mentioned it because I only just made the discovery myself. At this point, I don't know who has been using the beach or why." He shot a brief glare at Chad. "I saw no reason to frighten you."

The irony of that last statement made her wince. Nor was it lost on Grayson, judging by the suddenly ruddy cast to his skin.

She sank into her chair. "What sort of evidence did you find?"

"A cave filled with what could only be stolen goods. Crates, barrels, casks—a small fortune, by the looks of it."

"The other day you said you'd found evidence that your brother may have taken his own life." She frowned at the memory of his ravings. "That he'd got into trouble he couldn't get out of. This is what you meant."

He nodded. "My first thought was that Tom tried to recoup his finances through criminal means."

"That I do not believe, not a bit of it." The earl shook his head. "Not Tom. Far more likely he stumbled upon their lair and they . . . well, they eliminated the threat he posed to their operations. This is the root of the danger I spoke of, Nora. If you ask me, you should all leave as soon as possible. No telling when the brigands might return."

"Nonsense. We can't simply leave and allow them run of the place—"

"I'm afraid Chad may be right," Grayson interrupted. "When I found that cave I jumped to a conclusion. Now I realize my brother's death may have greater implications than I ever imagined. I'd never forgive myself if . . ."

He trailed off and again Nora wanted to grip him and shake him—shake loose all the truths he seemed to fear so desperately. That he cared for her, for one; that he cared deeply about so many things in this life. And that he was no killer, neither directly nor indirectly.

It would not have done any good. For now he insisted on shouldering the blame. . . . And Nora realized with a jolt that it must be as her lavender lady had told her. They must discover the truth and see it with their own eyes, their own hearts, in order to believe it.

Could Grayson ever be made to see the truth and believe in it? Dare she hope this discovery of his might be the first step?

"I'll leave with Jonny on one condition," she said evenly. "That you accompany us."

"Don't be stubborn, Nora." His voice rose, tinged with anger, and with the ever-present fear that now seemed so obvious to her, so pervasive. "I want you and Jonny safe, but I must stay and see this through. I owe that much to Tom."

She shrugged. "Then I am going nowhere."

"Don't be foolish," Chad blurted. "Gray, you're her husband. Persuade her."

It wouldn't be the first time Grayson had ordered her gone. Nor the first time she'd refused. But today, the urgency seemed far more on the part of the Earl of Wycliffe. Perhaps, in his heart of hearts, Grayson desired her to stay here with him, and be the wife she so wished to be.

With a decisive heft of her chin, she spoke before he could. "This is our home and I'm not about to let anyone run us off. I daresay it is highly doubtful any pirates will go to all the trouble of sneaking up to the house to murder us in our beds, but to ensure our safety we can hire local men to keep watch. I'm quite certain a coastal village the likes of this one will yield any number of young ruffians eager to wrangle with anyone threatening their own. If not, a letter to my father would certainly—"

Grayson held up a hand. "I've already instructed Gibbs to post a guard over the beach. I'll extend that to include the grounds around the house."

"You could be making a terrible mistake," Chad said.

"But it is my mistake to make." Nora lifted her

teacup and pretended to ignore their resigned expressions.

Soon afterward Chad excused himself to seek an hour's rest in the bedchamber always reserved for his visits. As his footsteps receded, Nora met Grayson's gaze. "You aren't at all convinced about these pirates, are you? Or you wouldn't have given in to me so easily."

"Smugglers, and what difference does it make what I believe?" He made a crooked attempt at a grin, not much more than a twist of his lips, but the sight produced a tiny thrill inside her just the same. "As you so recently pointed out, you are Zachariah Thorngoode's daughter, and you follow orders about as easily as you frighten or become discouraged."

"Would you prefer a biddable wife?" she could not help asking.

He hesitated, jaw going rigid and lips tightening around unspoken thoughts. "No."

"A different wife?" Why she felt the need to test him, almost taunt him, she didn't know. Perhaps to push him to his limit, from where he must either flee from her or turn and embrace her.

He did neither, but sat brooding.

Frustration propelled her out of her chair, sent her to stare out the rain-streaked windows facing the front park, silvered by a layer of mist. Feeling Gray's scrutiny on her back, his melancholy filling the room, she bent to rearrange a vase of flowers on a table beneath the window. Almost angrily she tugged the stems free and speared them back into the crystal vase, finding the delicate petals all too reminiscent of fingertips on flesh. . . . Of Grayson's fingers on her.

She slid a rose from the vase. Its sweet fragrance danced beneath her nose while the petals, glistening with dew, sent droplets trickling down her forearm. Lightly she brushed the rich red blossom across her lips, conjuring Grayson's kisses until she ached for them.

"No." The whisper grazed her nape and startled her. The heat of Grayson's length followed as his torso cradled her back and his hips nestled against her bottom. The feel of him set her body on fire. His lips moved against her hair; his voice smoldered in her ear. "If you must press for the truth of it, no, I do not wish another wife. I wish you another husband."

She longed to turn, to wrap her arms around him, but his unyielding stance held her pressed to the table's edge and would not allow it. Her gaze searched the clouds outside while her other senses reeled with desire. "And if I wish no other husband but you?"

"Then perhaps you are foolishly brave." She felt a gentling of his posture, an easing of the muscles pressing into her. An arm came up around her waist, his large hand splayed against her belly. "Or merely foolish."

"Grayson . . ."

A knock at the open door stilled the words on her tongue, words that eluded her, in any case. Beyond breathing heat into his name with the passion building inside her, she hadn't the slightest notion what she might have uttered next. Grayson stepped away, and she turned to see Kat entering the room.

"Sir. Ma'am." She curtsied twice. "Beg pardon for interrupting. There's a small matter in the art studio that requires my lady's attention."

"Is it Jonny? Is he all right?" Nora was already halfway to the door, her own concerns fading beneath burgeoning alarm.

"No, ma'am. Nothing to worry about. Lord Clarington is still at his books in the schoolroom. It's about his new canvas. He's painted something rather curious."

"I see." She stopped and turned back to Grayson.

"Go," he said. "He needs you."

*As do you,* she thought as she followed Kat up the stairs.

Grayson stood alone in the conservatory, ears pricked, senses alert, the hair on his nape bristling. Nora and Jonny were outside on the garden terrace, and Chad would be joining them shortly. In twenty minutes, Mrs. Dorn would serve an informal supper here at the wrought-iron garden table, a treat for Jonny on the special occasion of Chad's arrival.

Minutes earlier, he had tried asking Nora about what she had discovered upon entering her studio with Kat, but Jonny had been close by, and in a hushed tone she had promised to enlighten him later. Then she and the boy had taken one of the baskets used to collect clippings, and gone out to the terrace.

Now an odd sound had him staring down the dusky aisles between the potted plants and trees. Though the rain had stopped, steely clouds darkened the skies to an early twilight. Intermittent winds raised the creaking complaint of the oak trees beyond the terrace, and sent leaves and twigs tumbling through the air to stick to the conservatory's glass walls.

Inside all was quiet and still, or should have been. Grayson's nerves hummed with tension. Without moving he shifted his gaze once more to the terrace door.

It was shut tight, but as they had done moments ago, the potted dwarf maple trees beyond the bourbon roses stirred. Rustled. A hissing sifted through their leaves.

Grayson's heart thumped, sending the blood to rush in his ears and pound at his temples. He took a step, then another. Stopped to listen . . .

*"Gray."*

His lungs emptied; a murky haze swam before his eyes. Blinking, he gasped for breath and forced his feet to move. He held out his hands, feeling his way past the hothouse foliage. "Where are you? Show yourself, damn it."

*"Here, Gray. Here."*

The words filtered into his brain through the roaring in his ears, yet were they words, truly, or merely wisps of the breeze forcing its way past gaps in the casements?

He stood beside the roses now, straining his eyes. Not a breath stirred through the dwarf maples, yet as he stood waiting, a sharp, citrus scent drifted around him, so strong it could not have come from the potted orange and lemon trees on the opposite side of the conservatory.

"Charlotte? It's you, isn't it? I know you blame me for Tom. I blame myself. I'm so damned sorry. I never meant—"

*"Jonathan."*

Grayson's heart went still. "What about Jonathan?"

*"Must save him."*

"I'm trying. I swear to you, everything I'm doing now is for him."

*"No. Save him . . . danger . . ."* The whisper thinned, dissipated, but even as it did, the note of urgency, of bleak desperation, shimmied through the air to buffet him with physical force.

He bolted forward, standing now in the midst of the shoulder-high maple trees. "What danger? Me? Is that what you're afraid of? That I'm a danger to your son? Charlotte, wait. Please. Don't leave yet."

The citrus scent—the fragrance she had always worn in life—dulled to a vague tang. Then it too dispersed on the air. Grayson gripped the nearest branch, fisting his hand painfully around the bark as if to hold his sister-in-law's spirit a moment longer. "I swear to you on my life that I'd never hurt Jonny."

"Gray?"

He jolted at the sound of his name, spoken in a

masculine voice and filled with puzzlement. Pivoting, he beheld his friend's figure silhouetted in the conservatory's wide archway. Quickly he put space between himself and the maple trees.

"Were you talking to someone?" Chad directed a glance around the conservatory. His booted footsteps raised an echo from the flagstone floor as Grayson's heartbeat pounded down to its natural rhythm.

"I was . . . calling to Nora and Jonny. They're outside." He wondered how long the other man had been standing there, how much he'd heard. And whether his attempt to act naturally could fool his old friend. He forced a chuckle. "I don't suppose they heard me through the glass."

"You sounded upset." Chad reached him and stopped. His brow creased as he studied Grayson's features. "You look upset as well."

"It's nothing." Grayson put a hand on Chad's shoulder, then dropped it to his side when he realized his fingers were trembling. "Come, let's sit." He led the way to the garden table. "I merely thought it time they came in. It's growing chilly, and . . . with this wind, falling limbs could be a danger."

As he took a seat opposite Grayson, Chad nodded, though doubt hovered in his expression. "What the devil are they doing outside in this weather?"

Grayson shrugged. "Something about finding flowers worthy of being painted."

"Humph. I always say if one can't be racing headlong across the countryside, one might as well be indoors."

"Yes, I'm quite familiar with how you enjoy risking life and limb . . . and those of your friends and those of your horse. . . ."

He'd meant to make a joke of it, but his earlier irritation with Chad returned. This time, however, it wasn't about horses or taking foolish risks. Charlotte's fears for her son—good God, enough to raise her spirit from the grave—drove home his need to find answers. He should have spent all of today searching for those answers, but Chad's surprise arrival had distracted him from his task. Even now, he couldn't decide if his friend would prove a help or a hindrance.

In the days following Tom's death, Chad had been here, helping sift through Tom's effects and the estate records, poring over the unpaid bills and guiding Grayson in all the necessary financial decisions. Grayson's state of mind at the time had been less than dependable, but he should have been more involved in untangling the mess the estate had become—and uncovering the truth of Tom's death. Without meaning to, Chad may well have shielded Grayson from pertinent details, ones that might have determined a far different future for him.

And for Jonny and Nora.

"You were itching to jump that stream and you know it." Chad's flippant words roused him from his musings and scraped his anger raw.

"I itched to do many things today," he snapped, "but that most assuredly wasn't on top of my list." He shoved back his chair, the metal legs screeching on the stone floor. Once on his feet he turned his back on his friend. What he suddenly itched for now was to grasp the nearest potted palm and hurl it over sideways.

He heard a sharp intake of breath behind him, then the sounds of Chad gaining his feet. A heavy pause ensued, fraught with tension. Chad cleared his throat and said quietly, "You are upset, and perhaps I know the reason why. I believe I am intruding here. I'm sorry. I shall make my excuses to Nora after supper and be on my way. Sooner, if you wish."

Grayson released a breath, and with it his burst of temper. He raked his fingers through his hair and turned to face his oldest and closest friend. "No, I'm sorry. I don't know what came over me just then. Don't leave."

Chad stood studying him, his expression etched with concern. The terrace door opened. A gusty breeze whooshed through the oak saplings and dwarf maples, wispy palms and budding citrus trees. Grayson's back went rigid, his skin cold, but the only presence to seize the room was Jonny's. The boy bounded in and without the least hesitation hurled himself into Chad's open arms.

"Egad, it's good to see you, boy. Good heavens, you've grown nearly as tall as I am and twice as handsome." He held the child at arm's length and continued with forced jollity and an overly bright smile. "With you about, Jonny, a crusty old bachelor like me won't stand a chance with the ladies."

Nora entered from the terrace at a more sedate pace, a basket hooked over her arm. She stopped to force the door closed against the protesting winds. Seeing that her slender figure was no match, Grayson joined her in leaning his weight against the door, closing it with a thud and a click of the latch. The delicate trees inside stopped swaying, and an unnatural calm gripped the conservatory.

Desire, stark and startling, shivered through him. With strands of hair whipped free around softly flushed cheeks and her lamb's wool shawl blown half off her shoulders, she looked wind tossed and rumpled, as sensual as the flowers in her basket. The scents of rain and blossoms clung to her, emanating from the warmth of her skin. He found he could not step away from her, indeed, could barely remember the many reasons why he should.

If he could only believe he hadn't sent Tom from that cliff, he might be free to love her. God knew, the temptation to do so sometimes proved more than he could withstand. Earlier, in the drawing room, how easily he might have taken her in his arms. Had she sensed his yearnings? Had she heard it in his voice, felt the lust stalking through his body as he'd leaned over her? Had she detected the tremors of restraint shaking his frame? No, of course not. He'd merely frightened her—again.

Seemingly far away, he heard Chad talking to Jonny, but as if transfixed by a spell cast by the blustering weather beyond the glass, neither he nor Nora moved. He met a gaze brimming with questions and regret, and with longing too. Did she see the same in him?

Only when Jonny trotted over and relieved Nora of her basket did the spell release its grip. With an awkward nod she moved away, and he followed her to the others, thinking how normal this all might seem to the casual observer, the four of them safe and dry and sharing a few simple moments before supper. A little family, happily at home together.

It was a dream so painfully sweet, he might almost have accepted a devil's bargain to make it true.

When they reached the table, Jonny turned to her, an improvised spray of primrose and pansy clutched in his hand. His eyes large and solemn, he held it out to her.

"For me?"

He answered with a nod and a thrust of the little bouquet, a gesture so simple and sincere it made Grayson's throat constrict.

"Oh, you dearest boy. Thank you." She gathered the flowers and held them to her face. "These are my very favorites. How did you know?"

That earned her a fragile smile. She put her arms around the boy and squeezed, holding on until he began to squirm.

Gray tousled Jonny's hair, wishing he could bring smiles to Nora's face as easily, and almost envying Jonny's secure place in her heart. But like him, Jonny was trapped within a past so tragic, so desolate, he needed more than love to free him. He needed the truth. He needed the strength to forgive his elders.

He needed a miracle.

# Chapter 19

"I have something to show you," Nora told Grayson immediately following supper, once Chad had engaged Jonny at the parlor chessboard.

Her expression discouraged questions until they reached the relative privacy of the stairs. Until then, he felt content to merely walk with her, close at her side, where he could easily imagine slipping an arm about her slender waist, a gesture so carefree that, again, he might nearly have traded his soul to make it real.

She took him to her studio, explaining along the way about how she and her maid had devised a spacious canvas for Jonny, intended to encourage him to express anything and everything on his mind.

"A brilliant idea," he said as she opened the studio door. "I wish I'd thought of it long ago, when he first stopped speaking."

"Why would you have? Drawing and painting are second nature to me. They are what make me a rather quirky character, in Mama's opinion."

"She is correct, if by quirky she means beautiful, brilliant and entirely original."

The light of a nearby wall sconce caressed her glowing cheeks. Her lashes fluttered downward to shield her thoughts. She sidestepped away, took the candle from its holder and brushed by him into the studio.

He felt like an ass. He hadn't meant to flirt, not by

any means. No, theirs was not a relationship amenable to such trifles as flirting. It never had been, not weeks ago when circumstances had first forced them together, and certainly not now, with their present lives shaped by such misfortune.

As he watched her use the candle to light two lamps inside, it saddened him that he'd never had the chance to flirt with her, or court her as a beautiful young woman deserved to be courted.

"Come in," she called to him with a note of mild impatience. A bed linen lay spread at her feet, and as he moved to her side, he saw the bright designs that covered the first yard or so of fabric.

"Look at how many of these yellow circles he's drawn," she said with a sweep of her hand. "Have you any idea what they could mean?"

Grayson crouched and traced a finger around one of the dozen or so disks painted among Jonny's other illustrations. "Suns, perhaps?"

"Yes, that occurred to me too." She knelt beside him, so close he imagined he could feel the heat of her shoulder against his own. "But see how he's drawn half circles within each one. Instinct tells me there's something important about that, a deeper meaning than a mere copying of everyday sights."

"An artist's instinct?"

"I suppose you might call it that. . . ." Her chin angled over her shoulder, her gaze traveling to her shrouded easel, where his portrait lay hidden. The memory sent a shiver across his shoulders. Her gaze darted back to him. "I'm afraid I'm not terribly confident in my instincts lately, so perhaps I'm mistaken about Jonny's designs."

"I am. Confident in you, that is." His hand closed around hers. It felt so small and warm against his palm, so delicate. Some possessive instinct stirred to life inside him. But if he had learned anything about her in recent days, it was that she was by no means delicate, no flower to be preserved and protected. He pressed her hand to his lips, turned it over, nuzzled her palm. Need mounted inside him, painful, making breathing difficult.

He held her open palm against his cheek. "While I've been fighting my demons, you've been making a difference in Jonny's life. And mine. I think if it weren't for you, I might have . . ."

She drew her face close to his. "Might have what?"

"Given up. Given in." His head sank between his shoulders. "I don't know."

Her free hand cupped his jaw and gently but firmly forced him to look at her. "Do you still want me gone?"

For an instant her features blurred behind a blinding wave of panic. Want her gone? Good God, no. Her light touch, now a soft caress across his face, had the ability to anchor him to this world, to life. He'd be entirely adrift without her.

But what of her? Surely her world had been more tranquil, more rewarding, with her paints and brushes and artist society, than her life here at Blackheath Grange, than anything he could offer her.

She must have sensed his inner battle, for she came swiftly to her feet, hands on hips, eyes glittering down at him. "Never mind what you *think* I should do," she said severely. "You must decide what you want me to do. No more lying to me or to yourself."

"Nora, wait."

She was already at the door. Without turning she said, "I'm going to see Jonny off to bed. Should you decide you have anything to say to me . . . you may seek me out afterward."

Would he? His body clenched around an aching desire to be with her, hold her, love her. Could he trust himself not to hurt her? Frighten her? Could he restrain his demons long enough, at least, for one night's bliss in her arms?

Or would he instead prowl the house, sleepless for hours, and then finally rouse his groom to have his horse saddled? Could another reckless ride across the darkened, storm-drenched moors banish this particular demon—the one that refused to see the sense in letting Nora go?

Only by severing his ties to her could he ensure her future happiness, a future free of his past and of the ghosts that haunted him because of it. The part that loved her knew that to be true. Grimly he looked down at Jonny's yellow circles and acknowledged that the worst part of him, the hardened, selfish part that had caused so much sorrow—Tom's downfall and death, Jonny's silenced spirit—still couldn't manage to see past its own needs.

And, dear God, he needed Nora. So the question was, Did he need her more than he loved her?

Nora tucked Jonny in, bid him good night and returned downstairs. If Grayson decided he wanted to see her, the logical place for him to find her was in her bedchamber. But she had no intention of making matters easy, nor of waiting like a docile wife to attract her husband's notice. No, if he wanted her, if he had anything worthwhile to say to her, he would have to come find her—in the very room he claimed to abhor.

No more shrinking from things that couldn't be changed. If their marriage was to have a ghost of a chance at succeeding, they must each be willing to brave anything and everything—together.

But as she opened the library door, she discovered the room already occupied.

Standing at a bookcase in a circle of lamplight, the Earl of Wycliffe whirled when the door creaked, his expression registering surprise. An open book sat cradled in one hand, its pages gently fanning. Several books spanned the desktop. Three or four lay at his feet.

"Nora!" Flashing his easy grin, he pressed his free hand to his heart. "You startled me. I'd thought you'd retired. Don't tell me you're another night owl like that husband of yours."

"No. In fact . . ." She moved into the room. "Sometimes I wonder if Gray sleeps at all."

"He seems excessively troubled. More so than last I saw him."

She nodded. "It's this house. . . ." She trailed off. How could she explain about the ghosts that had been haunting both her and Grayson? Chad would think she'd taken leave of her senses.

He shoved the book he held back onto the shelf, went to her and took her hand in his. "You're correct about this house. It's full of sorrow, Nora, and is certainly no place for newlyweds. Add to that the possible danger Gray discovered, and it's obvious the two of you should take Jonny and return to London. Or, if you like, you may consider my Grandview at your disposal."

Nora was already shaking her head. "I do thank you, more than you can know. But we must remain here. I cannot fully explain the reasons, but it is of vital importance, to both Grayson and Jonny, that we all remain at Blackheath and . . ." How could she put it without revealing the strange, unearthly goings-on here?

And then she knew, because ghosts or no ghosts, the answer was the same. "We must face the past head-on, not run from it. We must all come to terms with what happened and learn to live with it. Live and move on, as a family."

"You're very brave, Nora." A sad smile tugged Chad's mouth. "I only hope Gray knows what a fortunate fellow he is."

He kissed her hand and released it, and bid her good night. On his way out, she called to him.

"Haven't you forgotten something?"

He turned, an eyebrow raised. "Have I?"

"Your book. I assume you were searching for something to read, yes?"

"Oh. Yes, of course. I, ah, didn't find what I was looking for."

"I see. Good night, then."

After he left, she returned the books he'd left lying on the desk to their rightful places on the shelves. She scanned the titles and, like the earl, found nothing to interest her. No, that wasn't quite true. This library contained no shortage of fascinating volumes. But none that could compete with the one question that claimed her thoughts tonight.

Would Grayson come find her?

She had left the door open, allowing the light from Chad's lamp to spill across the threshold. Surely for a man intent on being with his wife, that presented invitation enough. Drifting to the settee facing the hearth, she sank into the lush comfort of the down cushions. Outside the squally winds sent their somber echoes spiraling in the chimney. She considered calling for a footman to light the fire, but, tightening her shawl about her shoulders, deemed the room and the down cushions beneath her warm enough.

So she settled in to wait . . . and hope. Swinging her feet up, she stretched out and slipped one of the velvet throw pillows beneath her cheek. . . .

She awakened with a gasp on her lips and a weight across her shoulders. She struggled to sit up, discovering an arm pinning her in place.

"Shh. It's only me." Grayson crouched on the floor beside the settee, his face level with hers. His arm relaxed but its embrace remained, his fingers curling about her shoulder beneath her shawl. "I didn't mean to frighten you."

A smile spread across her lips. "I didn't know if you'd come. I'm glad you did."

He shook his head and studied her, his lush lips parting. "Why are you still here?"

The question sparked a little flame of guilt that heated her cheeks. "I'm sorry. I should have waited for you upstairs in my room, but I was rather angry earlier and supposed it would be a sort of justice to make you come to me here. It wasn't very nice of me, especially as I've yet to learn why you avoid this room."

His blue eyes darkened, and shadows fell across his cheeks as his head went down. "Tom and I argued in this room the last time I saw him alive." He flicked a nod toward the open space in front of the desk. "We were standing just there when I told him to go to the devil. By the end of the day, he had."

"Oh, good heavens, had I known that, I never would have—"

"It doesn't matter. This is merely a room. These four walls are not responsible for what happened." The rest of the thought went unfinished, but its echo reverberated in Nora's heart.

"Gray, men argue. Brothers say regrettable things." She gripped his free hand. It was rigid, as cold as a grave. She rubbed it between both of hers, trying in vain to warm it. "But they are not each other's keepers. Perhaps you wrong your brother in believing you drove him to take his own life . . . or to do anything. Perhaps he was stronger than you think, and some other reason entirely caused his death."

"God, how I want to believe that." His arm tightened around her, his fingers almost digging into her shoulder as he held on. "But when I asked why you were still here, I didn't mean in this blasted room, I meant here with me, in this marriage."

"Oh." Her first thought was the simplest. She loved him. But if she told him that, he'd only tell her not to, and claim he wasn't capable of loving her in return. So she said the one thing he could not refute. "I am here because I wish to be. Can you understand that?"

He shook his head. "No."

"Can you understand this, then?" Her arms went around his neck. She tugged him until their lips met, and held him there while she gathered her courage and slipped her tongue into his mouth.

His response was immediate, impassioned, his arms burrowing between her and the settee to wrap her tight. A rumbling erupted inside him, a sound that built, vibrated against her lips and filled her with fiery need.

"You're insane for staying," he whispered. "As insane as I am."

"Yes, and equally stubborn." She began opening the buttons of his shirt. "I know what I want," she breathed against his chest. She nipped his flesh, flicked her tongue across his nipple. "I want you."

He groaned and lifted her higher, crushing her to him. His hands groped at the fastenings down her back. "Beyond a doubt you'll live to regret this."

"My only regret would be dying"—she kissed him, gasped for a breath and continued—"without making love to you one more time."

His tongue swept her lips, speared between them and pushed deeply, a sultry prelude to the lovemaking Nora craved so acutely. He raised his head to meet her gaze. "Only once?"

Their hands went still. Their panting breaths stopped. They stared into each other's eyes.

And laughed. Laughed as they hadn't since their wedding night, following the fiasco with her eavesdropping mother and her overzealous father. Still, Nora couldn't quite decide if the tears tricking down her cheeks were merely mirthful or the result of the immense relief surging through her at the rare sound of Gray's laughter.

"Master Grayson? Is there a problem here? I can hear shrieking all the way down the corridor."

Nora shrugged her loosened dress higher onto her shoulders and started to sit up, but Grayson held her fast.

He poked his head above the back of the settee. "Leave us, please, Mrs. Dorn, and close the door behind you. We are not to be disturbed."

The woman murmured a terse "Yes, sir" and did as she was bidden.

"Now, then." His hand slipped beneath her sagging bodice to caress her nape, then skimmed the flesh between her shoulder blades, eliciting a quiver. Next he stood, scooped her into his arms and sat her in his lap on the settee. Their lips and tongues locked in moist combat until he gently pulled away.

"Make no mistake, Nora. I *am* what the scandal sheets say I am." When she started to protest, he held a finger to her lips. "We cannot sugarcoat it or pretend otherwise. I failed my brother and now he's dead. I murdered him, even if only in my heart."

"So be it." She combed the hair from his brow. "We shall not pretend you are a perfect being. You have made mistakes. Regrettable ones. We must learn to live with them. I must learn to live with you. Just as you, my darling, have had to reconcile yourself to the shame of marrying London's Painted Paramour."

With that she shifted in his lap until she faced him. Straddling his thighs, she yanked up her skirts to expose her legs. As she pondered how to continue, his hand obligingly tunneled beneath her petticoats. His palm settled against her underdrawers, spreading delicious heat through her nether regions.

"That is a shame I can most assuredly live with."

She unbuttoned his collar and worked his shirt from his body. He stripped her of her drawers and tossed them to the floor. Her bodice came next as Grayson tugged her sleeves from her arms, baring her from the waist up. Her hair came streaming down around her, its softness mingling with Grayson's sensual nibbles at her shoulders. He swung his legs onto the settee and sprawled out beneath her, his face and chest framed in the trailing fringe of her hair.

"The next move, my paramour, is yours." The once-hated epithet dripped from his lips like honey, smooth and sweet, setting her insides thrumming. She leaned over, nipped his lips, grazed them with the tip of her tongue.

Like a tenderly springing trap, his lips seized her tongue and drew it into his mouth. They played a teasing game of venture and retreat, caress and suckle. He found her hands and slid them to the buttons of his trousers. She broke their kiss, conjured her most scandalized expression and decided to do him one better. With a grin she slithered lower until her chin came level with his hips. Then she used her teeth to open each button.

A groan rumbled deep in his throat. His head thrown back against the cushions, his eyes became crystalline crescents sparking at her between his lashes.

With each opened button she kissed his exposed flesh, following the narrow trail of crisp hair lower and lower. His hands swept through her hair, his fingers tangling in the loose strands. A lust-driven laugh, low and throaty, broke from his lips.

"Ah, my *paramour*, what a wanton you are."

The sound of that word again, paramour, spoken in a rusty murmur, filled her with an overwhelming desire to fulfill his darkest fantasy, to be his wanton paramour in every glorious sense of the word.

Her heart beating frantically, she tugged his trousers below his hips and took him into her mouth.

A sense of power surged through her. It made her giddy, bold, to gaze upward along the taut planes of his body and watch the sensual tension shiver across his muscles as her touch guided him toward ecstasy. Her desire to take him there was exhilarating, intensely erotic.

As was the trust she sensed in him. Trust he hadn't dared bestow before now seemed hers for the taking, and it humbled her to see how completely he surrendered control to her.

His every motion, every grind of his throat, communicated his body's mounting response. Even before his hands found her face and lightly tugged, she'd known the time had come to recede, to let his passion ebb before rousing it again.

She kissed her way up his torso, letting her tongue slide over the contour of quivering muscle and sinew. Sliding higher until her thighs cradled his hips, she sat up and towered above him, her creature of darkness, her heart's desire. If his love had yet to grow, if he could never fully love a woman he had been forced to marry, the trust she perceived at this moment, even if only lust driven, was enough to kindle her heart forever.

She rose to her knees, positioned herself and then slowly and deliberately slid down on his erection, staring into his fierce blue eyes—eyes blazing with an emotion so unbridled it frightened her at the same time it thrilled her.

Flinging uncertainties aside like so much more clothing, she let his length fill her, spread rippling flame through her. "Is that a move that pleases you, sir?" She wriggled her hips. "Or perhaps . . . this." With a cry, she buried him deeper, consuming all of him.

He let out a moan. His hands slid up her sides, cupped her breasts. Pleasure spread in infinite fissures as he kneaded them, teasing the nipples between his fingers. Tiny diamonds of sweat glistened across his chest. Nora curled her fingers into the moist whorls of hair and rocked her hips, seeking leverage by tightening her knees against his sides. His arms rigid, he clutched her hips to guide her, becoming her strength when hers might have waned.

She clenched her muscles around him, squeezing, feeling the length and width of him shape and fill her. Together they moved as passion gathered into a dangerous coil, tight and ready to fracture. She felt it build to breaking, saw the glory of it in his face. It became too much, too powerful, and she let go, giving unhindered voice to the climax pulsating through her.

Afterward, she did not immediately question the glow surrounding them, thought it merely a resonance conjured by her perfectly blissful state. It wasn't until Grayson abruptly pulled to a sitting position that she recognized the unearthly quality to that light.

"What is that?" he whispered.

Her heart throbbed in her throat. Groping at her waist, she found her bodice and dragged it up to shield her breasts.

"Good Christ!" Gray's arm was like a steel band around her as a figure took shape at the corner of the hearth. His feet hit the floor. He stood, dragging Nora up behind him, his bare torso a wall in front her. "Nora, go. Quickly. Get help."

She peeked out over his shoulder. "It's all right," she murmured in his ear. "She isn't dangerous."

He turned enough profile toward her to shoot her an adamant look. "It's me they're after, Nora, not you. Charlotte and Tom want justice. I won't have you caught in the middle."

"Charlotte and Tom . . . and Jonny. Of course." She pressed her forehead between Grayson's shoulders as understanding dawned. "Gray, don't you see? She isn't here to hurt anyone. She's here to help. Its time to put our fears aside and discover what she wishes us to do."

# Chapter 20

"She was your brother's wife, wasn't she?" Nora murmured against Grayson's shoulder. It was less a question than a statement. "How did she die?"

Without taking his eyes off the apparition shimmering a few paces away, he struggled with one hand to button his trousers while holding Nora behind him with the other. "In childbirth. Four years ago. She and the baby both died."

"I should have realized who she was, but I suppose I was too frightened. I can see Jonny in her quite plainly now—the shape of their faces, the curve of their mouths. So very alike."

"Exceedingly so, though I see much of Tom in Jonny too."

"Her voice, that lovely musical accent I'd pondered over. She was Welsh?"

"Yes, from Cardiff."

They were whispering, barely moving now that his trousers were secure. A sizzling current ran under his skin, only partly the result of what they'd just done and the fact that Nora was pressing her length snug to his back and buttocks.

No, this was an energy he'd never before experienced, but what he imagined shivered through the clouds during a lightning storm. It vibrated through his limbs and raked his nerves raw.

"What the devil do you think she wants?" he murmured.

"She has asked me to search. To find the truth." Nora started to step out from behind him, but with a jolt of alarm he nudged her back.

"Stay where you are."

"It's all right. If she hasn't hurt me thus far, why would she now?" She moved forward to stand at his side. Her fingers curled around his, and he returned the gesture, holding her fast. "What is it you wish, Charlotte? Oh, do you mind if I call you Charlotte?"

No answer came.

"It's as if she cannot hear me."

"No," he agreed, "nor see us either. Look at her."

Charlotte, or at least the unsettling image of the woman Grayson once knew, stared with her oddly glowing eyes at some point across the room. One ivory hand fisted where her heart should have been. With the other she reached out, her face filled with such naked longing he held his breath and instinctively followed her gaze.

What he saw made him tug Nora to his chest and wrap his arms protectively around her.

"What is it?" She went still against him as she too saw what presently robbed him of speech. In front of one of the bookcases, another image wavered like heat off a dusty road. "Is that . . . ?"

Together they watched this new specter take on the shape of a man in a dark blue coat and gray trousers.

Grayson's arms tightened until Nora let out a whimper.

*"Thomas."* Like a musical note, high and clear, the name echoed through the room.

The sound filled Grayson with an inexplicable sense of despair that had him blinking back a tear. Against him, Nora convulsed softly with a sob. He looked down at her pinched features and knew that she too felt that same unaccountable despondency.

"The fireplace. Gray, there were no flames before."

Indeed, as he watched, small flares burst to life among the logs, though no kindling had been piled on top and certainly no match struck.

His gaze flicked back to Charlotte. She reached out with both hands now but didn't move forward, didn't attempt to meet her husband partway across the room. As he watched her, the already pale colors leached from her image, leaving her little more than a glimmering outline of light.

"What's happening to her?" Nora whispered.

"I don't know. I think she's grieving. Mourning for my brother."

"But why shouldn't they be together now?"

He had no answer. He peered across the room at the image he'd seen so many times before but had never truly accepted as real until now.

Tom's hands hung at his sides, but his expression mirrored his wife's powerful longing.

"It's as if they are suspended in separate realms," he said, "and cannot reach each other."

"That's it." Nora hugged him tighter and burrowed her face against his chest. When she looked up, tears magnified her eyes and glittered on her cheeks. "Charlotte said I must free Thomas and set his spirit to rest. I'm guessing that can only be done by uncovering the truth of how he died."

She turned to the misty shade that was now Charlotte. "Am I right? If we discover the truth, then you and Thomas can be together?"

For the first time, Charlotte looked directly at Nora. *"Do not give up. Please."*

"We won't fail you." Nora's arm slipped from around Grayson's waist. She held out her hand. "I promise."

*"Keep close watch over our Jonny."*

"Always." Nora's voice caught. "I swear it."

The hearth was fast becoming distinct behind Charlotte's waning figure. Grayson moved toward her. "Charlotte, please tell me . . . was it my fault?" He swallowed a lump of grief. "Did I send Tom to his death?"

Charlotte vanished, and he was left staring at fluttering flames. He glanced down the room to discover Thomas had vanished as well.

"Damn it," he hissed on a shaky breath, "why didn't I ask her sooner?"

"She would not have answered." Nora's hand came down on his shoulder. "We must learn it for ourselves."

He stood panting, staring into vacant air, his heart racing. "How can this be real? I can't deny what we just witnessed, but how can such a thing be possible?"

Nora turned him to face her and slipped her hands into his. "We conjured them. I'm certain of it."

"How could we?"

She rose on tiptoe and kissed him. "With the energy of our lovemaking. I'd never seen them together before. Have you?"

"Not like that."

"No. It was our passion that drew them here, that rendered their own yearning for each other unendurable. And now it is our task to make certain they spend eternity together. As a man and wife were meant to do."

Those words frightened him more than anything he'd seen today or any day previously. *Man and wife.* The notion left his heart aching, but also hollow. If in searching for the truth of Tom's death they discovered that he, Grayson, was responsible after all, how would he ever be able to seek happiness, find it, hold it and return it?

He dropped to the settee and drew Nora down beside him. "We'll find a way to free them, I swear it. But as for you and me . . . I . . . I simply don't know." Her hand was warm in his, trembling slightly against his palm. He covered it with his other hand and felt a chasm open up inside him. "It may not be in me to ever be the husband you deserve."

Nora dabbed her brush into the glob of sienna brown on her palette and lightly touched it to the canvas. Just a slight lift to the right eyebrow to relieve the gloom that had initially permeated Grayson's portrait.

Pausing, she shifted the easel a couple inches into the morning light. An hour must have passed since she set to work adding fullness to his lips, brightness to his eyes, softness to the shadows around his face. It seemed only minutes since she'd mixed her colors, but in that time her creature of darkness had transformed into the gentle, compassionate man she loved.

Yes, loved quite desperately.

Just as desperately, she knew she must find a way to free him of his past. Charlotte and Tom's love depended on the truth being known. Her future with Gray also pivoted on what they learned, for good or ill. Otherwise, even if he remained her husband in name, she could quite possibly find herself as adrift as Charlotte, spending the rest of her days mourning something she couldn't have.

While she painted, Jonny filled his expansive canvas in the middle of the floor. Every so often, she peeked at him, hoping something new might be revealed. She saw little else but more of those yellow circles.

She dipped her brush again when a thin breath of a voice reached her ears.

"Watch."

Her paintbrush tumbled from her fingers and skimmed the front of her sprigged muslin gown, leaving a brown streak before clattering to the floor. She waited for the telltale chills, the glowing light that always surrounded Charlotte's image. There was none, and realization sent a shock wrenching through her.

Suppressing a gasp, she craned her neck around the

side of her easel. "Jonny, dearest . . ." She stopped, calming the tremors from her voice. "Did . . . did you say something?"

His back was to her. He didn't move, not a muscle. She broke through her stupefaction and swept to his side.

With feigned calm she sat, tucking her legs beneath her and settling her skirts. "I'm here, dearest, I'm watching. What is it you wish to show me?"

When he remained utterly motionless, she grasped his chin on the ends of her fingers and turned him to her. His eyes were large with alarm, dark with dismay. Clearly he hadn't meant to speak, probably hadn't realized the word had passed his lips until Nora spoke in return.

She peered at his canvas, at all those yellow circles. Nothing new had emerged . . . except he had painted a swoop from one of those circles to a moundlike shape depicted in hues of green and gray.

What did it mean? What did he want her to watch? A frustrated demand for answers welled inside her, threatening to burst, tempting her to grasp his shoulders and give him a shake as she so often wished to do with Grayson.

She forced a cheerful smile instead. "That is a wonderful picture. You're showing great potential as an artist. Someday you'll be the teacher and I the student. But won't you tell me why you called me to come watch?"

Nothing. Only those large eyes looking up at her, solemn, sad, filled with secrets.

Her own eyes misted. For whatever reason, Jonny had spoken. A single word, little more than a gasp, but a word all the same. A beginning. In time he would say more; the certainty squared her shoulders. For now the most important thing was to assure him he'd done well and he was loved. So very loved. She reached her arms around him.

"My dear, dear boy," she whispered. "My clever young man. You know you are like my very own son, do you not?" She didn't wait for a response but hugged him tighter. He dropped his paintbrush onto the sheet. His thin arms slowly reached around her and he rested her chin against her shoulder, filling her with bittersweet joy.

"No matter what happens, your aunt Nora will always watch over you. I promise. And if there is ever anything you want, anything at all, you need only tell me."

She felt him pull away a little and realized she was smothering him. When she released him, he turned back to the sheet and retrieved his brush.

"Yes, Jonny, I'm watching. And listening. You needn't worry about a thing."

"Jonny spoke to me."

Nora entered the stables and made her quiet announcement just as Chad dismounted from his chestnut gelding and handed the reins to the groom. Since dawn he and Grayson had been out searching the grounds and surroundings for more evidence of smuggling. Later she would question them about their findings. For now, she believed her news took precedence over all else.

Seconds after the words left her lips, Grayson bolted out from his own horse's stall. He stopped short and both men gaped at her, their complexions blanching.

Then, with a quick glance at the groom who was leading Chad's horse down the center aisle to another stall, Gray strode to her, grasped her hand and brought her out to the windy stable yard. Chad followed a couple of paces behind.

"What on earth did he say?" Grayson demanded, his tone a shade gruffer than normal, but understandable under the circumstances.

"Only one word, I'm afraid." She clutched her

shawl before the breeze could tug it from her shoulders. "He said 'Watch.' "

"Watch," Grayson echoed, frowning beneath the dark hair blown across his brow. "Watch what?"

"That I cannot say. I gave him my full attention immediately, of course. We were in my studio, I at my easel and he on the floor at his canvas. I expected him to show me something extraordinary, but in truth he did not."

The disappointment on Gray's face made her wish she had tried harder to coax Jonny into speaking again. Made her regret that she and the boy had yet to reach a level of complete trust. "He painted a simple line while I watched, and that was all."

Chad mopped a handkerchief across his brow. "Perhaps the request had nothing to do with his painting."

"Yes, that occurred to me," she agreed. "Perhaps it has more to do with his fear of being left alone. After all, he must remember little of his mother, and lost his father not long ago. Soon after that, Gray left Blackheath and returned only for brief visits." With immediate regret, she whisked a hand to her mouth. "Forgive me, I don't mean to imply—"

"No, dear heart, you are correct. His father died and for the most part his uncle promptly abandoned him, leaving him to the care of servants instead of family." Grayson's remorseful gaze caressed her face with a regard so tender her throat tightened. "I don't wonder that because of you, Jonny dares believe he is safe again. That he is loved."

"If you ask me," Chad said, "Jonny is slowly healing because of both of you. A child needs two parents, after all. But then, no one has asked me, have they?"

"Your opinions are always welcome, my friend." Grayson's smile retained an edge of sadness, of doubt. Still, Nora once more experienced a rush of gratitude for Chad's presence. She couldn't deny that much had changed since his arrival, and though she would have liked to believe Grayson's rallying mood was purely the result of her love, she must give credit where due. In many ways she was still a stranger to Blackheath Grange, and to her husband's life. Gray's friendship with Chad went back decades. There were levels of trust and communication between them she could not yet hope to attain.

"Did you find anything during your ride?" she asked them. She pressed a hand to her hair to hold it in place and wondered if they would have another day of stormy weather.

"We searched some old ruins not far from here and a tin mine no longer in use." Grayson let out a sigh. "Both have plenty of potential as hiding places—in the foundations, down the shafts—but we found nothing. No sign that anyone had been there in recent months. We also spoke with several of the villagers and tenant farmers, none of whom ever saw anything suspicious."

They started walking back up to the house. "Are you certain they were telling the truth?" Nora asked. "Perhaps they've been threatened. They could be frightened of repercussions."

Chad shook his head. "It would appear that Blackheath's smugglers are ghosts, to have vanished so entirely without a trace."

At the suggestion, Nora came to a halt and experienced the same shock that visibly passed through Grayson; as she felt the blood drain from her own face, his complexion turned ashen. He slipped an arm around her and drew her close as they continued walking, sending a shaky breath into her hair as he kissed the top of her head.

"This once more leaves Tom as our only suspect." Grayson's arm weighed heavily across Nora's shoulders, but she wished she could as easily bear his emotional burdens.

"There is more to this," she assured him. "Just because we aren't seeing it yet doesn't mean the answer doesn't exist."

"True," he agreed. "But what if it is an answer none of us can live with?"

She had no answer for him.


"Master Grayson, this is an outrage."

He was on his way to his bedchamber to change for supper. Instead, Mrs. Dorn's complaint from just beyond the upper landing sent him about-face and down the stairs in hopes of eluding her.

"Master Grayson, please," the woman called to his back as he descended the steps. "I cannot remain silent."

Pretending not to hear her had never worked, not even when he was a child; she would only pursue him more zealously. Halfway down, he stopped and waited for her to appear at the top of the stairs.

Her scowl sizzled with animosity. Jonny's improvised canvas dangled from her fists.

"That belongs to my nephew—"

"*This* is part of a set of Irish linen bedclothes monogrammed by your great grandmother, Lady Amelia Camden Lowell." She gave the sheet a thrust. "And look at it. Ruined! This rubbish will never come off."

Grayson pinched the bridge of his nose. "We don't wish it to come off, Mrs. Dorn. We wish for Jonny to continue his painting as a way of communicating his thoughts and feelings to us." He started back up the stairs, hand extended to retrieve the sheet from the housekeeper.

She backed away as he reached the landing, her mouth opening on an obvious retort. Nora just then rounded the corner from the south wing.

"Is that Jonny's canvas you have there, Mrs. Dorn? May I have it, please?"

"No, you may not." The woman glared. "Canvas—poppycock!"

"Poppycock to encourage a child to express himself?" Nora held out her hands for the canvas.

Her face crimson, Mrs. Dorn whisked it out of reach.

"I understand your wish to preserve this house and everything in it," Grayson said with the patience due the woman's decades of untiring service. "You've been loyal to this family for many years. But this is a matter you do not understand."

"The way I do not understand banging hooks into walls and valuable pieces of furniture, or putting one's feet upon priceless seat cushions?"

"Please give the sheet to Lady Lowell, Mrs. Dorn," Grayson ordered softly. "Now."

She hesitated, gaze angling back and forth between them. Slowly she held out Jonny's canvas. Just before she released it into Nora's hands, she said, "You'll do more harm than good to that boy. Best leave him be."

Nora's eyes narrowed on the woman. "Henceforth my studio door will be locked. No one enters without my permission."

"As you wish, madam." The last word dripped with contempt. With an impertinent twitch of her eyebrows, Mrs. Dorn brushed by them and stomped down the stairs.

Grayson released a breath. "She's walking a fine line."

"That she is," Nora agreed.

His stomach clenched. "Do you wish me to dismiss her?"

She frowned in the direction the housekeeper had gone. "No. At least not yet. She's part of everything that happened here and I suspect she knows more than she's willing to say."

"Surely you don't believe she was involved in Tom's death." Despite Mrs. Dorn's disagreeable behavior, Grayson could not envision the dedicated servant ever harming a member of the Lowell family.

Nora shook her head. "I don't know what I believe. But I think we should watch her and not leave Jonny alone with her. For now."

Before he could comment, she slipped her arms around his neck and kissed him. He let the heat of it sweep through him, sought what comfort from it he could. But another piece of his world spun out of control. Mrs. Dorn had been part of the Lowell household his entire life. Holding her in suspicion was like leveling accusations at an elderly aunt.

*Chapter 21*

A t the breakfast table the next morning, Grayson helped himself to a second cup of coffee, his only source of energy after too few hours of sleep. He'd instructed Cook to brew it extra strong from now on.

Across the table, Nora also looked tired, but at the same time a glow suffused her cheeks. Absently she hummed a little melody as she ate her breakfast, and seemed more content than she had since their arrival here.

Last night he had knocked on her door, and without a word she had welcomed him into her embrace. In each other's arms, they had spent several hours during which neither ghosts nor the past had intruded. The world had been contained within the four posts of Nora's bed, a tiny paradise of heated, satiny flesh, fragrant, silky hair and the miracle of feeling, for that brief time, that he needed nothing more.

She had been awake when he finally rose and searched for his clothing, and with understanding glimmering in her eyes, she had let him go without questions. It was only later, when he was alone, that the memories had once more closed in around him like enraged pixies, tormenting him and denying him more than a couple hours' sleep.

Nora pushed her plate aside now and drank the last of her chocolate. "If it's all right with you, I should like to take Jonny for a ride in the coach this morning. The rain seems to be holding off and I think it would do him good to be out for a while, away from this house. And I have an idea besides."

"What sort of idea?"

"Well . . . I thought I might visit some of our tenants, perhaps bring them little gifts from our kitchens."

"A splendid notion." He narrowed his eyes at her. "Then why do I have the feeling there's more to it?"

Her gaze broke from his and dropped to the table, then rose with a bold gleam. "I thought I might ask a few pertinent questions—"

"No. I don't want you involved in this."

"I already am."

"I don't need you playing at being a spy. I want you here, where I know you're safe."

"Surely you don't expect me to stay locked in the house, nor Jonny either. And the local folk might be more willing to open up to a woman and child, especially if I'm careful to merely sound curious rather than suspicious." She forestalled his intended protest by moving to the seat beside his and kissing him. "We'll have our driver and a footman along to protect us," she continued, her breath warm against his lips. "Surely you can't object to that."

How could he object to anything she wanted? Even here, in the cool gray light of the morning room, she infused him with desire, with a fiery inclination to sweep her into his arms and carry her upstairs.

No, he found he could not deny her any request, even one against his better judgment. He stroked her arm up and down and leaned in for another kiss. "You are more your father's daughter than I ever dreamed. Like him, you know what you want, and you know how to set about getting it, though your methods are markedly different."

"I don't know if I've just been complimented or insulted."

"Complimented, to be sure."

"Then Jonny and I can go."

"Will you refrain from asking questions?"

She shrugged. "Can I help it if certain matters are bound to arise in the course of conversation?"

"I will send an *armed* footman with you. I would accompany you myself but Gibbs sent a note to my room earlier asking if he might meet with me following breakfast. Perhaps he has managed to trace the silver from the cave."

He sent her and Jonny off with repeated warnings to be careful, watched the coach disappear down the drive and turned to find his steward waiting for him at the bottom of the front steps.

"I've information that may be of consequence, sir," Gibbs said, his face grim.

A footman stood waiting at the open front door. Grayson signaled a dismissal to him and, as the heavy door closed, he walked with his steward around the house to the rear gardens.

"We'll have more privacy out here," he told the other man. "What have you learned?"

The breeze swept through the flowering trees and carefully trimmed hedges to ruffle the steward's hair, revealing more of his balding pate than he liked to admit having. He didn't bother shoving the strands back into place. "Someone has been to the cave."

"Who? When? Don't stand there gawking, for heaven's sake. Tell me." Gibbs's wounded expression prompted Grayson to say more quietly, "Sorry. Tell me everything. Who is our mystery pirate?"

"Just to confirm, sir, did you perchance visit the cave the night before Lord Wycliffe arrived?"

"In the dark? Hardly. What are you getting at?"

"One of the men I've hired to watch the beach overheard a village lad raving about having seen a ghost recently. The lad, Joseph Little, happened to be rowing in from fishing shortly after dusk the night before Lord Wycliffe arrived." Gibbs's gaze darted about the garden. "Lantern light drew his attention to the beach. He says he saw a well-dressed man making his way back up to the headland."

"A well-dressed man? How could he see that clearly if it was growing dark and he was out in his skiff?"

Gibbs regarded his feet, looking embarrassed. "There are rumors in the village concerning a, ah, ghost, sir, that haunts the beach and the cliffs. . . ."

"Yes, of course there are. Go on."

"So when Joseph saw the light, he quietly rowed in for a closer look. He had his spyglass with him and quite distinctly saw a figure in a frock coat and breeches tailored far too finely for a villager. He believed he was seeing . . . well . . ."

Grayson nodded wearily. "My brother's ghost."

"Sorry, sir."

"I still don't see what the devil this has to do with Lord Wycliffe."

"Nothing, sir. I was merely using his lordship's arrival as a frame of reference. Although, it *is* rather a coincidence. Not to toss suspicion at the earl, but few men in these parts could be considered well-dressed, besides yourself, of course. And as far as it having been the late Earl of Clarington, well, any rational man knows there are no such things as ghosts."

Grayson almost laughed at Gibbs's assertion, for he knew now of a certainty that ghosts in fact *did* exist. It was quite possible Joseph Little *had* seen Tom's spirit climbing the headland that night.

A sudden memory made him question that conclusion. *You should leave as soon as possible.* Those were Chad's words the other day. And months earlier, *Let me sort through Tom's things for you, Gray, and spare you that pain. . . .*

Had Chad's apparent concern masked a greater desire to push Grayson conveniently out of the way?

A sickening suspicion plummeted to the pit of his

gut. Then again, those were merely two memories plucked from a lifetime's worth. How many times had Chad taken the blame for their childhood mischief, in order to save Grayson and Tom from the brunt of their father's wrath? And what about later? How many scrapes had Chad helped Grayson out of at university? At London's gambling hells? Chad had always been there, always been a friend to both him and Tom.

That Chad could be anything else . . . it was inconceivable. Impossible.

He grasped at the most obvious hope available. "Lord Wycliffe didn't arrive until the next morning."

"Quite true, sir. Did he mention where he spent the night?"

"No, he didn't." Grayson had naturally assumed Chad spent the morning of his arrival on the road, coming from east Cornwall or perhaps even Devon. But he might have spent the night in either Helston or Mullion and still had time to travel to the beach and back, and then make his arrival here in the morning.

The notion gnawed like a festering sore.

With a shake of his head he dismissed the suspicion. "Surely a finely dressed gentleman, as you say, could have been any one of a half dozen others. Confound it, the Lowells are not the only landed family on the Lizard Peninsula."

But even as he stated the obvious, he realized that Chad himself was a landowner who hailed from the same peninsula, albeit some fifteen miles to the southeast, on the opposite coast.

"If you'll pardon me, sir, I am only the bearer of the information. It is not my place to tell you how to interpret it."

A gust of wind parted the clouds and Grayson squinted through a bar of sunlight to make out his valet's features. "What do you suggest?"

"Prudence. Have the utmost care where you invest your trust. Perhaps, sir . . ." Gibbs left off, looking uncomfortable.

"Perhaps what?"

"Perhaps the late Earl of Clarington made that very mistake and trusted where he should not have."

A hot denial rose to Grayson's lips, but its fervor cooled before the words formed. He needed time alone to think, to sort through everything he'd learned these past few days. He started toward the house, then stopped and turned. "Were you able to find out anything about the goblet I gave you?"

"It came from a silversmith in Sheffield, sir. One Oliver Samuels."

Grayson nodded and continued on, dragging heavy feet through the grass as a vague nausea claimed his stomach. The thought of Chad being involved . . . He considered how accomplished a liar Chad would have to be to have acted so surprised when he saw the cave, and again each time he denied the possibility of Tom's involvement in smuggling.

No. Chad was his friend, and Grayson didn't believe otherwise any more than he believed in Tom's guilt. Far easier and, in a way, less painful to believe in his own guilt.

Yes, that remained the one constant. No matter how Tom died, no matter what lengths he might have been driven to in the end, if he'd had a better brother, a brother he could depend upon and turn to . . . dear God, how much might have turned out differently?

"Run out that way, Jonny!"

Chad pointed into the field that bordered the road between Millford and Blackheath Grange, his other hand cupped around an unripe apple he'd picked up from the ground. He ran several steps himself, drew back his arm and sent the hard piece of fruit flying, a bright spot of green against the steel gray sky.

Chad framed his mouth with both hands and called out in a voice ringing with laughter, "Keep your eye on it! Don't look away!"

Nora held her breath. "Oh, I hope he doesn't trip," she murmured as Jonny trampled half-backward through ankle-high grass and heather. He raised both arms above his head, his hands outstretched and close together, ready to trap the improvised ball.

"Nonsense," Chad said, still laughing. "Run, boy, and watch that apple, not your feet."

A second later Jonny gave a little hop and snatched the apple out of the air as it arced above his head.

Chad gave a whoop. "Well done! Now toss it here."

For the next few minutes they passed the apple back and forth between them, Chad running into the field on the east side of the road, then Jonny into the western pasture and so on. Finally one of Jonny's tosses went wide and struck a rock border wall, smashing the apple to pulp.

"Ah, well, no matter." Chad clapped Jonny's shoulder, and both he and Nora were rewarded with one of Jonny's exceedingly rare smiles. Then the child returned to his earlier task of searching out interesting objects to drop into Nora's basket.

"I'd no idea he was so athletic," she confided to Chad.

"Have you seen him ride?"

"Only in the paddock."

Chad gave a low whistle. "He's fearless in the fields. Or he was. I don't suppose he's been out much beyond the paddocks since . . . well . . ."

"No," Nora agreed with a sigh. "I don't suppose he has." She shifted her basket from one arm to the other.

Earlier, the basket had brimmed with cakes, breads, fruit and meat pasties. She, Jonny and Chad had visited some half-dozen tenant families, becoming acquainted and dispensing their treats. Jonny had eagerly played with a litter of puppies at the Davis farm, and at the Conway household, Nora had been delighted at the chance to hold their new baby daughter. Such a lovely, precious little dear . . .

She hadn't expected the earl to accompany them this morning, but when the coach had reached the end of the drive earlier, there he had been by the gatehouse, out for a morning walk, he had said. Under any other circumstances she would have been pleased to have her husband's friend along.

Today, however, he presented an encumbrance to her intended purpose, which was to casually glean as much information as she could from the people she met. But each time she had tried posing questions about Cornwall's long history of smuggling and piracy, Chad would somehow steer the conversation onto other topics. After a time she had begun to wonder if perhaps Grayson had secretly sent him along to prevent her "playing at being a spy," as he had put it. She had finally given up and reverted to small talk and polite inquiries into the health and well-being of each family's members.

She sighed and watched Jonny as he ambled several yards ahead, plucking blossoms from the hawthorn hedges now bordering the road and picking up odd rocks and leaves from the ground. Though thunder occasionally rumbled in from the moor, the clouds were high and scuttling, not the sort that promised rain anytime soon. They had therefore opted to send the coach on ahead and walk home, and Nora was glad they did, for despite his silence, Jonny seemed to be thoroughly enjoying himself, as any little boy might.

She lowered her voice to prevent him from overhearing. "Taking Jonny out of the house today seems to have done him worlds of good. Tell me, does he look at all improved since you last saw him?"

"The last time I saw him was well before you came into his life, Nora." As they walked, the earl swung an arm outward, plucking a fragrant white blossom from the hedge. With a little flourish, he handed it to her. "And yes, he looks vastly improved."

"I'm glad to hear it. And thank you." She held the flower beneath her nose and inhaled its sweet scent. Oh, Chad might have foiled her plans this morning, but she couldn't bring herself to remain annoyed with such a good-natured, considerate man. Especially when that man had been her husband's closest friend since early boyhood.

"I must confide to you," she said, "that Grayson's mood has rallied greatly since your arrival. Before that he . . . he was not . . ."

"Quite himself?" Chad angled his head, offering an expression filled with sympathy.

"In truth, I can hardly say. In the short time I've known him, he has been . . . troubled."

"Indeed." Chad strolled with his hands clasped behind him, boots thudding out the rhythm of his long-limbed stride. "What has he told you about his brother's death?"

She considered before answering, wondering how much she should reveal. She was grateful for Chad's presence, certainly, yet she hesitated to betray any part of Grayson's confidence. "I . . . suppose it isn't news to you that he feels responsible."

"He has ever since Thomas's body was found."

Jonny returned to them and laid a handful of pink willow herb into the basket.

"Those are exquisite," Nora told him. "Thank you, sir."

When he ran off to continue his search, she became serious again. "Can you tell me anything about that awful day? I understand you were here at the time."

"True enough, but I probably know little more than you about what happened. Tom and Gray had argued that morning, a frightful row Jonny overheard."

"In the library."

"Yes, in fact, it was in the library, and Jonny had been listening outside the door. Afterward, Grayson stormed from the house, mounted his horse and galloped off. Thomas remained brooding in the library and I did my best to make myself scarce, thinking they both needed time to cool their tempers.

"After bringing Jonny up to his nurse, I'd fallen asleep in my room, only to wake to the chaos of the nurse shrieking that the boy was nowhere to be found. Soon after, we realized Tom had gone missing as well. That actually calmed my fears for a time. I surmised nothing more sinister than Tom taking his son for a walk. But when Grayson returned to the house and discovered the pair gone, he insisted on mounting a search. Didn't credit my theory one bit." Chad's head went down. Nora heard a breath hiss through his teeth. "A pity he turned out to be right."

"Gray must have been frantic with worry."

"More than that." Chad stopped walking, his features taut as he clearly struggled with a difficult memory. "He was gripped by a foreboding unlike anything I'd ever seen in him. And afterward . . . egad, Nora, I've never seen a man as haunted as Gray. The very next night I found him drunk and raving about how it had been no accident, that he was to blame. Never before or since have I witnessed my friend in such a state."

"Surely you didn't believe he—"

"Not for an instant."

As Nora digested this information, they walked on in silence. Jonny tossed another handful of blossoms into her basket, then broke into a run when the main gate of Blackheath Grange came into view.

She slowed to a halt and stilled Chad with a hand on his arm. "I understand it was you who found Jonny."

Surprise flashed in his eyes. Then he nodded. "The search party had split up. I found Jonny in the woods near the headland."

"Did he say anything?"

"Not a word." His face brightened. "Until yesterday, that is."

"Yes, but only that single word."

"It is a start. He wants only for time and patience."

They were nearing the drive now, and Jonny ran back to them, this time clutching a handful of rocks and acorns. Chad rumpled his hair and reached for the basket. "Perhaps I'd best carry that, especially if Signor da Vinci here insists on bringing home half the park."

"I'm stronger than I appear." Nora gave the basket a little swing.

Chad flashed his admittedly dashing smile. "A gross understatement, I'll warrant. Nevertheless . . ." He took the basket, clasping both hands around its handle. "But whether through strength or sheer determination, Nora, I believe you have the power to ultimately heal both Grayson and Jonny."

"It is my only wish," she said around the little pain that pressed her heart.

"Your only wish? Is there nothing you want for yourself?"

She heard the teasing in his voice and a wistful smile fluttered across her lips. "What more could I want? I have all the worldly possessions that can be imagined. But such things mean nothing without a family happily sharing them."

Chad brought them to an abrupt stop and surprised Nora by placing a hand beneath her chin. "Devil take Grayson Lowell if he doesn't realize what a damned lucky fellow he is."

The words bore an intensity that startled her. He'd said something similar before, but this time she felt awkward . . . uncomfortable, suddenly, to be strolling beside this man and allowing him to hold her basket while they discussed her husband's troubles behind his back. It did smack of a betrayal of Grayson's trust, and something of the old unease she had once felt around Chad came rushing back. He removed his hand and continued walking, but the imprint of his fingers lingered like shards of ice against her skin.

Up ahead, Jonny had roamed down the road past the gate. Confused and discomfited without quite knowing why, she seized the excuse to call him back, and was glad when the boy returned to walk between her and the Earl of Wycliffe.

*Chapter 22*

After his talk with Gibbs and learning that his best friend might be a liar, a thief and possibly involved, somehow, in the death of his brother, Grayson had done as any man in his position would.

He had quietly returned to the house, chosen a room where he wouldn't be disturbed, shut the door, and pummeled his fist full force into the nearest wall.

The pain shooting up his arm and jarring his shoulder provided a measure of morbid satisfaction, but did little to help his situation. Or alleviate his rising anger at . . . everything. Everyone. Tom for dying. Himself for not being able to prevent it. At his father for creating the circumstances that could only have led to tragedy. At Gibbs for raising a suspicion that left a rancid taste in his mouth. And at his boyhood friend for being the focus of that suspicion.

"Damn it, Chadwell," he murmured, "if you've been lying to me I'll break your bloody neck."

He cradled his throbbing knuckles in his other palm, all too tempted to thrash another object. Swinging around, he glared at the portrait hanging above the mantel. Three pairs of eyes stared back: a stern-faced tyrant who even now had the power to make him feel inadequate, and his two young sons doing their utmost to stand tall and look like the men Alexander Lowell insisted they be.

"What happened months ago?" he demanded of Thomas's youthful image. "What was on your mind that day? And where do I turn now to find the truth?"

The room seemed to close in on him, narrowing to no more than the width of the portrait. Those three faces filled his vision until his eyes watered from staring. A quivering energy emanated outward from the canvas, encompassing him, pulling him in, absorbing him whole.

The answer came, not from Thomas or in spoken words, but from the gleam of gold paint scoring his father's waistcoat.

Grayson froze at the sight of his father's fob. His pounding heart tallied the seconds while his mind worked it through.

"Good God, why didn't I think of it sooner?"

He bolted from the room and dashed across the gallery to the south corridor.

Outside Nora's studio he sagged against the closed door, hand gripping the knob. As Nora had told Mrs. Dorn, she had locked the door and taken the key.

He threw his shoulder against it, causing it to tremble on its hinges. Tucking his head, he backed away for momentum and rammed the door again. This time a splintering of wood echoed the pain that lanced his shoulder. Nevertheless, the door proved a stubborn barrier.

"Sir, surely there are better ways of opening doors than breaking them down."

Feeling both foolish and defeated, Grayson pressed his palms flat to the wood and didn't bother glancing up at Nora's maid. "Your mistress has the key, Kat. Can you suggest a better idea?"

"I believe I can, sir. As to whether I should, though . . ." With a doubtful expression she tapped a finger against her chin.

"I am your employer, am I not?"

"Oh, to be sure, sir, and I mean no offense. But I've known Miss Nora these many years and—"

"Kat, I value your loyalty to your mistress and I assure you she did not lock that door against me." He lowered his voice to a confidential murmur. "She merely wishes to prevent Mrs. Dorn from interfering with Jonny's project. Now, if you happen to have the key . . ."

"Keeping Dorn out— Why didn't you say so? I don't have the key, but if you'll stand aside, sir, I'll have that door open in a trice."

"I hardly think you . . ." He trailed off, watching the pretty, dark-eyed maid slip a pin from the bun at her nape.

"This should do the trick." She held it up and winked. "In future, sir, if a hairpin is not to be found, a cravat pin should do quite nicely."

He fingered his neckcloth, knowing full well he hadn't bothered wearing a cravat pin since returning from London.

As Kat knelt and set to work, Grayson revealed his impatience with the tapping of his foot until he noticed the nervous gesture and stopped. After several moments the lock clicked. Kat grasped the doorknob and pulled to her feet.

"There you are, sir."

She stepped aside and he opened the door. "I won't ask where you learned that skill."

"Very wise of you, sir. Suffice it to say I rarely need to put such expertise to use nowadays."

"Amen to that."

"If that will be all, sir, I'll leave you to your snooping."

"I am not . . ."

She'd already started off down the hall. Grayson shrugged and stepped inside.

The pungent odors of oils, pigments and turpentine

assaulted his nostrils as he crossed the threshold. Nora and Jonny had been painting earlier. Wrinkling his nose, he knelt before Jonny's canvas.

Reaching down, he traced one of those yellow circles, repeated so often among the other designs. His finger then followed the smaller half circle drawn in black at its center. His hand shook as a conviction burgeoned.

It wasn't a half circle. It was a *C—C* for Clarington. "Watch," Jonny had said to Nora. Not "Watch me," but "Watch."

The Clarington watch, which Thomas had inherited from their father and which Jonny should have inherited in turn, except that it had gone missing after Tom died.

For months now Grayson had assumed Tom had sold it. It hadn't been found on the body or in the house among his personal effects. But if it had been sold, why did it prey on Jonny's mind to such an extent?

How much importance could that watch hold that it prompted the boy to speak for the first time since his father's death?

Grayson sat back on his haunches, staring out the window as an ashen cloud rolled across the sky. A hawk swooped into view, its fingered wings wide and motionless, riding the wind currents as it silently hunted for prey.

Perhaps the watch didn't matter at all and he imagined meaning where none existed. Perhaps Jonny merely associated the piece with his father and wished he had it to remember him by.

But the more Grayson considered all those golden Clarington watches crowding the sheet, the more convinced he became that finding the real watch would provide a vital key to solving the mystery of his brother's death.

Jonny must be part of that key as well, but Grayson felt certain that without the watch, he'd never be able to break his nephew's silence and discover the truth.

He stood, wishing Nora were back so he could share this latest revelation with her.

Her easel stood facing the window, denuded of its cloth. A twinge of curiosity sent him toward it until his conscience stopped him short. Kat had accused him of snooping, and though he'd denied the charge, viewing Nora's work in progress uninvited would certainly qualify.

Still, the fact that it was a portrait of *him* should give him some right to snoop. The last time he'd looked, however . . .

He almost turned and left but instead held his breath and circled the easel. He raised his eyes to the canvas . . . and experienced a jarring mixture of relief and astonishment.

Not only did he *not* see his brother's image mingling with his, but Nora had made some extraordinary, if subtle, alterations. Though he couldn't quite say what the changes were—a shadow here, a touch of brightness there—he no longer spied a man battling guilt and a sense of failure. Saw no demons dancing in fatigue-sunken eyes.

The Grayson gazing back seemed far less burdened, far less haunted. He saw a man looking toward the future with hope, with a measure of confidence. And, he had to admit, the more he stared, the more he also detected an underlying current of desire—in his expression, in the very brushstrokes—as if the Grayson of the portrait stared out from the canvas and saw her, waiting for him with open arms.

Dear God, how he wanted to be that man! The sentiment tore a hole through his heart. What wouldn't he have been willing to give to trade places with that other, happier Grayson? To be the man Nora envisioned.

Perhaps, in time . . . was it too much to hope? Did he have the strength, the resilience, to fight his way past his demons and be that other, better man?

For Nora . . . and for Jonny . . . perhaps he did. He desperately needed to believe so.

"Sir?"

He choked back a gasp and turned to see Gibbs outside in the corridor. "What is it?"

"One more thought, sir, concerning what we discussed earlier."

Grayson didn't want to think about it, but knew he couldn't ignore the matter either. The Grayson in the portrait certainly wouldn't. "Yes?"

"The magistrate. Is it time to summon him? Bearing in mind, of course, that it could take a day or more for a message to reach him."

Grayson ran a hand through his hair. He hadn't wanted to call the magistrate for fear of incriminating Tom's memory in front of Jonny. Now he might be incriminating Chad. Or both men. And Jonny would be left with even more to mourn.

He filled his lungs and forced a single word past his lips. "Yes."

"Very good, sir." Gibbs turned to go.

"Wait. Have my wife and nephew returned yet?"

"I believe the coach turned in about a half hour ago."

"That's odd. Then where are they?"

He didn't wait for Gibbs to sort out an answer for him. Downstairs, neither Mrs. Dorn nor any of the other servants had seen Nora and Jonny. With the vague beginnings of panic prodding his steps, Grayson strode out to the carriage house. He found the coachman wiping down the sides of the vehicle with a soft white rag.

"Morning, Master Grayson. No, they sent me on ahead. Said they preferred to walk. I warned them it might rain, but the earl insisted it would do no such thing." He angled a glance at the sky. "So far, it seems he was right."

"The earl?" Alarm streaked across Grayson's back and sent shooting pains into his neck. There were two earls presently residing at Blackheath Grange, but unless some miracle had occurred this morning, of which Nora most assuredly would have informed him, the young Earl of Clarington could not have insisted upon anything. That left . . . a man he no longer knew if he could trust.

Pushing off on the balls of his feet, Grayson sprinted to the stable yard and shouted for his horse.

The sound of hooves crunching on gravel echoed through the trees and set Nora's already tense nerves on edge. Who would be cantering a horse on this part of the property, far from the riding lanes? Between the tree trunks, she spied flashes of Grayson rounding the nearest bend in the drive, his tall figure bent low over his mount's neck.

When he cleared the curve and came into view, the look on his face made her stomach clench. She quickly drew Jonny beside her, out of the Thoroughbred's way, and braced for ill tidings.

Grayson reined in as he reached them, the sudden stop sending gravel spitting in all directions. Pellets struck Nora's skirts, but she paid them no mind. She went to him and pressed a hand to his thigh, feeling the rigid muscles bunch beneath her palm. "What is it? What's happened?"

"You're in quite a furor, old boy." Chad spoke from just behind her shoulder. "What can I do?"

Grayson's gaze shifted between her, Chad and Jonny, his tension obvious in the angle of his chin, the thrust of his shoulders, the way he held the reins aloft as if poised for flight. He looked confused, disoriented, and Nora's concerns took a fearful tumble. Was he lapsing into one of his previous episodes? Would he begin ranting, threatening?

But then his posture relaxed and his hands lowered to rest on his thighs. "When the coach returned without you, I grew worried."

"Didn't Clements tell you we'd decided to walk?" Nora slid her hand to cover one of his. "It's such a rare morning without rain, we couldn't pass up the opportunity."

Grayson swung a leg over the horse's rump and dismounted. "I'm sorry. A terrible sensation gripped me that something might have been wrong." He wiped a sleeve across his glistening brow. Jonny had moved beside Nora, and Grayson handed him Constantine's reins. "If you wouldn't mind." When the boy silently accepted the responsibility for leading the horse back to the stables, Grayson added, "Thanks, old man."

"Sure you're all right? You're looking distinctly pallid."

At Chad's query, Grayson flinched, and made Nora flinch in turn as he took a brisk step closer to the earl. "And how is it you came to be part of this morning's outing?"

Chad's brow creased in a slight frown. He shrugged a shoulder. "I was out for a walk when the coach passed by."

"You were out for a walk?" A muscle worked in Grayson's cheek. "Before breakfast?"

"A bit odd for me, I realize, but I woke early and couldn't get back to sleep. But never mind about me. What happened to send you thundering after us? Surely this premonition of yours didn't arise from thin air."

"You are correct," Grayson said calmly, and Nora wondered if perhaps she had only imagined his anger a moment earlier. He waited for Jonny to lead Constantine a few more paces ahead of them. "Gibbs had a report for me earlier that made me worry about Nora and Jonny being abroad alone." His gaze swept his friend's length. "But they weren't alone, were they?"

Chad replied with a question of his own. "What did Gibbs say?"

"It appears you may be right about thieves prowling the property. A local man was out fishing the night before you arrived, and spotted someone down on the beach."

"Good heavens." A jolt of alarm had Nora instinctively craning her neck for a view of Jonny as he disappeared with the horse around the turn in the drive.

"Did he get a good look at this man?" The contents of the basket rattled lightly at Chad's side. Nora had forgotten all about Jonny's collected treasures. She reached to take back the basket, but Chad seemed not to notice her gesture. His attention remained focused on Gray. "Could this prowler be identified?"

"Regrettably, no." Grayson returned his friend's scrutiny. "It was too dark."

"A shame."

"Indeed."

"And all the more reason for the two of you to consider leaving Blackheath Grange." Chad held up a hand as if to forestall an impending protest. "For a time, at least."

"We've been through this," Nora put in. "And we decided—"

"You decided," Grayson interrupted. "And I went along with it because you have your father's skill at bullying people, though you employ decidedly more subtle means." Though couched in a jest, his assertion nonetheless rankled. She tossed him an incredulous look and searched his face for an explanation, but he noticed neither. All his attention remained focused on Chad. "We'll consider leaving."

*   *   *

"What was that about earlier?" Nora demanded the very instant she managed to corner Grayson alone in the drawing room following supper that evening.

Jonny had retired to his room with Kat. The glow of Chad's pipe floated through the darkness beyond the windows as he paced the terrace. For the first time since breakfast, they were alone. She intended for them to remain that way until she had her answers.

"What was what about?" Grayson looked as though he wished to slip away, but she had effectively trapped him between a pair of chairs, a sofa table and the pianoforte.

"Outside on the drive this morning." She set her hands on her hips and backed him up against a wing chair until he was forced to sit. "I know you had feared for Jonny's and my safety at first, but even after you discovered us safe, you seemed peeved for no reason with Chad. The two of you behaved like a couple of gamesters playing for high stakes, each vigilantly preventing the other from seeing his hand."

He grabbed her wrist and pulled her into his lap. When he'd settled her comfortably across his thighs, he pressed his lips to her brow. "All right, my lovely paramour. You have me. I've something important to tell you and I didn't wish to do so in front of Chad. I was disappointed not to catch you alone."

"Is that the truth? There is no trouble between you and Chad?"

Even as he kissed her and gave his assurances, she could not banish a niggling sensation that he was hiding something. Yet she said, "I can sympathize with you. You know I'd hoped to ask questions during my visits with the tenants."

"Yes, quite against my advice."

"Then you'll be relieved to hear that with Chad along, I learned nothing."

"How so?"

"His presence made such questions awkward, and he has a way of stealing a conversation, doesn't he?"

"He always did." A perplexed expression claimed his features, and Nora realized she had distracted him from his original intention.

With her fingertips she smoothed away his frown. "What did you wish to tell me?"

"Better if I simply show you." He raised her to her feet, giving her bottom a pat as he stood up beside her. "Come with me."

Minutes later, they stood in Alexander Lowell's former study, staring up at the portrait of the man, a boyhood version of Grayson standing to his left, Thomas to his right.

"What is it I'm supposed to see?"

Grayson stepped closer to the painting. "I actually spoke to this picture today, asking what the devil we were supposed to be looking for." He peered at her over his shoulder. "And to prove I've quite gone round the bend, the picture answered."

He gestured toward his father's image. "See the fob? Each Earl of Clarington inherits the Clarington pocket watch. It's been missing ever since Tom died."

Baffled, Nora shook her head. "Yes, but—"

"Jonny's yellow circles."

She felt her eyes go wide.

"They represent the watch, monogrammed with a *C*."

"Good lord. Of course."

"He's obviously obsessed with it. I'm convinced if we found it we could persuade him to speak. And then we might learn what happened to his father." His hand fisted as if around that scrap of hope. But another thought occurred to Nora.

"Gray, suppose Jonny already knows where the watch is? Perhaps he hid it away for safekeeping, and what we must do is persuade him to show us where."

"I hadn't thought of that." His hand opened and his

shoulders visibly slumped. "Perhaps he merely took it from Tom's bedroom after he died, his way of remaining close to his father. In that case, finding it won't help solve anything, will it?"

Her heart ached to assure him otherwise. Opening her arms, she embraced him, pressing his head to her shoulder and rocking him tenderly as she might have done Jonny. "I don't know. I only know that whatever happens"—she tightened her arms around him—"I love you."

"At times I wish you didn't." His lips moved against her neck, leaving traces of warm moisture. "And I thank God you do."

*Chapter 23*

They spent the next day searching the rooms frequented by Jonny. At times they split up, with Grayson exploring his nephew's bedroom while Nora resumed the lessons she'd begun with the boy. Later, he and Chad brought Jonny out to the stables to ride Puck, while Nora stole the opportunity to comb through the schoolroom.

Now Grayson climbed the stairs to the third floor to meet her in the old playroom, high beneath the eaves. Minutes ago he had watched Chad drive away in the curricle. He was traveling up to Helston today, ostensibly to speak with a solicitor about some new investments that had caught his interest.

*Ostensibly.* True, Chad had conducted business in Helston in the past, but why hadn't he arranged for these particular investments before he left London? Why suddenly now?

And was it an accident that Chad had accompanied Nora and Jonny on their visits to the tenant farms? While Chad might eagerly arise at dawn for a race on horseback across the moors, early morning walks were utterly out of character for him, always had been. Grayson suspected his friend might have been listening outside the morning room when he and Nora had discussed her plans, and had contrived to meet her later on the drive.

He groaned inwardly. He detested these suspicions concerning his friend, loathed himself for even entertaining such notions. Yet ignoring them, flatly denying them as false, could put Nora and Jonny at risk. And that was why, as soon as Chad had left, Grayson had sent one of his tenant's sons to ride to Helston and back.

He shook his skepticism aside and slipped a hand into his coat pocket, fingertips making contact with the object he'd put there. His search that morning had brought him to Charlotte's former bedchamber. He didn't quite know why. Perhaps it had been an act of defiance or challenge or simple frustration to stand in the room of the one person who seemed to know all the answers—but refused to reveal them. He'd gone so far as to call her name and dare her to appear. She hadn't, of course. But on his way out, the sight of three miniature paintings hanging in a row from a velvet ribbon made him wonder if Charlotte hadn't summoned him to her room after all. He'd removed the bottommost painting, and now he intended it as a surprise for Nora, one he hoped might make her smile.

It was a selfish hope, really. The tilt of her lips and the light in her eyes had the power to make him forget everything—regrets and ghosts and silent little boys—if only for an instant.

The playroom door stood open, spilling the odors of must and abandonment onto the landing, for even Jonny no longer played here. Grayson found Nora sitting on a small hooked rug with her skirts tucked beneath her, her arms folded around a porcelain-faced doll with golden curls and a ruffled gown.

She glanced up with a rueful expression. "I don't suppose Jonny would have hidden his watch inside a doll."

"That would be one of my aunt Pricilla's. She had quite a collection as a child."

"I've always loved dolls." Nora patted the gleaming

curls into place and fluffed the layers of yellowing satin skirts as lovingly as she might have done for a real little girl.

His chest tightened at the sight. "My guess is that playing at being a mama was a game you loved most as a child."

"Yes." With a sigh, her expression turned solemn. "But I no longer have the luxury of playing. Jonny needs a real mother, and at present, I am the only one he's got."

Outside, the breeze coursing beneath the eaves echoed of long-ago laughter. She stood and set the doll on a bench piled with other dolls and forgotten toy bears. "His parents need us as well. We have a job to do. Did you find anything in his bedroom?"

"Not a thing." Grayson feigned interest in the tattered coat of the rocking horse while battling a keen sense of chagrin. Nora's focus never wavered from Jonny's and his parents' needs, while his main concern these many months had been his own guilt.

He flicked a cobweb from the pony's moth-bitten ear, his other hand patting the small weight inside his pocket. He wanted only for the right moment. "I checked all the nooks and crannies I could think of. He keeps his room so tidy. . . . So unlike other boys his age."

"I know." She clasped her sleek artist's hands together. "I long to see a streak of dirt across his face, a tear in his shirt. Or find him sprawled on the ground, wrestling with a local boy." Her chin came up. "That is why we cannot give up. Why we must keep searching."

She knelt before a painted wooden chest against the wall and opened the lid. The contents clunked, rattled and jingled as she rifled through them.

"Funny you should say that." He knelt beside her. "About longing to see Jonny tussling about like a mischievous scamp. I have something for you."

He reached into his coat pocket and drew out the oval, gold-framed miniature portrait he'd found earlier that morning. "I'd forgotten all about this. I thought you might like it."

"Like it? Oh, Gray, it's wonderful." The little portrait filled her palm and she sat with her head bent over it, uttering a gasp of pleasure. "When was it done?"

"He was about four, I believe. Tom had commissioned a local artist to paint a family portrait, but that morning Jonny slipped away from his nurse for a romp in the garden. He wasn't gone long, but somehow managed to return as dirty and unkempt as a stable hand."

Touching a finger to the painted image, Grayson laughed softly through the pain evoked by the bittersweet memory. "Instead of the throttling Tom said the boy deserved, Charlotte scooped him up, sat him on a stool and insisted the artist paint him exactly as he was."

"Oh, I do like her so very much. I wish I had known her while she lived. . . ." She hugged the portrait to her bosom. She blinked, turning her face away.

Grayson caught her chin. "Charlotte would have adored you. Does adore you. I know she would want you to have this picture."

"This is the single most thoughtful gift I've ever received." Setting the little painting aside, she tossed her arms around him with a grateful squeeze that for an instant made him feel rather like the luckiest man alive.

She eased away, holding him at arm's length and beaming at him. "I have something for you too." She pushed to her knees, her hands gripping his shoulders for leverage. "You must come to my studio to see it."

"Do you mean my portrait?" He tugged her into his lap, turning her in his arms and cradling her as she had cradled Aunt Pricilla's doll. "I've already seen it."

She gasped. "You sneak! Never peek at an artist's work without permission."

"I thought being the subject of that work, not to mention the artist's husband, surely granted me a privilege or two."

"Humph." What began as a scowl melted into apprehension. "Well . . . what did you think of it?"

She poked his ribs when he didn't immediately answer. Truth was, he was searching for the right words to express his gratitude over the changes. Not that he cared so much how he appeared in a painting, but he did care exceedingly much how *she* saw him. As a good man. A compassionate man. A man worthy of her love.

When he could think of no words adequate enough, he rolled her onto the floor and anchored himself over her.

His mouth to her ear, he whispered, "It's perfect. Just like you. Thank you."

"You're welcome." Her arms came around his neck.

Desire flared and he kissed her again. Letting his chest graze the tips of her breasts, he rubbed back and forth against her while narrowing the V of his legs on either side of her thighs. With her moans to urge him on, he dipped his head and set his lips to her throat, then lower, across her bodice. She was as warm and pliant as a kitten beneath him. His loins ached with the knowledge that here on the top floor of the house, they were very much alone.

Her gasping breaths and her squirming body told him she was all too willing. But against his neck, her lips spoke to the contrary.

"Gray . . . perhaps we shouldn't. We're supposed to be searching. Besides, I've been away from Jonny for nearly two hours now. It's time I went downstairs to check on him and Kat."

"As usual, you're right." His arms tightened around her. He rolled again, setting her on top of him, and nestled her head beneath his chin. "But don't move away just yet. Stay in my arms a while longer."

In some ways, simply holding her, savoring the weight of her against his chest and inhaling the fragrance of her skin and hair, felt as good, as life renewing, as making love to her. Unhurried and tranquil, it conveyed a sense of permanence, as though his world might not fall apart tomorrow. He could have held her like that long into the night, and considered himself the luckiest of men.

But the truth remained, never far away. "We may never find it," he murmured against a lock of her hair that lay strewn across his lips. "The watch, I mean. Probably washed out to sea all those months ago."

"We're not giving up," she replied, her quiet conviction vibrating gently against him. Retrieving the miniature of Jonny from the floor beside them, she stared intently into it. "If not the watch, our search will yield something else of vital importance. Charlotte was very clear—"

"Charlotte was not at all clear. I believe *cryptic* is the correct word."

She stiffened against him. He'd spoken more harshly than he intended. He stroked her hair, kissed the top of her head. "Forgive me. I'm . . . tired."

Yes, but the weariness of so many sleepless nights combined now with a knife-edged fear: that the only revelation their search would yield was proof his friend had betrayed them.

He should tell her. Warn her. But speaking the words would give them all the more feasibility, and that was something he wished to forestall for as long as possible.

She lifted her chin, and he felt the weight of her gaze upon him. "You must not give up hope. I will not allow it. Do you understand me?"

"Ah, there you go, being Zachariah's daughter again."

"Your promise, please."

He raised them both to a sitting position and kissed her, tenderly, but long and fully. "You have my word. I shall not give up hope, not as long as I have you guiding me."

"Good." She looked regretful. "Now I must go down and check on Jonny and Kat. Care to join me?"

He was about to accept her offer, but before he could speak, the crunch of carriage wheels drifted from three stories below. Could Chad have arrived back so soon?

But it wasn't his friend whom Grayson hurried out to see. It was young Rob Massey, whom Grayson had hired that morning to track Chad to Helston. Grayson stood waiting in the Massey's barnyard when Rob rode in.

"I'm sorry, Sir Grayson, I never caught up to him." Reaching into his pocket, the youth pulled out the note Grayson had written that morning, a request for Chad to purchase some items that could not be found in Millford. That way, Rob did not have to know the true reason he was sent to follow the Earl of Wycliffe.

"You never saw him on the road?"

"Neither going nor coming, sir."

"He would have been in my curricle." Grayson couldn't help clinging to that hope Nora had spoken of in such adamant terms. "You *do* know my curricle, don't you? Gleaming black, with a removable canvas roof and the Clarington crest on the doors?"

"Of course, sir. Never saw it."

"Very well." A part of him withered, along with every happy memory he had of his friend. In their place stood the recent warning from Gibbs: *perhaps the late Earl of Clarington trusted where he should not have.*

He wouldn't make his brother's mistake. No, he needed a plan and fast, a way to distance Chad from

Nora and Jonny until he knew of a certainty whether or not their guest could be trusted.

"Thank you, Rob." He pressed some coins into the young man's hand. "Here's a little extra for your trouble."

Two days of renewed optimism. In that time, Jonny had finally spoken, and Gray had smiled, laughed and taken Nora in his arms again, into—she had believed—his heart. Two days of hope for all of them—dashed by suppertime that evening.

Now she found herself seated opposite a stranger at the dining table, while a puzzled Earl of Wycliffe attempted to dispel the tension between them.

"An excellent supper, Nora." Chad took a last bite of brandied apricot torte and leaned back in his chair. "Gray, my congratulations. Your new wife is a woman of many talents."

Gray's quiet reply of "Indeed" did little to reassure her. He hadn't done much more with his food than push it around his plate. Hadn't said more than a terse word here and there, his expression shuttered and impossible to interpret.

She felt him slipping away again. What had she done? She thought back to their encounter in the playroom. He had been so sweet, and so utterly thoughtful both in the gift he'd given her and in understanding why she had put off his amorous advances.

But the more she pondered it, the more she realized the shift in his mood had started much earlier, as early as yesterday morning when he had raced down the drive on horseback, certain some danger had befallen her and Jonny. And the way he'd acted toward Chad then, hesitant and aloof, as if his friend of many years had suddenly become a stranger.

Yet quite to the contrary, following Chad's return from Helston this afternoon, the two men had spent long hours in the billiard room, then went riding, and afterward cloistered themselves in the parlor, playing chess.

At no time had Gray asked either Nora or Jonny to join them. Even when Chad had inquired whether she could ride, Grayson had dismissed her horsemanship as rudimentary and insisted Chad's love of a good gallop precluded her from going with them.

Now, as she emulated Grayson in pushing apricots, pastry and rich sauce around on her plate, she sifted through the events of the past two days. By not agreeing to make love with him this morning, had she led him to believe that Jonny claimed the greater portion of her heart, and now he resented her for it?

Chad commented again about the meal, about her hospitality.

"It is my pleasure. I'll never forget how kind you were to me in London. . . ." She broke off as a thought struck her.

*Devil take Grayson Lowell if he doesn't realize what a damned lucky fellow he is.* Chad's emphatic declaration yesterday morning had left her disconcerted, and once more pondering that elusive quality that had always raised ambiguous feelings toward him.

Perhaps he had spoken to Grayson afterward, and conveyed some of her worries concerning his state of mind and the state of their marriage. And Grayson indeed might have taken this as a betrayal on her part, to have spoken about him behind his back.

She swallowed a sudden urge to cry. Across the table, Grayson tugged at his neckcloth, already askew. Even in a few short hours, the brackets around his mouth and eyes appeared to have deepened, the shadows to have darkened.

"I'll have you know I whipped your husband soundly at the chessboard today, Nora." Chad tipped his head with exaggerated pride. "Why don't you and I have a go at it this evening?"

"Nora doesn't play."

Her mouth fell open, her reply silenced by the blunt denial.

"No?" Chad regarded her curiously. "I believe I distinctly remember you telling Belinda you enjoyed chess very much."

"Why, I—"

"What my wife must have said," Grayson muttered in a voice she barely recognized as his, "is that she would enjoy learning. Thus far she hasn't had the opportunity."

"I see. . . ." The earl gazed back and forth between them. "I'd be happy to teach you, Nora."

"That would take days." Grayson folded his arms across he chest. The exchange left her speechless, heartsick.

"A game of cards, then?"

"There aren't many games that work well for three." Grayson pushed back his chair and stood. His fingers yanked his neckcloth free. "Remember that old dartboard the footmen hung below stairs? Let's have a round or two."

Nora too started to stand. As she did, Chad hurried to hold her chair for her. "How about it, Nora? Ever tossed a dart?"

Her chest aching, thoughts reeling, she gazed across at Gray, the length of the table seemingly an insurmountable gulf between them. His closed expression provided her answer. She shook her head. "Thank you, but no. I should tend to Jonny."

*Chapter 24*

Grayson adjusted his finger in the niche of the sliding panel and tried again. Like the first time, the portal gave a slight jiggle and budged no farther.

He wished merely to steal into her room, watch her sleep, kiss her brow, and assure her of something of the utmost importance. In her slumber she would not hear, but there were words he desperately needed to say.

He set his candle on the bottom step and used his other hand for leverage to open the panel. But as he'd already guessed, the problem resulted from no malfunction of the lock.

Somehow Nora had improvised a lock. He wondered when she had done this. Days ago, when he'd surprised her in his room and tossed his bedclothes and clock about in a rage? Or had she finally decided she'd had her fill of him tonight?

He wouldn't have blamed her. He'd been detestable all evening, but in the short time since his life had taken yet another bizarre twist, he hadn't been able to devise any better means of protecting her. *If* she needed protecting. Even now, he couldn't entirely be sure. The hope she instilled in him refused to die, and, despite growing evidence to the contrary, he clung to the notion that one of his hired watchers might witness

Thomas's ghost walking along the beach . . . and clear Chad of guilt.

There had been no such reports from the headland. And where had Chad gone today? Almost assuredly not to Helston. Gray's suspicions mounted like the many debts that had once gone unpaid. He loathed himself for hurting Nora—and God, he knew he had. But for safety's sake, he wished to keep her and Jonny as far away from Chad as possible for now.

He'd considered telling Nora the truth. Christ, each time he'd had to step between her and Chad with a cutting remark and a quelling look, he had simply wanted to draw her aside and tell her what he had learned.

But what *had* he learned? All he had were suspicions, and what might only amount to troubling coincidences. Before he'd be willing to condemn his friend, he needed more evidence linking Chad to the goods in the cave and, possibly—his gut wrenched as he contemplated it—Tom's death.

Tom might have trusted where he should not have. Yes, in the very same person Grayson had trusted all his life.

Had he invited a murderer into his home, into his family? Then *not* telling Nora might be the surest way to ensure her safety, for if Chad did prove guilty, and he detected signs that Nora knew of his guilt, what might he do to silence her?

Grayson didn't mind putting himself in danger. What of it? But he'd see both himself and Chad in hell before he'd allow anything or anyone to harm his wife and nephew.

He gave the panel one final, futile tug. Her message to him was clear.

*Stay out.*

He pressed the flats of his hands to the door. "Nora, forgive me," he whispered. "I will make this up to you. As soon I know you and Jonny are safe, I swear I will make amends."

The following day brought more storms. More questions. More of Grayson's inexplicable behavior.

He had ordered breakfast sent to Nora's room this morning, a gesture that gave her reason to rejoice. She had believed he would be joining her and they would share some rare time alone together. Perhaps his dour mood had passed. She had held the notion close to her heart as she waited for him. But he hadn't come. Alone, crestfallen, she had finally swallowed a few cold spoonfuls of porridge before pushing away the tray. Grayson, meanwhile, had breakfasted with Chad in the morning room, and soon afterward they had left the house.

Later she had found him alone in the drawing room. With little to lose, she had put her arms around him and kissed him, hoping to reignite the spark that had so recently flared between them. Had she only imagined his response, the heat in his lips, the shudder of passion that passed from the taut planes of his body into hers?

But at the sound of Chad's booted footsteps outside the room, Grayson had thrust her to arm's length, silenced her stammered protest with a severe look and left her to join his friend.

Thunder rumbled, rattling the windowpanes in the schoolroom and wrapping Nora in a sense of dismal isolation, despite sitting across the oaken library table from Jonny and Kat.

With a weary sigh she eased to her feet. When the boy questioned her with a lift of his solemn blue eyes, she managed a smile, a painful effort that tapped what little fortitude remained to her.

"You and Kat continue playing if you like. My head is aching. I'm going to lie down before supper." At his sudden frown of concern she added, "No doubt the result of your growing monopoly of the world's riches and my impending poverty."

She alluded to the game she had devised for him, presently cluttering the table at which they sat. For the past couple of hours, she, Jonny and Kat had moved tiny wooden ships around a map of the world, "sailing" according to the roll of a die from port to port to either buy, discover or trade goods accumulated along the way.

Thus far Jonny had bartered for tropical fruits in the West Indies, discovered gold in Mexico, bought silk in China, and was now working his way to India and the exotic spices to be found there. The first to make his or her way back to England with a large treasury and a cargo hold filled with riches won the game.

The boy fingered the stack of tiny silk squares cut from one of her old scarves. Beside that a pile of amber beads from a broken necklace twinkled in the lamplight—that was Jonny's "gold".

Despite his victories, he showed little enthusiasm for the game today. Nora had attempted inviting both Gray and Chad to join them, and while Chad had showed interest, Gray had waved her off.

*We've no time today for children's games.*

If they were continuing their investigations of the estate and surrounding areas, Grayson might simply have said as much. She would have understood, would have wished them luck.

The hardest part had been watching the disappointment wilt Jonny's eager expression. On the surface, he and Grayson had taken no great strides into their relationship. But Nora knew better. No longer did she see the frightened child who had once cowered at his uncle's touch. Jonny remained silent and Grayson continued to be tentative with the boy, but she had sensed, or thought she sensed, a sincere and growing desire on both their parts to, well, be a family.

But today Grayson had flat out rejected his nephew, and now with each halfhearted roll of the die, she had sensed Jonny's thoughts drifting farther and farther away until even the silence she had so grown accustomed to seemed ponderous.

The first raindrops pattered the windows. She leaned to press a kiss to the top of his head. "Do leave a trade route or two open for Kat. I'll see you both later."

Outside in the corridor the cheerfulness she had maintained for Jonny's sake abandoned her. Her back sagging to the wall, she scrubbed at the tears rolling down her cheeks, each one a scalding memory of Grayson's disregard.

*If you wouldn't mind, Nora, we've business to discuss. I daresay, it's nothing that would interest you.*

Curt and condescending, and as painful as if he'd slapped her.

What had she done to make him so despise her? Did he resent her private talk with Chad, or had he grown jealous of her affections for his friend? But that latter notion was madness. After all they had been through in so short a time, after all her assurances that she would never leave his side no matter what happened, surely Grayson could not think so little of her.

Perhaps it *was* madness. The notion sent a chill shimmying down her back. He had tried many times to warn her about his true nature. Perhaps she should have listened, and not invested her heart in a Grayson that didn't truly exist, that was no more than an illusion.

The corridor darkened with the approaching storm. She wanted only to reach her room, shut the door and give in to these abominable tears, if only for a brief time. Until a better plan occurred to her.

She had almost reached her threshold when the sound of Grayson's voice stopped her cold.

"Nora, wait. I wish to speak to you."

Yes, she wished to speak to him too, wished to give him a piece of her mind and demand why he would toss away love as though it were so much rubbish. But not now, not with her anger and wounded pride and these blasted tears between them. In her experience, tears never solved anything, only made matters worse.

Without turning to look at him, she strode into her room, flinging the door closed behind her.

Except that it didn't close. When a slam should have vibrated her walls, she heard only a thud. She whirled, glared, while her heart clogged her throat and impeded every scathing remark sizzling for release.

Lightning hurled his face into stark relief, his eyes fierce against the jagged definition of his features. He stepped into the room and closed the door softly behind him.

She backed away, for although he made no move to touch her, his presence surrounded her, suffocated her. Threatened to release those tears like floodwaters. Thunder boomed, reverberating through the room.

"What do you want?"

He moved toward her. "Nora, I—"

"No." She took another step back. If the past days had taught her anything, it was that he possessed the power to hurt her deeply. She needed space, and safety, between them. "Whatever it is, tell me from where you are."

"I know you're angry with me. I understand—"

"You understand?" The word, the audacity of it in light of his recent behavior, set off a firestorm inside her. "Don't you dare patronize me. You've been a cad of the worst sort and I . . ." The words trailed away. Rain lashed the house. Had she been about to wish him to the devil? Offer up an ultimatum?

"I can explain, if you'll let me. But I haven't much time." His face was a study in shadows, infinite ones, yet still so ruggedly handsome despite the ravages of sleeplessness and guilt. Within those shadows, his stormy eyes blazed with tenderness, possessing her, caressing her as they did only at the most intimate of moments.

She didn't want him handsome, tender. Irresistible. She *needed* her anger. Needed that self-righteous indignation to shore her up because, blast it all, he had made her love him, then treated her merely as a woman he'd been forced to marry.

And *that* hurt more than she had words to describe.

After all she had endured for him and from him. After all the good she had insisted on seeing in him.

And then she realized what he had said. "You haven't time to what?" she said. "Fit me into your demanding schedule? Never mind, then. You wanted to hurt me and you did. But you hurt Jonny as well. And that I cannot forgive." Indignation coursed through her in great, hot gusts. "Get out. I don't want you here."

No, because those damned tears were falling, burning her skin and stinging her eyes. She turned her back on him. Moments passed, taut and brittle, while her tears and the rain smeared the view outside and she thought certainly he had left the room by now.

She heard footsteps in the corridor, assumed they were his, but when she peeked over her shoulder to ensure that he had complied with her wishes, she discovered him standing behind her, a breath away.

His strong arms seized her, turned her. She gasped. He clutched her to him and kissed her, swallowing her cries of protest. Went on kissing her, filling her mouth with the taste of him and her own tears until the struggle melted out of her, until she could only lean into the solidness of his chest and cling to the one thing beyond her easel that had ever, ever brought her joy.

Even if that joy were little more now than the lingering smolder of a lightning bolt.

His hands were on her face, in her hair, cupping her cheeks. His lips moved against hers. "Trust me. That's all I can tell you. All I can ask of you. But do it." His fingers tightened, insisted. "Please."

Something in his entreaty caused the blistering resentment inside her to still, to listen. But the hurt ran deep, was still too new and raw to be ignored.

She pulled away, glowering at him from behind wisps of hair pulled loose by his roaming, claiming fingers. "That is all? No explanation? Nothing?"

Beyond her closed door, the footsteps became louder, closer. Grayson pricked his ears and held up a hand to silence her while he listened. The rain maintained its constant lament against the house, taken up by the somber growl of thunder.

"Gray? Nora? Are you up here?"

It was Chad.

Neither of them answered. In the tense moments that followed, she watched Gray's expression change, saw the tender urgency freeze to an icy disdain that sent her hopes plummeting.

"You have nothing to say," she challenged.

"Nothing else," he murmured.

"Get out, then." She shoved at his chest, but she needn't have. He was already backing away. Then he turned and was gone, shutting the door behind him.

A sob sent her lurching forward until she was up against the door, arms outstretched, fingers spread, cheek flat to the wood. She thought of Charlotte—wretched Charlotte, mourning what she'd once had, grieving for what she might never have again. Her heart splintered as, from the other side, the men's jovial voices drifted along the corridor.

"Dornie sent me up to convey a message from Cook," Chad was saying. "There's been some minor disaster in the kitchen and supper is going to be about half an hour later than usual. Simply can't be helped, I'm afraid."

"Not a problem, my friend. A quick game of chess?"

About an hour later, Nora heard a creak above her head.

The storm had lulled to a drizzle, rendering the thunder mute for now. Lying in the middle of her bed, she left off feeling thoroughly miserable, sat up and went utterly still, face tipped toward the canopy above her.

A minute passed. Then she heard it again. The whimpered complaint of an ancient floorboard. Not directly above her head, but off to her left, over her dressing room.

It could only be Grayson in the attic. But why? If he had tried to access her room through the sliding panel, he would have discovered the way barred. She had never removed the wire holding the panel and wardrobe in place. In fact, in the events of the past days, she had forgotten all about it. At any rate, the one time Grayson had spent in her bed, he had entered the room through one of its conventional doors.

Another creak convinced her she hadn't imagined the previous ones. Did he think she'd come up to meet him? Did he wish her to? Based on everything he had said and done these past two days, her only answer could be a resounding no.

Yet . . . the *no* that tolled inside her dissipated on a wavering note.

*Trust me . . . do it. . . .*

He'd added a *please,* but that had done little to soften the effrontery of his demand.

*Do it.* As if it were easy. As if darkness hadn't once more invaded his mind, as if—

Something brushed her, touched her. Surrounded her, like a cool embrace.

*"If you cannot trust him, Nora, trust yourself."*

"Charlotte?" As with each visitation, a chill raked the hairs on her nape and arms; her pulse sped to a canter. And yet something had changed. The currents running through the air and beneath her skin felt drained of energy. She probed the room's deepest shadows, searching for that uncanny light she knew so well. "Where are you? I cannot see you."

*"Time runs short. You must be your own guide. Must look into your heart and believe that what you see there is the truth."*

A burst of vexation sent Nora to her feet. "You speak always of truth, yet reveal nothing."

*"I've told you I cannot."* Another brush across her shoulders sent Nora spinning about, only to confront her bedside table.

"At least tell me what's happening to Grayson."

*"You do not need me to tell you about Grayson. You already know. Trust yourself, Nora. Trust. . . ."*

The voice faded, leaving her standing, trembling, alone in the middle of her room.

Did she—*could* she—trust herself? Her beliefs, her convictions, her ability to judge the world and the people around her?

She had loved him. Loved him still. Had she been utterly wrong to place her heart in his keeping? Her creature of darkness. *Hers.*

Why? Because within the darkness she had seen something in him no one else had. Because she looked at the world differently than most people. What did solid objects, defined and finite, mean to her artist's eyes? Eyes were frail things, easily tricked. Art had taught her to view the world with her instincts, her intuition, to see in terms of light and shadow, form and substance. The essence of a subject. The soul.

Had she seen his soul, or only what she wished, hoped, to see?

A small pair of pliers lay beside her hairbrush on the dressing table, left behind by Gibbs. She snatched them up and went to the wardrobe.

Just as she gave the wire one last twist to release

the wardrobe from the panel, a current of air fluttered against her cheek.

*"Do not leave Jonny. Watch over him."*

"I will never leave him," she replied to the emptiness. "No matter what, I shall always be here to take care of him. I swear it."

An impulse, raised by a startling wisp of thought, had prompted Grayson to make his excuses to Chad and race up to his bedchamber. From there he had wasted no time in opening the sliding wall panel and taking the steps two at a time.

In the waning afternoon light, the garret's small window angled a dull diamond pattern across the floor. Near his feet, the feather tick lay glowing in the murky shadows like a ghost at rest, which, in a way, it was. A phantom memory of this room's original purpose.

A hiding place. By God, why hadn't he thought of this sooner?

After he and Tom had first discovered this room with its sparse contents, a series of recurrent events during their childhood had fallen repugnantly into place. Their father seemingly absent from the house for hours. Maids neglecting their work but, oddly, not sacked for it. Their mother complaining of strange noises traveling down the walls of her chamber, sounds no one could trace to their source. Even now, Grayson cringed to think of his overbearing, self-absorbed father trysting with his lovers here, above his wife's head, and she none the wiser.

But this attic had once played a far more significant function, as a bit of research had divulged. Just as the sliding panels downstairs revealed no trace of what lay beyond, the feather tick, devoid of a frame, would make no telltale creaks in the night. The Lowell family, secretly and dangerously Catholic during Henry VIII's Reformation, had needed a convenient and secure place to hide their priest.

As a testament to just how perilous England's changing religious and political climate was then, the family had thought far enough ahead to realize the advantage of providing two ways into—and out of—this lair. One opened upon his bedroom.

The other . . . Nora's. It couldn't have been any more convenient.

He reached a decision. He would tell Nora of his suspicions concerning Chad. If need be, she and Jonny could take shelter here.

Planning to go to her, to break down the door between their dressing rooms if necessary in order to speak with her, he turned to descend to his room. The light patter of footsteps, slippers tapping on bare risers, stopped him short.

For what possible reason would she climb those stairs? Surely not to see him. He had played his deceit all too well these past three days. Yet as the sound drew closer, the air that should have occupied his windpipe was replaced by a piercing hope.

The attic door on her side opened, and still he mistrusted what his eyes told him. Surely the graceful shadow hovering on the threshold could only be another ghost come to haunt him.

"I heard you up here." Her whisper sent the breath surging from his lungs, brought tiny pinpoints of light dancing before his eyes.

In two strides he reached her and tugged her into his arms. Real. She was real. In his elation, he wrapped her tight, closing as much of his body as possible around her. "My paramour. You are here."

"I am here."

The words brought him to his knees and she with him. There seemed no divisions between them; they were of one breath, one heat, one body joined at the arms and torso and lips.

A single reservation prompted him to ease his cheek from the warmth of hers. He pulled back to gaze into her lovely, infinite eyes. "I won't ask you to forgive me. Not yet. But can you, do you—"

"Yes. I trust you."

The gift of that simple statement racked him with relief. He pressed her to him, surrounded himself with her, fought back tears as she folded her love around him.

Clothing came off, peeled away to blanket the floor and the pallet on which they sprawled. His world became the fire in her lips, the satin heat of her breasts, the scorching strength of her thighs squeezing for purchase around his waist.

As her moans filled his mouth, he drove into her, drove with his tongue and his loins and his soul.

"Yours." His whisper rasped in his throat, stinging with urgency. He drew nearly out of her, then plunged deep, deeper. "I am yours."

"Yes. Mine." She pushed up against him, impelling him deeper still. "As I am yours."

With a heave he rolled with her, setting her on top. She smiled down at him with the glory of a goddess and rocked her hips, swaying him toward sheer bliss. Rolling again, he arched above her, moving in and out, sliding, delving, churning their passion to a frenzy until her cries sent the room spinning about his head, and with a roar of redemption he unleashed his passion inside her.

*Chapter 25*

A trifling thought drifted languidly through him, unable to do more than make his eyelids flutter.

It must be nearing suppertime.

Then another thought: Chad could damned well eat without them.

Followed by another, one that admittedly spit venom through him. Chad could go to the devil.

But Nora always settled Jonny down to his supper in the schoolroom with Kat before descending to the dining room, and he knew tonight must be no different.

The rain had picked up again, slapped against the little window by gusts of wind. A cloud-ridden twilight lingered beyond the dusty panes, unable to penetrate the eaves. Darkness draped the room.

He didn't need to see her to know she was there, her scant weight feather soft in his arms, her breathing butterfly delicate against his skin.

How he envied her ability to sleep so peacefully. How he loathed having to disturb her. He drew a long, luxuriating breath as a portion of her tranquillity flowed through him, relaxing him in a way he had not experienced in weeks. Months.

He kissed the crown of her head, nestled in the curve of his neck. "My paramour. Time to wake up."

"Hm." She burrowed deeper against his chest. "No."

"I'm afraid so, my love. Jonny will—"

She pulled up abruptly. "Yes, Jonny. He'll be waiting for me."

When she would have pulled to her feet, he caught her wrist and tugged her back into his arms. "You needn't run off this instant. Another minute or two shan't make a difference."

After what they had just done, he didn't have the heart to tell her about Chad. Not yet. What harm in waiting until after supper?

"It's grown so dark," she said.

"I'll go downstairs for a lamp." With a sigh he eased out from under her, then dragged his discarded shirt around her. "This will keep you warm till I get back."

He located his trousers and stepped into them.

"Gray, wait. Perhaps there are candles in the escritoire."

"Could be, I suppose." In bare feet he shuffled to the little writing cabinet. He opened the drawers and the glass-encased shelves, feeling inside with his hands. "No, there's nothing."

"Did you check the bottom cabinet?"

He smoothed his hands down the front of the piece until his palms closed over a pair of knobs. He gave a tug. "It's locked." He found his shoes and shoved his feet into them. "Don't move. I'll go down for a lantern."

"Do be careful," she called after him as he half felt, half sensed his way by memory down the staircase.

When he returned, the lantern swinging in his hand revealed her sitting up, her slender figure engulfed in the folds of his white linen shirt. Stealing a peek at him, she allowed the garment to slither down one arm. She tossed him a kiss over one exquisitely bared, alabaster shoulder.

"I thought you'd never return."

He knelt beside her and kissed her shoulder, running his tongue over its silky smoothness. "Mmm. You taste good in my shirt. You'd best beware, woman, or Jonny shall have to make do on his own tonight." His lips traveled up her neck and closed around the tip of her ear, making her shiver and laugh and squirm.

He was thinking he must make a point of doing that more often when she swatted him. "Jonny must *not* make do on his own." With a sigh she reached for her shift and corset. "Will you help me? Then I must run down and slip into a fresh gown, or the entire household will suspect the worst of us."

"Let them."

He swept her hair aside and pressed one last, lingering kiss to her nape while his free hand fondled the curve of her bottom. She released a wistful sigh, but still managed to issue a glared warning over her shoulder. He reluctantly resorted to his best behavior and helped her lace her corset after she tossed her shift over her head.

She helped him on with his shirt, her fingers delving beneath to fondle his pectoral muscle. "I like this," she murmured. "Very much."

He caught her wrist and yanked her against him, tipping her back in his arms. She lost her balance, and he knew his hold was all that kept her from falling. He leaned in and kissed her until he felt the breath leave her, and couldn't but admit he enjoyed the sensation of rendering her helpless in his embrace.

It was because she didn't fight him, because her yielding body communicated nothing but her complete trust in him . . . along with a desire that could not be denied, despite her obligations downstairs.

"I told you to beware, my paramour," he growled. "Think I was jesting?"

She looked giddy as he helped her upright.

They gathered their remaining clothing, preparing to descend the separate staircases to their bedchambers. When he raised her chin for a final kiss, her gaze slid beyond his shoulder.

"Why is it locked?"

He drew back. "Why is what locked?"

"That." She gestured with a flick of her chin. "The escritoire."

"Who knows? May have been locked for decades. Centuries."

"No." She moved to it. "It isn't that old." She ran her fingers over the rounded edges, the carved medallions on the drawer fronts. "Not very old at all. Who used this room?"

"I don't know for certain. Perhaps my father. My parents occupied our suites when they were alive. Tom and I didn't know this place existed until he inherited the house."

She straightened and faced him, her expression somber. "Did Thomas begin using the room then?"

He couldn't help smiling. "I teased him about it, saying he secreted his doxies up here. He denied it so vehemently we nearly fell to fisticuffs." His heart gave a painful squeeze. "Charlotte was all he ever needed. All he wanted. After she died, he did take occasional lovers, but he never brought them into this house."

"In memory of her." Nora's voice wavered with emotion.

"Yes, and because this was his son's home."

"But your brother knew the room existed."

"Well, yes, but what are you . . ." His throat ran dry. "My God."

She moved aside as he fell to a crouch in front of the desk.

"Damn it. Why didn't I think of it?" He gripped the wooden knobs and gave the doors a futile tug. "It only makes sense. This is the one place he could hide things where no one would ever stumble upon them."

"Perhaps the key is in one of the drawers?"

He had already opened the drawers during his

search for candles and had found nothing. He checked again. "They're empty."

"Perhaps on one of Mrs. Dorn's key rings."

"Hardly likely." He thought a moment. "Do you have a hairpin?"

Her fingers made a quick search through her hair. "I believe they've all fallen out, thanks to you. Check the floor."

They both crouched, palms sweeping the floorboards. "Here." She handed him one.

"Learned this little trick just the other day." He inserted the pin into the cabinet's lock and twisted. Twisted again. Pulled it out and tried once more. His fist rammed the door. "Confound it. She made it look like child's play."

Nora lifted his hand to her lips, kissing the raw knuckles. "Who did?"

"Your maid."

"Ah. Like so many of my father's staff, Kat is a woman of many talents."

"Talents I apparently lack. Hang it." He pushed to his feet and backed up. "There are more direct methods of opening a door. Stand clear, my love."

He lifted a foot and swung it dead center at the cabinet doors. The splintering of wood brought a burst of satisfaction. He kicked again, and the doors caved inward with a crash.

Nora stood at his shoulder, and together they stared down into the jagged hole. A quivering energy filled the room. Grayson felt the hair on his neck stand on end, felt Nora shivering beside him.

"I can feel them, Gray. Tom and Charlotte. They're here, in this room." Her hand groped for his, fingers convulsing around his own.

"I know. I believe they are telling us that the thing we've been seeking is inside that cabinet." His pulse points hammered with the certainty of it.

She nodded and released him.

"I suddenly find myself unable to move," he whispered.

"Shall I look?"

He almost said no. Almost didn't want the answers—answers with the power to brand him a murderer and his brother a criminal. Or possibly his best friend of both.

But then he thought of Charlotte and Tom, alone and grieving and caught between worlds; and Jonny, fearful and silent in a world of his own; and Nora, a world of hope and joy he had thought never to visit again.

He gave a nod. She knelt and reached inside.

"I've got something."

He heard a rustle of paper and shut his eyes.

"Gray, I'm sorry. . . . There's no pocket watch. These appear to be invoices of some sort."

She held out the stack of papers to him, but he shook his head and moved the lantern closer. "You read through them, please. Look for names and places."

Brow crinkled in concentration, she shuffled through the sheets. "This is odd. There are two copies of each, except the directions vary."

He peered at the pile in her lap. "What do you mean?"

"These are bills of lading for shipments of goods. Here." She pointed to the top of a page. "The destination indicates a location in Marseilles, France. Yet on the next page, the exact same list of goods is directed to . . ." She inched closer to the lantern. "To Hadley and Company, London."

Bile rose in his throat and for a horrifying moment he feared he'd be ill. He swallowed once, again, hands fisting for want of the appropriate neck to strangle.

"Gray." Her eyes sparked with alarm. "What is it?"

"Hadley and Company." His voice shredded, ripped apart.

"You know what it means?"

He rose and staggered to the window. Gripped the sill and stared out at the wind-whipped trees, stooped and twisted beneath the weight of the storm.

God help him, this was a truth he'd never wanted.

Despite the pain knifing his throat, his chest, everywhere, his voice was eerily calm. "Those goods made it to neither Marseilles nor London."

"How do you know?"

He turned, meeting her perplexity with infinite bleakness. "Because they are in that cave on the beach." He turned back to the window. "And God help me, now I know who put them there."

With barely a sound she came up behind him. Her length snuggled against his back and her arms slipped round his waist, cocooning him in warmth, in her gentle compassion. The knife inside him twisted less viciously because of it. Because of her. He turned in her arms and wrapped his own around her.

"Years ago, when Jonny was just learning to speak, he couldn't quite get his little mouth around the *CH* in Chad. So he called him Had. Didn't take long for it to evolve into Hadley." An ironic smile grew. This, at least, was a safe memory. "Chad fancied the nickname so much he began using it for his business concerns. Like that warehouse on the Thames."

"An earl in business?"

He shook his head. "When Thoroughbreds pull plows. No, he is the owner of several lucrative enterprises. He employs others to run them for him."

She went very still against him. "What are you saying, then? Surely Chad is not a . . ."

"A thief? Worse?" He cupped her chin, ran his thumb across her lips. "I wish to God there was some other explanation. I know my brother's financial straits made him desperate. Somehow he must have involved Chad."

"But isn't Chad enormously wealthy?"

He opened his mouth to agree, then clamped it shut on a dizzying wave of recollection. His legs wobbled, and Nora's arms tightened to steady him.

"The Holbein."

"What are you talking about?"

"The Wycliffe Holbein. It is one of the family treasures. Remember the night of our betrothal party? Belinda wanted you to see it, but Chad claimed he'd lent it to an exhibit." He pressed his fingers to his eyes. With his other hand he held fast to Nora. "He didn't. He sold it."

He watched understanding darken her expression. "Poor Chad."

"Poor Chad?" Perhaps she didn't understand, not at all.

"Yes, to be in such a dire position. To have to . . . good heavens—Uncle Had." The last words slid out as a hoarse whisper. Her fingernails dug into his forearm, threatening to pierce the skin.

"What did you say?"

"Uncle Had. Kat told me Jonny said that once in his sleep. At the time I thought he might have meant you, that his uncle had . . . done something."

She gazed out the window, tinged to charcoal by the waning twilight. "He's been so kind . . ." Her face snapped back to his. "This explains your behavior. You were keeping him away from me. From Jonny too. You were protecting us." She threw her arms around his neck and kissed him soundly. "Oh, you dear, courageous, gallant man! And to think I doubted you."

He returned her embrace, lifting her off her feet, and for an instant he felt as though the entire world had just been set to rights. Then he put her down and pressed his lips to her hair. "Forgive me for bungling it as badly as I did. I thought far better for me to hurt you than for him."

"Do you believe he would?"

"My love, we cannot trust him. I haven't proof be-yond his involvement in theft, but I think . . . that is to say, I believe he . . ." Even now, he couldn't voice it.

"I never once considered . . . Mrs. Dorn, possibly. She's been so strange, so ill-humored. She seemed to be hiding something. But Chad?" She shook her head. "What do we do?"

"To keep him at ease, we should maintain our pre-tense. I'll be his friend and remain distant toward you, my hurt and confused young bride. I've already had Gibbs send for the proper authorities. A magistrate should be arriving within the next day or so. I hope," he could not help adding.

He took the invoices from her and tucked them into the waistband of his trousers.

Nora frowned. "Do you suspect he knows about this room?"

"No. If he did he would have devised a way to steal up here and reclaim these records long before this. My guess is he came to search the house and cover his tracks."

"Why now?"

"Because I'm here now. After Tom's death I left Blackheath Grange. I returned only rarely and stayed as briefly as possible. Chad had no reason to visit an empty house. It would have looked suspicious if he had."

Her eyes opened wide. "I just remembered some-thing. The other night . . . I might have inadvertently caught him searching the library. He'd been combing through the books, and he appeared startled when I entered the room. He said he wanted something to read, but he didn't bother taking a book with him when he left."

"No. He'd been looking for something, to be sure, but not to read." Smoothing the hair from her shoul-ders, he traced his fingertips along the delicate lines of her collarbones, raising a little shiver and a ghost of longing in her eyes. "Come, my paramour. If we are to appear normal, we must be going down for supper soon."

The warmth of her palm on his cheek detained him. She rose on tiptoe, bringing her face level with his. Her features were tight, her eyes luminous. "This explains a lot. But whatever else he might have done, I still believe he is your friend. And I do not believe he hurt your brother."

"*Hurting* my brother is not the issue."

"It isn't in him. Not to do what you suspect."

"How can you be certain?"

Both hands cupped his face and dragged him close. She kissed him, then said against his lips, "I was certain about you, wasn't I?"

# Chapter 26

Dressed in rose silk, her hair restored to respectability and a false smile pasted on her face, Nora turned into Jonny's room—and discovered it empty.

An alarm went off inside her, quelled the next instant by approaching footsteps and Kat's easy voice humming a carefree tune.

"Good evening, ma'am." Carrying a bundle of folded clothing in her arms, she bobbed a curtsy and crossed to the clothespress. "Is his lordship ready for his supper?"

That little alarm set off another wail. "I came to ask you that very question, Kat. Where is he?"

The maid arranged stockings and underthings in the top drawer, a stack of shirts in the second. Then she turned, her brows gathering above her dark eyes. "Why, with you, ma'am."

"No, he isn't." Nora's heart fluttered, spreading spasms of fear through her. "I left him with you in the schoolroom."

"Yes, that was earlier."

"Do you mean to tell me you left him alone?" Fright, misgiving and anger twisted inside her. "After I explicitly ordered you never to do so?"

The other woman pulled up straighter with an indignant shake of her shoulders. "Certainly not, ma'am. The earl came for him."

"The earl?" Her voice was faint, tremulous, drowned out by the blood pounding in her ears.

"Yes, ma'am. Lord Wycliffe said you wished to see his little lordship, and so—"

Nora hoisted her skirts and started running. "Search for him, Kat," she shouted over her shoulder. "Search everywhere."

She maneuvered the corridors as fast as gown and petticoats and constricting corset would allow, becoming dizzy for want of a full breath as her legs pumped beneath her.

Less than a half hour ago she had told Gray she didn't believe Chad was capable of violence. Now Jonny was gone and she couldn't be sure, could no longer abide by instinct and sheer faith when it was the child's well-being at stake.

She found Grayson exiting his bedchamber, neat, dashing, ready for supper. Without preamble she grabbed his arm and hauled him inside. "He's somewhere with Chad."

"Who is?"

"Jonny. Chad took him. From the schoolroom. Kat told me. I'm not sure how long ago. We must find him—find him this instant. We must tell the servants to start searching. . . ."

"Slow down." He grasped her shoulders, gave her a gentle shake and drew her to his chest.

Against his hard length she sought strength, solace, reassurance; found all three for the briefest moment before pulling away. Jonny was missing; she had no right to be comforted. Breath heaving, she fisted her hands around his lapels. "We cannot sit here when—"

"I've no intention to. But I need you calm. Rational." His hands closed over hers, easing their grip on his coat. She met his gaze and nodded. "Good. Now, then. You mount a search of the house in the event they are still here."

He crossed the room, and a twinge of exasperation

eclipsed her fears. How dare he seem so composed, so methodical. "What are you going to do?"

He stopped and regarded her with no more agitation than if she'd asked what he wished for supper. "If Chad does indeed have my nephew, I fear there is only one place he would take him. One place where Jonny's life would hang in the balance. I'm going to the cliffs."

Horror flooded slowly but surely through her, like the tide that swallowed the beach each day. "But . . . they can't have gone out . . . it's grown dark . . . the storm . . ."

She gestured feebly toward the rain-lashed windows. Jonny, out in this weather, with a man who might very well wish him harm . . .

"You said you didn't know how long they've been gone. Probably left during the lull in the storm. Perhaps one, two hours, now."

"While we were . . ." With a groan she glared up at the ceiling as if she could see through to the room above, as if her gaze could set the blasted place on fire. All that time making love, imperiling Jonny's life. Her eyes fell closed. Her legs gave out and she sank to the bed. "Heaven forgive us."

He was before her in an instant. His hands gripped her again, shook her again. "You mustn't do that. We haven't time."

He released her and sprinted for his dressing room. When he didn't immediately return carrying a cloak as she expected, she rose and followed him.

She found him crouched beside an open cupboard, fiddling with something in his lap, something she couldn't see because his back was to her. She heard a sound like a marble rolling, a tamping, a series of clicks.

When Grayson stood, she saw the pistol in his hand.

The smooth wood and cool brass of the Boutet .58 caliber filled Grayson's palm with a sense of surety.

How ingenious, how intricate the workings of trigger, magazine and spring-loaded striker.

How empowering.

He reached back into the cupboard, grabbed a handful of extra bullets and the mercury pellets that fired them, and dropped them into his coat pocket.

Straightening, he confronted Nora's anguished stare. "He has my nephew. I'm ending this tonight."

He brushed by her, needing to distance himself from the indictment in her eyes.

"Not with that." She followed at his heels, her voice rising to a precarious summit. He braced for the tears that would surely follow.

"I want my nephew back. And I'll use any means I must."

She caught up to him at his chamber door, her hand banding around his wrist. "And Chad?"

He forced himself to meet her gaze, heartsick to be the cause of her pain. "I plan to ask him why he killed my brother."

"You don't know that."

"I know all I need to know. He's a thief and a liar, Nora. Why should he have drawn the line at murder?" He pulled from her grasp and pounded down the corridor. Her scampering footsteps sounded behind him.

"Even if he didn't draw that line, you must. Please. For me and Jonny."

Her plea thrust him off balance. The staircase bucked beneath his feet and he nearly plummeted, only just catching the railing in time.

The gargoyles carved into the newel posts seemed to echo her command: *you must, you must,* but in hissing, taunting voices. To Grayson, it was an affirmation of what he already knew he must do.

The very thing of which he had once been accused.

Fratricide.

Except this time it wasn't his brother. It was his

closest friend, a man who might as well have been his brother.

He crossed the foyer in four great strides, was out the door when he stopped beneath the portico, frantic to be off but unable to leave it like this, unable to leave *her* believing he finally had gone mad—truly, irreparably mad. And that she had been wrong to trust him.

She scrambled out the door behind him, arms snaking around his waist. He felt her trying to drag him inside.

"Gray, killing him will mean destroying yourself."

"I don't matter." He spoke to the blustering wind, to the rain pelting the drive, while she heaved sobs against his back. "If Jonny saw what happened to his father that night, if he knows who murdered Tom, then he isn't safe. It's up to me to do something about it."

She circled him, thrust her face in his. "We'll find them together. But I'm begging you, do not take the gun."

How could he deny her when she looked like that? So desperate, so anguished. So filled with love.

But he thought of Chad winning her regard with his abundant charm, winning his entire family's affections through the years and playing them all for fools.

He kissed her, hard and urgent.

"Forgive me." Then he broke away, rushing headlong into the storm.

Nora dashed inside, lingered long enough to shout commands to a flustered Gibbs. Then she too set off into the rain.

She was within ten or so paces of the stable doors when Gray rode out, his horse already spurred to a trot. Splashing by her, he cleared the first paddock gate and urged his mount to a canter.

"Wait for me!" she shouted, straining to be heard above the wind, rain and his horse's squelching hooves.

"You'll be safer here," he yelled back before breaking into a full gallop and vanishing down the riding lane.

"Slow down," she said, knowing he couldn't hear her. "You'll break your blasted neck."

Yet she intended taking the same risk. Gathering her dampened skirts, she made her way into the stable. A cough erupted from her as the scents of horse, hay and pine, made all the more acrid by the wet weather, closed around her.

As rain dripped from her hems, she blinked away bits of floating hay and scanned the small selection of geldings and mares. Some stared quietly back over their stall gates. Others snorted and pawed the floor in their storm-induced agitation.

Which one to pick? It had been more than a decade since she'd ridden, and then only her shy Shetland pony.

The sight of a lantern hung near the end of the line of stalls sent her scurrying down the aisle. "Is anyone here?"

Edwin, a groom's assistant about her own age, poked his head out and tugged his cap brim in greeting. "Evenin', my lady. Can't say it's a good one."

"I need a horse, quickly."

"Come to the right place, ma'am." He sauntered out and placed the brush he'd been holding into a box with other tools.

"A tame one I can handle, but not too sluggish either."

"Aye, ma'am." He moved up the aisle and gestured to the misty cob Nora knew well. "Puck here's a safe wager. Used to gentling our young Lord Clarington, but still got a fair scrap of spirit in 'im."

"Yes, he'll do."

As if the cob comprehended their conversation, Puck's gray muzzle appeared over the stall gate. Nora offered a hand, let him catch her scent, then ran her palm down his sleek neck. She'd seen Puck carry Jonny smoothly over the lower jumps in the paddock. She had also seen the horse veer from the higher ones, even when the eager child on his back attempted to steer him in that direction. No doubt Puck would see her through the forest without mishap, would bring her safely to his master.

"Please hurry."

When the groom wandered in the wrong direction, she called out sharply, "Didn't you hear me? Where on earth are you going?"

"Tack room, my lady. You'll be wanting a saddle, will ye not? 'Tis a might wet tonight to be going about bareback."

"Yes, yes, of course. But please do hurry."

He returned with saddle and harness and set to work. Though it seemed an excruciating eternity to Nora, within minutes he walked Puck out to the aisle. "Pardon me for saying, ma'am, but if you've a mind to catch Sir Grayson . . ." He trailed off, shaking his head. "Not at the rate he set out and not in this weather, ma'am. Perhaps I should—"

"No. Please just help me up."

With a dubious lift of his brows he stood at Puck's side and bent low at the waist. Nora gathered the reins and placed her foot into his clasped hands. He boosted her up, giving a second push when her wet skirts threatened to haul her back down. Once he had adjusted the stirrups to the length of her legs, he held up a crop to her.

"Oh, no, I couldn't . . ."

"Don't have to use it, my lady. Just rub it so 'gainst his shoulder to let 'im know ye have it." He demonstrated against his own arm. "Else the clever lad'll know you for a novice and may decide to have a bit of fun with you."

"I see. Thank you, Edwin."

Outside, she pointed the Welsh cob toward the headland, unsure of the distance, and not knowing what obstacles might lay in her path. This weather assuredly had felled trees and flooded gullies. She would be half-blinded by the rain besides.

"I can do this," she murmured. "*We* can do this." She patted encouragement against the horse's neck. "Bring us safely there, Puck, and quickly."

A shadow fell between her and the lane. A figure draped in black lurched out of the darkness, taking shape at Puck's side. Like talons, long fingers clutched at the bridle. Nora bit back a cry. Instinct sent her riding crop lashing outward, but she drew it back without striking as recognition took hold.

Like a disembodied ghost, a pale face framed in bedraggled gray wisps hovered beside Puck's shoulder. "Lady Lowell, if you care at all about Jonny, put a stop to these inquiries."

"Why, Mrs. Dorn? What are you afraid of?"

"The truth." Tears slid down the lined, quivering cheeks. "It will only hurt the boy."

Nora leaned over Puck's neck, locking her fingers around the housekeeper's wrist. "If you know what happened that day, Mrs. Dorn, you must tell me."

"I cannot."

"Don't be afraid."

"He . . . it was . . ." Indecision and obstinacy warred across the careworn features. Nora waited immobile, afraid to either frighten or anger Mrs. Dorn back into silence.

"I did it," she breathed. "I pushed him."

Shock struck Nora a blow that nearly knocked her from the saddle. Hand shielding her eyes from the rain, she stared down, taking the woman's measure.

Mrs. Dorn's defiant gaze faltered, and Nora knew. "You're lying."

"No. He owed me money. A great deal. He had promised to pay me but continually put it off and . . . that day he dismissed me."

Nora bent lower until her face came level with the other woman's. "This is ludicrous, and I haven't time for it."

She clucked to the gelding but Mrs. Dorn groped for her hand, squeezing it in both of her own. "Leave Jonny alone. It was me. I killed his father."

Frantic to be off, Nora had been struggling to pull free of the woman's stubborn grip. But that last mention of Jonny brought a realization cascading through her. She stopped tugging. "You've been trying to protect Jonny, haven't you?"

"He has nothing to do with this. Nothing."

"You've been hostile toward me since I arrived, especially when it came to Jonny. I resented it, but now . . . now I believe you only have his best interests at heart, that you'd even relinquish your freedom for him. For that, Mrs. Dorn, I forgive you every slight you've ever done me."

As the housekeeper gawked at that pronouncement, Nora snatched the reins free. "We will discuss this later, of that you can be certain. But now I must be off."

A cluck of her tongue and a tap of her heels coaxed Puck to a canter.

She didn't know whose instinct, hers or the cob's, conveyed her through the drenched forest, where the storm made a sodden unity of sky, trees and turf. The pins scattered from her hair until the heavy mass streamed down her back, over her shoulders, in her face. Flashes of lightning blinded her, disoriented her. She squeezed with her knees for balance, leaned well forward and gave Puck his rein, praying they would emerge from the trees to find Grayson, Chad and

Jonny laughing at what would turn out to be an extraordinary misunderstanding.

She didn't know how long she bounced in the saddle, thighs burning, aching fingers snagged in Puck's mane, before the distant roaring of ocean waves thrust past the hissing rain.

"Do hurry, Puck," she cried, her voice lost in the tumult of water inundating the earth now from two directions, both sea and sky. In vain she tried flinging the hair from her eyes but in the end had no choice but to trust the gelding's ability to follow the trail.

At a break in the trees she pulled back on the reins. Across the terrain, boulders and thick brush made for dangerous footing. After a few more yards, she climbed from the saddle, tugging when her wet skirts clung to the leather.

Beyond the cliffs, lightning sizzled across the water. Thunder rolled in the distance now, and the rain fell less insistently. Her legs trembled from exertion, threatened to buckle beneath her. Dropping the riding crop, she shoved shanks of sodden hair from her face and strained to see into satiny darkness.

"Grayson!" she tried to shout, but her voice was a drowning gasp. She cupped her hands around her mouth and filled her lungs with air. "Chad, Jonny!"

No response.

Panic quaked through her. What if she had emerged a mile or more in the wrong direction? The path had been wide and clear, but perhaps she'd missed a turn. Perhaps the others weren't here at all. Perhaps she was too late.

On unsteady legs she stumbled toward the cliffs. Her shaking fingers lost their grip on her skirts and her next step tangled with her hems. Down she plunged, splashing onto the turf, her cheek smacking the ground and stinging against a clump of nettles.

As she dragged herself to her hands and knees she

spotted the moving shadows, velvet specters silhouetted against the glistening night.

"Grayson!"

He and the others loomed near the edge of the headland some fifty yards away. Scrambling to her feet, Nora ran, heedless of the puddles sucking at her shoes, the brambles tearing at her skirts.

Parallel to the precipice, Chad and Jonny stood together facing Grayson. Unable to hear what they were saying, Nora skidded to a halt and completed the triangle. Gasping to catch her breath, she clawed the hair from her eyes.

"Gray. Chad. Please . . ." A dozen entreaties shrieked through her mind. *Please do not do this. Please come back to the house. Please keep Jonny safe. Please do not kill each other.*

It didn't matter that fear ravaged her voice and rendered her mute. They seemed not to notice her at all.

She craned her neck. Was Grayson holding the gun? She saw no sign of it, but that didn't mean it wasn't within easy reach.

His voice boomed above the waves and rain, the growling thunder. "I'll say it once more. Let the boy go."

Nora held out her arms, ready to sweep Jonny into them when he ran from Chad. But he didn't run. Instead he leaned into the earl's side and slipped his hand into Chad's larger one.

"Jonny, darling," Nora shouted. She swept toward them, and all three flinched in their sudden awareness of her presence. "Won't you come help me? I've lost my way and . . . and I've brought Puck. Won't you help me bring Puck home?"

Grayson's head snapped in her direction, then turned just as quickly back to Chad. "Nora, what are you doing here?"

"Ah, Jonny, here is your aunt Nora." Chad spoke

as if they were enjoying a picnic, except that his eyes never wavered from Grayson. He gave Jonny a forward nudge. "I think she needs you, lad."

Fear tingled through her limbs as she waited for the boy. Every instinct, every throb of her racing pulse shouted that no one must move, nothing must happen, until the child was safe.

"Despite what you apparently think, Gray," Chad called across the expanse separating them, "I didn't bring him here. He brought me."

Grayson leveled a dangerous smile at the earl. "I might believe that but for one essential detail. I already know you for a contemptible liar."

Nora stood with arms outstretched, aching for the feel of Jonny filling them, willing him, with all the energy she possessed, to come to her.

Chad spared her the briefest flick of his gaze, then bent to speak to Jonny. "This is hardly proper weather for a lady to be caught in."

"Uncle Chad's right, Jonny," Grayson put in, his tone easing for the boy's sake. "Please take Aunt Nora back to the house."

As if suspended in a dream, she watched Jonny step away from Chad, hesitate and walk slowly toward her. The next moments brought the small figure into her arms, his wet cheek pressed to her bodice, thin arms clasping her waist. She wiped his wet hair from his brow and hugged him tight. Relief made her weak and she sank to her knees, using her arms to shield him as best she could from the rain and from danger.

"Take him and go, Nora."

Grayson's command had her pushing to her feet, but no sooner had the words left his lips than he whisked an object from his coat pocket.

Metal gleamed in the rain. The pistol. His arm swung upward, taking rigid aim at Chad.

Nora fell back to her knees. She must protect the child—this child who was now as much hers as he had ever been Charlotte and Thomas's. But she must also prevent her husband from committing an irrevocable mistake, one that would destroy them all.

"Nora, I said go."

"I won't leave you. Not unless you give me that pistol."

Jonny struggled in her arms, and it was all she could do to keep hold of his slippery clothing.

"Damn it, Nora, get him out of here."

The child seemed suddenly crazed, pushing against her, trying to pry loose from her arms.

"Jonny, please stop. It's all right, we're going back to the house now." Fisting bunches of his shirt to restrain him, she struggled to her feet.

He went stiff, every limb refusing to budge.

"Nora!" A hoarse warning from Gray.

"I'm trying. He won't come with me."

Grayson glared at the man opposite him. "What did you tell my nephew to make him act this way?"

"Not a thing."

"Damn you to hell."

Chad shrugged. "Yes, probably."

"Why? Tell me that much." The pistol trembled in his hand, then steadied with a forward jerk.

Nora's heart fractured inside her. "Grayson, don't do it." Tears streamed, mixing with the rain on her cheeks. "If you pull that trigger, your worst demons will have won. You'll have done the very deed you've condemned yourself for all these months."

Jonny struggled. She summoned the last of her strength to hold on, to him and to all she held dear. "You'll destroy everything good inside you. You'll destroy *us*."

"The worst has already come to pass." His face turned toward her, a mask of pain and regret. The pistol's barrel drooped. "My brother is dead. Dead by Chad's hand."

"Then the guilt is his. Don't make it yours."

"Too late. He and I already share it." He repositioned the pistol, his aim dead-on.

Terror spiraled through her and broke from her lips. "Charlotte! Thomas! You brought us to this. If you ever sought to help us, help us now."

Jonny chose that moment to shove loose. Breaking away, he scrambled across the headland and threw himself in front of Chad.

*Chapter 27*

In horror Grayson felt his hand tighten around the pistol, felt his finger flex on the trigger at the exact moment his nephew stepped in front of the man he intended to kill.

Nora's scream racked his soul. As if controlled by strings, his arm jerked to his side, fingers flinging the gun to the ground. A ribbon of lightning robbed him of sight; the crack of thunder deafened him.

Had the gun fired? He felt no sting in his palm, no burn from the powder. Or had he grown too numb to feel?

His body swayed. He swore his heart stopped beating.

"Jonny!" He stumbled forward, hands scrubbing tears and rain from his eyes. He tripped, fell to his knees, scrambled to his feet. Through spinning relief he saw the boy still upright, arms outstretched as if to shield the man behind him.

But Chad was no longer standing. He was crouching, head bent over Jonny's shoulder, arms clutching the boy from behind, hands sweeping his small torso. "Are you hurt? Jonny, say something, damn it. Please."

Then silence. Until Jonny pushed out of Chad's arms and squared his shoulders. "He . . . he didn't do anything, Uncle Gray. I d-did. It was . . . my fault."

Each word, stammered in a voice Grayson hadn't heard in nearly a year, pummeled him physically, painfully. Miraculously. Relief and elation rode a tumultuous tide of remorse, of guilt. He shoved his feelings aside and focused on what mattered most—the boy.

"No, son. No." His throat closed around all the things he wished to say. Pushing to his feet, he reached for his nephew. "It wasn't your fault."

"It *was*. I'd heard you and Papa arguing that day. It made me so angry." Jonny sidestepped toward the cliff.

Grayson's insides ran cold. He held out his hand, afraid to move another muscle lest he frighten the child over the edge. "Jonathan, come here. Come to me. Please."

He received a shake of the head in reply. "I was so angry at both of you. I thought I should be earl now instead of waiting, that I could do a far better job than either of you. So I took Papa's watch—the Clarington watch—and came out here to prove I could be the earl." He backed closer to the edge, looking out over his shoulder at the thrashing ocean below.

"Please don't go any farther." Grayson didn't understand what Jonny was trying to tell him. What had the cliffs to do with being Earl of Clarington? Trying to ease toward his nephew without being obvious, he forced his clenched jaws open. "Come here and tell me what happened. Yell at me, call me any names you like, but please come away from the cliff."

Jonny went still. His face was grim, hard, aged beyond his years. "I did what Papa said you and he used to do as boys."

"Good God."

The stunned utterance burst from Chad, who now knew as well as Grayson what Jonny meant. As boys, all three of them used to challenge each other to lean out over the precipice, a foolish game of courage they were damned lucky to survive. Thomas had always tried to lean out the farthest, his way of proving his worth as the Clarington heir despite their father's disdain.

Grayson held up a hand behind him, forestalling any intentions Chad might have to rush forward and intervene. Behind him, he heard the soggy drag of Nora's skirts as she pulled to her feet. Her soft sobs rode the wind, then quieted.

She had always known exactly what to say to Jonny, known in ways Grayson could never fathom. But this was between him and his nephew, was something no one else could mend.

He took an infinitesimal step closer. "It was brave of you, Jonny. But leaning over cliffs is not the way to be a nobleman. Your courage is needed for far more important matters. Matters I'd like to teach you about, if you'll allow me."

"You don't understand, Uncle Gray." Where Jonny's features had appeared older moments ago, now they crumpled like a child's as he began to cry. "I dropped Papa's watch over the edge. I didn't mean to—it slipped. It caught on a root and when I tried to reach it, I nearly fell.

"I clung to the vines and held on a long time. I don't know how long. But finally Papa came and found me. He dragged me up, and then he tried to reach the watch. He said I must have it because it belonged to all the Earls of Clarington. And then he . . . he . . ."

Jonny pivoted so quickly Grayson's heart hit his throat. "It was here," the boy cried an instant before he dropped to hands and knees and scooted to the brink.

Grayson lunged and dove, scrambling after him. Mud and earth oozed through his fingers and sucked at his legs. Rocks and pebbles slid from under him, showering down the cliff face.

His hands clamped around Jonny's legs, but pulling

only succeeded in dislodging more earth and rock. He felt himself slipping. From somewhere above, Nora shouted his name, a sound framed in anguish. His head went over. His shoulders. His torso slid. The blood rushed to his brain, dizzying. The void seemed intent on swallowing him . . . and his nephew, dangling below him.

"Jonny," he ground out, "do not move."

"I have it, Uncle Gray. I found it. The watch. It's here and I have it."

"To hell with the watch!"

A weight came down on his legs, anchoring him in place. Hands fisted on his coat. "I've got you, Gray. I'll pull you up."

But as Chad tugged, Jonny began to slip from Grayson's grasp.

"Stop! I'll lose him."

"Then I'll reach around you and grab him."

That meant Grayson would have to relinquish his hold on his nephew. A chilling suspicion that Chad might push them both over nearly sent a protest from his lips. Only the realization that Chad could easily have made his escape in the past few moments but hadn't led to a renewed surge of faith in his friend.

A faith he had no choice, for now, but to heed.

"Hold on to him for all you're worth," Grayson shouted up at him, "and don't worry about me."

"Nora, lean on Gray's legs. Hold his coat."

Across Grayson's legs, Chad's greater weight was exchanged for hers, but not before he slipped another inch on slick earth and rock. Nora snugged down harder, curling her fingers around his coat. "Gray, I've got you. I swear I will not let you go."

He believed her. Good God, he believed her all too well, knowing that if he and Jonny went over, she'd likely go with them. Sorrow engulfed him, along with the wish that if anyone met the sea tonight, it would be him alone.

Chad leaned out over him, reaching, stretching. Still too far away to grasp the boy.

"Please help us." Nora's plea was little more than a breath, yet it reached Grayson's ears and ran through him, giving him the strength to hang on to his nephew's ankles.

"I've got him!" With a grunt Chad heaved. Jonny seemed to hover an instant in Grayson's vision, then surged up and over him, barely skimming his back as Chad drew him onto solid ground.

And then Grayson was sliding, slipping. Like a rabid animal the black Atlantic foamed on the rocks beneath him. Sea and sky streaked in his vision as his mind reeled, all sense of direction lost. Only the sudden smack of his chin against firm ground assured him he wasn't falling, that he had been dragged back up onto the headland.

Exhausted, shaking, gulping in breaths that knifed his lungs, he rolled. The last drops of the abating storm splattered his face and plastered the hair back from his brow. For one hideous moment he felt alone in a wet void. Empty. Barren. His trembling arms lifted, groping at the air. "Nora? Jonny?"

In an instant Nora was in them, her weight thudding against his chest. "I'm here. Jonny's safe. It's all right."

"Thank God, oh, thank God." Relief scoured through him, and for a moment all he could do was lie there while the blood resumed flowing through his veins. Holding Nora tight with one arm, he lifted the other. "Jonny?"

A small body jarred his side. "I'm sorry, Uncle Gray. I'm sorry." His hand opened against Grayson's chest, and he felt the small round weight of his brother's pocket watch pressing against his heart. "I'm sorry. . . ."

"I know, son, I know." *All too well.* He stroked his hand up and down Jonny's small back, absorbing the boy's shivers into his own body. "It'll be all right now."

"How can it? I was angry, but I didn't mean for Papa to die." The boy's voice shredded, then re-emerged in hiccupping sobs. He lay rigid against Grayson, his tears pooling warmly through Grayson's wet shirt. "I never meant for it to happen."

Nora slid an arm around him. "No one believes you did."

"It was an accident and nothing more, do you hear me?" Grayson shut his eyes and hugged the two of them tight.

Minutes passed as Jonny sobbed against him, asked for forgiveness, cried his father's name. His hands fisted in Grayson's shirt, pulling, pushing, delivering sharp little punches to Grayson's side as he struggled with emotions breaking free for the first time. Grayson let him, finding contentment in the knowledge that they were all safe, in the feel of their bodies snuggled against him, soothing the crushing fear of the last moments.

Gradually the fight drained from Jonny's limbs. Grayson nudged his tearstained face. "It was *not* your fault."

"I—I didn't wish to ever tell you."

"And so you kept silent," Nora finished for him.

The truth of her statement burned through Grayson. As unbearable as his own remorse had been all these months, it had been nothing compared to what the child had suffered, and all alone besides.

Continuing to hold them close, he sat up. "Your father loved you, Jonny, more than anything else in his life. Everything he did, he did for you. For your future. We argued that day because we had both made mistakes. Grievous ones. But more than anything he wanted to right those mistakes for you, to see to it you had everything in life you could ever want or need."

He nestled the child closer, pressed a kiss to his

damp brow. "I want the same for you. I intend to see that everything your father wanted for you comes to pass. And I promise you we'll keep his memory alive. We shall never forget him."

"Or your mother," Nora added gently.

It was then Grayson remembered Chad. He crouched not far away, wet hair spiked where he'd raked his fingers through it, eyes glazed and staring. Even in the darkness, his lips were white, bloodless.

"He simply flew up into my arms," Chad said to Grayson's unspoken question. "I barely tugged. I hadn't even got proper hold of him. I . . . don't understand it." His fingers shot through his hair again.

A shiver swept Grayson's shoulders. He traded a glance with Nora, and a flash of understanding passed between them. She smiled and crept out of his embrace.

"It's all right, Chad. " She patted his shoulder. "We were none of us thinking too clearly. I believe necessity merely endowed you with a strength you never knew you had."

"I suppose you're right. What else could it have been?" He didn't look convinced. He stood, moved closer to Grayson and Jonny, and eased to a crouch again.

"I can attest to how much your father loved you, Jonny. Before he died, he'd made up his mind to be strong for you and fix all that had gone awry." His gaze angled to Grayson. "We told ourselves we were indulging in a bit of privateering. The sort of smuggling that's been a Cornwall tradition for centuries. Almost too late we realized there was nothing quaint or conventional in what we were doing. In the end we couldn't go through with it. That's what he tried telling you that day."

"I didn't give him the chance." The old pain twisted, gave a stab.

"It's not your fault. You had no idea. And no inkling that Tom swore, and made me swear, to end our misdeeds and return everything to its rightful owners."

"To the Sheffield silversmiths."

"Among others." Chad's head went down between his hunched shoulders. He looked defeated, his vitality deflated. Both hands speared through his hair, tarnished from gold to russet by the rain. "Gray, the scheme was mine. I want you to know that. We were to use my connections and my warehouses in London to redirect the merchandise from its rightful destinations.

"It seemed a gentleman's crime that would yield no victims. Or so I told myself. For a time I convinced Tom of it too. At first he believed I'd merely found a shifty buyer and a means of avoiding the export taxes. When he realized the goods had been intercepted from reaching legitimate buyers, he put an immediate end to things. You see, what neither of us ever understood about Tom, what no one understood, was that in his quiet way he was stronger than you and I put together."

"I'm beginning to see that now." His throat constricting, Grayson studied his friend for a long moment. "But you still haven't answered my question." He swallowed. His hand came down on something cold and metallic on the ground, something forgotten in the past few minutes. His fingers closed tight around it. He cleared his throat. "Why, Chad? Why did you do it?"

"What you also have never understood, because I did not let you, is that I inherited a bigger fiasco than Tom did. Damn our fathers." Chad's hand fisted on his knee. "Both believed being a Peer meant attending Parliamentary sessions each spring and throwing lavish entertainments the rest of the year. But no." He shook his head; his fist uncurled. "That would be shirking the blame, which rests squarely on my shoulders."

Standing, Grayson passed Jonny into Nora's waiting

arms. With a gesture he bade her to walk the boy a short distance away, just out of hearing range. Clutching Tom's pocket watch, he faced his friend, who pushed to his feet as well.

"A ship went down off the coast about a year ago. Most blamed the weather. But I heard the word *scuttled* whispered in more than one place." He stepped closer and grabbed a handful of Chad's sleeve. Not a muscle in Chad's body resisted as Grayson yanked one shoulder higher than the other. "Were you responsible?"

"No. I swear, the goods we diverted—"

"Stole."

Chad conceded with a nod. "The goods we stole never made it as far as a ship. We were to redirect them to London and sell them on the black market, but we never got that far."

"And when you claimed to have gone to Helston the other day, where were you really?"

"You had me followed."

"Of course."

Chad's lashes fell; he released a breath. "Mullion. I went looking for a ship's captain, an unsavory fellow named Dick Gavin, who was to have emptied the cave at my order."

"Did you give that order?"

"No, of course not." His mouth tightened. "I told him all deals were off, that I was out of it and he could look elsewhere to make his profits. I swear it, Gray."

Grayson released him. Studied him and pondered. Allowed Chad to stew in uncertainty while a lifetime of memories ran through his mind. Their years as boys, as students, as arrogant bucks enjoying their first taste of freedom.

The pranks. The dares. The carousing. The conquests.

The tragedies and heartbreaks. And through it all, a friendship so solid he never once questioned or

doubted or looked elsewhere for the borrowed fortitude a man occasionally needed.

"Good God, Chad." He hissed a breath through his
teeth. "I might have shot you."

"You wouldn't have."

"You took an awful chance."

"Perhaps I deserved it."

Grayson hesitated, lifted an appraising eyebrow.
"No. But there will be a reckoning. I've sent for a
magistrate. I'm sorry, but I felt I had to."

Chad shook his head. "You did the right thing, what
I would have done in your shoes."

"I'll speak in your defense, Chad. Now that I understand what happened, I'll do whatever I can to help you
out of this." He held his friend's gaze. "Just as you
helped me out of countless scrapes through the years."

"Thanks, old boy." A glimmer of a smile restored
something of the cavalier, good-natured friend Grayson had known all his life.

"Do something for me," he said.

"Name it."

"Take my horse and get Jonny home."

"You can still trust me after . . . ?"

"You just saved both our lives." Grayson found he
needed to look away from the gratitude swimming in
his friend's eyes. "You and I are guilty of similar
crimes, aren't we? You stole outright. I stole more
subtly by marrying an innocent woman with a generous dowry." He offered Nora a remorseful smile. "I'm
sorry for that."

She nodded, and with a brimming but nonetheless
steady gaze, bestowed a forgiveness he knew he hadn't
begun to earn. He nodded back, trying to convey his
vow to spend the rest of his days doing so. He glanced
down at his nephew beside her.

"Jonathan."

The boy ran to him with an eagerness Gray hadn't

seen in nearly a year, that pinched the back of his throat. "Yes, Uncle Gray?"

Using the diminishing drizzle as an excuse, he scrubbed a hand across his eyes. "I want you and Uncle Chad to ride home on my horse—"

"But Aunt Nora said she brought Puck."

"That's right." Nora pointed down the headland. "He's not far from here."

"All right, son. You and Chad find Puck and bring him home. When you get there, change out of these clothes immediately and have Mrs. Dorn bring you both something hot. Aunt Nora and I shall be right behind you."

Chad and Jonny started away, but a weight in Grayson's palm had him calling them back. When Jonny turned, Grayson held out his hand. "I believe this is yours, Lord Clarington."

Jonny hesitated, seemed almost about to refuse, then gathered the pocket watch in both hands.

"One more thing," Grayson said. "Blackheath Grange was once a great estate. If you and I work together, it will be again. Can I depend on you?"

He doubted the boy understood how he could be of assistance, but at the moment it didn't matter. The small chest swelled and Jonny's chin inched higher. "I'll help you, Uncle Gray."

"Good man. Thank you."

As the two set off, Grayson moved to Nora's side and wrapped his arms around her. "He was lying."

She jolted against him. "You mean Chad?"

He nodded.

"Good heavens, Gray, we can't let them go off together, we have to—"

"It's all right. I meant he was lying by shouldering all the blame. I know him too well. He did it for Tom's memory. For me and most of all for Jonny. By making it appear Tom hadn't fully comprehended the illegalities of their plan, Chad has given Jonny the gift of his father's honor to cherish for the rest of his life."

She relaxed in his arms. "I was right about him then, wasn't I? He is your friend and always will be."

"Yes, and yours and Jonny's too. Beyond a doubt he and my brother nearly made a grave mistake, but then, none of us is perfect. Least of all me. I'm certainly no one to judge them."

"No. *Self*-judgment is your indulgence. Do you perhaps feel it's time to start believing in the honorable, compassionate man I see whenever I look at you, or must I alter your portrait to its former brooding state?"

He laughed softly. "I don't deserve you."

"That's true." She grinned, rose on tiptoe for a kiss, then nestled her cheek in his dripping collar.

"You've never stopped believing in me," he added.

"Also true."

"I didn't make it easy."

"A gross understatement, sir."

He tightened his arms around her. She was toying with him and ah, didn't she have every right in the world? He'd dragged her through perdition and back. It was time he offered her the heaven she deserved. "I love you, Nora. My brilliant artist, my unrivaled beauty, my enticing little paramour. We both know I am nothing without you—"

Her grin widened. "I believe we established that a while back."

"You're not going to make this at all comfortable for me, are you?"

"Indeed not." She pressed her lips to his neck, her soft breath infusing him with heat. "I intend to make you *un*comfortable for the rest of your days." To prove her point, her hand grazed his length to settle at the juncture of his thighs. He flinched as her nimble fingers took firm possession of him. "Rest assured I shall keep you on your toes, sir."

"You do love me." Though couched as a statement, it was a question born of his lingering inability to believe himself worthy of such a woman; a question with the power to humble him, redeem him or undo him.

"I have loved you since our wedding night," she assured him. Her grasp eased to a caress that threatened to inflame him, even there on the cold, wet headland. "Since the moment you made me yours and convinced me there could never be anyone else."

He lifted her face in his hands, leaning in close to rub his nose across her incredibly adorable one. "Where did it come from, this extraordinary faith?"

"My love, an artist sees the world with remarkable clarity. You'd do well to remember that the next time you attempt to shield your heart from me."

"I believe you capable of peering into my very soul. Mine and Jonny's. And I thank God for it. For you." He pressed her closer. His mouth found hers, and their kisses sent flames to lips gone wet and cold with rain.

Still, she shivered in his arms, prompting him to run his hands up and down her back to warm her. Her chills traveled into him, raising the hair at his nape and turning his back to gooseflesh.

A soft light enveloped them, and he understood.

Apparently so did Nora. "It's them."

"I know. Charlotte, Tom?"

"Shh." Nora held her fingers to his lips. Then she pointed in the same direction Jonny and Chad had gone. "There."

The surrounding glow shimmered and brightened. Grew warm as it never had before. Their shivers abated, and with arms around each other they watched two shapes gather as if drawing energy from the scant light around them.

Side by side, the lady in lavender and the man in the dark blue coat took form. Hands clasped, they hovered well above the ground.

"Oh, Gray, they're together." A sob choked Nora's words. She pressed her face to his shoulder. "We've done it, we've set them free."

The pinching of his own throat allowed him only to nod, hold her tighter and gaze in awe at his brother and sister-in-law.

*"Thank you."*

Two voices, mingling as one, seeped from the very air around them, caressing them with the gentlest of touches.

"You're very welcome," Nora whispered.

*"Gray, can you forgive me?"*

The sound of his brother's voice sent tears to burn his eyes. He held on tighter to Nora, felt her returning the pressure. "We both made mistakes, Tom. Can you forgive *me*?"

*"A thousand times over. Gray, don't harbor regrets. . . ."*

Tom's voice thinned, became little more than a breath of air. The images wavered. It was Charlotte who spoke next.

*"Take care of our son. Make him yours."*

"We will." Grayson's voice faltered. He pressed his lips to Nora's brow, seeking strength and finding it. "We already love him as though he were ours."

*"And love each other well,"* they said together, voices blending.

"That is our promise." He took Nora's chin between his fingers and turned her tearful face to his. Her smile was never more beautiful. "To you and to each other."

The specters were fading now, their light shrinking, cooling, growing fainter. *"Jonny will be so delighted with his baby cousin. . . ."*

The last word dissipated on a stirring breeze, and darkness settled again.

Releasing Nora, Grayson dashed several steps forward. "Wait. Please. There's so much more to say. . . ."

"Baby?" Nora's hands were pressed to her stomach, her face filled with alarm. "Surely," she whispered, "they did not say *baby*?"

The truth of it rolled through him like a rushing tide. A child. Their child. Of course. What better way to celebrate the renewal of their own lives, theirs and Jonny's, than by welcoming a new life into their little family?

He went to her, turned her in his arms and tucked her back to his chest. They faced toward the sea, toward a distant promise of moonlight glimmering in the parting clouds. Pressing his nose to her hair, he breathed her in, let her love flow through him and released the guilt and grief of these past months to the last of the storm's gusts. His arms circled her abdomen, to hold and protect the precious life within as he savored a well-being he thought never to know again.

"My darling paramour, I believe *baby* is exactly what they said. But one can hardly consider it prophetic on their part, not with the way you and I tend to have at it."

She gave a backward push against him. "Scoundrel."

"That I am."

She snuggled deeper into his chest. "I want a hot bath and a warm robe. And later, after Jonny's asleep, I want your warm body next to mine all night long. Let's go home, my love."

"Home," he repeated, as hand in hand they made their way up the headland to where Constantine waited beneath the trees. He swung Nora into his arms, set her on the saddle, and climbed up behind her.

He held the reins in one hand and wrapped his free arm around her middle. She settled into his embrace with a sigh. For a time, they rode in silence, until the house came into view through the trees.

"When I was a child," he said to her, "I believed Blackheath Grange the very center of the world. But these past months I thought I would never think of this place as home again, not in any true sense of the word." He fell quiet as a warm wind swept the clouds aside to unveil a multitude of stars pricking the night sky. Moonlight gilded the windows of the house, giving the illusion that the lamps were all lit, the manor filled with people.

He realized it *was* filled, with the people who mattered most. His family. His best friend. And soon, his son or daughter.

"I believe again, Nora. In home, in the possibilities of love . . . most of all in you, and in the kind of man I can be because of you. And do you know what I plan to do?"

She turned around as far as the saddle would allow, angled her head, and smiled up at him. "I can't begin to imagine." The lusty gleam in her eyes suggested she had an idea, but Grayson doubted she would, in this particular instance, be correct.

He smiled back at her. "I'm going to court you. Properly, as I should have done from the beginning."

She gave a little laugh. "A bit late for that, isn't it?"

"Not for a man who's been given a second chance." His fingers splayed across her belly. He leaned around to kiss her, glanced up at the starry sky, laughed and kissed her again. "I intend to do a lot of things differently from now on."

She leaned back against him, her hand covering his where it lay against her. "Just be happy. The rest will take care of itself."

Read on for an excerpt from
Allison Chase's next novel,

*Dark Temptation*

A NOVEL OF BLACKHEATH MOOR

Coming from Signet Eclipse
in November 2008

Where the stark expanse of Blackheath Moor met the rocky thrust of the Cornish coast, Sophie St. Clair hurried along a dusty road to the one place in the windswept countryside expressly forbidden to her.

The air today shivered with an intense, startling sort of light she had never experienced before coming to Cornwall—as crisp and sharp as springwater on a winter's day, it seemed to brighten colors, deepen outlines and render futile any attempt to be inconspicuous.

Sophie knew she presented an all too apparent blotch on the nearly treeless landscape, a small, dark figure scrambling along a pitted road bordered by a patchwork of heather and gorse, miles and miles of it, beneath a sky so thoroughly unblemished, it rivaled the brilliant blues of her mother's most prized Sevres porcelain.

Only minutes ago, after calling out a quick reassurance that she was going for a walk along the beach, she had put as much distance as quickly as possible between herself and her aunt Louisa's house. One hand gripped her bonnet brim to fight the tug of the wind, while the other steadied the satchel slung over her shoulder.

As she topped a rise, the sight of the gray slashes of four stone chimneys and a bit of peaked roof sped her steps. She was almost to Edgecombe, a sprawling property perched between the moors and the sea, abandoned these several years since the death of its last owner.

Even now, the details of the death of the previous Earl of Wycliffe remained sketchy. There had been rumors of a fire, but the family had refused to discuss the matter, and with Edgecombe being so remotely located, no one had been able to verify the truth. As far as Sophie was concerned, Lord Wycliffe could rest in peace. Her interest lay in events that occurred centuries earlier.

As a girl she had read the history and the tales, pored over details both fantastic and improbable. Edgecombe had captured her youthful imagination, but never once had she thought she'd have a chance to see the estate firsthand. Not until the incident last month that altered the course of her life.

Her first glimpse of the place had been little more than a jagged shadow thrown across the evening landscape, framed by the window of her grandfather's barouche, the driver of which had conveyed her from London and summarily dumped her at Aunt Louisa's front gate. But from that first glance, she had felt the call of the somber stone gables beckoning with an invitation that could not be ignored.

"Stay away from there, girl," her aunt had warned when Sophie broached the subject yesterday. "Don't you so much as point your toes in the direction of that old wreckage of a house."

"Oh, but Aunt Louisa, it's wonderful. Dark and brooding, and poised so precariously at the edge of the land. And the history—"

"Mark my words, Sophie. Strange things happen there; things a girl like you has got no business knowing about. Things that turn men's hair gray and their souls black."

"Are you speaking of ghosts, Aunt Louisa? Surely you don't believe—"

"Never you mind, girl."

The admonition had only strengthened Sophie's desire to see the house for herself. Reaching the drive, she halted before a pair of wrought-iron gates—closed, locked, doubly secured by a boat chain coiled several times around it and by a padlock twice the width of her palm.

*Keep out.* The gate's message echoed Aunt Louisa's words of warning. The two flanking stone pillars and the high granite walls that marched away in either direction issued the same command. *Stay away.*

"I hardly think so," Sophie whispered.

The house itself stood but a stone's throw beyond a short drive that opened onto a cobbled forecourt. An imposing pair of gargoyles kept watch from either side of an elaborate portico, topped by a gothic arch. The windows were shuttered, emphasizing the air of abandonment permeating the property.

Along the north boundary wall, she discovered another, smaller gate that might have been easily missed, half hidden behind a tangle of hawthorn growing beside it. Sophie shoved the spiky branches out of her way and found the latch. No chains barred her way. With a fluttering breath of excitement, she slipped inside.

A slate path led her past a dry fountain and across a wooden footbridge. Bushy ferns and tall, bristly spikes of bulrush choked the narrow brook below. From there she made her way up the garden slopes. A set of steps mounted a grassy surge to a terrace, onto which several sets of French doors opened from the house. Sophie climbed the steps, took in her surroundings and enjoyed a private laugh at Aunt Louisa's superstitions. Edgecombe was only a house, after all. Filled with history and misty legend, yes. But ghosts?

She perched on the top step, removed the satchel from her shoulder and reached inside for her pen, pot of ink and leather-bound writing tablet. Tucking a windblown lock of hair beneath her bonnet, she flipped to a blank page.

*A house crouched at the edge of the world,* she wrote, *defying the elements—wind, storms and sea—to attempt their worst and be damned.*

Well. She'd need to modify that last word, of course. Grandfather St. Clair, owner and editor in chief of *The Beacon,* one of London's weekly newspapers, would never set it to print. Just as he never published any of Sophie's feature pieces under her true, decidedly feminine name. No, if she wished to be employed by *The Beacon,* she must do so under the pen name of Silas Sinclair and, furthermore, must stick to such topics as her family deemed appropriate for a lady.

*Sophie St. Clair, nice girls do not ask bothersome questions; nice girls leave news reporting to men, for it is hardly a pastime appropriate for wellborn ladies.*

*Sophie, can't you for once behave as the proper, wellborn young lady you are?*

How she loathed *proper.* Despised *appropriate.* Detested *nice.* Despite a lifetime of trying to emulate all three concepts and more, she had always fallen a lengthy stride short of success. If curiosity killed the cat, as her mother always warned, then Sophie had flirted with death all her life.

Pen hovering above the page, she studied the house. A quick count of the shuttered windows suggested fifteen or so rooms, laid out on either side of a square tower that had, two centuries earlier, served as the seaside fortress of Sir Jack and Lady Margaret Keating.

According to the legends she had read as a child, Sir Jack had been something of gentleman buccaneer, a pirate and a smuggler, yes, but not a killer. Together, supposedly, he and Lady Meg had ruled the seas from Cornwall to northern France to Ireland and back, dispersing much-needed goods among people who could not afford the excise taxes. After his death at the hands of the Royal Navy, however, they say Lady Meg snapped, embarking on a high seas rampage of murder and pillage until she, too, had been caught and hanged.

*Be a nice girl, Sophie.*

Yes, very well then. Today, she would try to think architecture, not violent pirate history. She set her pen to the paper.

*A gaunt sentinel from an ancient time, whose granite walls seemed quarried from an ancient haze, with mysteries and memories trapped within each chiseled block . . .*

The whirling breezes abruptly dropped, replaced by an utter stillness that immediately felt . . . unnatural. A weighty silence fell over the trees while the birds roosting in their boughs went quiet, as though caught in a state of hushed expectancy.

Uneasy. Apprehensive. She glanced up at the house.

A cloud covered the sun, casting a gloom across the view and raising a sudden prickliness down her spine. She passed a gaze over the house. A fluttery sensation quivered in her stomach. Had the shutters on the bay window in the far corner always been open?

She sat quite still, watching. Waiting . . . for the wind to pick up, the trees to resume their creaking, for the house to remain as dark, empty and unchanging as ever.

The house did not comply. As Sophie watched, a curtain in the exposed window moved, fluttering aside, then falling back into place.

In an instant she was on her feet, her hand flying to her mouth as her writing tablet slapped the terrace and her pen clattered down the steps. Her pulse racing, she backed away until her foot met with insubstantial air, and she nearly tumbled down the stairs.

With a quick maneuver she caught her balance. Hooking the satchel over her shoulder, she straightened and found herself staring directly into a face on the other side of the window. Through the mullioned panes she could make out a tumble of fair hair, darker brows knotted over piercing eyes and a full mouth bracketed in lines of displeasure.

He stood in shirtsleeves and a waistcoat, one hand fisted against the buttons. He glowered long and hard at her, rendering her immobile, locked in a silent battle of scrutiny. Good heavens, she was caught!

A whisper of logic brought a measure of reassurance. She was a neighbor, after all, or at least a guest of this man's neighbor. There was nothing for it but to offer a friendly apology for trespassing and hope the man, be he servant or nobleman, possessed a forgiving nature. Or a sense of humor.

She raised her hand to wave, but he had vanished. The sun burst from the clouds and the wind picked up, plucking at her skirts and whipping loose hair in her eyes. She shoved it back under her bonnet and waited, expecting the man to come walking out of one of the terrace doors. A minute passed, and another, with no sound or sign of movement issuing from the house.

Confused, Sophie descended the steps, was about to turn and leave when an impulse sent her back up to the nearest set of doors. Rapping several times at the door, she called out, "Good morning. Is anyone here? I'm dreadfully sorry to be trespassing. I believed the place to be empty. My name is Sophie . . . Sophie St. Clair, and I'm a guest of the Goodwins down the road. Perhaps you know them?" She knocked again. "I say, won't you come out and become properly acquainted?"

Nothing.

"How insufferably rude."

At the bottom of the stairs a realization brought her up short. Only moments ago clouds had blocked the sun, but as she scanned the sky now, she detected not the faintest trace of a cloud, not in any direction. She shielded her eyes with her hand and peered out at the horizon. Rare though it was for an English summer day, nothing but unending blue stretched above the Atlantic.

She made it as far as the footbridge, when a rustling sifted through the bulrush along the banks of the brook. The sound brought her to a halt. It was more than the wind stirring the plants, more . . . solid. The rub of fabric, the catch of a thread.

Sophie stood motionless, listening, searching her surroundings. "Is . . . is anyone there?" she asked in a small voice, one that hardly sounded like her own.

Her knuckles whitened where she gripped the rail. Leaning out over the stream, she scrutinized the bank. At the thud of a footfall on the wooden planking beside her, she pulled back with a gasp. Seeing nothing, panting for breath, she braced to run. And then she felt, quite plainly, a graze against the back of her hand. Not the wind, not a falling leaf, but fingertips—cool, slightly rough, as if from an old callus and then . . . the sound of her name tingling in her ear.

"Sophie . . ."

# LYDIA JOYCE

## *SHADOWS OF THE NIGHT*

Fern and Colin Radcliffe were to
have a conventional marriage. But
after a shocking wedding night, Fern
strikes out at her new husband in a
fit of passionate independence—
and awakens a craving in both
husband and wife to cast off
society's rules and mores.

They spend their honeymoon
alone at Colin's isolated estate—
exploring a world of pain, pleasure,
and power. But their exploration is
interrupted by a devastating secret
from Colin's past—a secret that
threatens their future together,
and their very lives...